THE

DREAD

KING

LAUREN CATE LEAKE

ALSO BY LAUREN CATE LEAKE

THE DREAD DESCENDANT SERIES
THE DREAD DESCENDANT
THE DREAD PRINCE
THE DREAD KING
DREADFULLY YOURS

MURDEROUS LOVE: AN ANTHOLOGY
FEATURING MARRY, KISS, KILL

COVER ART BY JESS KUESPERT

ISBN 9798992059250

This book is for you, Little Vipers.

And a little bit for me.

8

Content Warning

This book contains MANIPULATION, NON CONSENSUAL SEXUAL RELATIONSHIPS, GRAPHIC LANGUAGE, ABUSE, AND VIOLENCE.

PLAYLIST

Every Breath You Take by Chase Holfelder
back to friends by sombr
In My Room by Julia Wolf
The Serpent by Besomorph
Dangerous by Sleep Token
The Death of Peace of Mind by Bad Omens
Hold on Till May by Pierce the Veil
Cold as Ice by Foreigner
My Immortal by Evanescence
God Went North by Nothing More
The Old Religion by Florence + the Machine
Who's Afraid of Little Old Me? By Taylor Swift
Gilded Lily by Cults
Animal I Have Become by Three Days Grace
Hazy Shade of Winter cover by Gerard Way
The Pretender by Foo Fighters
Watch the World Burn by Falling in Reverse
Kiss from a Rose cover by Wake Me
Gravity from Hazbin Hotel
The Line by twenty one pilots
Tell Dante (Cinematic) by Project Elmsie
God is a Weapon by Falling in Reverse
Stars by Grace Potter & The Nocturnal

PRONUNCIATIONS

Maeve *like wave*

Malachite *like kite*

Abraxas *sis not sass (though…he has that)*

Reeve *like leave*

Vaukore *vow/core*

Vexkari *vex/car with letter "E" sound*

Ambrose *like gross (I can assure you he is far from it)*

Spinel *spin/elle*

Peur *pure*

Zimsy *zim/zee*

Orator *or/uh/tor*

Morana *more/an/uh*

Morte *more/tay*

Elven Lands
The Dread Lands
Sinclair Estates on Earth
MOUNT MORTE
THE DARK PEAKS
CASTLE MORANA
THE BERYL CITY
THE TOWERS
THE GREYWOO

SANCTUM
THE CELESTIAN PALACE
DEEP
CRYSTALMORE
LOWER ATERNIAN TOWNS
Heims
The Dark Planet
Aterna
Vaukore

15

If you did not read the bonus chapter from The Dread Prince, and would like to do so before reading the Dread King, it will appear next. It is Chapter 54 from Reeve's perspective.

Chapter one of The Dread King begins on page 35.

Chapter 54

Reeve

It had been quite some time since Lithandrian had been to Crystalmore and visited Reeve. Despite her Elven pride and pious nature as a long reigning Queen, even she couldn't deny its marvel. She'd even bestowed him a quick compliment. The palace of gleaming crystal and Magic held Lithandrian's attention as Mal stood at her side, introducing her to Magicals whose names Reeve hadn't bothered to learn.

The Immortals in attendance were just as elated to see the Elven Queen and her husband as the Magicals were. The duels being hosted in Aterna were symbolic of something greater than had been seen in centuries: a Magical utopia.

If only all the fawning Magicals and Immortals knew just how close the table was to tipping.

Reeve didn't need to know all the details of said tipping table. He took one look at Maeve where she stood, alone and distant from the rest, and knew hell was close to breaking free in this new "utopia."

She watched Mal with heavy and worn eyes from the balcony.

No gown. She was fitted in her attire as Malachite's Dread Viper. Reeve couldn't deny she wore it well. She was born to be a symbol of power. The green cloak pinned by gold jewels at her shoulders flitted up in the breeze dancing across the water of the Black Deep behind her.

She did not look at him as he arrived at her side. Her arms remained folded across her chest as she watched Mal smile with nothing of the sort on her face.

"If you've come to mock me," she said weakly, "I'd ask you to withhold your desire to toy with me."

He continued to observe her silently for a moment. She looked like sleep was a foreign idea. He chose to believe the bloodshot nature of her eyes was a result of exhaustion and not tears.

"Your eyes are red and swollen. Perhaps you need to retire."

Maeve still did not look at him. Her gaze remained on Malachite.

"Have you ever read *Strange Case of Dr. Jekyll and Mr. Hyde*?" she asked, her voice nearly cracking.

Reeve's chest tightened. "Maeve," he began softly.

Too softly, because she looked up at him at last.

Her eyes begged for him to let it go. To just humor her, and not to care. And so he answered. "I've read it."

She looked back across the party until her eyes were on Malachite once more. With a slow breath, she ran a gloved hand across her throat, her fingers tracing each line of dark Magic that ran through her veins.

Malachite's Magic.

"I am always steps behind, wondering what version of him I will come upon," she said.

Tears pricked at the corners of her eyes. He wanted her to leave before she combusted and lost control of her emotions. From what he could feel, she was one wrong look away from those deadly fingers having a mind of their own.

"Do you think it's wise that you attend the opening ceremony? You appear under duress."

Maeve nodded as she looked up at him with a frown. "Is this the part where you sympathize and try to make me forget all the secrets you harbor? All the pain your careless choices caused me?" she scoffed and laughed darkly. "There's too much green in his eyes. If I leave, I'll regret it later."

Reeve's insides twisted. "What?"

"If I leave—" she began to repeat herself, but that wasn't

at all what Reeve was interested in hearing again.

"No," he said, trying and failing to sound casual. For there was nothing casual about the fearful Magic that slowly stepped down his spine. "What did you say before that?"

Maeve's eyebrows pulled together.

"About his eyes?" Reeve pressed her further, but it was too late.

Her walls reformed at once, and she protected him as she always had.

"I didn't say anything about his eyes," she said, her face flat and emotionless.

He couldn't even blame her for her well-placed mistrust. But he fucking hated it, nonetheless. He inhaled, long and slow, calming the rage that begged to lash out.

"Some advice," he said at last, "if you insist on staying: set right your face and do your job as his second. Because right now, you are only infuriating him more by not being at his side."

"And what of my fury?" she fired back lowly.

He smiled. "A beautiful thing when used properly."

He jerked his head towards the party. "Go," he said gently. "Try to enjoy your evening."

He tried to drown out their argument. He tried to keep his attention on forcing drinks on Abraxas and upping his bets on the duels. He tried not to watch Maeve attempt to get away from Malachite across the hall. She was smart to want to leave now, as he'd tried to get her to do prior to the ceremony starting. Reeve knew he was right: she was on the verge of breaking.

No.

Malachite was on the verge of breaking her.

Ice, sharp and cruel, penetrated her skin where he gripped her. Reeve ignored that he felt every bit of it on his own forearm and kept his eyes off the pair.

"Backing down so easily?" Malachite said lowly, tormenting her further. "It's a good thing Ambrose is dead and doesn't have to see how fucking weak you've become."

Reeve's eyes whipped up to them. He nearly Obscured to Mal and buried his fist in his face at such disgusting words.

But he remained in control.

Maeve did not.

Something snapped inside her, and he felt what remained of her control shatter completely, just as he feared. Magic rushed down her arm as two deadly fingers snapped together with electric intentions. Green lightning danced across her knuckles as her furious eyes looked up at Malachite.

Laughter and conversation faded as tense whispers flitted around him.

The lively party music tapered off slowly until there was nothing but an uneasy silence. Crystalmore's most talented cellists looked at the Dread Viper and her sworn Prince fearfully as the pair stared down one another.

The entire hall's attention was on the glorified and romanticized deadly couple.

Maeve's heart beat in a determined manner, and he felt her next breath would unleash all her, now untamed, fury. He could divert everyone's attention or break the tension with a joke, but Reeve was rather tired of playing games.

And part of him wanted to watch her do it.

He wanted to see her on full display, showing the world just how worshiped she should be. Malachite may have worn the crown, but she was the one he'd willingly bow to if she ever grew the courage to take the power she was born with.

He wondered if she herself had forgotten her own spell—

her own Magical handiwork that could make them all, even Mal, forget she'd attacked the Dread Prince himself. And then he realized. . .He felt it. . .

Part of her wanted to do it, too.

She'd regret it. It would make things harder on her than they already were. She was drowning in the waves of Malachite's storm. So he'd stop her from making such a mistake, but selfishly it wouldn't be at his own expense, covering for their reckless behavior with a joke or a deflection.

Because there was another way he could stop her from releasing the crackling lightning at her fingers. . .

Reeve knew it was wrong to be so selfish, to use the bond between them against her will. But he no longer cared what was wrong when it came to her. If she was going to fight him every step of the way, if they were going to bring their toxic Magic into his world, then he'd be damned if he continued to tiptoe around her feelings.

Even if it meant she hated him more for it. Another lie he'd told. Another deception. Ironic, he thought, that he was the one deceiving her mind.

Malachite's chin lowered as his eyes sparkled with a green evil that still haunted Reeve's dreams. He needed only one reminder of their color before he muttered, "Fuck it," and tossed back the rest of his Aternian Absinthe.

Don't, he said into Maeve's mind.

He felt the shock drown out her Magic, as the green lightning threatening to explode from her fingers fizzled into nothing. She turned across the hall with wide eyes and her brows pulled together in horror.

He kept his face calm as he watched her arm fall limp to her side. He didn't need to look at Malachite to know his far too green eyes had followed her gaze. Maeve's mouth fell open slightly. An expression of pure disbelief plastered across her face.

Reeve lowered his chin. *Don't*, he said again, ensuring

she knew without a doubt it was indeed his voice in her head.

Her heartbeat skyrocketed at the confirmation. Reeve looked away from them as Malachite grabbed her arm and whispered in her ear.

"Primus, Merlin, and all Seven Realms," hissed Abraxas, pouring himself another glass of Aternian Absinthe.

"Since when are they so at odds?" whispered Drystan.

Abraxas made a horrible sound as he forced down the liquor and looked back at his cousin with sad, drunken eyes. With a sigh, he replied, "Since Uncle Ambrose."

Mal's voice echoed across the hall. "Fiercely loyal, this one." He chuckled charmingly. "She thought I was in danger."

The atmosphere shifted at once. Relief swept across the hall and Mal joined Lithandrian with a soft smile, leaving Maeve in the middle of the hall. Some even applauded her.

"Pour me another," said Reeve with a laugh, plastering on a smile.

Eryx poured himself and Reeve drinks and toasted Abraxas. "You Magicals love drama."

Reeve laughed and watched as Abraxas turned another shade lighter.

Maeve's breathing barreled forward as she stared across the hall at him with rage he deserved, but didn't have the ability to handle in the middle of a fucking party. He did not meet her gaze but spoke smoothly across her mind.

Stop staring at me and pull yourself together.

Abraxas watched her go with uneasy eyes that darted between her swift exit and where Malachite sat next to Lithandrian, watching the duels with relaxed amusement.

"Walk with me," said Reeve.

Abraxas looked up at him and blinked heavily. He slipped a hand into his pocket and pulled out a small vial. He downed the contents in one gulp and braced himself on the bar with his head hanging low.

With a sharp breath, his eyes popped open and he looked

up at Reeve, completely sober.

Reeve grinned. "That's quite a party trick."

"I happen to have access to the world's best alchemist."

Reeve gestured ahead as they began their walk around the coliseum.

"I've heard the Mavros girl is quite skilled. Seems the rumors are true."

"She's incredible," said Abraxas. "She's the Maeve of potions. Creating new concoctions all the time."

"Like your little pick me up?"

Abraxas nodded and laughed as they walked down the pale crystal steps, venturing deeper into the Celestian Palace. "Yes. Though there's far more she's capable of than that."

The open corridors let in the salty breeze coming off the Black Deep.

Reeve pulled a small box from his pocket. He opened the ornate tin and offered Abraxas one of the white cigarettes. Abraxas took it with a sly grin.

"High Lord," he said with a shake of his head. "I had no idea you were this sinful."

Reeve pulled one out for himself and placed it between his lips. "I'm immortal," he said with a shrug.

"Must be nice," said Abraxas as he lit both their tips with a gentle snap of his fingers. "My mother would become positively mental if she saw me smoking this."

In unison, they took a long drag and stared out over the Black Deep.

"Now," said Abraxas with a sigh, "I know you did not bring me here to smoke in secret. My cousin's current state plagues you, does it?"

Reeve placed his elbows on the bannister and pulled on his cigarette. "My concern is for your Prince. As rulers of this realm, it's wise to be concerned about my friends across the sea."

Abraxas laughed and turned back towards the palace. He leaned against the railing. "Goodness, Reeve, I thought we were friends. And here you wound me with such lies."

Reeve looked over at him. "The Dread Hand is so good at detecting them, hm?"

Abraxas looked down at him with a knowing expression. "The Dread Hand sees everything, High Lord."

"And what do you see this evening?"

Abraxas sighed and chewed his lip. "I'll give you the truth, Reeve, despite the fact that you remain playing games with me. I see my two best friends each doing their best to ruin everything I am working so hard to create."

"Ruling and romance don't always complement one another."

"Yes," muttered Abraxas. "Because the pair of them simply being the crown and the sword worked so well the first time. I've never seen Mal so distraught. And I shared a room with him for four years at Vaukore."

Reeve scoffed. "You mean to tell me she denied him?"

"For a time."

"Hmm," said Reeve with a soft smile.

Abraxas looked over at him with a satisfied smirk. "You're holding your deck awfully low, Reeve. I can see that royal flush."

"If my hand of cards is visible to you, Rosethorn, it is because I do not care if you see them."

Abraxas' brows flicked up as his cigarette was at its end. The butt end vanished after his last drag.

"Jealousy is a hard emotion for Mal to swallow. Thank you for not pursuing her."

Reeve's defensive and jabbing reply slipped from him before he could stop himself. "There are many reasons I do not pursue your cousin. Fear of him isn't one of them."

"No," said Abraxas, looking away from him. "I imagine not. You stay away from my cousin for her sake." He smiled sadly. "You are speaking to the one other person who knows just how hard it is to watch them be together."

Reeve's face dropped at his honesty. He paused as he

realized the hand of the Dread Prince had just confessed his affection for the Dread Prince himself. "Does he know that?"

Abraxas paused a moment and then shrugged. "It doesn't matter." A genuine smile spread across his face. "I am happy it's her." He pushed off the bannister and faced Reeve fully. "Thank you for the cigarette, High Lord, and such wonderful hospitality."

Abraxas turned on his heel and retreated into the palace, back to the festivities, leaving Reeve alone. A chorus of thunderous applause echoed down the chamber where Abraxas headed.

Reeve didn't follow right away. The party would last long into the night. He fought his desires to see her for a time. As the duels continued and the wine flowed, he retreated to his chambers in solitude. But he desired to explain, even though he knew the Magic holding his tongue wouldn't allow such truth.

Perhaps it was the raw and honest way Abraxas spoke to him that drove him across the Black Deep and onto the balcony outside Maeve's chambers at Castle Morana. He knew he shouldn't be there. It was only a matter of time before Malachite grew tired of entertaining and would return to the castle.

It was only a matter of time before Malachite, or the darkness dwelling in his mind, would see the Magic between Reeve and Maeve.

But Reeve stood, nonetheless, and faced her, prepared to answer her questions. He folded his arms across his chest as the glass-paned doors slipped open and she appeared.

"How are you in my head?" she demanded without a greeting.

She did not leave the doorway and he didn't look at her. The green hazy mist surrounding them trailed by at a crawling pace. How could she stay here? So stifled and dark. Sinclair Estates had suited her, despite her brooding and dark temperament. The sun kissed stone and vibrant garden blooms complimented her essence.

This place was a tomb.

"You know how," was all the Magic holding his tongue allowed him to say.

"No," said Maeve sharply. "That's ridiculous."

His eyes darted over to her at last. "Is it any more ridiculous than the charade happening all around us?"

She tensed. Her jaw clamped in tightly.

Her next words were the ones that nearly stopped him from coming at all. He readied his indifferent and deflecting lie.

"How long have you known?" she asked.

"That doesn't really matter."

She shook her head and looked up. "I must be a joke to you."

She leaned against the frame of the doors. He turned towards her and took her in at last. She had changed from her posturing uniform as the Dread Viper, and now wore casual clothes. At least, as casual as attire for a Sinclair got. The neckline of her sweater was embroidered with golden floral vines.

"Is that what you think?" he asked quietly.

She provided no reply. A chilling breeze picked up across the balcony, and she hugged herself tightly as the constant haze of the Dread Lands moved to cover the moons.

The space around them darkened.

"It doesn't mean anything," she said.

He ignored the unfamiliarly insecure tone of her voice.

"I know," he said calmly.

"I choose Mal."

Reeve cursed himself for coming.

She continued. "I have faith he will pull through this."

"I know that, too."

She fired quickly once again, "You aren't owed me because of some ancient—"

He interrupted her gently. "I never said I was."

Silence, painful silence, settled between them. He watched her defenses drop as she stared at him. Her heartbeat slowed to a calm and steady pace as he felt each and every slow breath she took.

"I can't tell him this," she said softly.

More fear.

"I can promise I don't need your protection from—"

"Oh shut up," she snapped.

Reeve's Magic slammed to attention and he fought a smile as she continued.

"This isn't just about you or me."

On that account, she was correct. Still, he found himself unable to repress his desire to protect her. Since Ambrose's death, her Magic only called to him more.

Just as it had that night he returned to Earth after years, just in time to watch Malachite duel. He hadn't been expecting to come face to face with the Dread Descendant that evening. He had merely grown tired of wondering how she was.

Wondering if her Magic had manifested in the ways her mother's had. In all the ways Ambrose feared it might.

Wondering if she was beginning to remember all the things she altered where he was concerned.

But, despite the way her Magic called to him, none of the things he worried over had come to be the problem.

It was this damned place yet again that threatened Magic's existence.

It was Shadow. He was nearly certain of it.

"Things are changing, Maeve," he said.

Her eyes whipped up at him, as though she nearly forgot he was there.

Reeve continued. "I know you can feel the darkness that is growing here."

She tossed her head back slowly and closed her eyes. "Shut. Up."

Reeve ignored her and continued speaking over her. "I

can feel it all the way across the Black Deep."

"Did you not hear me say shut up?"

"No, I did," he snarled. "But say it again. I love hearing the hatred you harbor for me singing off your spoiled fucking tongue."

She pushed off the doorframe and closed the gap between them at last. The usual look of disdain she held for him was amplified.

She smelled addictively wicked.

He hated that.

He bent forward until their noses nearly touched and smiled at how easily he riled her up. "You're too easy."

She hesitated a moment and then stepped back from him. "How did this even happen?" she asked with a huff. "I thought you already had a mate. I'm not even an Immortal."

Leandra's face shot across his mind. Her golden hair and dark eyes. He lingered on the thought of her for only a moment, grateful the image of her was a pleasant one, and not his final memory of her broken and lifeless body.

"She was not my mate, despite the love that we shared," he said.

Her brows pulled together, not in anger, but in empathy.

His chest tightened as the soft side of her he so rarely was allowed access to slipped through.

"But I thought. . ." she began with a small shake of her head. "I asked you about her."

"You referred to her as my mate. I did not correct you. I loved her, yes," he continued. "Despite no Magical fated bond, I loved her fully. Painfully and achingly so. The way you love your Dread Prince."

Her lips parted. "You've known this whole time," she said softly.

He couldn't lie to her further. Not when they were piling up higher than his liking. So he ignored the truth that he'd known about their bond for many years, and deflected entirely.

"I won't say anything," he said, hoping to calm the panicked way her heart was still beating.

"To anyone?"

He paused a moment and then was brutally honest with both himself and her. "It is not in my best interest to announce to the world that my mate is Malachite's Dread Viper."

She looked away from him and ran her fingers across the stone bannister. "It is not, nor it cannot come to good."

Reeve looked down at her and attempted to smile, but it quickly faltered. It was becoming harder to pretend for her. "You read Hamlet?"

She avoided his gaze, but he could have sworn the beginnings of a playful smile pulled at the corner of her lips. "You gave it such a glowing review."

His own smile naturally flourished then. "And?" he prodded.

Maeve shrugged. "It was. . ."

Malachite's Magic appeared close by, Reeve felt his incoming presence at once. Maeve inhaled sharply, having felt it too. Her eyes slid to a close at once as her grip on the bannister tightened.

Reeve didn't hesitate.

He left her on the balcony before Malachite could find them, and returned to the Celestian Palace. The opening celebration continued across the crystal halls, where Reeve was certain Eryx and Drystan were providing too much Aternian Absinthe to Abraxas and Alphard. He proved himself right when moments later he joined them in his study, and Alphard's eyes were barely open as he tried to look at the deck of cards in his hands.

"Look alive," said Reeve, clapping him on the shoulder. "My men are trying to take all that Mavros gold."

"He's got plenty," said Eryx with a smile as he upped his wager.

Abraxas groaned and threw down his cards, a light shade

of green on his cheeks. "That's it. No more Aternian Absinthe. Not one drop."

With a triumphant smile, Eryx pulled the stack of gold (and Abraxas' rather expensive watch) towards himself from the center of the table. Reeve watched the Commander of the Senshi Warriors enjoying himself more than Reeve could remember having seen him do in ages.

He wouldn't tell Eryx and Drystan about Malachite's changing eyes until the morning. Nor about the familiar and haunting Magic he felt on Maeve's balcony. The one that lingered in the air and drove him to desire to steal Maeve away from such a place.

If a part of Shadow remained in the Dread Lands, despite his defeating her three hundred years ago, then it wasn't just Maeve Reeve had to worry over.

It was the state of all seven realms.

PART ONE

Chapter 1

Maeve

I am not yours, and you are not mine.

The voice forced its way into the cracks of her mind with desperation.

The feeling of smooth, cool skin brushed against her cheek in the darkness. His voice continued, low and filled with something between a promise and a threat.

And yet, I want you all the same.

She inhaled sharply as Magic slipped down her spine. That same desperate, seeking feeling trying to take root.

Another voice, entirely different, one she could name, entered her mind.

"Maeve."

Alphard Mavros' voice cut through her mind, yanking her eyes open, leaving the prickling skin on her cheek feeling bare. Her eyes settled on the teacup before her, steam swirling above the amber liquid.

"Maeve," Alphard said again, his voice unbothered and absent.

She looked up at last, the entire breakfast room coming into focus. Maxius sat next to her, eating his food with careful precision. Alphard looked through their mail, setting aside the newspaper.

"Have you taken your potion today?" he asked, flipping through the various envelopes.

Maeve didn't answer. Her hand moved to her cheek, where the Magic she'd felt slowly faded at her touch. At last, Alphard's eyes landed on her.

He slid a vial of pale liquid across the breakfast table. "Drink."

Maeve took it without argument, realizing she couldn't remember how long she'd been taking them. A side effect of the "episodes," Astrea would remind her.

Rebelliously, Maeve left some at the bottom of the bottle, bitter she needed Astrea to make her potions at all. Her fingers slipped into her pocket, brushing against a small strip of blank parchment. Something that unexplainably grounded her on days when her mind felt far from her own.

Her mind settled, and the voice she'd heard felt like a fast-fading dream she could hardly even recall.

"A royal invitation," said Alphard, tossing a glowing square of parchment on the table.

"A royal invitation, where?" asked Maeve with a groan, already knowing the answer.

"Castle Morana," answered Alphard.

Maeve frowned. "I hate going there," she muttered.

"I know," said Alphard.

"You can just go without me," she replied.

"Doubtful," said Alphard as he looked up at her and slid the parchment across the breakfast table towards her.

Beneath the swirling and performative invitation to a ball at Castle Morana was Abraxas' elegant stamped seal. Beneath that was a brief note.

Non-negotiable, cousin.
Brax

"He really does know everything," said Alphard as he stood.

Alphard's fingers twisted gently through Maxius' hair in the seat next to him. Maxius barely noticed; he was fixated on Spinel pawing relentlessly at the window. Ice edged on the large panes as endless snow fell in the bitter cold. It had been winter for as long as Maeve could remember. Never-ending ice and snow covered everything from the Greywood to the Dark Peaks.

"How are things?" asked Maeve, before Alphard could leave.

Alphard's brows raised.

"Abraxas says you are likely to return to the front lines of The Elven Lands soon if their capital doesn't fall."

Alphard frowned. Maeve hadn't forgotten how he'd come back

the first time he'd been sent off to fight. How distant. How on edge he was.

"You neglected to tell me that," said Maeve pointedly.

Alphard sighed. "I don't want to talk about this in front of Maxius."

"Your son deserves to know if you are heading into war," she replied. "Even if you don't think I do."

Maxius peeled his eyes away from the window and looked up at Alphard at last.

"He's six." Alphard's eyes narrowed slightly at Maeve as he dropped his affectionate hold on Maxius. "The Dread Prince has been away for some time. Until he returns, I have no idea where I'll be."

With that, he left them in silence.

After a moment, Maxius' attention returned to the window where Spinel begged for entry.

Maxius signed, *Open*, with his small hands.

Maeve raised her brows at Maxius. "Go on," she said, nodding her head towards the window. Maxius' lips pulled together. He blinked once, but the window remained closed, despite Spinel's frantic pawing.

At his initial failure, Maxius looked up at her with frustrated eyes. She felt no Magic radiating from him. Maeve smiled softly. Maxius returned his attention to the window and tried once more.

Nothing.

Maeve's eyes drifted to the locket that hung around his neck. Thoughts threatened to slip into her mind, thoughts that bordered on reality, but she knew to be false.

Maxius stood in frustration and slammed his fist on the table. The glass shattered with a sharp ring.

Maxius startled and then quickly smiled up at Maeve in triumph. Spinel jumped onto the floor and fussed at them before slinking away to find warmth with Maxius hot on his heels.

Maeve shook her head and muttered, "That's one way to do it," as she relented and downed the rest of her daily potion.

Zimsy rounded the corner of the breakfast room, narrowly dodging Spinel and Maxius. She immediately pulled her robe tightly around her with a quick shiver. "It's freezing in here."

Maeve breathed a laugh and repaired the broken window with a quick twist of her wrist. "Yes, but at least he's performing Magic."

"Oh, good!" she chimed, taking a seat at the table. "What's this?" she asked, snagging the invitation between two of her delicate fingers.

"A royal invitation," answered Maeve grimly.

Zimsy read over the elegant square of parchment. "It's a month away. Gives you plenty of time to fake an illness."

Maeve laughed. "Brax is too sharp for that."

"Looks like it's a rather important event," said Zimsy, placing the invitation down and pouring herself some tea. "Any idea what they could be announcing?"

"No," said Maeve. "Maybe they expect the war will be over then."

"Maybe the Elven Army finally surrendered."

Maeve knew Zimsy didn't approve of the war in the Elven Lands. Maeve didn't concern herself with politics and war, but since Zimsy was passionate about it, she had already decided to agree with her friend.

"How long has it been now?" asked Zimsy.

Maeve's brows raised.

"Since the Elven Queen was overthrown by her own people," elaborated Zimsy.

"Over a year," said Maeve.

Over a year since Lithandrian's people staged a mutiny and established militant control. How the Elven Army managed to obtain Magic no one knew.

Their sudden ability to fight with Magic was a mystery to all citizens of the Dread Lands. Not even Abraxas himself understood. Not that it mattered to Maeve.

She never thought of her crowned Prince beyond the occasional reminder of his existence. They hadn't been close at Vaukore, and in the years she and Alphard had lived in the Dread Lands, she'd never even laid eyes on Malachite Peur. In fact, rumor had it the Crowned Prince had been away for some time, searching for an explanation and counter to the Elven people's newfound Magic.

Chapter 2

Maeve

Maeve's fingers traced over the worn strip of paper, at a loss for the hundredth time why she had never been able to part with it. She looked up at her reflection in the vanity mirror, tucking her legs beneath her on the stool. Zimsy had braided her hair perfectly for the non-negotiable ball at Castle Morana. Her gown was green, an attire required by all those who visited the castle.

Her gaze lingered on her face. Pale, icy eyes looked back at her, foreign and cold, stark against her dark lashes. She hated them.

Portraits and paintings, even the few photographs of her that existed from her adolescence, depicted her with deep-blue eyes. Sapphire blue. Like her father's, like her sister's.

Even like Antony's, in what little memories she had of her brother.

But Maeve's eyes were now a hollow, winter icy blue-white, with no explanation of why or how.

Her fingers still lingered across the small strip of parchment as something sharp slid across her mind. She could nearly see herself properly in her reflection — with blue eyes she missed with every look at herself.

Her hand gravitated towards the feathered quill on her vanity.

She scribbled across the worn paper, daring to mark the blank slate at last.

Why does this strange bit of parchment call to me?

She stared at it for a moment, yanked open her vanity drawer, and tossed it inside.

Castle Morana was just as she remembered: magnificent in its grand appearance, dripping in Dark Magic, but entirely devoid of warmth.

"This room gives me the creeps," said Alphard in a hushed voice as they stepped into the Throne Room. He wore his Bellator Captain's uniform, his chest decorated with various pins representing his power and status. Within the Bellator, those who fought for the Dread Prince, Alphard was second only to Roswyn.

"As a top-ranking Dread Knight, I can't imagine why you wouldn't want to attend, Al," said Abraxas, appearing at Maeve's side.

Alphard didn't look at Abraxas. His gaze was now fixed upon a redhead and her husband. Maeve and Abraxas exchanged a glance.

Her cousin's cheeks were flushed, and his eyes sparkled.

"Hello, Brax," she said with a smile.

Abraxas leaned towards her and quickly kissed her cheek. "Glad you could make it."

"The invitation didn't seem optional," said Alphard.

"Royal things rarely are," said Abraxas with a dazzling smile.

"Evening, Mavros," said Roswyn, appearing in their circle with Emerie at his side.

Alphard nodded his head once, barely acknowledging him.

Roswyn cleared his throat.

Alphard tore his eyes away from Victoria Damario and looked at Roswyn. His brows raised in annoyance.

"We're at Castle Morana, Mavros. You should address your superior properly."

Alphard's brows pulled together. "Fuck off."

Roswyn's stone-cold glare faltered, and he loosed a small laugh. They shook hands like old friends, Magic zapping between where their palms met—something that Maeve noticed each time the two men greeted one another.

"So what's all this for, Brax?" asked Maeve.

Abraxas took a sip of his drink and shook his head. "You'd have me spoil the surprise?" he asked with a chuckle.

He locked eyes with someone across the hall and toasted them. "Got to run," he said and disappeared, the crowd parting effortlessly for the Hand of the Prince.

Roswyn and Emerie's attention was pulled elsewhere, leaving Maeve and Alphard to themselves. Maeve's grip on his forearm tightened where their arms linked. Alphard looked down at her as she stalled beside him.

"Do you feel that?" she asked breathily, referring to an incoming of Magic that had the hairs on her arms standing up.

Alphard looked around them and paused. "No, Maeve," he replied, his voice filled with pity as he scanned the room.

Maeve cut her eyes up at him. She slowly slid her arm from his at his tone. A tone she often heard when he grew tired of her strange thoughts.

She opened her mouth, prepared with a sharp retort, but stopped short as an oppressive Magic entered the atmosphere. Alphard's eyes widened slightly. The room stilled, conversation halted, and the firelights flickered and dimmed.

Maeve turned from her husband, her heart racing in the presence of this power that barreled towards her, towards them all.

But she was certain with every drop of Magic that ran through her veins, that the Magic which pressed down on them all like a weight, called *her* name. Alphard whispered something to her as she stepped from him, but she didn't hear it. Her thoughts were consumed by a new and exciting feeling that ate at her with each second that it intensified. It was unlike any feeling she could recall ever experiencing as it raced towards her at super speed.

Alphard grabbed her wrist gently.

His Magic slid across her skin, trying to ground her as he had done many nights when her own mind felt like an enemy. But this was no "episode." This wasn't a feeling Astrea's potions could tame.

This was something entirely *Magical.*

A breath swelled in her chest as the green glass ceiling above them vanished in an explosion of viridian light, exposing the hazy night sky of The Dread Lands. Giant swirls of darkened Magic barreled down on them, slamming into the hall with a triumphant strike. The darkness was no mere mist alone; it was a Morconis, and the largest of them all in the Dread Prince's fleet.

The creature's long, black, inky body tensed as it landed on all fours in the middle of the hall. They were majestically dark, slick, creatures of night, with razor-sharp teeth and long, eel-like necks with wings that were like those of a dragon. Though their massive wings appeared tattered and torn, Magic still allowed them to fly. Magic had brought them back to life. They, like the rumored army of the undead that lurked in the Dark Peaks and the Greywood, were reanimated corpses. Given second life through Magic.

His Magic.

As striking and commanding as the creature was, nothing compared to the man who sat atop it. His Magic continued to bear down on her with constricting force. His entrance to Castle Morana was nothing short of a spectacle, but Maeve knew from the Magic radiating off the handsome Dread Prince, he was much more than show.

Her heart thrummed against her chest as the corners of her visions blurred anything that wasn't him. She couldn't even feel Alphard's grip on her wrist anymore. The only feeling that remained was his overwhelming presence.

He dismounted the tall beast elegantly, landing on his feet with a stare so intensely calm, it should have been sinister. Magic shot across the floor beneath him upon impact. He tucked his hands behind his back as guests fell to their knees.

All black suited the pale Malachite Peur, though none called him by that name who weren't his closest adversaries. Abraxas was among the few who called him Mal.

Without Alphard's hand tugging her down with him, Maeve herself wouldn't have remembered to bow. It wasn't out of disrespect or rebellion that Maeve was frozen in place.

No. It was the Dread Prince's green eyes that had been locked on hers since the moment he appeared that caused her trance.

"A joyous evening," exclaimed Abraxas, his Hand pin proudly gleaming on his chest as he bowed with worshipful admiration. "The return of our Prince to his throne and another realm nearly one with ours!"

Chapter 3

Maeve

"Alphard Mavros," said a cool voice.

The voice split across Maeve's mind like a whip, duplicating itself over and over, growing in its intensity until Alphard's hand took her own subtly at their sides. His right hand formed a fist and pressed into his chest, where a bright red brand of the Dread Mark lay beneath his clothes.

Malachite lowered his head, and Alphard dropped his salute.

"And Maeve Mavros," said the Prince, turning his attention towards her. "Formerly Sinclair."

His eyes moved quickly to the black lightning bolt-like lines that danced up her neck, but Maeve didn't miss it. She was used to the stares of curiosity at her unique markings, but being beneath his gaze felt like an honor.

"I was hoping to steal her for a dance, Alphard," said Malachite, slipping his black leather gloves off one finger at a time.

Maeve's stomach flipped.

Alphard took a swig of his drink and didn't miss a beat. "That'll save me the trouble."

Malachite didn't humor him with a laugh. He merely extended his now ungloved hand to Maeve, his bright green eyes on her. Her eyes lingered on the scar that ran across his eyes, splitting his brow.

He was devastatingly dark.

Realizing her stare, she quickly placed her hand in his. She nearly recoiled as a crack of Magic sliced down her throat and settled at her heart.

The Dread Prince's eyes shot to their hands. Maeve took a steadying breath as his icy fingers curled beneath hers, trapping her in his grip. He guided her gracefully onto the ballroom floor, never dropping her hand. He rounded on her and stopped. She looked up at him, certain by his glance down at her chest, and the small smile of victory that played at the corner of his lips, that he could feel just how unsteady her heart was.

His Magic had calmed since his arrival, like he was keeping it close to himself.

Malachite closed the gap between them. In one step, Maeve instinctively lifted her free hand and allowed him access to her waist. His hand did not settle above her hip as she anticipated. His slender fingers reached around her fully and pressed against her exposed back, drawing an involuntary inhale through her lips and bringing them closer than necessary for such a formal dance.

He was bold.

His eyes followed her hand as she placed it on his shoulder.

Magic swelled between them. Maeve looked at their joined hands and realized his Magic trickled down her arm in soft waves. The feeling settled into her bones. With a contented exhale, she allowed herself a breath closer to him.

An image slipped across her mind, something dreamlike and impossible, as her thoughts often were.

"Have we danced before?" she asked softly, already certain of the realistic answer.

Malachite's chest rose and fell, his eyes also on where their hands joined. "No," he answered simply.

Their heads turned back to one another in synchrony, and he began to move her across the ballroom gracefully, joining those already in their dance.

"Thank you for coming," he said.

Maeve didn't move her attention from him. "It's an honor to be here."

Malachite chuckled.

More Magic swelled between them. She ignored it, doing everything she could to write it off as his own, overflowing power.

"You sound like your cousin," he elaborated. "So political."

Maeve smiled softly. "Given unto us from a young age."

His gaze slid to her hand that rested on his shoulder. The one stamped with three stars. "Pureblood divinity."

Maeve's smile faltered. His eyes returned to hers.

"Are you ashamed of your Father's house of Magic?"

"No, my Prince," she replied, feeling the weight of too many eyes on her.

"Then it is your mother's unknown heritage that haunts you?"

Maeve nodded softly.

"You requested special permission from the crown to visit Earth, correct?"

"I did, yes."

"Your father is buried there."

She nodded. "He is, yes."

"How did he die?"

Maeve swallowed, grateful he continued to send calming Magic through her, intentional or not. "I wasn't there. My grandmother was with him. His heart gave out."

Mal's mouth pulled into a thin line. "Such a strong Magical. A Supreme. The Premier. Taken down by something that plagues Humans."

Maeve broke their gaze at last and stared straight ahead at his chest. Laughter from a couple near them drifted into her ears.

Malachite spoke softly and gently. "My apologies, Mrs. Mavros."

She didn't look back up at him. The song came to a close. They stopped dancing. Light applause filled the room as Maeve prepared to pull away from him and thank him for the dance.

But Malachite's hold on her remained. She looked up at him. Another song began, and he moved once more, in a much slower waltz. She stayed in his control without comment. His interrogation continued.

"Visiting your father's grave is not why you travel there, though, is it?"

Maeve hesitated. "No. It's not."

"So you admit you lied to me?" he asked lowly.

She tensed beneath his grip. "I didn't know it was you directly that granted my request, but yes. I lied."

"What is it you do on Earth, then? No lies this time."

"I practice Magic I am developing," she admitted.

His brows raised in a silent command. She continued.

"Memory renewal spells."

"You are in need of those?"

Maeve didn't respond right away. She swallowed and glanced across the hall. Watching as her husband and Roswyn were swarmed by younger Bellator, hanging on their every word, honored to stand among the soldiers closest to the Dread Prince. His Dread Knights. His command rang across her mind: no lies this time. Her voice was soft as she said, "Sometimes I feel like I've forgotten large parts of my life. There are memories I have that feel more like stories. Discrepancies in them all. I'd like to develop a way to retrieve lost memories. Humans have memory problems in their older age. There is a woman in America who allows me to try and unlock her lost memories."

If he felt some emotion from her response, he did not show it. "She is aware you are a Witch?"

She looked back up at him. "Most days, we are meeting for the first time. It is rare if she truly remembers me."

Malachite looked away from her, observing his party with casual enjoyment.

"If you require something of the Crown, Mrs. Mavros. You need not lie. There is nothing happening in the six realms that I don't know about."

"Forgive me," said Maeve. "I'll be more careful in the future."

He looked back down at her, satisfied. "While we are being so truthful, I am interested in your memory work. I'd like to discuss it with you in a more private setting. Preferably at your earliest convenience."

"I'll have to see if I can squeeze you in between rearranging my library for the hundredth time and picking out new drapes with my grandmother Agatha," she said dryly.

His head cocked to the side. "You sound rather bored with the golden life I created for you in these lands."

"You'd be bored too if you never got to pick your own drapes." Maeve sucked in sharply, realizing just how candidly she was speaking to her crowned Prince. "I'm sorry-"

Malachite smirked down at her. "I can assure you the work I have for you will interest you far more than window fabrics. Though I'm certain your son keeps you the most entertained. He appears to be what? Six now?"

Maeve's smile blossomed, and Malachite's performative charm faltered.

"Yes," she answered. "He is my greatest love."

Malachite's grip loosened, as his expression returned to that of a Prince.

"That must be wonderful," was all he said.

Maeve's smile faltered then. Malachite had no heirs. No companion he shared his secluded and secretive life with.

"I'm told your son only uses one finger to produce Magic."

Maeve nodded. "It happened once. He struggles to channel even the simplest of Magic most days."

"Regardless, you understand how incredible that one moment is, I trust?"

Maeve nodded again, softly. "I believe the restoration of Magic is to your credit. He is able to flourish here."

"You had him here, yes? And not on Earth? Before you were wed?"

"Yes," she said with a small laugh. "I'm afraid I was carrying him. . .preemptively."

The Magic pulsing through his fingers retracted, bringing her heart rate back to a racing speed as he withdrew his calming effect.

Maeve's cheeks flushed at her own admissions. Such bold things to confess to her Prince. The song ended, and this time, Malachite let her go. Her arms fell to her sides, and she took a small step back. He reached for his pocket, pulling out the black leather gloves he had removed prior to their dance, and began working his long fingers back into the fabric.

"The surname Mavros feels so strange to call you," he said, his voice detached and plain.

"You're the crowned Prince," she replied. "I'm certain you can refer to me however you please."

"Is that so?" he asked, a hint of playfulness in his tone. His now gloved hands landed behind his back. "What would you have me call you?"

She hesitated. Words she couldn't find on the tip of her tongue. "Maeve seems sufficient," she settled on saying.

"I look forward to working with you. . . Maeve."

Chapter 4

Maeve

The corridor was dimly lit at Blackstone Tower as Maeve slipped off her heels in the foyer, home at last. Her bare feet padded against the cool, dark tile in silent solitude. Alphard remained at Castle Morana with Roswyn, though Maeve elected to return home the first chance she got.

She could feel Maxius' slow flicker of Magic where he slept a floor above her. Her thoughts lingered on Malachite's words, on his remarks about her son.

A single finger. Maxius' use of a single finger, though it had only happened once, was truly remarkable, as the Prince stated. But it mattered little when controlling even the smallest bit of his Magic was out of his reach a majority of the time.

She rounded the corner to the kitchen. With a soft snap of her fingers, the firelights illuminated the space.

"Enjoy your dance, cousin?"

Abraxas leaned against the center counter, a cigarette between his fingers.

"Don't smoke that in my house," she replied, moving towards the teacup cabinet without answering his nosy question.

Abraxas put out the tip of his cigarette with his free hand, and it disappeared. "At least offer me a drink then."

"You've never needed permission to make yourself at home before," she remarked, grabbing the tea bag she wanted.

Abraxas leaned over the counter, propping his chin on both his hands. Maeve endured the silence between them with ease, knowing Abraxas was squirming behind her. She continued to prepare her tea and then joined him at the counter.

"Did you have a good evening, cousin?" she asked, blowing across her hot tea.

"You know," he replied, leaning towards her. "I know about every single thing that Mal wants. Needs. Plans. Everything. So imagine my surprise when I look across the ballroom and see him dancing with my cousin, having such a private conversation that I know nothing about."

"The Prince isn't allowed to dance with his subjects?"

Abraxas' eyes narrowed, true frustration showing through on his face.

"Did you see him dancing with a singular other subject? Have you ever seen him dance with a single subject?"

"I haven't seen him do anything, Brax. I haven't seen him in years. What are you obsessing about?"

His fingers drummed against the counter. "No gloves," he remarked.

"What relevance is that?"

"I can't remember the last time I saw him without them."

Maeve brushed off the thought and suppressed the shiver that threatened to run down her spine, recalling the feeling of his fingers on her spine as he held her in place. . .his smooth, cool fingers wrapped around her own. . . his—

"He wants something from you. And didn't run it by me," said Abraxas, yanking her from her thoughts.

"Aww," said Maeve with mock pity. "That must be so hard."

Abraxas pulled a fresh cigarette from his pocket with an exasperated sigh.

"No," said Maeve sharply. "You're not smoking that in here."

Abraxas groaned as his head fell dramatically onto the counter between them. "I wanted his return to be perfect," he muttered.

"And it was," she replied calmly, bringing the teacup to her lips and taking a hesitant sip. "The entire evening was wonderful. Can't you feel the Magic that has already shifted here at his return?"

Abraxas' head rolled against the counter in a dramatic display. "What did he want from you?"

"That's none of your business, Brax," said Maeve gently.

His head shot up as he pouted at her. Maeve laughed.

"Pathetic," she said with a smile.

"Alphard will be furious if you get involved in this war," he said. "Rightfully so. There's no reason you need to be—"

"Don't try and make your curiosity about my well-being."

"Can't it be both?"

Maeve shook her head at him in disbelief and sipped on her tea. "When this cup runs out, I'm going to bed, Brax."

"No," he whined, as she was nearly done.

She tilted her head back and drank the remaining tea.

Abraxas sighed and stood from the counter. "No one is ever as forthcoming with information as I am," he muttered, relenting that she wasn't going to give him the information he wanted.

"Goodnight, Abraxas," said Maeve sweetly.

He waved her off without a glance and headed for the door.

Maeve took the back set of stairs from the kitchen, climbing higher into the house to check on Maxius before going to bed. She pressed open the door to his room gently, ensuring he wouldn't wake. He slept soundly on the bed, his lips parted slightly through even breaths. The covers around his legs moved, and Spinel appeared between the draping fabric.

He jumped from the bed, dropping into a quick stretch before trotting across the room. He rubbed against her legs, purring heavily. Maeve pushed off the doorframe and continued through the house. Spinel stayed in step with her up the curved stairs onto the third floor. Maeve stopped short as she turned down the hallway to her bedroom.

A soft green glow illuminated the corridor from the slim crack in the open door, spilling from the bedroom and onto the deep mahogany floors. Spinel meowed and continued forward without her, slipping in the small opening of the doorway and disappearing into the glow.

Maeve followed the black cat and, with a gentle wave of her hand, opened the bedroom door. The soft green light narrowed down to one point in her room: her vanity. Maeve raised two fingers.

Spinel rubbed against the legs of the vanity, meowing loudly, his wide-set eyes glowing and refracting green. She twisted her two fingers, and the drawer popped open, flooding the bedroom in green Magic.

Spinel jumped on the vanity silently and peered over into the open drawer.

Maeve stepped hesitantly across the room and picked Spinel up. She held him close as they peered into the drawer together. The soft green glow resonated from the small scrap of parchment she couldn't part with. The same one on which she'd written: *Why does this strange bit of parchment call to me?*

The words she had written were gone, replaced with a sentence she did not write, in a handwriting that was not her own.

Perhaps for the same reason it calls to me.

Her jaw fell open. Spinel meowed once and jumped from her arms. She picked up the piece of parchment as the words vanished. The handwriting was unfamiliar, jagged, but elegant, script.

Maeve grabbed a nearby quill and dipped it in the ink jar, ready with a response, as a cold trickle of Magic swept down her spine. Her connection to the spell on this unknown strip of paper intensified, validating her affection for it. She wrote the words with confidence.

Who are you?

Maeve waited only a moment, and her letters vanished. New ones appeared that glowed bright green, in that same elegant script.

I would ask you the same.

The words disappeared as Maeve read them. She steadied her breathing and wrote back once more.

I did not make this Magic. Did you?

Her words vanished, and a reply came back at once. Soon, she and her unknown pen pal were writing back and forth at a rapid pace.

I believe so.

You can't tell me anything else?

What else is there to tell?

So you know nothing of this parchment?

Nothing that could be true.

The words were like a stab to the gut. She spent so many nights hearing those words from Alphard in response to her "episodes."

Maeve, none of that is real. Maeve, that isn't true. Maeve, that never happened. . .

Magic cracked tightly across her mind as her fingers touched the parchment once more. The sensation was familiar. One she associated with feeling the word no one ever dared utter about her, despite the things she saw. Despite how certain she was at times that the visions, the reality her mind showed her, was real.

Insane.

She was insane.

She set down her quill as the ink vanished and stepped back from the vanity. "No," she whispered. "I won't do this to myself."

Another reply appeared, the script unhurried and beautiful.

You shouldn't question what's right in front of you.

Alphard's Magic entered the house nearby. She felt each step he took towards the bedroom. She slammed the vanity drawer closed and turned away just as he appeared in the doorway, leaning against the frame for support.

"You're in a state," said Maeve cooly.

Alphard smiled at her. "A night worth celebrating. You know how Roswyn likes to celebrate."

"I can smell how Roswyn likes to celebrate from here," she replied.

Alphard watched her as she removed her jewelry and began unwinding her hair.

"You should be careful with him." Alphard's voice was low.

"Surely you aren't talking about your sworn Prince. Whom you slaughter and claim land willingly for?" Her eyes met his in the mirror. "Save me the lecture."

"Then you know exactly how serious I am."

He pushed off the door and closed it behind him with a flick of his wrist. He crossed the room, and Maeve turned towards him. She placed her hand on his chest, preventing him from coming any closer.

"I don't need you to treat me like I'm a child," she said softly, looking up at him.

Alphard raised his right hand, where a faint line of scarred Magic ran across his palm, and held it on display for her.

"I swore to protect you," was all he said.

Maeve studied the scar on his hand, a memory of Antony surfacing. His blue eyes, eyes she lacked, that matched the stone in the ring each of the Sinclair children had been gifted by their father— her father's eyes as blood poured from them—

"Hey," he said gently, warmth flooding into his tone.

Maeve's eyes slammed closed. With a single breath, she opened them once more and looked up at him.

"Thank you for your concern. I'll be careful."

Alphard nodded and moved his hand to rest over hers, where it still lay flat against his chest. He ran his fingers along hers, his expression shifting to a faraway thought.

Maeve hadn't missed how his gaze lingered all evening on one woman.

"I know," continued Maeve. "I know you wish she were yours to dance with all evening."

Victoria Damario had been Alphard's before his engagement to Maeve. And in private, she was still his now. Though his moments with her were few and far between.

Alphard looked down at her. "Does our arrangement still suit you?"

"Yes," she assured him. "You're free to do as you please. And so am I."

"I don't see you doing much that pleases you."

Maeve made a noise of disapproval. "I'm picky."

Alphard laughed, his fingers constricting around hers. Maeve's breath caught, her mind racing back to Malachite's hands on her own. How even such reserved touches left her wanting them again.

"I guess I should feel honored then," he said, his free hand finding her hip and tugging her closer.

She didn't pull away from him as his lips found hers. Nor when he guided her backwards towards the bed. She allowed her mind to slip to thoughts of another as they pleasured one another. And she was certain Alphard did the same as he took her.

Chapter 5

Maeve

Zimsy's eyes were wide as Maeve crossed the downstairs corridor towards her.

"What?" asked Maeve casually.

"The Dread Prince is here," she whispered quickly.

"Oh," said Maeve, looking past her towards the foyer.

Zimsy's shoulders fell, and her mouth popped open. "You don't sound surprised at all."

"I'm not," she replied, as though it were a question.

"You didn't think to tell me he would be coming?" Zimsy hissed.

"You don't live here," said Maeve as her brows raised. "By your own choice," she added as a reminder.

"Well, I'm still here all the time," said Zimsy.

"I know, Zim," agreed Maeve grimly.

"Please," said Zimsy as she rolled her big, round eyes. "You can't even braid your own hair."

"Yes, I can," said Maeve indignantly. "Anyway, where is he? I just have this feeling we shouldn't leave him waiting, you know, being the Prince and all."

"He's in the gallery, looking at all the paintings," relented Zimsy.

Maeve turned on her heel and made her way to the front of the manor. When she rounded the corner, Malachite stood with his back to her. His gaze was fixed on the largest portrait in the space with a golden frame and firelights illuminating it all around.

The portrait of Ambrose Sinclair dominated the space.

Malachite stood with his hands in his pockets, his cloak draped over a nearby chair. Maeve waited respectfully for his attention to fall on her. After another moment, he looked over his shoulder at her.

His green eyes flickered with Magic that made her spine

straighten.

"Maeve."

His voice was cordial, but his stance was casual. She bowed at him, as she knew was expected of her, and moved towards him, each step feeling like she was surrendering something. She kept a slight distance between them, stopping beside him in front of the portrait of her father. The Prince looked down at her from the corner of his eye.

"Apologies for coming unannounced."

Maeve shook her head. "Not necessary."

Malachite looked back up at the wall, taking a step farther down as his eyes scanned the various paintings.

"Are you still willing to assist me?" he asked.

Maeve made a small sound of agreement.

"Really?" he asked, his eyes on a small painting of Alphard and his father. "You haven't been. . . coerced into changing your mind?"

Maeve didn't smile. "I'm not so easily swayed."

Malachite looked back at her. "So I'm told." His eyes moved away from her, his expression unreadable. Even his Magic remained coiled tightly around himself. "Your cousin, my Hand, was quite adamant I leave you out of my affairs."

"My cousin is very protective."

"Of me or you?"

Maeve tensed beneath his words, but Malachite left no room for an answer.

"Abraxas is my most trusted advisor and friend. Perhaps if he thinks our union would yield problems for me, then I should heed his words."

Maeve didn't move towards him. "May I speak candidly?"

"I would prefer it if you did so without asking permission first."

She didn't need to be told twice. "I don't care what Abraxas says."

Mal turned towards her fully now, a hint of satisfaction on his face, and allowed her to continue.

"If you want my assistance, it would be an honor to serve you."

Mal's chest rose and fell quickly at her words. His brows raised, as though challenging her to take her admission one step further.

Maeve thought of the way his fingers danced down her spine, and confessed to herself that she didn't care that he was dripping with dark energy, with warning.

She'd help him with whatever work he asked of her, just for the chance to feel his hands on her again. So she sealed their fate as he waited patiently for her to do so.

"And moreover, I want to help you."

Malachite's head angled slightly to the side, drinking in her confession. "Your husband will allow such a thing?" he pressed.

Maeve couldn't help but smile up at him. "Don't insult me."

Mal's own smile blossomed at last. "Let's begin, shall we?"

He stepped towards her. "What's the easiest way for you to view a memory of my own?"

"From directly inside your mind."

"And the way I'm actually going to let you view it?" His voice remained calmly collected, despite the weight of his question.

Maeve matched his demeanor. "You can place it in my mind."

Mal made a face like that was obviously his preferred method and stepped towards her.

"But," she continued, "the accuracy of what I see will be skewed that way."

"How so?" he asked.

"Your interpretation of the memory can corrupt it. Whereas, in your mind, I can see things even you can't see."

Mal looked away from her, considering her words.

"It's pure that way," she added.

He didn't consider it for long. Mal's eyes landed back on hers. "No."

She nodded.

"Then, before I look, I have a few questions, if that's alright."

"You may ask them. Though I cannot promise a response."

They sat on two tufted benches, opposite one another in the middle of the gallery. Maeve stared out the frosted windows as she began her questioning.

"Why do you want me to see the memory?"

His reply came swiftly, without hesitation. "Because it feels like a lie."

"In what way?" she asked, looking back at him.

Mal's green eyes never left hers as he answered her. With each word, his voice slipped into a magnetic drawl, entrancing her attention completely.

"In the way that shoes one size too big are obviously wrong with each step you take. In the way that stale bread is clearly no longer fresh. And some days, with some memories. . . they are wine that tastes like water."

She knew such a feeling well. The potion she kept in her pocket at all times in case of an emergency weighed heavily at his words. How often had she tried to explain that exact feeling to Zimsy? And Zimsy looked back at her with a soft, generous smile, assuring Maeve that she wasn't crazy, but that she shouldn't dwell on such ideas.

That was easy for them to say.

"Maeve."

With a quick blink, she realized she'd been staring at him.

"Sorry," she muttered. She crossed her legs and continued with their conversation. "So you'd like for me to see if there are any anomalies?"

Mal nodded, his eyes fixed on hers and his mouth slightly parted. If there was a question on the tip of his tongue, he did not ask it. He stood and stepped across the gap between them. She remained seated as he loomed over her. He removed the glove on his right hand with sensual precision, his eyes never leaving hers. Maeve sucked in a tight breath as his hand moved towards the side of her face.

His brows raised in a silent question. She nodded in approval, her eyes fluttering closed.

Mal's finger touched down on her temple with the smallest movement, and white light erupted across her vision, drowning out the gallery and Mal's tall, slender frame before her. His projected memory appeared in full force around her, blazing to life from black mist.

The Throne Room at Castle Morana manifested into view. The Dread Prince stood before his throne, Abraxas beaming at his side, and named Roswyn his right-hand man. Maeve herself remembered the day Malachite Peur was crowned Prince. She stepped closer to the men, observing them, reaching her own Magic towards them. The memory felt real.

Roswyn kneeled before Mal and placed his fist across his chest in a heartfelt salute.

Ice slammed into her own chest, coursing through her bones, causing her to grip her heart with a sharp cry. The Throne Room vanished in a blink and was quickly replaced by the gallery at Blackstone once more. Mal took a swift step back from her, his curious green eyes on where her hand gripped at her chest.

The pain began to slip away, and she removed her fingers.

"That was strange," she whispered, "considering there were no obvious anomalies overall."

"You wouldn't call that," he gestured to her aching chest, "an 'anomaly'?"

"When you visualize that day, what about it specifically feels strange?" she asked, ignoring his rhetorical question. "In what you shared with me, where does doubt leak in?"

Mal stared down at her for a moment, seemingly contemplating answering her at all. At last, when he spoke, he kept his reply short. "Where Roswyn is concerned."

Maeve's brows pulled together. "While I admit that feeling such defensive Magic from a memory is rare, it is curious that the pain I experienced inside the memory correlated with the very thing you feel is out of place. However. . .I felt nothing that would lead me to believe it harbors any sort of deception. My professional opinion is that the memory is rooted in reality."

"And you have no reason to not trust your senses?"

Maeve stalled at the words. "Pardon?"

Mal whipped his glove from his pocket at slid it back on his hand. He twisted his wrist, checking the time on a golden watch with emerald inlay and two serpents for hands. Her eyes narrowed at the familiarity of it.

His voice changed, returning to the princely way he'd conversed with her at the ball. "Thank you for your time. I hate it seems I've wasted both ours."

The blow, intentional or not, didn't go unfelt by Maeve. She didn't stand as he stepped away. Only the sound of his cloak whipping around his shoulders filled the space, and he was gone.

Thoughts filled her mind, slow and testing at first, creeping in like light through small cracks. She knew to press down on them. She knew better than to allow them to gain a footing in her mind. But her failure before Mal made it all the more tempting to give in to them.

Each step to her bedroom echoed across her mind, drifting further towards the back as new sounds, new ideas took their place. Voices she couldn't place, even after years of hearing them, slipped through those terrifying cracks.

Her bedroom door closed silently behind her with effortless Magic. As she moved across the room, she lifted the fabric of her sweater over her head, slipping it off and tossing it on a nearby chair. She stepped closer to the tall mirror and ran her fingers across the starburst of white skin that sat just above her heart, wondering if the scarring she'd never quite remembered getting suddenly mattered. Or if it was even real.

Chapter 6

Maeve

Alphard was not present for Christmas. He was called to the front lines in the Elven Lands with the remaining Dread Knights. Abraxas was certain the realm would fall soon.

"It'll be swift," said Abraxas. "He'll be home before spring."

Spring. Maeve hadn't seen a spring in years. Winter was all that remained in the Dread Lands. Astrea sat at the piano in the corner, playing a soft melody that Grandmother Agatha hummed as she leaned back in her chair with her eyes closed. She occasionally sat up to speak to the children, but then returned to enjoying the soft tune. Astrea's youngest, nearly a year old, lay cradled in Maeve's arm.

"Where's he been?" Maeve asked, still uneasy about the Prince's visit weeks ago. "Why isn't he fighting? And where did they even get Magic that could possibly stand against ours? And how does he rule if he's gone for so long all at once?"

"That's why he has me," said Abraxas with a smirk and a flick of the pin gleaming proudly on his chest, signifying his place as Hand of the Prince.

Maeve sighed. "That's only one answer."

"Something wrong, cousin?" he asked wickedly. "Your little adventure with Mal not go as planned?"

Maeve didn't need to answer. By the smug look on his face, she was certain he knew Mal's only visit to her had been swift, uneventful, and hadn't been repeated.

Abraxas laughed. "Don't be sour, Maeve. Alphard fighting for those he loves, for his Prince, is good for him. Just as it is all the Bellator and those special Dread Knights. If Mal could waltz in and take the realm, which. . .with this Magic would be tricky. . .I still don't think he would. Having an army proud to stand by your banner means something to him. It's not like Vaukore, the realm and the school were naturally his as our ruler. As for the Magic, we have no idea. The Magical signature differs from Dread Magic. And lastly, as for Mal, his absence has been in solitude, growing his strength and studying the Magic he needs to conquer in the Elven Lands. He doesn't want to rule a pile of rubble. He wants a realm intact and worth ruling."

Maeve, though she was satisfied and grateful for his honesty, pretended not to care, waved him off. "Whatever you say."

Lyrux appeared at Abraxas' feet with a wrapped present in his hands.

"We'll open presents later, love," said Brax. "Go put it back under the tree."

His son pouted and huffed, but returned to the Christmas tree where Arianna's twins, Anselm and Aislin, and Astrea's oldest, played. Maxius was the oldest of them all, but by far the most innocent in nature.

"Juliet bought him even more presents than last year," said Abraxas. "Ridiculous."

"Don't act as though you weren't counting your presents at his age as well," replied Maeve. "Primrose used to say at age three, you only said 'mine' in regards to anything and everything."

"Yes, well, she was an old bat, wasn't she?" he replied with a smile.

Astrea's fingers halted their tune. She looked over her shoulder towards the foyer.

Alphard stepped through the archway, and Maxius' eyes lit up. He rushed towards him at once, leaving his cousins behind. Alphard scooped him up with one arm.

"Look at you," remarked Alphard, his smile wide at the sweater Maxius wore. It had been his as a child, handed down to Maxius by Alphard's mother, Irma.

But Maeve's attention couldn't linger on Alphard for long, for her husband was not alone. Her heart hammered against her chest as Mal lowered the hood of his cloak behind Alphard. The Prince observed Alphard and Maxius, his face calm and collected as always.

"Mal," said Abraxas cheerfully, his head dipping into a bow.

"What a surprise."

Mal reached out his gloved hand to touch Maxius' small face and stopped short. The gesture was so tender that Maeve's insides fluttered.

"I figured no child should be without their father on Christmas," he said as Maxius smiled up at Alphard.

Maxius tugged on Alphard and signed for him to come and see the desert he helped make.

Arianna rounded the corner. "Dinner is ready," she said as Alphard passed her with Maxius in his arms. Her eyes landed on Mal. With a startled sound, she dipped into an awkward bow.

Mal didn't seem to care.

Agatha corralled the children out of the living room, but not before passing my Mal and giving him a soft smile.

"Handsome as ever," she noted.

Mal smiled at her, genuinely smiled. "Thank you, Agatha."

It was no secret that Maeve's grandmother, Ambrose's mother, had been quite encouraging of Mal's place on the throne long before all their lives began in the Dread Lands, both with her words and her gold.

"Would you like to stay for dinner?" asked Abraxas casually. "Zim and Juliet probably prepared enough to feed an army."

"No," Mal answered swiftly, with little emotion in his voice. "I'd like to speak to Maeve and then I'll take my leave."

Abraxas rolled his eyes. "Fine," he said with a sigh. "But if you're after my place, cousin," he added, turning towards Maeve, "I'll remind you that though I never need it, I use a single finger now too." He pressed a kiss to her cheek, smoothly slid the sleeping baby from her arms, and left them alone.

Maeve shook her head, stretching her arm where Astrea's youngest had been asleep for quite some time.

"A Supreme who doesn't fight," remarked Mal once they were alone.

The silence between her and the Dread Prince grew heavy and thick. Voices from the dining room carried across the house. Mal looked to the glass-paned doors that led into the atrium. His eyes cut back to hers, and she followed the silent command. With a gentle wave of her hand, the doors spread open for them.

Mal observed the various plants and shrubs growing in the unusually warm space.

"Between Zimsy and Agatha, there's hardly enough room for everything they grow," said Maeve.

"Magic keeps them alive?"

Maeve shook her head. "Agatha enchanted the room to maintain the proper temperature, but they take care of the plants themselves." Maeve ran her fingers over a large, green leaf. "But I'm certain you aren't here to discuss gardening."

When she looked over at him, his gloves were gone. He stepped farther into the atrium until he stood before a large hydrangea bush her grandmother had brought from Earth. His long fingers brushed against one of the blooms. His voice was smooth as silk as he spoke, not looking at her.

"Was there anything you discovered after my last visit?"

Maeve swallowed. "I'm sorry. No."

"No?" he asked, a brow raising as his eyes landed on her. He turned towards her fully. "This will be so much easier if you are honest with me."

Maeve chewed the inside of her lip, suddenly nervous under his impatient eyes.

"It seems like you already know the answer you seek," she said, trying to keep her voice steady.

Mal crossed towards her, each step relaxed and unhurried. Maeve held her head high.

"I seek your cooperation, not your deception."

She held perfectly still as his fingers moved towards her chest. They curled around the fabric of her shirt gently, pulling it aside with reverence, revealing the white starburst scar that sat over her heart.

His eyes fixed on her skin. "What is this from—" he began, his cold fingers brushing over the scar.

His question halted, his voice catching in his throat as she winced.

Her vision flashed white. The image that appeared in her mind flooded her blood with an overwhelming sense of panic. She sat on dark, silken sheets, completely naked, looking up at Mal with flushed cheeks and worship in her eyes. He kneeled before her with a single finger pressed against her chest. His toned and exposed stomach glimmered in the darkness.

The vision melted away as quickly as it had formed. Mal stood before her in the atrium once more. She slapped a hand over her mouth as her eyes widened. She looked up at him at once, and it was clear Mal had seen the same scene she had.

"That's not real," whispered Maeve beneath her hand, twisting away from him. "That was my uncle's flat in London—" she rambled.

"The Hapswitch House."

Maeve turned back towards him and shook her head. "Why would you know anything of that place?"

"Welcome to my mind, Maeve," he said coolly.

Maeve's breaths quickened. The thick, humid air stung with each jagged inhale. She'd never been more desperate to down one of Astrea's potions, to soften the thoughts all talking over one another in her mind.

"Do you not feel it?"

Maeve looked over at him. His gaze was distant.

He continued in her silence. "Do you not feel the extraordinary signature your Magic holds?

"Could that be the future? What we saw?"

"No," he answered plainly. "There's no scar over my eye in what we both just witnessed."

"Then perhaps it's not real at all," said Maeve.

Mal looked over at her. "That's quite a jump just to rationalize the thoughts you are having. Tell me honestly that didn't feel real to you. And remember when you answer, that I am your sworn Prince."

"I don't have the luxury of believing what I see in my mind."

"And who convinced you of that?" he challenged.

"I did," she replied, more bite in her tone than she intended.

"So what made-up story did you concoct to explain that scar across your chest?" he asked, his cool demeanor cracking slightly.

"An accident. I was told there was an explosion from an experimental potion in Alchemy when I was at Vaukore, and—"

"You were told? You don't remember?"

Maeve's mouth opened and then closed.

"And those?" he continued, gesturing to her inky dark veins.

"I don't remember," she admitted quietly, realizing that the corners of her eyes were filling with tears.

Mal nodded, not in agreement with her, but as though she had proven him right.

"I thought," he began, "if I could understand why you were suddenly appearing in my mind, a girl I'd barely brushed shoulders with in school, then maybe I'd understand what it will take to seal my rule over the Elven Lands. But each time I converse with you, the one who understands memories better than any Magical alive, the less I understand anything. What a paradox you are."

"I'm sorry I wasn't of better service to you," she said, keeping her voice flat.

Mal shook his head. "You speak in past tense. We are only just beginning."

Chapter 7

Maeve

It was foolish.

She was a fool.

Maeve stared at the empty bottles and glass vials of her specially brewed potion. They weren't empty because she had consumed them all. No. They sat empty in her bathroom because she poured them all out. Every last drop, sunk down the drain.

Now, two days later, as pain sliced across her head like a line of needles and one achingly familiar voice whispered incoherently in her mind, she held each bottle up and begged for even a drop to hit her tongue. The small sliver of parchment on her bathroom vanity lit up green, but she had already turned and left in desperate haste, missing the message:

You don't need them, Little Viper.

The gates of Castle Morana stood tall before Maeve as they opened in a sinister silence. Her steps felt muddled as she moved through a protective barrier that encapsulated the Prince's castle, each step against the stone path echoing in a strange void.

"Mrs. Mavros," said one of the guards as she neared the steps. "Alphard isn't here, he's—"

"I know where he is," she answered swiftly. "I'm here for his sister, the healer."

The boy straightened. "Of course," he answered, without any further questioning.

Something shifted in her stomach that made her uneasy. Nauseous. She wasn't welcomed so easily into the castle through any means of her own. It was Alphard's station that granted her unvetted access.

She shook off the childish feeling, pressing further against that voice, the things it wanted to show her in her mind. Soon she'd be downing a bottle of silent ecstasy, and it wouldn't matter anymore. Maeve never visited Astrea at Castle Morana, an unexpected perk of being her sister-in-law, she supposed. Regardless, she knew where the Healing Wing sat in the castle.

She didn't knock. She pulled open the doors without announcing herself.

Astrea's head whipped over her shoulder, where she stood healing a young Bellator. He lay shirtless on an exam table, a violent wound across his front.

More whispers flittered across her mind, each word like a claw trying to snag hold of something solid. She pushed her Magic against it, harder this time, silencing the desperate voice.

"Get out," said Maeve to the boy.

He looked up at her with disgust. "Who do you think you are talking to?"

Astrea placed her hand on his shoulder as the air crackled with Maeve's unsteady Magic. "We were done here anyway," she assured him.

She helped him back into his shirt, his eyes flicking up at Maeve in uncertainty. As the door finally shut behind him, Astrea didn't need to speak. She crossed her Healing Wing and ran her fingers down a tall cabinet, unlocking a tight, Magical seal that protected Maeve's potions.

Maeve slid into a wooden chair, counting her breaths with closed eyes.

Silence passed.

Too much silence passed.

"I'm out," said Astrea, her voice quiet.

Maeve's head whipped up. "What?" she quipped, certain she'd misheard her.

Astrea stared at the empty shelves with her lips pulled tightly together. She closed the cabinet door and opened it once more. She turned towards Maeve.

"Have you been taking some behind my back?" asked Astrea.

Maeve's eyes narrowed.

"I gave you two weeks' supply at Christmas," said Astrea.

"I know," groaned Maeve, pressing her palm to her eyes. "I poured them down the drain."

Astrea sighed. "What the fuck, Maeve?"

Maeve's head shot up, her disposition growing more dangerous by the minute. "Don't speak to me as though you aren't supposed to have plenty stocked up."

Astrea gestured to the empty shelves. "I did. They didn't disappear on their own."

Maeve looked from the shelf to Astrea, and then swallowed hard.

"How long will it take you to make more?" she asked, as something like laughter echoed across her mind.

Astrea hesitated. Maeve's heart sank.

"How long?" she pressed again.

"At least a few weeks," said Astrea softly. "I had over a month's supply here. I wasn't due to begin brewing more for weeks."

Maeve's hands rolled over her face. "Who knows you brew this for me?" she asked.

"No one," she answered quickly. "Well. . ."

"Well?" asked Maeve.

Astrea's shoulders lifted. "I mean, Abraxas knows, of course. Everything goes through the Hand."

"No," said Maeve, standing. "It doesn't. My cousin uses that as an excuse to know everyone's business."

"Abraxas would never do this to you," argued Astrea softly.

"I know that," said Maeve. "But Primus, love him. He can't keep anything to himself, asked or not."

"Why would someone take your potions? I brew them

specifically for you. They're useless otherwise."

Maeve suspected. She had an idea. But the accusation was heavy. Dangerous.

If she was correct, the command was clear. She wouldn't be relying on Astrea's Magic any longer. And so she remained silent and left the Healing Wing without a goodbye.

"You looked beautiful that day," said Agatha, joining Maeve in the tearoom, and looking up at her bridal portrait where it hung over the mantle.

Maeve hugged herself close, her fingers picking at the skin around her nails. "I don't remember this day anymore."

She didn't remember breakfast. Or yesterday. Or when Agatha arrived.

Pain pressed into the corners of Maeve's head, drawing white light into her vision. With a steadying breath, she pressed into the sensation, her stomach at war with the impending feeling of helplessness. Without her potions, her mind would soon begin to fall. The voice would grow louder, the visions that never made sense would force their way into her line of sight.

Maeve shook off the feeling as Agatha pressed towards her slowly, her cane wobbling with each step she took.

Maeve turned from the portrait and stepped towards her grandmother. "I thought Mrs. Mavros was healing you," she said, observing her wobble that had gotten much worse.

Agatha grunted. "Only so much to be done for an old Witch like me. These lands have prolonged me past any life on Earth."

Maeve helped her to a seat. Agatha sighed with relief as she relaxed into the plush cushions. She rearranged the teapot and cups to her liking. Maeve took a seat as well.

Tea. She was there for tea. Maeve remembered at last.

Her fingers slipped into her pocket, running over the tattered and worn slip of parchment that earlier had read *Quit fighting so hard* in glowing green, elegant handwriting.

"Zimsy and Arianna coming?" asked Agatha.

Maeve shook her head. "No."

Agatha looked up sharply, her eyes catching something like excitement. "My granddaughter desires a private audience?"

Maeve smiled and loosed a tiny laugh. "Nothing so formal."

Agatha settled back. "Then pour the tea, child."

Maeve did, and when she was done, she looked across at her grandmother. "I want honesty in its purest form. Don't hold back."

Agatha barked. "And here I was certain I never did."

Magic rippled across Maeve's mind, the voice in her head stronger with each moment that passed. Maeve's head tossed back at the sensation.

"I've stopped taking my potions," she admitted. "I can't even remember if I decided that or not. I don't remember getting to the bathroom. I don't remember gathering them all."

Agatha sighed. "I've been saying since you started, you needed to get rid of those things."

"Those things," began Maeve, "are the only reason I haven't completely lost my mind."

Agatha shook her head, her eyes snapping shut. "No. No," she argued, and her eyes popped open. "Your husband and his sister convinced you those potions were good for you. Have you forgotten what happened when you took too much? It took you a month to remember Maxius' name without being reminded." That was a low blow. But one Maeve accepted. "I have told you time and time again, you would find your way through those episodes. A potion blocking the natural course your mind desires to take. . ." She shook her head once more. "You of all people should know how dangerous that is."

"Why me, of all people?"

"Because there was a time when you relied on the inconsistencies in your mind to guide you further in knowledge of the mind. Now you cling to those potions like a lifeline, like a child's teddy."

Maeve pulled the top of her shirt to the side. "Where did this come from?"

"An explosion at Vaukore, in Hummingdoor's class," answered Agatha, bringing a fresh-baked madeline to her lips.

"Do you think it's strange that this mark would be exactly where I'd have a Dread Mark, if I were granted one?"

The treat stilled in Agatha's mouth. She swallowed and pondered before replying. "You're asking the wrong question." She shook her head. "A Supreme doesn't need logical explanations. That scarring is Magical, potion or otherwise. What do *you feel* in it?"

Maeve knew, as she had known since the moment The Dread King's fingers touched hers. "It's. . .my Magic."

"But?"

Maeve looked down at the floral teapot. "Burying another's Magic."

"Whose?"

"The Prince's."

Magic pulsed through her, down her darkened veins, and cooled the slip of parchment sitting hidden in her pocket.

Agatha nodded. "And still you doubt what you feel."

"I feel this even with my potions."

Her grandmother laughed. "Then why are you even asking me?"

"Because everyone, even Brax and Zimsy, thinks I'm. . ."

That's not real, Maeve. That didn't happen, Maeve. You aren't remembering correctly. You're wrong. You're wrong. You're wrong.

". . . crazy."

Agatha leaned forward slightly in her chair and forced such an intense and motherly eye contact that Maeve struggled not to look away. "No one," she began calmly, "thinks you are crazy. You asked for honesty, Maeve, and I will give it to you. Your projection of yourself is not what those who love you see. Least of all Zimsy and Abraxas."

Maeve nodded and shifted the subject swiftly before her courage left her.

Quit fighting so hard.

"I've started remembering Maxius' birth. Carrying him."

Another slam of Magic barreled through her, egging on her confessions.

"Alphard wasn't there," continued Maeve. "I can see it, just barely in my mind, Mrs. Mavros and Astrea helping me, but Alphard's not there."

"Is there some significance in that to you?"

Before she could answer, the voice she'd drowned out with each potion slipped into her mind, its words crystal clear as water. Her teacup slipped from her grip, spilling its liquid onto her lap and rolling to the floor. The voice no longer needed to pry its way in. There was no forced entry. There were no more chemicals to dull it. It spoke unhurriedly, like a predator stalking towards its already wounded prey.

And Maeve welcomed it.

Hello, Little Viper.

Chapter 8

Maeve

Just a little blood, Maeve, please. Please. Please. I can't sleep, I can't eat—

Abraxas' laughter burst into her ears.

I need it, Maeve, please don't do this to me—

"Did you hear me?"

Warmth drained from Maeve's entire body as Abraxas slammed into view. She swallowed hard, digging her nails into her palms as the voice in her head echoed into silence.

"Did you hear the joke, Maeve?" asked Abraxas.

The Ballroom at Castle Morana flickered to life behind him. He stood with a glass of liquor in his hand and an expression of expectancy. But Maeve's eyes were elsewhere. A wave of pain rolled through her head as her eyes remained locked on Mal's across the hall. He listened to Roswyn and Mumford with bored interest, his green eyes fixed on her.

She didn't recall coming to Castle Morana. She didn't remember getting dressed in formal attire. She didn't know what the occasion was for a hall full of people. The voice in her head slipped through the cracks, returning as a whisper, growing louder with each word.

"Whoa," said Alphard, his hand finding the small of her back. "You alright?"

Just a little blood, Maeve, please. Please. Please. I can't sleep, I can't eat—

"I just need a minute," she choked out, turning on her heel and squeezing one eye shut to dull the ache in her head.

"Bring me another brandy, then, will you?" Abraxas shouted after her.

Neither of them followed after her, for which she was grateful. She passed through the hall with her head down, her nails so deeply embedded in her palms that the skin tore.

She rounded one, two, three corners until she stopped. White light tore at the edge of her vision as she held herself upright against the wall. The firelights flickered in the dark, driving her eyes closed.

Just a little blood, Maeve, please. Please. Please. I can't sleep, I can't eat—

She pressed her back against the cold marble wall, desperately searching for something to ground her.

"You seem quite distraught."

Maeve pushed off the wall and turned sharply in the shadowed corridor. She swallowed quickly as Mal moved into the flickering glow of the firelights. She fell back against the wall once more, looking away from him, as a roll of pain rippled through her head and down her neck.

"It's. . . none of your business," she said at once. Hearing how sharp her voice was, she sighed. "Apologies, I only meant—"

"I know what you meant," he replied casually. "Your husband's sister is my personal healer. Perhaps you should pay her a visit."

Maeve nodded. "Perhaps I should," she replied, unwilling to tell him Astrea couldn't offer her any help. Unwilling to admit to him that the medicine she needed was gone.

A small smile pulled at the corner of his lips. "Deception comes so easily for you."

Maeve's control of her expression dropped. She didn't care that he was her Prince as she glared at him.

Mal chuckled lowly. "It was a compliment."

"Allow me to accept it and take my leave," she said, feeling a wave of light flickering towards her. The voice grew more desperate with each pass it made through her.

Just a little blood, Maeve, please. Please. Please. I can't sleep, I can't eat. She's consuming me completely.

Mal's chin lifted as his Magic searched her. "You're in quite a state. Your Magic is completely unstable."

Maeve took a lengthy inhale. "Why does my state *concern* you?" she asked breathily.

Mal's eyes moved down her entire body. The action caused her head to slam back against the wall as that same voice cut across her mind again.

No, not voice.

His voice, she realized at last.

It had been his voice all along. She squeezed her eyes shut, begging his voice in her head to shut up. To stop whispering things she knew not to believe. "You," she whispered.

"Judging by your expression, I'd say right about now you're realizing that I've been in your head for quite some time. I must say it accelerates my ego that I figured out it was you in my head first. Would you like to see what currently plagues me where you are *concerned?*"

Maeve shook her head, squeezing her eyes shut even tighter.

"Too bad," said Mal.

He closed the gap between them faster than she could register and placed both his hands on the side of her temples. She didn't resist, curiosity getting the best of her as she allowed the memory to play out across her mind.

Her birthday at Sinclair Estates. Before her father's death. A small party where only a handful of family gathered for dinner. But Mal's memory did not match her own. He himself sat, one leg crossed over the other, in a large armchair, watching her open gifts as her family drank and conversed.

Maeve pushed back on Mal's Magic that slid into her mind. With a groan, she flung herself back to the darkened hallway at Castle Morana. Mal did not retreat. His hands hovered over either side of her face.

Maeve didn't care that he was her ruler, her superior. She felt everything from deceived to toyed with. And so she spoke far more boldly than she should have. "How did you come to this memory, for I know it is not yours. That was my birthday. My party. You were not there."

She waited for his reply, and when it didn't come, she pressed him further, her voice demanding and her heart fast. Too fast.

"How did you get this—"

Mal cut her off, his voice deadly calm. "I did not answer the first time."

Maeve groaned, a mixture of pain and anger, as she pushed off the wall and made to slam her hand into his chest. The corridor tilted slightly as she attempted to push him away. Electric Magic burst from her fingers as she made contact, sending her back into the hard wall.

He pressed another vision forward. And another. Each one was more intimate than the last. Each one showed time that couldn't possibly have passed, private moments she was certain were lies. His protection. His possession.

His hand in hers at her father's funeral.

Despite her knees buckling beneath her, Maeve threw up what little energy she had to force the vision away. Mal loomed over her once more in the darkened corridor at Castle Morana.

Just a little blood, Maeve, please. Please. Please!

"Get out, get out, get out," she cried, gripping the sides of her head as dozens of his words filled her mind. Some tender and some furious.

His fingers pressed against her throat, tracing her dark veins.

"And one more, for good measure," said Mal, his voice too calm. Too sinister. Too deadly.

With ease, he forced another vision into Maeve's mind. The darkness around her vanished and was replaced by a hazy morning light.

Mal held Maxius, moments after his birth, in one gently cradled arm, as Maeve remained collapsed against him in the large bed. He continued to hold her tight, sending visible, calming, and healing Magic through his fingertips.

"A boy, Malachite," said Irma Mavros with pride. "Just as you said. Congratulations."

Mal didn't tear his eyes away from the small life in his arm.

"Well done, Astrea," muttered Irma, giving her daughter, who had delivered Maxius and kept Maeve completely calm, a soft smile.

Mal looked down at Maeve and adjusted himself to press a kiss to her hair.

"My Little Viper," he praised. "Look what you have given us."

The vision shattered like glass, falling in a hundred reflective pieces and plunging her into darkness.

Chapter 9

Malachite

Her pale eyes darkened as she went limp against the wall. Mal caught her smoothly, scooping her up into his arms. In all his visions, her eyes were a signature Sinclair blue. Another mystery to solve. Her head rolled against his shoulder as her eyelids slipped closed.

"That was too easy, Maeve."

He fed his Magic deep, calling for Astrea through the brand of Magic on his healer's chest. He felt her on the move at once, successfully beating him to their destination, just as he hoped she would. He carried Maeve across Castle Morana, staying in the shadows until he reached The Healing Wing.

The doors were already swung open. Astrea swore under her breath as she took in the sight of Maeve.

"She collapsed in the corridor, outside the ball," said Mal, keeping his voice smooth and even. "I came upon her just as she nearly hit the floor."

"Lay her down," instructed Astrea gently.

Mal draped her limp form across the exam table, watching as her head rolled to the side. Her Magic was unstable, erratic, and so, *so* very dull. His lip curled at the feeling, just how dampened she was from the poison Astrea and Alphard had been forcing down her throat for fuck knows how long.

He knew little of her, but he didn't need to know her to feel the Magic that once poured from her. It lingered on her skin like perfume. It begged for release.

"How long has she had these episodes?" he asked Astrea, knowing her answer might still be a lie, through no fault of her own.

"Since we left Earth," replied Astrea.

Wrong. Not possible. "Think harder, Astrea," he urged.

The command of Magic struck her brutally. She gasped, her eyes widening. "I misspoke," she breathed, confusion on her tongue. "It's been three years."

Three years.

Three fucking years.

"But," Astrea began, working her way through whatever lie Mal had just destroyed in her mind. "That doesn't make sense."

Mal ignored her revelation. It wasn't Astrea's confessions he longed for.

"Why did she stop taking her potions?" he asked, misleading her to divulge more information as her puzzled expression remained.

Astrea shook her head. "She hates taking them. She has, in the past, refused them for a day or two, but never gone without like this. Not since the first time she had such a breakdown over Maxius."

"When was that?"

"About two years ago."

"And what happened two years ago?"

Astrea stumbled over her words for a moment, then said with clarity, "She was in pain, said something sharp was splitting across her mind. She could barely move. When I finally got the pain under control, she was able to speak. She kept crying, saying she'd made a mistake. That Maxius would never forgive her. She was hysterical and inconsolable."

"What did you do then?"

"I did all I could think of. I knocked her out with a sleeping potion and then figured out how to calm her mind from the things she was seeing. She was miserable for over a month while I did everything I could to calm her."

Maxius.

He'd seen only a fragment of the boy's birth surface in his mind, what he'd shared with Maeve moments ago. The thought had lingered since then, the possibility of what he saw. The boy was never alone, not truly. If he wasn't being guarded by Maeve or Alphard, it was the Elven girl who watched over him.

Zimsy. Mal remembered her in bits. She was once Maeve's servant on Earth. That had clearly changed. Still, she'd not stand in his way if he wanted to take the boy himself, to see what lingered in his young mind.

But Maeve. . .

Her Magic swarmed Maxius like a blanket of metal. He hadn't even been able to lay a hand on him at Christmas. His fingers touched electric steel as he tried to brush the boy's face.

"It'll be weeks before more potions are ready for her," said Astrea as her hands hovered over Maeve's body, checking her.

"She won't be taking those anymore."

Effortlessly, his Pathokenesis abilities took hold of his healer. Astrea's hands stilled. She glanced up at him. With a nod, her only reply was. "Yes, my Prince."

At least his gift worked on his healer. He looked down at Maeve, her chest rising and falling with shallow breaths, and wondered how the woman before him was immune to his sway. Each time he had tried to manipulate and affect Maeve in such a way, he failed.

Little Viper. He remembered he'd called her that once. Was that her title in his Court? Or something else entirely? Regardless, she harbored secrets. She kept the chains in his mind intact, and he was going to shatter them all.

He'd never loved taking by force. Being given had come to be much more satisfying. He craved her submission. Her willingness. He'd take it all from her if he had to, but just like his war with the Elven Lands, he enjoyed a little play.

If it meant she'd glare at him again, he'd thoroughly enjoy watching her squirm.

"What happens when she wakes? I have no idea if she'll be out of her mind or. . ."

Mal anticipated Maeve's anger. Even now, as his Magic felt for hers, he knew he was awakening something catastrophic. Perhaps that's why she called to him so persistently. He had to know just what had been buried. And *why.*

Mal's fingers moved towards her, slow and steady. His index finger traced the underside of her jaw with meticulous memorization.

"That won't concern you from here on," he replied. "Though before I relinquish Maeve from your care, I have one last thing I need you to do."

Astrea waited for his command in silence.

"Leave, and forget this encounter."

Astrea nodded, another Magical command she couldn't avoid, and merely said, "Goodnight, my Prince," as she dipped into a formal bow and left the Healing Wing.

He stared down at Maeve for longer than was necessary. Outside of the Magical pull, beyond her voice in his head, and past the true reason he sought her out. . . she was lovely.

Chapter 10

Maeve

Are you mine?
Her voice.
In every meaning of the word.
The Dread Prince's voice.

Maeve rolled across cool bedding, pressing her palms into the mattress with a groan. She lifted herself off the bed, her hair across her face, and her body aching. She brushed her wild hair back with her fingers and grabbed the glass of water she spotted next to the bed. The cup barely touched her lips when the memory of the night before, or what she assumed was the previous night, flooded her mind. With shaking fingers, she discarded the cup back on the nightstand and tumbled her way out of bed.

Maxius.

The visions she had seen—NO. The vision Mal had *forced* on her played at super speed in her mind over and over.

My Little Viper.

His Little Viper. His?

She was in the family room in a blink, Obscuring to the point of Maxius' Magic. He looked up from the elongated couch, a piece of parchment in his lap, and a small quill in his hand. He smiled softly at her and then returned to his writing. Spinel was curled halfway in his lap as Lyrux petted him with small hands and watched Maxius write.

The truth begged to be acknowledged; it knocked so politely at her chest, it made swallowing such a life-altering pill nearly feel like relief. But she pressed down on the feeling. Even as she looked at her son and the resemblance stared back at her with undeniable certainty.

"Maeve," came Abraxas' voice.

Her eyes slid to the other end of the room.

"What are you doing here?" she asked, but the question was not directed at her cousin.

Mal sat in one of her armchairs, one leg crossed over the other, and his chin propped lazily on his gloved fist.

"Alphard headed back to the front lines this morning," said Abraxas, as casual as stating the forecast, but his eyes darted back and forth between his cousin and his Prince. "Mal suggested a brief discussion and to see him off here. Left just a bit ago."

Maeve's eyes didn't leave Mal's. He watched her with unexpectant eyes. She crossed closer to him, fully aware she was in a set of thin silk pajamas she had no memory of changing into, and that her hair was untamed.

"Can I speak with you in private?" she asked, her throat raw.

"No," replied Mal swiftly. "My Hand will remain present. Speak freely."

Maeve's mouth opened with a soft sound of annoyance. Abraxas didn't even attempt to hide his pleasure.

"You disappeared last night, Maeve," said Abraxas, reveling in the tension that sat thick in the room. "Zimsy said you came home earlier than she expected you. Where'd you get off to?"

"Yes," said Maeve, tension coiling at her fingertips as she refused to break eye contact with Mal. "Where did I get off to?"

Mal lost their stare down without a care. His green eyes dipped to her fingertips and then took his time trailing them back up her body.

"How should I know?" he replied as his gaze found hers once more.

Her chin lowered with a sharp exhale. If he wanted it all out in front of Brax, then by all the Gods, she'd do it.

"The things you showed me last night, are those your memories or something you believe to be false?"

Mal's bored expression didn't falter. His breathing didn't even accelerate. He remained leaning against his knuckles in an infuriatingly handsome way.

"I have no idea what you are talking about," he said smoothly.

Maeve's mouth fell open at the bold lie. "Excuse me?"

Mal's brows lifted, and a small laugh vibrated in his throat. One that sounded like pity. Maeve's eyes narrowed.

"Are you getting enough sleep?" he asked, his voice casual. Unconcerned. Carefree. "You look. . .flustered."

She remained standing, despite how he relaxed further into the chair.

"But," he continued, his voice dropping to a low hum, one that pulled her spine tall, "your Magic is so much more stable than last we met. Any changes in. . .consumption?"

Suddenly very aware that Abraxas' wide eyes had not peeled away from either of them, she swallowed hard, fixing a forced smile on her face. Mal was challenging her to accuse him in her own home, in front of his Hand.

"I stopped taking my potions," she decided to say.

Mal's free hand shot up, silencing Abraxas before he could berate her. "Wonderful. Maybe now you can be of use to me."

His voice was cold. Distant. But so effortlessly *addicting*.

Maeve smiled bitterly, showing teeth and pressing down on the laugh that wanted to burst forth. Mal grinned, fully satisfied to be under her skin.

"Maxius," called Mal, never shifting his eyes from Maeve. "Are you done?"

Maeve looked over her shoulder as Maxius slid off the couch and crossed the room towards them with the bit of parchment in his hand.

"I asked him to write down what he knew about his Magic for me," said Mal, answering her unspoken question.

"What do you mean?" she asked, her fingers brushing through Maxius' hair as he stepped by her.

Maxius bowed his head and presented Mal with his work. He turned towards Maeve and signed, *What I feel in my Magic*. He pointed to the parchment, which Mal now read silently. *I wrote how it feels when I. . .fail.*

Maeve cupped her fingers under his chin. He looked devastatingly like—

Mal's voice broke her thought, bringing Maxius' attention back to him.

"That feeling in your chest," began Mal, pressing a single finger against his own chest, dragging it up across his neck, his lips, his nose, and then settling centered above his brows, "it must travel to your head first."

Maxius held up a single finger, extending his arm straight out.

"Yes," said Mal, understanding him. "Then back into the hand."

Maxius didn't break their hold. *In my head, it hurts, like hitting a wall,* he signed and pointed back down at the parchment.

Mal continued to read in silence, his fingers trailing over his lips in thought and bringing heat to Maeve's cheeks. He nodded and looked back up at Maxius. Then at Maeve.

"No," she answered, her voice quiet.

"I can help him, Maeve."

"I will not lower the shields on his mind," she said, finality in her voice.

"And if your sworn Prince commands you to?" he asked.

If he wanted to play a game, she'd play. "Command away, *my Prince.*"

Mal smiled with full charm. So good at the game.

"I'll give you time to choose correctly," he replied. "I have plenty of time to ensure things are. . .unveiled." He looked back down at Maxius. "Practice what I showed you earlier in the meantime."

In the meantime, as if he knew she'd relent. Or that he'd eventually force her. She didn't know which she hated more. Maxius nodded.

Mal stood and grabbed his traveling cloak. "See to the complaints from Vaukore, Abraxas. Give them whatever they need."

Vaukore. Magic pressed against her mind, distant and foggy from her time there. Gaps. There were too many gaps.

"Whatever they need?" asked Abraxas with a laugh. "Larliesl will claim the entire dueling hall needs remodeling."

"Then see it done," said Mal, heading out of the room. "Vaukore is our realm to oversee. Mine to rule. Yours to manage."

He didn't wait for Abraxas to reply again as he left them, though it appeared Abraxas, as he picked up Lyrux and settled him against his side, had nothing more to say to his Prince.

Maxius signed, *Breakfast?*

Maeve nodded, and he slid past her out of the room. Maeve ran her hands over her face and said, "Shut up, Brax," from behind her palms. She turned on her heel and followed Maxius to the kitchen. Abraxas wasn't far behind her.

"I prepared some fruit," said Zimsy, turning away from the stove as they entered the kitchen. "It's already on the table." She nodded her head towards the breakfast room.

"I'll make some pancakes," said Maeve.

Maxius shook his head with large eyes as Zimsy said, "No," with a laugh. Maxius smiled up at Zimsy and signed, *She burned them the past three times.*

"I know," said Zimsy grimly.

"I can see and hear you both," said Maeve, reaching for a teacup on a brass hook but finding it hard to argue as she had, in fact, burned the pancakes the past three times.

She pulled open the drawer of tea bags and found it empty. Warmth slammed into her side as Maxius wrapped his arms around her. She looked down at him with a soft smile.

He was so clearly Mal's child that the thought choked her.

Acceptance slid through her like a shockwave.

How, how, how?

She kept her composure and ran her fingers through his dark hair. He released his hold and signed, *But you make the best tea.*

She ran her thumb along his cheek. "Would you like some?" she asked, masking the fear that swarmed her. The fear of the unknown. The ever-present *why?*

He nodded, and then Zimsy pulled his attention away. "Maxius, will you carry this tray to the table?"

Maeve watched as he helped her at once, his face scrunching slightly as Lyrux attempted to assist, but nearly toppled them both over. Abraxas followed Maeve into the pantry, hot on her heels. She pulled open the cabinet where the box of tea was stored.

"What, and I cannot possibly express this enough," began Abraxas, "the hell was that?"

"Oh," laughed Maeve, the sound bordering on hysteria. "I'm sorry. I thought the Hand knew *everything.*"

"Oh, he does," he assured her with a nod, his tone taunting. "He sees quite well, cousin. He just saw his Prince flirting with his cousin," he hissed quietly.

"No, he wasn't," she assured him darkly. "He's playing with me."

Abraxas laughed and muttered. "I think for Mal, they are the same."

"I'm glad this is so amusing to you," she said, shaking her head.

"Oh, it absolutely is," he assured her.

She slammed the cabinet door closed and turned on him. "Stay out of it."

Abraxas snorted as she moved past him and back to the kitchen. "Yeah, right."

Chapter 11

Maeve

Mal returned to Blackstone each day. Each day, he watched Maxius. Taught him a training exercise. Encouraged him. And each day, Maxius failed to truly perform the way Mal instructed him to. Frustration never developed on the Prince's face, though it was prominent on Maxius'.

Maeve watched them each day. She couldn't find it within her to deny Maxius the potential to find his power. She couldn't deny Mal his request to be near the boy. Not that it had been a request. She wondered if he'd ever command her to lower the shields around Maxius' mind. It wouldn't matter if he did. She had already made up her mind where that was concerned.

And the answer was no.

She watched as her son's anger piled up with each failure. A visual reminder of why she never pushed him. She remained silent as he blew out the windows, the glass shelves, the picture frames, the vases, and the firelight fixtures. Mal watched with unmatched patience as his Magic never manifested much more than violent and uncontrolled destruction in a close vicinity.

When their lesson ended, Maeve left the shattered mess. She'd mend it all later, not in front of Maxius. Her son turned sharply and made for the stairs.

"You need to eat something," she stated calmly, standing and heading towards the kitchen without acknowledging Mal.

I don't want to, he signed, not looking at her. *I want to go to bed.*

"You'll feel better if you eat even something small, love."

Maxius shook his head, his scowl never softening. She reached for his hair as she moved past him, the gesture familiar. He swatted her away with a sharp hit. Residual Magic from his outburst trickled into her skin like tiny flecks of ice.

"Maxius," said Mal, his voice cool and low.

The boy's eyes shot to him as he swallowed hard. They stared at one another. Maxius, with his heavy and frustrated breaths, and Mal, with his unsettling emotionless control.

"You're working hard," said Mal. "That requires you to eat."

I'm just failing, signed Maxius, his movements fast and sharp. *Like always.*

Only then did Maeve see the tears swelling along the bottom of his eyes. Her lips parted. Mal spoke before she could offer him reassurance or comfort.

"Failure," said Mal, his eyes locked with Maxius' glassy ones, "is the only path to success."

Maxius' lips quivered. His fingers balled into fists at his side.

"Breathe," said Mal, his tone soft.

So soft it made Maeve's chest ache.

But Maxius did. He breathed. And his tiny fists uncurled at his sides. He swallowed, and by the fourth breath, his eyes were dry.

"What if," came Zimsy's voice as she rounded the corner, dressed in a thick coat, a fuzzy head wrap, and gloves, "we went to your favorite restaurant in the Beryl City?"

Maxius ran his fingers through his hair and looked up at Zimsy. She already had his coat and hat draped over her arm. His breathing began to settle.

"I'll come with you," said Maeve.

"You've been hogging him for weeks," said Zimsy. "This will be just Maxius and Aunt Zim time, hmm?" She smiled down at him again as Maxius took his coat from her and slid his arms in the sleeves.

"Thank you," Maeve mouthed to her, acknowledging that he needed space, and happy she had such a friend she trusted him with.

Zimsy took his small hand in hers, and they left. Maeve turned towards Mal. His eyes followed Maxius until the pair vanished from sight.

"Do you have to push him so hard?" she fired immediately.

Mal nearly rolled his eyes. "If you think this is me pushing him hard, I'd encourage you to prepare yourself."

"And if I say he's done with this? That you're done coming here?"

"Then the command won't come as some trivial power play as your Prince that I know you don't respect. It will come in full demand of my strength versus yours."

She angled her head to the side. "Did you send Alphard to the front lines so that you could step in this way without hindrance?"

Something between a laugh and a scoff hummed through him. "As if he could hinder me."

"Could I?"

Mal's expression shifted, suddenly interested. "I don't know. Could you? Have you performed Magic in the last year beyond lighting all these pretty candles and the occasional Obscuring? Or maybe you can change the color of the drapes? It must be so hard playing the role of the oppressed housewife with all that Magic crawling under your skin unused. It's unfathomable how you can stand it."

"You're awful," she said, shaking her head. "And I've been so compliant, so *silent*—"

"Then speak up," he hissed, his eyes turning wild and the mask fading. "You think I push you so you remain soft?"

"What does it matter?" she said dully. "If he is yours, then who am I to deny you your son? I've accepted that truth. But why must you drag my dignity into this? What does my Magic matter?"

Mal's eyes searched hers with a look of disbelief. Then his expression twisted, understanding washing over his features. "You don't understand," he said, his voice full of realization. "You think all this is only about Maxius."

"Isn't it?" she pressed.

Disappointment flashed in the way his eyes narrowed. Then a different resolve settled into his expression. He stepped towards her, and she didn't dare step back. He peeled the glove from his right hand with such predatory grace that her tongue slid across her bottom lip without a thought. Another step closer, and his left glove was off.

He was going to touch her.

He held out his hand expectantly. She was hesitant to trust him again, to let their skin make contact after the last time he'd forced her to see such forgotten things. But the pull was strong. A flicker of Magic at her core asked sweetly to feel his skin on hers again. It yearned for his attention.

She looked from his hand back up to his face.

"Aren't you at all curious what once was between us?" his silky smooth voice hummed.

She shook her head, but her fingers brushed his, submitting to his beckoning call, and her eyes dipped down to his lips. His fingers curled beneath hers, and his elbow retracted slowly, forcing her to yield a step towards him. His free hand found her front, knuckles brushing up her waist. His fingers unfurled, snaking across her back until he had her wrapped fully.

Their chests pressed together in forced intimacy as he closed in on her, never releasing her back. He tugged her impossibly closer, pulling her to the tips of her toes as his nose brushed down over hers.

She tried, but failed to conceal the small gasp that slipped from her at the contact. At his cool breath on her lips. Close enough, she could claim them. Close enough for his to claim hers.

"Are you that starved?" he asked, his voice low.

She refused to answer. Refused to give him the satisfaction of a clever response. The truth gnawed at her. The desire to taste him, to know what his slender fingers would feel like tracing across her thighs, to hear both his praise and his degradation, bubbled up inside her.

Foolish thoughts.

"You don't think about it?" he hummed, inhaling slowly as his head dipped and his nose brushed behind her ear. "Don't you wonder what it was between us that created a life?"

"No," she said, hearing the lie in her own voice.

His cool lips brushed across her ear, and a surrendering moan spilled from her throat.

"Is it just me you feel so compelled to lie to?" An amused hum vibrated up his throat. His grip tightened with bruising force, causing her to suck in sharply. Magic pulsed from his palms and fingers, each flicker growing hungrier. Deadlier. "I'm curious." His hand moved lower on her back, his fingers ghosting across her skin. "I think about it." Her eyes fluttered to a close. "I can admit I wish I remembered what drove me to find completion inside you."

Maeve whimpered at the words, warmth rolling across her core, buried between her legs.

Why? Why didn't she remember?

"One thing you can be certain of, Maeve, is that we are in this together."

His words were both a threat and a promise as his power pressed down on her like a blanket from all angles. Heavy and oppressive.

He let go of her hand, his fingers slipping across her scalp and carding through her hair as he pulled his face back, taking in her expression. She opened her eyes and looked up at him through heavy lids, fighting off the dizzy heat rolling through her.

"Much better," said Mal as he observed her with a frown that somehow suited him. His fingers twisted at the base of her neck, gathering her hair and angling her head up at him.

Maeve's teeth ground together. "What are you doing?"

Mal's frown deepened. "Breaking you."

He flicked her forehead faster than she could register.

The living room at Blackstone disappeared, replaced by utter darkness. A void. The vision didn't slam into view. It crept up slowly, manifesting in soft plumes of Magic and filling the space around her. Glittering gowns and massive emerald green banners whispered into view as she was forced to watch the scene unfold.

The Throne Room at Castle Morana.

She spotted herself immediately. Bright-blue eyes that felt right and real, that were in keeping with her father's. With her siblings.

Mal, no scar running across his face, with The Dread Crown atop his head, smiled down at Maeve, where the fanged serpent pin Roswyn now wore gleamed on her chest. She wore pants and boots, and a long coat that matched his set. Combat attire that still held every ounce of the femininity and beauty she loved in a gown.

Maeve felt a twist in her chest as she watched herself. "I was your second." It was partially a question, her voice dampened, hardly moving anywhere across the vision. . .the memory.

The hall was silent as all watched Ambrose Sinclair step towards their newly crowned royalty. Her father's handsome and kind face held such adoration for Mal as he held out his hand with the pride of a father.

"Premier Sinclair," said Mal.

"My Prince," replied Ambrose.

The silent hall then burst into applause.

Mal turned away, and when he moved back to Ambrose, something slender and gold sat between his hands. A goblet.

"A gift," said Mal, presenting the goblet to Ambrose. "For your allegiance and dedication to my cause."

Ambrose took a hefty exhale, clearly honored. He hesitated to grasp the goblet's serpent-like handles.

"Bring us some wine," called Ambrose. He grinned up at Mal. "Our new Prince deserves a toast."

As guests' goblets and glasses were filled, including the gold glittering one Mal gifted Ambrose, her father stepped onto the stairs of the throne and raised the goblet high.

"A toast! To the new age of Magic, to the end of living in the shadows and hiding from the world. To our Savior and his Viper, my darling daughter."

Cold Magic shot through her.

Mal's Viper.

His darling daughter.

Maeve's mouth went dry.

Ambrose continued. "I knew from the moment the pair of you stepped into my home that this day was soon to come barreling forward."

There were a few clamors of excitement as her younger self and Mal locked eyes.

"To the Dread Prince!" cheered Ambrose. "May your reign be true!"

Ambrose raised the goblet to his lips, and everyone followed suit. Ambrose stepped past Maeve and clapped her shoulder, a gesture fitting for The Premier and the Prince's Viper. He stepped closer to her mother, no, Clarissa, and Arianna.

"Breaking you", Mal had said before plunging her into this moment of happiness. A smile pulled at her lips as she enjoyed watching her father in this way. He oozed perfected dominance in such a warm and protective way. He was strong, stronger than most, and knew that gave him a duty to keep others safe.

To keep her safe.

Ambrose lifted the Dread Goblet to his lips once more.

The smile faded from her younger self's lips. Her own glass of wine had been discarded, and her curious eyes locked on Ambrose.

"Daddy–" she started, but he didn't hear her over the music and the crowd.

He coughed.

"Daddy!" she shouted, louder as she pushed through the guests.

Ambrose brought the Dread Goblet to his lips, drinking quickly, in an attempt to satiate his coughs.

Maeve tried to move towards him with her past self, but she was frozen, a captive audience and nothing more.

Alphard's father whipped his handkerchief from his pocket and handed it to Ambrose. Her father coughed into the bright white cloth.

Red spattered through the fabric instantly.

Maeve's whole body went cold.

"Irma!" screamed Mr. Mavros as her younger self broke through the crowd, at last arriving at her father's side.

Ambrose faltered. The goblet fell from his limp fingers and clattered on the emerald and silver floor. The echoing sound of its heavy thud repeated again and again, like a church bell.

Her younger self gripped his shoulders and forced his gaze to hers. He collapsed to the floor, taking her with him.

Blood slipped from the corners of his eyes.

From his nose.

From his ears.

Horror, acidic and oppressive, slithered through her at the sight.

Irma was at their side in a blink, her hands over his face, which was turning a yellow shade of sickness. Bright red lines shot from his lips, spreading across his cheeks.

Ambrose's eyes went black. Empty.

And he collapsed forward into her younger self, who had grown a sickening shade of pale. Her father didn't blink. He didn't meet her eyes. He stared past her at the ceiling with collapsed, black eyes.

The Throne Room froze in place. Slowly, each particle of the memory floated into the air. If it took seconds or an hour, Maeve didn't know. Eventually, she was alone in a void, unable to move. Unable to speak. Time passed in an uncertain quantity until footsteps, unhurried and light, found her ears.

Death hung in the very air she breathed.

Mal manifested from nothing, standing in the void just over where Ambrose's body had been. He looked down, as if he could still see the blood. The way it ran from his eyes and slid along his jaw. The way his lips turned a color no daughter should have to witness.

"Do you understand now?" Mal's cool voice slithered across the darkness, his eyes still cast downward. "This is about more than an intimacy we may have shared."

Bright white light struck like lightning, and her next view was before her in a blink. Her white knuckles gripped around a wrist. Her eyes trailed up the fingers she held captive, realizing at once they belonged to Mal. The Healing Wing at Castle Morana shifted into focus behind their hands.

Her grip tightened, and his fingers relaxed against her hold. He didn't fight her as quick, erratic breaths slipped from her. Her stomach clenched. Her throat was raw with screams she couldn't remember voicing. More screams, more sobs, desired release.

Her gaze slid over slowly, hesitantly, to Mal's frame. His eyes were glimmering emerald beauties, each of them swimming with a cool elegance.

"You're alright," his voice hummed.

"You—" she began with a broken voice, attempting to rise.

Mal's ungloved finger pressed against her lips. "Shh." He pressed her back down onto the examination bed, forcing her to lie flat.

She didn't, couldn't, tear her eyes away from his. The only thing that kept her from bursting into tears was his petrifying gaze. The very thing that brought her to tears was the only thing that grounded her. His gaze slipped into something unexpectedly gentle. The game was forgotten as his free hand moved to her stomach.

"Breathe, Maeve," he said lowly, his tone shifting to something soft.

Her name on his lips sent Magic creeping up her spine. She wanted to scream at him. She wanted to point two fingers at him and show him just how infuriating his brief presence in her life had been thus far. Unrelenting and selfish. Taking and never giving.

Abraxas appeared at her other side, his hand finding her free one. "You're okay, Maeve," he said, with far too much concern for her lighthearted and pestering cousin.

Her eyes shot to him. Pain erupted across her entire body. Magic gripped at her mind like hundreds of sharpened talons, each one pulling her in a different direction. Calming Magic slid down her arm and across her sternum. Desperate begs were on the tip of her tongue, but as the waves of paralyzing dread passed over her, no words formed.

How could she forget the way he died? She wanted to forget again.

"Her Magic is so unstable I'm afraid it's going to shatter, Mal," Astrea's voice drifted over her.

She was cold. Freezing. Her body shook. She wanted warmth. Another plea that her tongue refused to voice. Fear ran freely through her, sinking its hooks in wherever it could until she felt completely chained.

"Mal?" Abraxas said, confusion in his tone.

"It has to shatter," he stated, though there was regret in his voice.

No.

NO.

Quakes of terror and uncertainty twisted through her. The only thing she could hear was her own fearful screams.

Fear is the absence of Magic.

Her father's constant reminder slid across her mind, the words feeling like three gentle squeezes to her hand.

Her Magic flickered. A reminder of its presence. A reminder that though she pressed down on it well, it too had hooks and claws. She, too, had a say.

Whatever spell was on the verge of shattering in her mind, the thing Mal would do anything to break, she *would not* let it. Pride or instinct, she didn't know what it was that drove her to act, to push back against the chains in her mind. The claws in her Magic wanted to rip and destroy.

How long had it been since she tasted her Magic so fully? It provided the warmth she sought at once, crashing through her like waves of divinity. She drank it all, letting every molecule and every shard of power take root inside her. It nestled into each corner of her existence. Nothing could ever feel so unexplainably hers but this.

Her mind fell quiet. No chains or claws. No hooks. Just warmth.

Chapter 12

Maeve

She flew through the halls of Castle Morana, abandoning the unfamiliar bed she woke in, still in her pajamas, uncertain how she even knew where the Dread Prince's study was in the massive castle. Or how she knew he was there. But she did. Staircase after staircase. Corridor after corridor, until she felt his presence grow stronger with each step towards a large, rounded door.

It slammed open violently with a flick of her wrist.

"Enough of this game," she cried out. "You win."

Mal didn't smile. He looked up from his desk, stacked with books, and met her eyes. "I wasn't aware we were playing. It's only you who hasn't understood the weight of any of this."

Her eyes burned, tears threatening to loosen at any moment.

Her father. Bleeding. From his eyes, his mouth—

"You took my potions," she seethed, finally voicing the truth, as if there was any weight to it now. "I want them back now."

The image of her father in her arms with dead eyes. Dead eyes with blood pouring from them. Lifeless and cold.

Her palms dug deep into her eye sockets as she let out a throaty groan. "Why, why would you show me that?" she exclaimed.

His eyes didn't deny it as he said, "I needed to see your mind without restraint."

Maeve shook her head.

"Would you have preferred I order you to stop consuming them?"

"Yes," snapped Maeve. "At least there would have been honesty in that. And I want them back."

Mal relaxed as his brows raised. "Honesty?" he began, ignoring her demand a second time. "Is that what we are being with one another? Don't even begin to answer that. I am afraid your infuriating response will conjure anger I work endlessly to tame."

"You had no right to do that," she pressed him. "Just to play hero and make me better—"

"Don't start lying to yourself now," said Mal darkly. "I meant what I said. I needed to see your mind clearly."

"Why?"

"Why?" he repeated, almost mocking. He scowled at her despite her fragile state. Mal's chest rose and fell. "Those potions muddle your mind. They make you pathetically weak."

"They are meant to. I cannot grasp reality without them."

"And you are certain what is reality and what is not? Who is to say what is in your mind is not a reality itself? Did I not show you just how far from reality what you cling to is?"

Maeve shook her head in disbelief. "Stop," she said, her voice shaking. She turned from him and made for the door. "I have gone down this road before. I have been on the brink of madness in my own mind, doubting my own thoughts, and you will not pull me back there."

Darkness swirled before her as Mal appeared in her path, stalking her backward. "I will drag you to the depths of hell if that's where the truth lies."

"Stay out of my mind," she warned, countering his steps as he closed the space between them.

Mal shook his head. "If only I could get there to begin with. I thought removing the potions would allow me access. But no. I had to force-feed you memories in your vulnerable moments just to get through to you. Reading your thoughts has been the first failure I've experienced in quite some time. You alone seem to be immune to my persuasion."

"Poor thing," said Maeve with a scowl as she collided with the tall back of an armchair.

The corners of his lips pulled up as he trapped her.

"I enjoy the thought of watching you fight," he said. "It's so. . .refreshing." His eyes dipped down to her two fingers, pulling together tightly at her side. "You'd strike your sworn Prince?"

"I thought you wanted to watch me fight," she challenged back.

Mal hummed in agreement. He moved away from her, crossing

back to his desk. "I'm not sorry for doing what was needed. You needed to see the severity of what has been lost in your mind. And before you say the words again—no, you cannot have them back."

"I need them," she argued, hating the desperation in her voice.

Mal leaned back in the black leather chair. "No. You want them."

Maeve crossed the space between them, placing her hands on his desk and bending towards him with pleading eyes. He scanned her face and spoke softly.

"You'd rather remain in ignorant bliss than remember the true nature of your father's death? You'd rather go back to liquid lies and never question why you forgot it in the first place?"

Silent tears streamed down her face. Mal lifted his hand with slow confidence, wiping away each one. "One of us has to make the hard decisions, Maeve. I don't care about the consequences. I will have answers."

She shook her head, her knees giving way beneath her as she kneeled before his desk, her wet cheek now flush with the wood. Mal's thumb moved across her cheek. His paralyzing green eyes danced with flecks of brown and hazel. She'd never noticed that before. No. They had never been so very hazel before.

"Such pretty eyes, even if they aren't yours," he remarked.

His thumb stilled. Maeve's stomach rolled as a monumental shift in Magic swept over them. His jaw clenched, fingers tensing against her skin. Maeve froze, unable to look away as his eyes flooded green, saturating and overtaking each fleck of brown.

She pulled away from the desk, rising cautiously as the foreign Magic lingered. Mal's head rolled back, and with a sigh bordering on ecstasy, the Magic lifted. He leaned back in his chair, suddenly looking exhausted, and looked up at her with hollow features.

No flicker of flirtation or enjoyment. Just tired eyes.

"Go," he said, clipped and strained.

"What—" she began.

"If you make me repeat myself, I will force you to watch Ambrose's death again."

Maeve stepped back from the desk, anger swelling up in her chest. She swallowed all the nasty things she wanted to say to him as she pitied him for the first time.

It seemed the Dread Prince held secrets of his own.

Chapter 13

Maeve

Mal left her alone for longer than she could stand. And that was infuriating. Even as she traveled to Castle Morana, the hour late, she knew he wasn't there.

"Maeve," said Abraxas, genuine surprise in his voice as she entered the Hand's study. Lyrux played on the floor beside his desk. He spotted Maeve, wobbling to a stand, and reached for her. "It's late," continued Abraxas. "To what do I owe the pleasure?"

Maeve bent and picked up the little blond. His eyes were Juliet's, but everything else in his small, round face would grow to look identical to Abraxas. "It's past your bedtime, surely," she said to him.

"You look rested," noted Abraxas, setting down the papers he perused. "Better than last I saw you."

Maeve didn't comment. She slid into an expensive chair, settling herself and Lyrux back comfortably.

"Where is he?" was all she asked.

She prepared herself for a snarky comment, but her cousin merely looked back down at his papers and softly cleared his throat.

"There will be an announcement within the week," he began, "regarding the Elven lands and some adjustments to Mal's title."

"That's not what I asked."

Abraxas smiled, not at her, but in the way she noticed he smiled at parties, when speaking to council members, or high-ranking Bellator. Abraxas didn't reply. His eyes lifted to Lyrux, sprawled across her chest, drifting to sleep.

"He finally won then?" asked Maeve.

Abraxas' voice was anything but gloating. "Yes."

"Why don't you sound happy?"

His eyes remained distant, thinking, calculating. "Because I am not certain the cost was worth it."

"And what cost is that?"

Abraxas looked back down at his papers, his fingers running over the cream parchment, hesitating to speak the truth. With a sigh, his shoulders slumped, and he leaned back in his chair. "A Queen."

If a heart could stop at two words, Maeve's did. She deflected the nauseating pit that opened in her stomach. "He will take the title of King?"

Abraxas nodded. Silence settled between them.

She felt so foolish for ever having thought of him while Alphard was between her legs, for playing the image of his fingers ghosting across her face again and again.

His intentions were clear now. He'd merely wanted to make her vulnerable, like he said. He needed her guard down. Nothing more. His interest lay in his parentage with Maxius alone.

But. . .for the first time in what felt like ages, she trusted her Magic.

And she knew something deeper lingered between them.

"Who?" she asked at last.

Abraxas' shoulders pulled up. "I'm not certain. She's offered him her power in exchange for ruling beside him, and the glory for conquering the Elven Lands."

"His ego agreed to that?" She scoffed, unable to hide the hurt in her voice.

"Mal doesn't have many goals. There is only one goal. All the realms. Under his crown." Abraxas looked up at her at last. His eyes widened slightly. "Oh," he said, seeing through her at once as a grin split wide on his face. "I knew it, cousin."

"Seal your lips, Brax," said Maeve, her stomach rolling with unwanted energy.

Jealousy. It was pure jealousy.

"I'm right, aren't I?" he offered, his tone casual and confident.

"Does it even matter?" asked Maeve softly, her fingers winding through Lyrux's soft locks. "It is but a dream," she said softly. "One I will surely be denied."

"Ambition propels him to her. But there is deeper Magic in you that calls to him. I can see it." He paused. "I can feel it."

Maeve laughed, a mixture of embarrassment and vulnerability. "You really do know everything."

Abraxas bowed his head at her in thanks.

She shook her head and groaned. "Here I am, openly admitting I want another man, while my husband is off fighting a war."

"Oh, please," said Abraxas, his chin lowering. "He's been home twice to see a certain redhead and didn't even visit you."

Abraxas knew it wouldn't sting her, and it wasn't said with the intention to. Maeve had known for quite some time that Alphard's heart lay with another. She'd even suggested they part ways amicably, but Alphard insisted he couldn't do that to Maxius.

She dreaded the day she'd have to tell him the truth. Maxius too. She'd been putting off the reality of it, at least until she and Mal had a better understanding of just how much of what they believed was a lie. The truth was a terrifying thought. The possibilities of what once was were many.

"When will he be back?" she asked, standing smoothly to hand off Lyrux to Abraxas.

"Soon, by dawn I imagine," he replied, taking Lyrux in one arm and positioning his head on his shoulder.

Maeve bid her cousin goodnight and didn't tell him she was headed for the Prince's study.

There were no enchantments around the doors. No protective barrier to keep Mal's study private. She wondered if that was because no one would dare invade his space, or if it was an invitation for her to. She closed the door behind her, leaning against it for a moment and taking in the large room.

Glass-covered shelves housed everything from books to vials, all organized and labeled. She crossed the study, observing each shelf. Some of them were filled to the ceiling with dark objects that pulsed with Magic. None of it compared to Mal's. She'd never felt something so paramount and consuming.

She couldn't imagine a force greater.

She stopped before an entire cabinet of pages. Worn and blank. Curiosity got the better of her. She pulled open the glass doors gently with a wave of her palm. As she sifted through the various pieces of parchment, she confirmed they were truly all empty. Hundreds of pages, stacked in the cabinet with nothing on them.

Thunk.

Her heart stilled at the sound from behind her. Turning, she saw the firelight on Mal's desk was now aglow, casting light onto the only object sitting on the oversized piece of furniture.

The ring she'd seen on his finger, The Dread Ring, she knew it to be called, sat at the center of his desk like an offering. The dark stone of the ring appeared almost molten against the small and enchanted flame that sat on his desk.

She shifted her own ring, the one her father had given her, with her thumb, as the unavoidable feeling that The Dread Ring too belonged on her finger thrummed through her.

She yielded a step to the thought.

It couldn't hurt just to try it on. Just to feel even a flicker of him through the Magic that resonated from the stone. Maybe then she could let the notion of him rest.

A lie. There were times when his stoic gaze was on her that she could swear he was running through her very veins.

Another step closer to the ring.

No one else has fucked you, Maeve, because you know they'd never be crawling through your skin like I am.

She stalled, a heavy curse stinging from her lips as his voice, a memory buried deep, sliced across her mind. Her fingers were steady as they brushed down her neck, hovering over the black inky veins she'd been scarred with.

Another step, and she stood above the Dread Ring. It hummed

with Magic, his Magic and ancient Magic all mixed into one. She stared at it until its pulse was one with hers. Her fingers hovered above the skulls holding the dark stone in place.

No one else has fucked you, Maeve, because you know they'd never be crawling through your skin like I am.

No one else had touched her when those words were said. The venom in his voice as she begged it to play again and again in her mind was just as intoxicating as the words themselves.

The implications.

She hadn't even realized her fingers touched down on the Dread Ring until her head shot back, her eyes rolling with it. Consequence be damned, she gripped the ring fully, sliding it onto her finger with a breathy exhale. It fit perfectly. Maeve smiled at the triumph. Wicked thoughts flooded her mind. She couldn't tell where surfacing memories ended, and where new ideas began. It didn't matter; they were all centered around one singular desire: Mal's body with hers.

A bright green glow interrupted her fantasy. The cabinet with hundreds of blank pieces of parchment illuminated the study with heavenly light. She crossed back towards it, and this time, the cabinet opened for her.

Black ink filled each sheet in hasty script, until the words they held were fully visible to her.

She hadn't even made it through all of the papers, all of the endless scrolls of parchment, when Mal stood before her in the darkened study, silent, and not questioning why she was seated behind his desk.

The Dread Ring remained on her finger.

He ran an exhausted hand across his face. He was thinner. His skin was pale. So pale the deep purples of his veins were stark against his skin, exposed by his rolled back sleeves. Beneath his eyes were shadows.

"You shouldn't be here," was all he said.

"What are these?" she asked without hesitation.

He stopped and surveyed her. His expression changed. He crossed the space between them and didn't touch the stack of letters piled on the desk.

"You went through my things?"

She could feel the tether on his temper go taut.

"There are no dates," she continued, ignoring his question. "Only endless ramblings and paragraphs of years' worth of writings. Years of you apologizing to me. Years of your regrets listed again and again."

"Maeve—"

His voice was nothing but a warning. She didn't heed it.

She picked up one of the letters and read it aloud. "'If you will not save Maeve, deliver her from this darkness. It is I who cannot be saved. It is I who cannot be saved'." She set it aside and read another one. "'Something that is buried deep in one who is not mine calls to me. She breathes across the room and my pulse rushes'." Maeve looked up at him. "What is it that haunts you? Even now, I feel its ever-present gaze."

Mal's voice shook with breaking control, "Maeve, stop—"

Maeve ignored him, continuing to read his entry. "'Dark hair, blazing blue eyes. Skin, smooth and warm. The darkness has her eyes, but she is cold and her hair is white'." Maeve slammed the paper down and looked up at him. "You know more than you have told me."

"I do," he seethed, that temper a breath away from shattering.

"Then why are you keeping me in the dark?"

Mal drew the breath in, and shatter it did.

"Because we both know it was *you* who did this!"

Maeve swallowed. Mal continued.

"And I have yet to determine if you did it with my consent or not."

Maeve fell still, suddenly aware of the dangerous Magic pressing down on her.

"Why didn't you tell me from the start?" she offered softly.

"There is Magic holding my tongue, and you are lucky it allows me to speak to you at all."

"That Magic I felt here before? The darkness you refer to in these writings? The one that caused your eyes to burn green and your skin to—"

"Enough," he said, his eyes closing. A hand brushed across his face in exhaustion.

"No," argued Maeve calmly. With the slightest shake of her head, she refused to back down. "You dragged my baby boy into this. You will not put his life in danger."

Mal's hand dropped. That frown that somehow made him more enticing was directed fully at her. "Our."

"What?" she snapped softly.

His chest rose.

Up.

"Our son."

Down.

His Magic withdrew, no longer looming threateningly over her.

"Again," he said hollowly. "You shouldn't be here."

She leaned forward in his chair. A blatant challenge. "Why, the moment you read these," her fingers danced over the piles of letters, "didn't you come to me?"

"Because until recently, they were blank. We've been under a spell for far too long, Maeve."

She relaxed at his words, at some tiny shred of honesty at last. And so she offered him some in return.

"I want to break this spell of lies."

Mal didn't move towards her. He remained planted on the other side of the massive desk. "I've searched the Dread Spellbook. I've searched every writing on memory charms, spells that ensnare the mind, and nothing ever comes close to even touching on what this is. The Library here, the library at Vaukore. There is nothing."

"If I did this," she said hesitantly, eager not to anger him again, "then why was it you who felt it breaking before me?"

"Those damn potions," he drawled, as though it was obvious.

Maeve nodded softly, looking back down at the letters.

"Could these be a trick as well?" she asked, her voice quiet.

"You are far too clever to believe that."

The Dread Ring pulsed on her finger as though it begged her to feel every dark and intimate moment of their past again.

"And how would you know anything of my cleverness?" she fired back softly, brows flicking upward.

His slender fingers traced across the desktop between them absentmindedly. The motion made her stomach tight.

His voice was velvet. "You are in the dead blooms of hydrangea in the gardens. Your scent lingers in my chamber bed. In the Entrance Hall, I taste blood, and I know it is yours. I know little of you, and yet I know that you are mine."

The words slammed into her like a physical blow.

The room darkened, shadowing everything but him. In a mist of black Magic, he stood beside her, his glistening eyes locked on her. Magic swirled under her chin, pulling her towards him. Only then did she realize there were small flecks of deep brown in them.

"You know that too," he said lowly. "Don't you?"

"I don't have the luxury of believing what I feel."

Mal's fingers reached out, gently tapping along her temple. "You are of sound mind, Maeve."

The magnetic pull between them intensified, pulling her towards him from where she sat.

"What does it matter? I hear rumor that another is to be crowned your Queen," she said.

Mal's eyes traced over her face meticulously before he said, "And yet. . .I crave you. I do not want her."

His eyes widened as their green color darkened and the small trace of brown vanished. Magic barreled up around them. He turned from her, falling, and braced his hands on the desk with a loud slam.

His shield of Magic slammed around her before she could conjure one of her own. She stood from the desk and stepped back carefully, placing distance between herself and the sudden darkness.

Mal's head hung. The firelights in the room flickered. The darkened state around them that had previously enticed her, drawn her to him, slowly morphed into something unwelcome.

He stumbled slightly, placing himself on the opposite side of the desk once more. He did not look back at her as he commanded her with a strained voice. "Go."

She disobeyed.

She sent her Magic out, feeling that new darkness, assessing its threat. Her Magic hissed through her veins with fearful warning.

Maeve crossed back towards the desk with careful steps. He turned and he looked up at her with heavy eyes, still bracing himself. Eyes that were now swimming in new shades of green. "I told you to leave."

She placed her hands on the smooth wood between them and took a steadying breath. "If my Prince commands it, I will go. But if Mal would have me stay. . ."

She saw it then: the conflict reflected in his eyes as the green in them fought for dominance.

"She is here, isn't she?" asked Maeve quietly. "The one you are meant to marry? The one who offered you victory in the Elven Lands in exchange for a queen's title?"

Mal did not look away from her. "Sharp as a thorn, you are, at last. Freeing your Magic was worth your animosity." He turned towards her fully. He contemplated his next words and finally said, "Part of her is always with me."

Maeve nodded and leaned over the desk. The darkness seeping through the walls buzzed in threatening disapproval.

"You should fear her," he said, his voice slipping in and out of control. "If you only knew. . ."

Maeve's head dipped to one side, observing him. "Fear is the absence of Magic."

She pressed her palms into the desk and closed the space between them, locking her lips on his.

His body tensed as Magic skyrocketed around them. His hands grabbed her face instantly and pulled away, as if burned. Maeve melted into the feeling of his skin on hers.

The green in his eyes flickered and dimmed. Warm tones of brown swirled to the surface. Maeve smiled triumphantly, with no understanding of just how deadly the Magic she challenged was.

How with just a kiss, she had broken her own forgotten promise to that darkness.

Mal's hands dropped, fear prevalent across his beautiful face.

"Tell me, *Mal*," she said, as she propelled herself on top of the desk until she kneeled before him, "that you want me to leave."

She placed her hands on his chest and looked into his wild expression. His fingers slid up the sides of her thighs hesitantly, drawing a hum from her throat. Maeve's head dipped back, and her eyes closed. Mal gripped at her waist, her back arching in approval. His thumbs pressed into her with bruising force, bringing a laughter of arousal from her lips.

She looked directly at him. Her fingers brushed a few stray hairs from his forehead and then carded through his hair until her hands rested against either side of his jaw. "You're exquisite," she whispered. "I won't run from you this time."

She pressed her Magic into the darkness, piercing it with everything she had, and at last Mal breathed fully as his eyes darkened. His hands moved further up her body, exploring freely, until his fingers locked around her face. His grip constricted, knotting up her hair and propelling her chest into his.

"I do not want you to leave," he said at last.

Maeve sucked in a breath. "And what do you want?"

His lustful eyes bore into hers.

"I want you just like this: on your knees before your Prince."

"My soon-to-be King," she replied.

With a sharp inhale, his mouth was on hers, their lips fighting for dominance. His hands hooked behind her knees and pulled hard. She gripped him tightly as her behind slammed into the wooden desk. Mal moved himself hungrily between her legs as he bit into her bottom lip.

Her fingers wound through his raven hair as his tongue trailed down her neck. Bliss settled deep in her stomach. Reason and sensibility nowhere to be found.

"When was the last time you were touched in such a way?" he murmured into her skin.

"I can't recall ever being touched so sinfully."

Mal nipped at the base of her neck, bringing her shoulders tensely up. His teeth sank into her skin, freezing her entire body like trapped prey. His mouth clamped down harder, causing her fingers to twist tightly through his hair, desperate to inflict pain of her own.

His teeth pulled from her skin with a sharp exhale, and his forehead trailed across hers. Together they shared one breath. Mal slid a finger over her bottom lip, rolling it down.

"You are a dangerous dream," he said. "My mind is filled with nightmares, and they do not enjoy sharing me."

His lips met hers, and his tongue dragged across her own.

"Now that I have tasted you," he said, pulling back, all points of his contact tightening, "I know with certainty that there is much we've yet to remember."

Maeve scooted closer until the heat between her legs met the growing and bulging desire beneath his hips. "Remind me."

Chapter 14

Malachite

Mal stood at the edge of the Dark Peaks, Mount Morte behind him. The Greywood extended farther than he remembered, circling back to The Beryl City. The Dreaded Dead that lurked there moved in silence, observing him, but never moving without command.

Her command.

The waters of The Black Deep vanished over the horizon.

Vanished.

He couldn't shake the feeling, as he had for quite some time, that something about that horizon was strange. That it lacked. That it too was a lie.

The Dread Stone, the last piece he needed, remained out of his reach. Not a trace of it. Not a single writing or clue as to its whereabouts. Still, he knew it was out there somewhere. He'd overturn every single stone in the Elven Realm to ensure it wasn't hiding there.

He'd wandered through the Greywood endlessly searching for answers, answers he was on the brink of finding. He'd delayed his Queen for as long as he could. Now she'd grown strong enough to manifest a body. One with eyes too beautiful to possibly be hers.

Her skin was paper white. The first time he saw her form, she was nearly transparent. Every muscle and vein in her body visible through her thin skin. Now, her hair had grown long and straight and whiter than snow. Her lips were cold and distant. Like kissing a phantom.

Maeve's lips were the first warm thing he'd felt in. . .

And now that he'd had her fully, regret sat deep between his ribs. The Elven Lands and his victory there felt disappointing in comparison to the way she lost herself beneath him. He now ruled a fourth realm.

And he didn't fucking care.

Acid burned against his mind, a silent reminder of what he gave in exchange for power. That it would not be Maeve who warmed his lips any longer, that it was his Queen who spoke of heirs.

That was the bargain. The vow.

A Magically-binding promise of an heir in her belly, and all would bow before him. A pact made before he knew. . . Maxius needed him. Both Maeve and his soon-to-be crowned Queen would have to endure the truth that the Magic, stifled and trapped within Maxius, was his to unleash.

Back in the North Tower, he silently crossed his chambers.

Maeve slept soundly in his bed. Before he left her, Mal adjusted the duvet over her exposed back and placed a heavy shield of Magic around her, aiding in her sleep.

She looked just as he'd left her.

The bedding shifted beneath him as he moved over her, pulling back the covers. She stirred slightly, lifting her arms above her head in a sleepy stretch. Morning light peeked through the windows as he watched her frame twist towards him. The cool air prickled across her skin, making her even more devourable.

The black veins that ran the length of her body pulsed beneath his touch. He delighted in the way her body responded so eagerly to him. His fingers dipped past her navel, each hand pressing into her thighs and spreading her legs slowly.

She groaned.

"So, you are awake?" he murmured, lowering himself to the bed with his face dangerously between her legs.

Another groan. He lifted the barrier of his Magic that he knew aided in her sleep. She never slept through the night at Blackstone.

He pressed his lips to the soft skin on the inside of her thigh. Her knees pulled up instinctively. He pressed them back down with steady hands. With a content sigh, her pale eyes met his. Her thick black lashes against those icy eyes made her ethereal.

"Hi," she said, sleep still thick in her voice.

Mal didn't reply. He smiled at her and pressed another kiss, closer to her center, into her chilled skin. Another. And another.

Her fingers found his hair. "Can it always be this way?"

His eyes found hers, though he did not stop his slow and steady onslaught of kisses. The truth wasn't an easy admittance.

"So much peace. Just you and me," she continued, her eyes closing as his lips kissed down just above her hip.

"Peace," he repeated, crawling over her body until their chests pressed together and his nose nearly brushed hers, "is fleeting."

She tilted her chin up until they shared one breath. "Are you speaking of us or of war?"

Mal hummed in approval. "So quick to make assumptions that you understand either."

Maeve frowned. He grazed the tip of his nose over hers. Back and forth. Back and forth.

"I end one war and am already preparing for the next."

She hesitated beneath him. "Earth?" she questioned at last.

"Sharp as a thorn," he commended her.

"Earth will fight hard," she remarked, something like doubt in her voice.

"But I will fight harder," he said with a small smirk.

"You travel to Hiems often?" she asked.

Mal nodded. "I am their Prince."

"Hmm," murmured Maeve.

"Why?" he pressed casually.

"I dream about the realm often. At least, I think it's Hiems. Truly, I've never been."

"Would you like to see it?"

She pressed back into the pillows, her eyes darting between his.

"You'd take me to the ice planet?"

"My planet," he corrected, his fingers raising to brush hair from her forehead. "What are your dreams about?"

She looked up at the ceiling. "My brother," she answered softly. "I think. That wolf that trails you, the one from Hiems. He reminds me of him."

"Mordred is his name," said Mal. "He tells me your brother was a werewolf."

Maeve nodded, her eyes still not meeting his.

"Death circles you like a vulture," said Mal, reaching for her hand and swiftly slipping the Dread Ring off her finger. Her eyes snapped to his, color draining from her cheeks. "Can you feel it? All the destruction you could bring?" His lips moved towards hers. "I am insatiable for it."

He kissed her tenderly, savoring her warmth.

There would be no warm kisses in his future.

A content sound slipped from her. He pulled his lips back.

"With every touch," she began, "I can feel Magic unraveling inside me. You were right. It was me who cast this spell." Mal watched her throat as she swallowed. "I'm scared to let it rip completely," she confessed. "If I do break it, I'm scared of what that will mean."

He kissed her lips once more, withdrawing slightly, and said, "It's not a question of if. It's when."

"And when you have a queen. . .where will I be?"

He didn't answer. He knew that moment with her was fleeting. As death circled Maeve, his own reaper breathed at his back.

"I don't have an answer for that," he admitted, his voice even.

A heavy breath shifted through her, but she did not complain. She didn't have time to as his mouth claimed hers.

Chapter 15

Maeve

Maeve pushed on Abraxas' chest, gently moving him aside, and kneeled before Maxius, fixing his hair for the celebration at Castle Morana. "You've recited your speech twice already, Brax. Go away."

"You're in *my* wing of the castle," he retorted. "The whole wing is mine." He huffed and continued pacing across his lounge. "'Go away'," he muttered. "You go away."

Maeve looked over her shoulder at him incredulously. He began to recite his speech a third time, despite her protests.

Juliet and Lyrux were already downstairs. Abraxas was, uncharacteristically, stressed as he marched across their luxurious residence inside the castle. Alphard had returned home as well. Though Maeve was certain he was relishing all the attention and praise he was already getting at the festivities.

Maxius let Maeve fix him as he played with his fingertips.

Maeve talked over Abraxas. "Victory, blah blah, all thanks to our new Queen, blah blah blah." She pulled on the buttons on Maxius' overcoat a little too hard. His eyes shot to hers. "Sorry," she said, smiling softly.

Will Mal be there? Maxius signed.

"Yes," she replied, careful to keep her voice devoid of any emotion. "Though I think tonight you should address him properly in his crowned title."

Maxius shook his head and signed, *He said not to.*

"Well," said Maeve affectionately, her heart heavy, "aren't you special?"

Maxius smiled and crinkled his nose.

Abraxas was still muttering his speech under his breath as Maeve stood and took Maxius' hand in hers. With a long and grounding exhale, she prepared to meet Mal's Queen.

Abraxas' speech was just as irritating the fourth time she heard it. She stood by Alphard, just below the throne's dais, awaiting Mal, who officially claimed the title Dread King, and his new savior queen's entrance.

Applause rolled through the hall. Abraxas oozed the perfect amount of confidence and humility as he had the honor of announcing such a monumental step for The Dread Lands. His arm spread wide as he turned towards the center of the dias.

Magic coiled up Maeve's throat, her black inky veins hissing in warning. She retreated a step, pressing back against Alphard. His hands steadied her hips as the corners of Maeve's vision flickered white.

"Hold it together, my girl," said Alphard, his voice low for only her to hear. "You can do it."

His thumbs traced slow circles on her hips, a motion he'd made many times in the past during her episodes.

Abraxas' voice became a distant whir of sound. His dazzling smile and his bright blond hair blurred into one fuzzy image. One of Alphard's arms slid around her front, holding her up just as Maeve's legs began to turn to mush.

Two figures appeared on the dais, blurs of black and white. Mal was there; she'd know his silhouette anywhere. And she could only assume the white mass of light in her decaying vision was his new Queen making her grand entrance with Abraxas' perfectly practiced words of gratitude.

Alphard's voice was distant in her ear, but suddenly, both arms were around her, yanking her to the side.

Glass shattered close. Or far? Maeve didn't know. A blade flicked across her mind, and the Throne Room snapped into darkness.

A voice, distorted and eager, filled the void around her.

A game? A game of crowns? A game of broken hearts? A game of death? I win them all.

The infinite black space beneath her feet swallowed her whole, tipping her body backwards until the green glowing lights of the Throne Room returned to her vision. Alphard's distinct scent filled her nose, bringing her mind back to the celebration at lightning speed. She gripped at his chest, fabric coiling beneath her fists, and pressed her forehead into him. His arm remained in a tight hold around her. The spell ripping open inside Maeve, threatening to reveal unknown truths, tore further. Maeve winced, desperate to keep it sewn together.

The hall was silent. Completely still and silent, save for Roswyn's sharp and encouraging tone.

"It's alright, Em, let it happen."

Maeve pressed her heels into the floor and turned, still gripping Alphard tightly. A crystal goblet lay shattered across the marbled floor at Emerie and Roswyn's feet.

Emerie's eyes were completely black as Roswyn held her upright. Her voice was raw, and words not her own spilled from the Seer's blush-painted lips.

"Three were made and given away. Bound in gold and silver chains, the Magic lay, buried beneath another from the protection of the father." Her fingers curled into themselves as her breathing became labored. "When the night devours the sun, when the holy three join one, the Dread Stone will stand alone."

She gasped like a sword had just sliced through her stomach, and doubled over. Roswyn's strong arms were already lifting her back as he supported her weight fully. When Emerie's eyes flooded with color, they were already on Mal. She trembled against Roswyn as she took long and strained breaths.

Roswyn held her close, pride beaming in his voice. "Another Em.

Well done."

Maeve's attention whipped to Mal. His wide green eyes were set on Emerie. Astrea appeared suddenly. With a snap of her fingers, the broken glass vanished, and her hands grasped Emerie's face. The healer checked her briefly and then smiled. "Well done," she whispered in agreement.

"The Dread Stone."

Maeve's shoulders dropped. The voice from the vision she had just had. It was unmistakable, it was—

Maeve's eyes locked on the woman next to Mal.

His Queen.

"What a way to step on a Queen's entrance," she said, her blue eyes on Emerie.

Abraxas made to smile, but it quickly vanished as he took in the new Queen's frown.

Emerie stood and bowed to her, her breath still lagging. "Apologies, my Queen."

Magic swelled at all ten of the queen's fingertips. It poured from her lips and pooled at her feet. Maeve was so entranced by it, so stunned by the greenness of Mal's eyes and the dead expression on his face, and utterly caught off guard by his soon-to-be queen's beautiful appearance.

She had convinced herself that this dark queen who held power over Mal was a creature from a cave. Something lacking in grace. But this woman was more striking than even the Elves Maeve had seen.

She was decadent in an all white gown.

But her Magic was wicked.

She was a match for Mal where strength was weighed. But their Magical signature was distinctly different.

Her long white hair cascaded across her shoulders, shiny and straight.

Her laugh echoed across the hall, unsettling and forced. "There's no need to apologize when making such grand prophecies, is there?" She giggled.

Alphard's grip on Maeve tightened.

Abraxas cleared his throat, drawing Judyth's eyes to him.

How did she know her name?

"Would you like me to continue with your introduction now, your grace?"

"No," she said with another hollow laugh. "Let them enjoy a night of victory."

"All thanks to you," said Abraxas, bowing.

The entire hall followed suit. Abraxas then quickly instructed the music and serving to begin.

"Emerie," said Mal, stepping down from the dais towards her. "Anything else?"

"No, my King," she said, adjusting easily to the title change Abraxas had just announced. "It would appear the stone you have been searching for was split into three parts."

Abraxas, a drink already in hand, offered one to Alphard. He took it without question, a hand still wrapped around Maeve. "Alright there, Em," asked Abraxas, sipping his drink. "Ruined my speech a little."

Emerie smiled in apology.

Maeve wanted to thank Emerie for upstaging her own episode, but held her tongue as Mal's attention shifted to her. They stared at one another in aching silence. His face was stone cold. Maeve felt each step that his new queen took down the dais towards them. Mal's expression never changed as she drew closer.

"And you are?" she asked as she arrived at Mal's side, one arm snaking around his, down until their fingers joined.

Maeve swallowed. Alphard's hand rested against her back. Sweat pooled at the base of her neck.

Abraxas pulled his drink from his lips quickly and introduced Alphard.

Magic raced down Maeve's spine as the queen's blue eyes rested on her. They were so familiar.

So very. . . Sinclair.

Maeve's mouth fell open as Mal's words rang clear across her mind.

Such pretty eyes, even if they aren't yours, he had said.

The pale queen laughed. "I know all about our beloved fighter. I meant the stunning little thing hiding in his shadow."

She was suddenly so grateful for every lesson Agatha and her father taught her. "Class and cleverness" was always the lesson for the children of the Sacred.

Regardless, those titles didn't matter in Mal's world.

"This is my wife, Maeve," Alphard's voice interrupted her thoughts.

The queen's eyes never left Maeve. "A pleasure," she said, as she rested her head against Mal. Long, white fingers slithered across his chest, resting possessively.

Maeve did not bow. She smiled, her Magic buzzing beneath her skin in challenge.

Maeve knew then, without a shadow of a doubt, that she had met this woman before. She remembered her.

Shadow.

And she knew with even more certainty that in the eyes of the pale queen with striking irises that didn't belong to her, Maeve wasn't meant to be there.

She had vowed not to be there.

Chapter 16

Malachite

Mal's fingers traced across the Dread Crown, slowly dipping down the curves of the intertwining serpents as he held it in his lap at the foot of his bed. Even as Shadow ran her fingers down his bare chest, draped over him from behind, the thought of another's warm lips lingered.

"The Dread Stone," said Shadow. "And you'd nearly given up on that idea."

Mal didn't reply.

"Can you still sense its Magic?" she asked, her fingers dipping around the curve of his abdominal muscles.

"I can," he replied. "Or. . .I suppose all three of them now."

"You heard the little prophet," she muttered, a mocking tone in her voice. "They'll be one again."

"The holy three," said Mal, his mind running over Emerie's prophecy, "joining as one."

Shadow's cold lips trailed along his shoulder. The weight of her was crushing, as it had been since the moment she chained herself to his Magic.

"Holy three," he muttered, his fingers still tracing his crown.

He stood, putting distance between himself and the woman at his back. Forgetting the new prophecy and placing his crown on its stand, he reached for his robe, desiring at least the illusion of warmth. Or maybe to prevent Shadow's lips from assaulting his skin further. Her skin was nothing like Maeve's. It didn't heat where he kissed. It didn't blush where his fingers traced.

Shadow groaned and lay back on the bed. The sound was like that of an animal. "How many times am I going to have to rid your mind of this brat?"

Mal stilled.

"It's becoming tedious," continued Shadow, staring up at the ceiling. "Maybe I should just let the pair of you break the spell, and you can see for yourself what a traitorous snake she is."

Mal did not move towards her. Shadow's blue eyes landed on him. She grinned, delighted. "Poor little Dread King. So lost between two deceivers."

Mal was on her in a blink, a mist of black Magic in his wake as he Obscured on top of her. His hand pressed into her throat, a warning.

"Leave her out of this."

"How can I when you intend to fight for sweet Maxius to remain close?"

Mal's jaw tightened.

Shadow reached up, brushing his hair from his face.

"I don't care if Maxius inherits the throne. The crown," she said, taking his hand from her throat and placing it on her flat stomach. "I just want your blood, Dread blood, in my children."

"More than one?" asked Mal, his dead eyes locked on where she held his hand in place.

"I'll create as many little Dreaded ones as you give me, my King."

Mal looked back up at her. "Why? If you don't intend to see them rule?"

She smiled, but her eyes hardened. She sighed and dropped his hand. Mal pushed off her, his head dizzy, as she moved across the room without making a sound or leaving a single trace of Magic. Her voice was no longer coated in sweetness. "I've told you before, my motives aren't really relevant to you." Another sigh. "I hate when you're so ungrateful. I have given you so much, and promised so much more."

"And when do you propose we move on Earth?" he asked as a wave of her Magic crashed over him, muddling his thoughts. He struggled to remain upright and could have sworn he heard a distant laugh.

"Earth is not next, young King," she replied.

Mal glared up at her. "Then what is? The Dark Planet is nothing to rule. It's a barren wasteland."

She turned back to him, her long white hair swishing at her waist. "I'm going to tell you the truth about your dear Little Viper, now, Malachite. And all the things she, and that wretched Immortal, have taken from you."

Mal's eyes remained devoid of any hint of feeling, but his mouth turned down at the second mention of Maeve. "Immortal?" he questioned, no idea who she referred to.

Shadow nodded. "He gave me the very name you call me," she said, a satisfied and toothy smile creeping across her pale face. "And soon your Little Viper will remember him, too. And then she will remember the vow she made with me."

Mal's scowl deepened. Oh, how he regretted Shadow's existence. Her chokehold and her attention. "Why would she have made any arrangement with you?"

"Because she," said Shadow, stepping back towards him and taking his face in one hand, "does not love you." Magic stiffened through him, slowing his breathing and rinsing his mind in rushing cold water. "Does she?"

His eyes closed, succumbing to the deadly thrum of Shadow's power. "No. She does not."

Shadow's grip tightened fractionally, all-consuming numbness spreading from her fingers like vines. "Do you love her?"

Mal looked up at his captor, his demon, and his Queen, and spoke with certainty. "No."

Chapter 17

Maeve

Maeve lingered in the doorway of Mal's study. She adjusted the sleeve of her gown in the silence, wondering why he'd called her there prior to that evening's events.

Alphard was to be publicly honored for his efforts in the war and for his allegiance to the crown.

Maeve arrived at Castle Morana early, as she had been instructed to.

Mal played with the Dread Ring on his finger as he reclined at his desk, eyes on her. Hazel swam in them. A pathetically small comfort for her.

"Where is your Queen?" asked Maeve, tucking her hands behind her back and testing the waters.

Mal's eyes traced down over her at the gesture. A predatory smile kicked at the corner of his lips. "Is that jealousy in your tone, Mrs. Mavros?"

"Of course not," said Maeve smoothly.

"I know you're a better liar than that."

A silent moment passed between them, Mal's green eyes holding her hostage.

"Apologies, my Prince," she said softly. "I suppose I should have bowed formally and thanked you for honoring my *husband* this evening."

A swift breath rose across his chest, and he stood. Maeve's chin lifted slightly higher.

"You're going to tell him before his promotion," said Mal lowly. "About Maxius."

"What?" she asked, her teeth tightly together.

"And it's King now," he added, closing the gap between them gracefully. "I won't repeat myself."

Maeve swallowed.

"Because," he continued. "I'll be telling Maxius tonight myself."

She opened her mouth to protest, but the words came out as nothing more than a quick, throaty sound. Magic held her tongue as his head cocked to the side. The realization that he'd been loose with her, he'd given her space to think she stood a chance against him, washed over her.

It took hardly anything from him to stop the very air in her lungs. She froze beneath his power. Her Magic remained still and unmoving.

His brows raised. "You're not even going to fight back?" He smiled lazily. "Tonight will go smoothly, then."

He passed her, releasing his invisible hold on her throat, and commanded her as he walked away. "Go and break his heart."

His unhurried footsteps were long gone before she moved.

Alphard wasn't there to be honored. Maxius wasn't there to watch.

They were all there to be exposed for the lie.

Her lies.

"I need to speak with you," she said, pulling Alphard away from a Dread Knight in the main floor's corridor without an apology or even a slight courtesy.

"You're shaking," he noted as he followed her out of the hall without question.

"Where are Zimsy and Maxius?" she asked, rounding a few guests.

"Should be here any minute," he replied, looking over her.

Once they were a decent distance from guests and court and council members, Maeve turned on him in the corner. She kept her face calm, as there were still nearby eyes.

"You need to take Maxius and go."

Sensing the panic washing over her, he didn't hesitate.

His hands captured her face. "Maeve," he said, no trace of frustration in his voice, his tone reminiscent of when she had her episodes. "Nothing is wrong. Maxius has been invited here as a great honor on the day I am to receive a promotion."

"No," she hissed. "That is not why we are here. You do not understand."

Alphard's eyes locked on something behind her. His shoulder fell slightly, and Maeve was certain it was his beloved redhead, Victoria, that caught his eye.

"Listen to me," she snapped, electric Magic zapping at her knuckles.

Alphard's eyes looked down at her side as his brows pulled together.

"Something is wrong—"

He grabbed her hand and pulled her from the hall. They turned one corner, and he looked down at her.

"Is this about Victoria?" he asked hotly.

"What?" she replied, her face scrunching in confusion. "No. This is about Maxius and you and me and. . .everything." Words poured from her, fearful her chance to speak would be cut short. He had to hear it from her. Not from Mal. "I can see so much now. Every second, I see more and more like. . . like this spell is ripping apart against my will."

"Alright," he said hesitantly. "What do you see?"

Tell him Maxius isn't his.

"I've altered things in our minds," she replied. "Everyone's minds."

Alphard nearly laughed, but just as quickly as his expression shifted to one of disbelief, he turned serious.

"What?" she asked.

Alphard shook his head. "No. No," he reasoned with himself. "You couldn't do that. There's no way. That's just, just, unheard of."

It was clear something unsaid ran through his mind, and he wrestled with the thought.

Maeve urged him further. "I have to confess something because I'm concerned what hearing it from someone else will do. I do not think we are here as honored guests. I think Mal knows it was me who did this."

She had to tell him; she had to before Mal did. This Mal, the one entranced by his white queen, would not be merciful or kind in his deliverance. She'd felt the possessive way Mal's Magic reached for and desired Maxius' for weeks now.

Fear sank into Alphard's expression. Maeve pushed forward, even though the words that needed to be voiced confirmed she had deceived Alphard.

"Maxius is his."

Alphard held his hand up, his eyes moving rapidly. He sighed, closing his eyes. "I shouldn't have even let you get this far into this delusion. I keep telling Astrea you aren't okay and you need the potions back—"

Maeve didn't think twice. She didn't hesitate. She dove into his mind, breaking through his Pureblood mental shields with far too much ease, and showed him just how real her words were. His eyes flooded white. She showed him the memories she'd collected so far of Maxius' birth, of Mal as his father. Memories she hadn't let herself enjoy. Not yet. Maybe not ever. His mind remained pliant under her grip.

And then she showed him the one thing she'd come to see clearly that could make him snap. She showed him the night she appeared on his doorstep, bruised and frightened, just before he was meant to marry Victoria.

She only let the memory play out once, and then she withdrew from his mind. Alphard's eyes opened and latched onto hers. His chest rose and fell as his expression became vacant.

They didn't have much time. She couldn't allow him moments of digestion.

"Alphard," she said gently.

His mouth hung slightly open as he stared at her. "What have you done?" he asked darkly.

"Listen. I am afraid that all of this spell is about to crumble, and neither you nor I will be immune from Mal's reaction."

"He knows," said Alphard. It wasn't a question. "He's known Maxius was. . .is his."

"Yes," she replied.

His face hardened. "How long have you known?"

Maeve hesitated, stumbling over the truth of just how long she'd been certain Mal was Maxius' father. "I wasn't sure," she began.

Alphard's face twisted. He tilted his head back, biting hard into his bottom lip. "I have always had these thoughts about Victoria, things that felt so real. . . Fuck, Maeve." He looked back down at her, denial and reality colliding. "Fuck."

"I can fix this," she offered, aching to find Zimsy and Maxius and get them away before the spell completely shattered.

Alphard laughed once. Then twice. Then he was hysterical. Maeve stepped away from him.

"Fix this?" His laughter bounced wildly off the marbled walls of the corridor. "It is because of you we are here! It is because you are insatiable. You have never been and can never be satisfied."

"That's not why I did this! That's ridiculously unfair—" she argued back.

"Fair?" shouted Alphard. "Did you know that I couldn't deny you?"

"What?"

"Did you know," he repeated, bending towards her, "when you came looking for a way out, that Magic would force me to say yes?" He held up his palm, where a faint scar was visible. "Did you know that because you were in peril, and because I promised to protect you, I couldn't say no?"

"No," she replied hastily. "Roswyn bears the same scar—"

"Indeed, he does, because somehow, despite the fact that you never hesitate to choose yourself, all those around you aren't so selfish. And we continually choose to protect you."

"You did that for Antony," she fired back.

"Yes! Because I loved him and I love YOU!" He stepped back from her, shaking his head. "She was mine. She was a breath away from being mine."

"I know," said Maeve. "I'm sorry. I couldn't think of another way —"

Alphard turned on her, nothing but fury in his eyes. "You can alter the entire fucking world's memory and couldn't come up with any other explanation for Maxius? The possibilities were endless, Maeve."

"I wanted him to have a good father in his life," she said defensively, her voice breaking as tears swelled at the corners of her eyes.

"Oh," said Alphard, a laugh of disbelief burning through his throat. "Don't start crying now."

"From the looks of that memory, it appears I saved all our necks," she fired at him.

"And now you have put us both on the chopping block," he snarled.

"I'll fix it!"

"By doing what, Maeve? Have you thought this through at all?"

"I'm not going to stand here and do this with you," she snapped. "Maxius needs us now."

Alphard's eyes were blown wide. "What he needs is the truth. A truth which he likely already feels. Like calls to like, after all."

"What are you suggesting then? What great plan do you have?"

"That you stop digging and confess what happened. Allow Maxius and our King their truthful relationship. He's the fucking heir, Maeve!"

"And abandon the notion that the only reason this happened was to protect him? What a dumb thing to suggest, Alphard." She shook her head.

"Knowing you, it was probably only about your protection," shot Alphard.

"You ass—"

"Am I interrupting?"

Both their heads snapped sideways at the new voice. Abraxas stood with his hands in his pockets, looking rather annoyed. It was uncommon to see a scowl on his playful face.

Alphard ran a hand through his hair, turning from Maeve and shaking his head. "For fuck's sake," he muttered.

Maeve turned without another word, making her way towards Abraxas. Silently, she passed him. He joined her in step, uncertainty radiating from him. They left Alphard there in the corridor.

"What did you do, Maeve?" he whispered. "I am seeing some strange things in my head, and there's only one Witch I know who has an obsession with memories."

"I royally screwed up, I think," she answered as they swiftly made their way back to the Throne Room. "I need to find Maxius."

"I was sent to retrieve you both," said Abraxas. He stopped and yanked her back gently. His eyes scanned hers tensely. "Primus," he hissed. "I cannot shake the feeling that something is about to snap in half."

And it was. Her spell had been splintering and cracking for weeks now. The tear was so large that it was becoming more painful to hold it together than it would be to let it spiral out of being.

But Maeve couldn't bring herself to do it. Not yet. She had to get to Maxius first.

"I know, Brax. I feel it too," she assured him. "But right now, I need to find Maxius."

She slid from his tender grip and continued into the main castle.

She felt Maxius arrive as he crossed the protective barriers around Castle Morana, the protective barrier she kept around him solid and unharmed. Thank the Gods.

She turned the corner, the grand stairway at her feet, and stalled.

Mal stood at the center of the Entrance Hall, a dazzling smile that held just enough humility to ensure he was beloved by all on his face as he greeted those arriving. His crown of serpents glistened against his dark hair. Zimsy and Maxius stepped through the castle doors.

Maeve gripped tighter on that unraveling Magic swimming through her. Not yet. Just a little more time. She stepped down, gasped as icy Magic gripped her ankle, holding her in place. Mal turned, his smile dropping as his green eyes locked on her. He looked her up and down, his eyes narrowing slightly in disgust. He shook his head in silent command.

The look sent a shock through her chest. She didn't fight against the Magic keeping her at the top of the stairs. Not with that look on his face.

Mal looked back towards the castle doors as Maxius stepped towards him. Zimsy released his hand and dropped into a bow before Mal. Maxius bowed, but kept his excited eyes on Mal. Mal dropped into a low kneel, coming face to face with his son. His mouth moved, but Maeve was too far away to hear his words. Maxius' face changed, a nervousness taking over all of his boyish features. He looked into the Throne Room and then back up at Mal.

In front of so many? he signed.

Mal nodded in response. Then he stood and stepped to the side, letting Zimsy and Maxius pass. The Magic gripping her ankle vanished, and she flew forward at once. He met her at the base of the stairs, his hands tucked behind his back. Her heart swelled when she saw flecks of brown and hazel swimming in his eyes.

Hope settled in her bones. She sighed swiftly at the sight of him.

"You didn't tell him?" she questioned at once, hoping he could sense her gratitude.

Before she could continue, Mal's eyes flicked up to the top of the stairs behind her. Alphard and Abraxas stood together, arguing heatedly.

"Something to share?" said Mal, his voice carrying up the stairs.

The two looked down at them. Alphard's jaw tightened.

Abraxas hurried down the steps to Mal's side. "Everything is ready for you," said Abraxas.

Mal didn't reply. His eyes moved up to Alphard, still at the top of the stairs, and then once more to Maeve. He left them without another word and returned to greeting his guests at the center of the Entrance Hall. Though Maeve noted his smile was gone. Abraxas lingered by Maeve until Mal cut him a sharp look from the corner of his eye, and Abraxas hurried to his side.

Maeve didn't wait for Alphard to join her. She rushed into the

Throne Room, her eyes scanning for Maxius. She spotted him at once in the packed Throne Room. The upper balconies and galleries were full as well. Maxius was signing to Arianna. His hands moved so fast and with such enthusiasm, Arianna appeared to have a hard time keeping up. But she didn't squash his excitement.

Alphard appeared at her side, watching him with her.

"For what it's worth," said Alphard, his voice strained. "I will never be angry for the time I had with him."

"But will he be angry at me?" she asked softly as they stood and watched him.

Without waiting for an answer, she made to move towards him. But Abraxas appeared between them both, grabbing their forearms and hauling them towards the empty throne.

Their new Queen was nowhere to be seen.

"Brax," said Maeve, beginning her argument.

"Trust me, cousin, just shut up and allow this to unfold without a public scene."

Maeve bit the inside of her lip and listened as Abraxas continued. The change in his tone told her he knew a bit of truth at last.

"I'm going to pin this stupid new honorary broach on your chest, Alphard," said Abraxas, "for all your excellent combat in the Elven Lands. And then Mal is going to bring Maxius forward and announce him as his heir. And then, Maxius is going to show everyone all the wonderful Magic Mal has shown him, and then everyone is going to leave in one piece. Yes?"

Maeve and Alphard shared an apprehensive glance at Abraxas' chaotic order. Neither of them argued as he placed them at the base of the throne dais. Abraxas took his place by the throne as the hall fell silent.

Mal entered with little time for acknowledgement. What would normally have been a formal walk to his throne was unceremoniously swift and direct, causing an immediate tension to settle in. Everyone, including Maeve and Alphard, dipped their heads as he passed them. He did not look at either of them as he ascended the steps to his throne.

Once seated, Abraxas stepped forward and picked up a golden pin from a wooden stand on the dais. He faced the hall and began what Maeve knew at once to be a well-rehearsed speech.

"It is my honor as Hand of the King," began Abraxas as Maeve dared a look at Mal.

His gaze was fixed on nothing in the distance. A vacant stare on his handsome face. Magic rippled through her, her own spell slicing open wider against her will. A few shifts of breath scattered the hall, and Abraxas stumbled over his words as she struggled to hold the Magic together.

"Stop."

Mal's voice was unsettlingly calm.

Abraxas turned towards him and raised a soft brow.

Mal regarded him for a moment and then tilted his head. "Do you serve me, Abraxas? Or another?"

Abraxas nearly faltered beneath the question. Maeve had never seen him under such duress. "You, my King. Always you."

Mal made a contemplative sound, as though he was undecided if Abraxas was being truthful, and his eyes lifted back to Alphard. "And you?"

Alphard wasn't dumb enough to let his rage out on Mal, but Maeve felt his temper swell.

"A captain of the Bellator, named a Dread Knight" continued Mal, "who I recently promoted to commander, now receiving another great honor. Where does your loyalty lie?"

The question was veiled, but clear to Maeve: Mal was aware that Alphard had willingly helped her deceive him. Mal stood and stepped down from his throne, his eyes still on Alphard.

"Do you think a man who swears fealty to another, and then breaks his word, should be honored in my world?"

Alphard scowled. "No, my King."

Mal circled them with a nod. "On that, we can agree." His eyes landed on Maxius. Maeve's heart hammered against her chest. He held out his hand and beckoned the boy with two fingers. Maxius looked to Maeve for approval. She offered him a single nod, knowing her protection over him was not easily broken.

Mal's eyes still held a trace of their true color.

Maxius stepped forward, leaving behind Zimsy, and Arianna, and his cousins. The tense silence drew out his journey across the long hall. Mal's fingers curled around themselves, soft Magic kindling. His eyes narrowed slightly as the locket around Maxius' neck pulsed with Magic. Maeve held a tight breath, realizing, no doubt at the same moment Mal had, that the Dread Locket rested on Maxius' chest.

When he arrived before Mal, the Dread King looked back at Alphard.

"Continue, Abraxas," he commanded. "But know this, Mavros." He looked back down at Maxius. "It is only for his sake."

Relief swept through her. Relief that swiftly vanished as words spilled from Alphard's mouth and he stopped Abraxas' hands from pinning the broach to his uniform. "No."

"Alphard," Abraxas snapped under his breath.

Mal looked over his shoulder at him, a confident challenge in his voice. "No?"

Alphard took a step towards Mal, Magic pouring from his palm. "You're right. I don't deserve this honor."

Mal turned towards him fully, standing between him and Maxius. Alphard continued, his temper swelling with each curling movement of his fingers.

"And that's fine with me," continued Alphard smugly, "because the next time you bruise her, I won't just take her from you. I'll kill you where you stand."

Maeve moved between them at once. It was only a few steps, but she Obscured, placing her back to Alphard and keeping her eyes on Mal.

"He doesn't mean that, Mal," she said swiftly. "There is other Magic speaking for him. Magic that forced him to agree to help me in the first place."

"Is that what you told yourself, Mavros?" Mal asked. "That you had no say?"

Alphard nearly growled as their Magic pressed towards one another. Maeve continued to try to reason with Mal.

"He made a promise with my brother, a blood pact to protect me."

Mal's lip curled. "I'm well aware. I can see it dripping from his hand now." Their Magic continued to confront the other's, testing who would snap first. "You know what else I can see?" His arm raised, his eyes never leaving Alphard's, and pointed at Roswyn. "He bears the same vow."

Mal nodded triumphantly, right as Alphard tensed.

"And he," seethed Mal, "did not touch what was *mine*."

Maeve's breath caught.

"You may have forgotten it, thanks to the treacherous viper standing between us, but I made it clear to you that you were forbidden to marry her. Forbidden to touch her in the ways only I should touch her."

Mal stepped back slightly, his eyes slowly becoming more green, and lingered across Maeve's body.

"You did both," said Mal darkly.

Swirls of Dark Magic manifested from the ground beneath him, snaking up his legs and wrapping his torso. As it grew higher, the darkness lifted in color, turning iridescent and solid, until Shadow stood clinging to Mal like a vine.

Her voice was almost childlike as she whined against him. "Malachite. Let's move this along now."

Hope flickered out like the end of a candle as his eyes became fully green.

"If a fight is what you seek, Mal," spat Alphard, "then I'll gladly give you one."

Shadow moved towards the throne, casually placing herself upon it. Mal made a small sound of disgust and turned towards Maxius. "What a waste of my time that would be."

Maxius, whose brows were pulled together anxiously as he watched the tension unfold between them, looked up at Mal.

"There's only one with Magic that could rival mine," said Mal. "And I know just how to pull it out of her."

He moved with devastating grace. His arm slid across his front as one slender finger, dripping with Magic, too much Magic for the child before him, crackled across his hand. As he took aim at Maxius, the boy instinctively mirrored the King, pointing one tiny protective finger up at his father.

Chapter 18

Maeve

Lightning shattered through the hall, cracking into the jet of light that burst from Mal's fingertip. It ricocheted into the vaulted ceiling and slammed into a sculpture of an oversized serpent. The creature's marbled head severed, crumbling to the floor with massive force. Debris from the hit scattered across the hall. Light dust from the destroyed fixture plumed in the air.

Maxius fell backwards, looking at his fingers in shock. But he, and the entire present company, swiftly realized it wasn't the young boy who fired such an extraordinary force of Magic.

The Dread King's eyes were already on Maeve, where she stood between him and Maxius.

On the electricity bouncing between her fingers.

On her protectively fierce expression.

The air crackled with threatening Magic between the King and the one who had blocked his path of Magic.

"You are out of your fucking mind," said Maeve slowly and carefully.

Shadow smiled from the throne, her grin so utterly satisfied that Maeve desired to spit in her face. She giggled and stood, crossing behind Mal and wrapping her pale arms around his chest.

"Didn't I tell you, my King?" she began.

"On your feet, Maxius," commanded Mal. "We are not finished."

Maxius obeyed with haste, exhausted breaths rolling through him.

"Yes," said Maeve lowly. "You are."

She turned and faced Maxius, her eyes landing briefly on her sister. She twisted her fingers through his hair, his frightened gaze locked on hers.

Do not fear. Fear is the absence of Magic, she slid into his mind.

Maxius' eyes widened. He nodded. Maeve smiled softly down at him as his breathing evened.

"I will not let harm come to you," she spoke aloud this time, ensuring her promise was heard by all, and gently tapped his temple.

He slipped to the floor, his landing light as a feather, as Maeve rendered him unconscious. She would not scar him further by witnessing the scene that was about to unfold.

She turned back to Mal and Shadow.

Shadow's pleased grin remained plastered on her face. But Mal. . .

Mal's dead eyes and pale lips held nothing but rage. Calm and sinister rage. And every ounce of it was directed at her.

"Have you remembered what you did yet," his cold voice began, "or do you need reminding?"

Shadow rose to the tips of her toes and planted a long kiss to Mal's jaw. He didn't peel his eyes away from Maeve. She rested her head against him and pouted. "Look how sad you've made my King." She moved back to the throne swiftly, like a madwoman, and draped herself across it. "There's no use fighting, now, *Little Viper*," taunted Shadow. "I showed him everything."

"That must be nice," replied Maeve. "I seem to be the only one of the three of us in the dark."

"An easy fix," said Shadow with a sigh, her gaze shifting upwards towards the glass ceiling. "There's no point in my trying to prevent it now. We tried this your way, and you failed. Now, we do it my way." She angled her head and looked directly at Maeve with a sigh, as though this was beneath her. "Though, I will enjoy watching you realize just how much of this is your fault."

"Enough," said Mal, his voice ripping Maeve's attention from Shadow.

"Apologies, my King," said Shadow.

As though it wasn't she who possessed him.

As though it wasn't her power looming over all of them.

Maeve couldn't fix her mistakes, not if she didn't know what they were. She wouldn't be able to right the wrongs if she had no idea of the truth. She begged forgiveness for the things she didn't remember. She prayed Alphard would understand. She prayed that the unknown would unfold itself with grace.

As though he sensed her next move, Mal spoke. "I wonder if when you break the spell you'll feel guilt for any of it."

"It's you who are under a spell," said Maeve softly, the reality she created ripping open inside her mind with each surrendered word until she let go completely.

Magic slipped free from her, unraveling in a spiral of destruction. Pain snapped across her knees as she buckled under the weight. Loss and gain flooded her veins. Too much, too swiftly to understand all the changes, all the rewritten memories, and the contradictions of new and old, as her spell shattered.

Verification for the things she suspected, and the things Mal showed her, hung heavy in her mind. Her father's death and falling in love with Mal at Sinclair Estates. Maxius' true childhood, the one she'd hidden more than once now, hit her in blooming waves.

A weight lifted from her chest, one she'd never felt before its absence, only to be replaced by the worst memory of them all: her betrayal. Her abandoning of Mal.

It was her blood that unsealed Shadow. She went to Mount Morte, ignoring Mal's commands not to. He had tried so hard to protect her, to keep them all safe from Shadow. And she had failed to do the same in return.

Her cheeks became soaked as she kneeled in the Throne Room.

The floor between them may as well have been coated in blood. Her father's blood. Arman's blood. The blood she'd willingly and unwillingly spilled for Mal.

"Tears?" Shadow's voice cut across the silent hall. "You'll have to do better than that to sway the Dread King. Can't you feel it radiating from him? How utterly furious he is?"

"Stop it," she whispered, her gaze down.

"You didn't just take his son from him," said Shadow, sitting up in the throne, ignoring her completely. "You broke *all* those sweet promises of companionship, protection. You vowed to fight for him until your last breath!" Shadow's voice edged on something hysterical. Maeve looked up at her at last. The Shadow Queen frowned deeply and continued.

"Meaningless words," she muttered. "You live and breathe despite such bold betrayal."

Maeve shifted her focus to Mal.

It was truly a horrible feeling, not being able to deny such blatant proof that she had broken every word between them. That he'd begged her not to abandon him to the wicked and vile creature that now occupied his throne.

But she did.

That she'd promised on bended knee to be his second, and fight for him.

But she ran.

"The worst part is," began Shadow, her voice crackling with Magic, "is that if you had told him the truth, he might have understood your reasoning. I hadn't fully consumed him yet then." Another bored sigh. "That isn't the case anymore, of course." She straightened her back and crossed her legs. "Malachite."

Mal turned towards her, looking over his shoulder.

"I've grown tired of this," she said, her blue eyes on him.

Maeve's blue eyes. Those were her eyes.

Something between a laugh and a cry broke from Maeve's throat as she remembered trading her eyes for Shadow's pale ones. The white Queen's scowl landed on Maeve at her outburst.

"What now, Little Viper?" said Shadow, the affectionate name sounding like acid in her voice.

Maeve nodded in understanding, pressing one foot into the floor and slowly standing to her full height.

"First," she said, swallowing hard. "You're going to stop calling me that."

Shadow's eyes narrowed ever so slightly at being given a command.

Maeve inhaled slowly, pulling inward every bit of Magic that occupied her soul, her veins, and her mind, and let it run wild through her. She exhaled, marveling at the expanse of it and the control she maintained.

She was awakened.

She extended her arms, electric energy pulsing across her knuckles, begging to be used. Lightning had shot from her fingertips only moments ago. Rare and destructive Magic that, with each breath, she remembered just how she'd used it in the past.

"You do not command me," said Shadow.

"Second," said Maeve, dropping her hands to her side as Shadow's lips thinned into a tight line. "You are the one who failed. Not me. Though," she held up two fingers, observing how sharp the potential in them was, "the way I'm feeling right now, I think I'm grateful."

Shadow scowled.

Maeve looked back up at her. "When you asked for my eyes, I didn't understand it then. But I do now. You loosened your hold on his mind. That's why he broke through. There is no deception of Magic that drives him to me. Like calls to like. You loosened your reins on his mind with the pathetic notion he'd truly fall for you." Maeve shook her head. "Didn't you?"

The blade struck its mark.

Darkness swallowed Shadow's eyes. "Since you've remembered so much now, then you'll do well to remember that we had a deal. And that your son's life hangs in the balance of that deal."

Maeve continued her slow breaths, just as she'd been taught by her father. In and out. In and out. Each set stoking the Magic flowing freely through her.

How could she have buried such an undeniable extension of herself?

"I kept my bargain," continued Maeve. "I stayed away. Your failure to win his heart is not my burden to bear."

Shadow was anything but bored now. The air turned oppressive, volatile as darkness wrapped her pale body.

Maeve turned her attention to Mal. "I did fail you, though."

His green eyes shifted. Maybe it was just a trick of the thickening mist of darkness, but she swore a tiny fleck of hazel drifted through them.

She looked down at her chest, and the starburst scar of Magic remained. She remembered then how she had removed it. That hadn't been an illusion, or a lie, or a trick of mind Magic. That removal was real. Her chest ached at the feeling, recalling how desperate she had been to protect Maxius.

"I won't fail again."

She anticipated the blow. As Mal's Magic coiled back and prepared to strike on Shadow's behalf, Maeve readied two fingers at her side.

Chapter 19

Maeve

Something reminiscent of a smile tugged at Mal's lips as his eyes watched her fingers with predatory intent.

"There's so much more than even I could have imagined," said Mal. "You hid him from me. . .multiple times. You even hid him from both of us."

"Because that *thing* draped across your throne puts Maxius in danger."

"In my defense," said Shadow, a mock hurt in her voice, "I was content with keeping him alive so long as you kept him away. It's his *dear daddy* here who wants to absorb his power. That's the part I can't allow."

Mal turned sharply over his shoulder and focused his attention on Shadow.

"He only wants that because you have poisoned his mind," seethed Maeve.

Shadow barked a laugh. "Surely you understand the irony of such an accusation coming from yourself?"

"You've corrupted his Magic," argued Maeve. "It's not the same."

Shadow's eyes narrowed. "He will always be driven to become one with the Dread Magic that lies dormant in your son. It's written in Magic. It's a shame you aren't more in tune with your own blood, Little Viper. There's so much you can't see. It almost makes me pity you." She paused. "But you are in my way. And so is your son."

Maeve attempted to settle her mind. She'd never get him out of this if she couldn't think straight. Shadow's oppressive Magic blurred her thoughts, dragging some and spiraling others.

"There's a way out of this," said Shadow, her voice slick with deception. "I'll give you a little do over."

Maeve stilled.

"Tell her our price, Malachite," said Shadow.

Mal turned his attention back to Maeve. Her heart ached at the sight of him. At how his eyes held nothing even close to what they once did.

"The spell you created to alter the world's memories. You will give it to me."

Maeve hadn't been expecting that. She'd assumed some blood sacrifice, or a vow of Magic, would be demanded of her. Mal continued.

"When I began hearing you in my head, the first thing I did was scour the Dread Spellbook for anything resembling a spell that ensnares the minds of all into one unified thought. Nothing came close. As I spent more time around you, I realized you had the potential for such a thing. Which only made me more curious about you. The power of the Dread Spellbook is that it contains, automatically, all Dread Magic known to exist."

The power to alter the world's perception would be far too dangerous in Shadow and Mal's hands. She loosed a long breath, reality forcing its way to the forefront of her mind as she stood between Maxius' sleeping body and Mal. It was dangerous in her hands, too, it seemed.

"I can't give you that," said Maeve softly.

"This is not a bargain," replied Mal smoothly.

"No," she said, more bite in her tone now.

Mal's lip twitched. "Maeve," he warned.

"No," she repeated.

"No?" said Shadow with a laugh. "That's fine." She rested her arm against the arm of the throne, flexing her fingers. "Malachite," she called, his attention turning back to her. His eyes glistened at her draw of Magic. "Kill the boy."

Mal turned without hesitation, power thrumming at his hands as he stalked towards her. Maeve's insides twisted violently, and her Magic snapped to attention. To battle. To whatever unfortunate end.

"Mal, please wake up," she begged softly.

Shadow laughed. "You did this, Little Viper," she mocked. "You alone set me free. He was so weak from keeping me back. From keeping you safe and away from all my Dreaded Dead and creating barriers to keep you from where I slumbered at the top of Mount Morte. But he could never have unleashed me. That was only you."

Mal stopped before he reached her, their position a reminder of so many duels from their past. But those ended in his praise. His kiss.

This one would not be so lovely.

"I won't let you harm him," said Maeve. "You know that."

"It will take all of you to stop me."

Maeve sighed. "Then so be it."

Maeve jumped quickly, slipping into Alphard's mind, far easier than she had ever jumped before, and moved behind Mal. He swirled around and blocked the burst of Magic from Alphard's fist, as she let go of her hold on him. Mal sent Alphard flying across the hall. Maeve Obscured, placing herself closer to Mal's back, and slammed two fingers into his back.

Her Magic rippled through him, successfully landing and drawing a throaty groan from him. She Obscured again, putting distance between them as he turned on her, shaking off the impact of the spell.

"Shadow dulls your senses of my Magic," remarked Maeve. "I could have never landed that before."

Alphard glared at her, now back on his feet.

Mal was on her in a flash. Their hands collided in a burst of Magic, sending each of them sliding away from each other. Maeve Obscured again, careful to keep herself between him and Maxius as they dueled. Mal blocked one advance with ease. Then another. And again. He didn't fire back at her until his fourth block.

His foot shifted to the side, sharp Magic shooting across the floor and yanking her forward. The back of his knuckles collided with her cheek. The force of the hit was enough to blur her vision, but the Magic that penetrated her at contact caused her to cry out.

She Obscured quickly, placing herself behind him. He turned with speed she could barely register and a single finger pulsing with Magic, ready to strike her chest. She dropped to one knee, and his blast of Magic exploded over her head. With a quick slice, she struck his legs, landing a hit. Her victory was short-lived as Mal's free hand coiled in her hair and yanked her up and against his chest. His other hand snagged her forearm as she moved to make contact, electric Magic dancing across her fingers.

His grip tightened.

The bone snapped, shattering in half.

Maeve's reaction was delayed as her eyes widened and her mouth parted. Nausea rolled through her toes, up to her stomach, and exploded. Her cry that rang out across the hall was primal, like stabbed prey surrendering. Mal gripped her harder, drawing her even closer.

"You will not take him from me again," he whispered, his voice calm and even despite the horrific hold he maintained on her broken arm.

"I can help you, Mal, please," she begged through staggered and shallow breaths. Pain tore through her in wave after wave, each one crashing harder than the last. "Together, we can rid your mind of this dark possession."

"How can I believe a word that comes out of your traitorous mouth?"

Shadow smiled triumphantly from the throne.

"Give me the spell," he commanded.

"Anything else," stuttered Maeve. Begging now, and hating every bit of how it sounded in her voice. She had never begged like this. "Anything else you ask and I will give."

"The spell, Maeve," said Mal, shaking his head like he thought she was stupid.

Mal released her with such a forceful shove, she landed on the floor, unable to brace herself fully. She cried out as her torture increased. It wasn't solely a snapped or shattered bone that ailed her. Toxic Magic ate at her skin. He stalked across the room, his eyes on a new target.

Zimsy.

Maeve scrambled, Obscuring, only partially there as the pain of her broken arm thrumming through her weakened her Magic. Zimsy stood with her back tall as the guests around her scrambled to put space between themselves and Mal's pursuit.

"Zim," began Maeve, but her throat closed instantly before she could tell her friend to run.

Mal prepared a single finger as he continued to move towards her.

"It seems cruel to attack you this way, when you can't perform Magic," said Mal.

Zimsy's chin lifted. She raised her hand, palm flat towards Mal, as Magic swirled against her skin. Mal stilled. He sneered.

"You? How could you possibly perform such Magic?"

"Mal—" called Maeve, forcing herself to her feet.

Lethal Magic rippled from him as he turned back towards her. "Don't you dare call me that." He whipped back towards Zimsy, pointing at her. "How is it you came to possess Dread Magic? Your Curse was broken, effectively ending any shared Magic granted to you for the purposes of serving in slavery."

That last word brought a sharp breath up through Maeve, anger brewing deep in her chest.

Zimsy swallowed hard. "When Maeve broke my Enslavement Curse, some of her own Magic slipped into me," explained Zimsy, her beautiful face on Mal. "It's not much," her eyes shifted to Maeve, "but I am honored to have it all the same."

The air turned thick, like the atmosphere before thunder rolls. Green light pulsed at Mal's finger, Maeve's senses feeling it before it ever manifested.

Her next words weren't heard over the blast of Magic.

"You can have the spell, just leave her—"

Zimsy's body lifted from the floor beneath Mal's power, agony spread across her delicate features. If Maeve was breathing, she'd never felt more suffocated.

"Stop, please stop—" screamed Maeve.

Zimsy's body contorted in the air, her hands snapping backwards in an unnatural way.

"STOP!" Maeve wailed, turning back towards Shadow, her screams echoing off the stone walls as she fell to her knees. The poisonous Magic penetrating her shattered arm fried her mouth.

Shadow didn't move an inch. Her eyes were glazed in a

bloodthirsty, hypnotized way that made Maeve's heart shatter. She couldn't tell where Mal ended and Shadow began.

The sounds were horrific.

Mal continued until Zimsy's arms were twisted in all directions. Exposed bones shattered at the tips. Blood spilled to the floor, pooling up beneath her.

Maeve didn't even know if she was screaming anymore. The entire room was hauntingly still. Frozen in fear.

Mal watched Zimsy for a moment longer before letting her slim body slam to the floor. Maeve pushed off the ground to rush towards her, but Abraxas grabbed her waist, firmly pulling her back. She shook in his grip as another wave of spinning nausea passed through her. Her cheek prickled with growing, sharp Magic where Mal had struck her.

Zimsy didn't move. Maeve couldn't even see if her chest rose and fell.

"Stop," whispered Abraxas in Maeve's ear, his voice dry and strained. "Stop fighting."

Maeve pulled against his arms around her, but her hands met a bar of steel around her. She was pathetically weak. Mal's Magic along her arm pulsed in satisfaction.

Mal flung an arm out behind him, where Alphard made a break for Maxius. A solid beam of Magic zapped across the Throne Room, sending Alphard into the wall with enough force that he fell and did not rise again.

"Let her go, Abraxas," commanded Mal.

He looked away from Zimsy's body. With the wave of his hand, she disappeared from the floor, black mist in her wake. Abraxas' arms around Maeve loosened, but Maeve didn't move away from him, and he did not drop his hold.

"Do not think you will be sliding by unscathed, Abraxas."

Mal didn't move towards them, where they clung closely to each other on the floor. His lip curled up at them.

"Betrayed by my two closest allies," he said evenly, no trace of the lethal power he'd just used affected him. "I should have seen it myself, Abraxas. I should have known that you would choose her over me if it came to it. Punishment for not returning your feelings after all this time?"

Abraxas went stiff behind her.

"This one stings, Abraxas, I must admit. Knowing you conspired to help her erase my memories, when I gave you reign and power over anyone else. I trusted you with my world, my life. . .with her."

"She is my blood, Mal," said Abraxas carefully. "We did what we thought was best."

Mal laughed. "Your blood?" His eyes slid to Maeve, then back to Abraxas. "Have you forgotten she is not of Pureblood? That you bear no relation to her mother and therefore none to her?"

Abraxas shook his head. "I have not forgotten. She is still my blood."

Mal merely nodded. "We'll see exactly what your blood means to you by the time I'm finished with you."

Maxius remained across the hall. Slow breaths rose and fell from his little chest. How would she ever tell him about Zimsy?

The sounds of her mutilation echoed across her mind in such a paralyzing and distracting way, she couldn't prepare herself for Mal's advance. Abraxas shoved her to the side, placing himself before Mal. Mal's hand shot out, gripping Abraxas' face.

Abraxas flinched as Mal's fingers tightened, forcing his mouth open. He raised his free hand, and with one sharp movement of his pointer finger, blood sprayed his chest. Thick, bright-red blood poured from the corners of Abraxas' mouth.

"It's like you have all forgotten that what runs through me is not the same as you!" exclaimed Mal, seething with fury.

Abraxas' body hunched over as Mal stood and released him. Only then did Maeve see her cousin's tongue fall to the marbled floor in a pool of blood. Juliet's muffled scream slammed straight into Maeve's chest.

Mal's words settled against her. The weight of them. The truth of them as he stepped towards her. He was, even without Shadow to aid him, different from the rest of them. He was born better. Stronger.

It was in his blood.

Maeve scrambled for Maxius, her face hot with dried tears and her body on fire as each movement was nothing but agony. Mal raised a single finger, threatening Magic branching in all directions, and called out to her with a voice of warning.

"You have others in this room you love, Maeve. Do not continue to get in my way."

She didn't have it in her to Obscure again. Getting to Maxius would take all she had left. Even then, once she did, where could she run with him? Her Magic continued to drain from her grasp with each pulse of Mal's lingering force on her body.

He was right. She'd never grasped just how superior he was.

He'd never used it on her.

She crawled towards Maxius with one good arm and hadn't even realized she was moving. He was far. Too far. Mal's footsteps echoed across the space, taunting her with how unhurried they were.

A blur of motion appeared before her. Her body twisted, compressing against another as someone Obscured her, and they landed next to Maxius. Pain shot through her entire side at the contact. Maeve looked up at Arianna.

Her sister's voice was icy as she uttered the words she'd never given Maeve. "Usque ad mortem, Sinclair."

Her sister dropped her hold on her and stood, leaving Maeve on the floor next to Maxius. Mal continued his steady pursuit towards them. He reared back his arm and fired at Arianna. She stepped forward.

Bright blue lightning scattered across the hall, uncontrolled and wild. But it was not from Maeve's fingertips that it poured.

While Maeve kneeled before Maxius, chanting Magic with a voice nearly not her own, Arianna Sinclair stood with two fingers furiously pointed at Shadow. Smoke dissipated from Arianna's fingertips, as her face was lit with discovery.

Her eyes lifted from her fingers to Shadow.

Arianna's blast of lightning was stronger than Maeve's had ever been, even if it lacked the control Maeve had previously perfected.

"It seems the Sinclair sisters share in their electric abilities, Dread King," commented Shadow, just inches from the throne Arianna had just exploded.

Arianna crossed the hall boldly towards Mal, towards Shadow, not a single step held a drip of fear. "You controlled the Dreaded Dead, did you not?" she asked, her question directed at Shadow.

Shadow smiled at Arianna's fury. She relished the pain in Arianna's eyes so sinfully, it seemed, that she did not feel the Magic pouring from Astrea and Juliet. Their whispers were barely audible as they assisted in placing protective enchantments around Maxius.

"I did," said Shadow proudly. "I do. Did I take something precious from you?" Her voice lacked all remorse, already knowing the answer to her inquiry.

Knowledge of the past, knowledge she herself had not hidden, flooded Maeve's senses. Arianna wouldn't last long against Shadow, and so Maeve knew time was limited. Though she was grateful her sister was clever enough to bait Shadow into gloating, giving Maeve the time she needed.

She placed two fingers on her palm and sliced the skin open in one swift movement. Placing her bleeding palm on Maxius' chest, she offered everything for his protection.

Absolutely all of her.

Pain began to cut through Maeve as her offering took hold.

It happened all at once, through her entire body. Death's hands grabbed her mind, each of her bones, holding her in an iron grip of observation. More hands appeared and began clawing with long, sharp, dirty fingernails across her bones. An icy prickle walked slowly down her spine, piercing each segment, meticulously covering all of her. They stalled, Magic giving her a chance to turn back.

Spinel appeared in the archway across the hall, his bright and wide-set eyes locked on her. Maeve's brows pulled together as his sudden appearance at Castle Morana shifted through her. Always at Maxius' heels and always curled near him.

And now he was here. When she was on the verge of pouring every bit of her Magic forth in order to protect Maxius.

Spinel's head dipped to one side, and Maeve took it as a silent encouragement. He disappeared silently back into the shadows behind him, and she accepted the exchange of Magic as more lightning cracked wildly behind her.

At once, those filthy hands that had fastened themselves to her very essence began scraping and clawing with relentless and unyielding intentions. They drowned her. Again. Again. And when she was certain she was drained completely, they pulled more air from her lungs, only to crush them again. Again. And Again. Maeve begged them to stop. Each dirty fingernail that ripped her skin felt like a hundred lashes, the pain building with each claw that stripped away her Magic.

But in the absence of Magic pouring from her in sacrifice, she felt a beam of power that stretched farther than she could understand. It had no destination. No end that she could rationalize. But the Magic vibrating along the thread was pure. It was a friend. She pulled gently on the strand of Magic and pleaded for her son.

Get him out of here.

The line of Magic sharpened at her call.

Her blood was on fire, forged of something new. The hands worked diligently until every fiber of her Dread Magic was sucked from her.

Her center tilted as she slumped sideways. She barely saw the pale-blue crystal slowly encasing Maxius vanish with his sleeping body.

Chapter 20

Reeve

The mountains across the Black Deep turned dark, black as night, as Maeve's scream echoed through the halls at Celestian Palace in Aterna.

No one stirred. The water crashed lightly against the stone steps below. There came no footsteps of panic or calls of confusion.

For her scream had only reached one set of ears in Aterna. Traveling across ancient Magic, it struck its mark.

Her voice was broken and begging in his ears.

He'd been waiting for this day. Overseeing the training of every boy and girl old enough to enlist in the Senshi Cadet Corps, strengthening the Magical borders that separated them from the Dread world.

Wondering if she'd find him before he'd be forced to find her. That perhaps the Gods would spare him the misery of having to take her against her will, guaranteeing her already festering hatred.

He tore his eyes away from the distant land and placed his gaze on the banister outside his chambers, where Spinel sat like a chiseled statue with glowing, pale red eyes.

The goblet of wine in Reeve's hand shattered furiously as he looked back across the dark water at The Dread Lands beyond, where they knew not he and the Aterna people existed.

Where she was tearing apart her Magic willingly.

Where he would soon be.

Get him out of here.

An audible sound of pain left Reeve's throat at hearing her voice for the first time in years.

Reeve shook his head. "Gods dammit," he muttered, feeling that constant pull towards her tighten as she wrapped her Magic around their bond. His stomach clenched, feeling her shred open the spell he himself had cast.

The one meant to protect his people, to keep her far away from him.

He closed his eyes, drifting into the space of their connection, feeling her relentless tug on the Magic that bonded them. In the endless darkness that surrounded him, was Maeve Sinclair. She sat not ten feet from him, with red eyes and swollen cheeks. Too many bones exposed, and her skin void of color, save for the bright purple beneath her eyes. Her dark hair framed her sunken face, as lifeless pale eyes shone across the darkness at him.

Reeve shuddered a breath as he took in the sight of her. He could never have imagined her in such a state. The Witch he once knew was full of Magic and power, her eyes unnervingly sharp and her cool demeanor present at all times. This girl before him now, was far from the daughter of Ambrose Sinclair. This girl was the consequence of so many wrong choices.

He should never have left her that day. He should have taken her then and gotten it over with. Now she was paying for his own pride and fear.

"Get him out of here, Reeve."

Her broken whisper echoed across the nothingness twenty times over before it grew silent in the connection of their minds once more.

Reeve shook his head, which lay in his hands.

"Gods dammit," he muttered again.

Reeve gasped as a moonlit darkness snapped before him, and the vision of her vanished. Spinel rubbed against his arms as Magic visibly crumbled in the distance, his own Magic, across the Black Deep. He ran his hand along Spinel's back, petting him as he made a promise to himself: this time, he would not lose her.

PART TWO

Chapter 21

Maeve

Explaining what being a Magical felt like had always been impossible for Maeve. She had no frame of reference for what it felt like to be Human. Normal. Without blood forged in power. She'd never been able to grasp the magnitude of strength she carried, or the physical weight of what ran through her that granted her supernatural ability.

Until then.

Now she was starved.

Her fingers felt rotten. The center of her chest was hollow. Carved out. A heavy weight, oppressive and constant, locked on the edges of her mind. A solid chain. It wasn't there before.

"I have to say, I wasn't expecting you to act with such desperation."

Mal's voice was a dark hum.

"I'm not complaining, though," he continued, her heavy eyes focusing on him at last. "A spell I could have never cast with all that Magic running through you."

With his hands tucked behind his back and his posture pristine, he loomed over her in the empty room. There were no windows. The only source of light was a small firelight that floated alongside him as he crossed the vast room.

Her own prison cell.

"The thought really only occurred to me after your Elven friend reminded me just how easily I could bind you to me, despite the fact that I vowed to never use my Pathokenesis abilities on you. This works much better. The same Enslavement Curse used on Zimsy."

Zimsy.

She would vomit any moment, she knew it.

"Unable to disobey me," he said, dropping into a crouch before her. "It's unfortunate that I had to use Magic to assure it. You had so many opportunities to get in line."

"Zimsy didn't deserve that," she said, her voice cracked and sore.

"Perhaps she did not deserve it, but you most certainly did deserve to watch."

A nightmare. This was a horrible nightmare. She buried her face in her knees, the images of Zimsy and Abraxas, their blood pooling on the marbled floor.

Her father's blood pooling on the marbled floor.

"Look at me."

She shook her head, still buried in her knees. At the disobedience, a whip of Magic pierced her mind, the shock ringing through her whole body. Her head shot up, back slamming into the wall behind her as she looked up at him.

Her head throbbed. Her body took the blow like a full-force curse filled with malice. Sweat pooled at her forehead and neck, between her breasts. She nearly toppled sideways.

The pain of Mal's Magic was entirely different without her own. Exaggerated and so, so deadly.

"Still so rebellious," he murmured. "I doubt that will last long, judging by how that small act of defiance seemed to affect you."

How had Zimsy ever survived this feeling? Had Zimsy even survived Mal?

She held his gaze, hot tears threatening to spill down her cheeks.

"Pathetic," he said dryly.

Such uncaring cruelty from the lips that had once promised her nothing but affection pushed tears from her eyes. He was lost to her. She pushed down on the guilt that it was her fault.

Shadow's possession was so paramount within him, she could barely sense anything of the Mal she'd once shared a life with. Created life with.

Mal's hand reached forward and pressed against her temple with not an ounce of tenderness. "Incredible," he said, though it was far from a compliment. "Those shields in your mind are even stronger."

His hand withdrew, and he remained crouched before her.

"Give me the spell," he commanded.

Maeve's jaw tightened and her eyes squeezed shut, anticipating a long blow as a result of her disobedience. But it never came. That oppressive chain in her mind lay still. She waited another moment and slowly looked back up at Mal.

He nearly rolled his eyes. "You are infuriating."

Mal stood and stepped away from her. "Where is Maxius?"

"I don't know," she answered, truthfully and without hesitation.

No whip of Magic bore down upon her.

"Then I guess we'll find him together."

She remembered it then, that thread of warm Magic she'd begged to take Maxius. To keep him safe. It was there, barely burning, like the edge of a wet leaf struggling to maintain a fire.

Her mouth fell open as she remembered him fully.

Reeve.

Too many thoughts. Too many colliding thoughts.

"Come," said Mal, extending his gloved hand for her. "My right hand is needed."

His right hand?

"How am I to be your right hand if my Magic is gone?" she asked, taking his hand at once, fear of another shattering blow sharpening her reflexes.

Mal's frown remained as he pulled her to her feet and steadied her with his Magic. It formed around her like a second skin and did not lift. "You have an eternity with me, Maeve," he said. "I plan to make it count."

The words rang true, like another piece of the puzzle that her mind had forgotten.

"An eternity?" she questioned.

"Haven't remembered that yet?" asked Mal.

Maeve shook her head in disbelief. "You're wrong."

"I'm not wrong. I remember it perfectly. Oh, you were so easy to manipulate then, vain little thing that you were. You didn't hesitate to exchange part of your Magic for Immortality."

He pointed a finger at her. A small orb of gold mist drifted towards her. She held out her hand and accepted it. As the swirling memory brushed the tips of her fingers, white light flashed into vision.

She'd somehow suppressed her memory of this particular bargain. She gave Mal her blood in order to access the hidden Library in Castle Morana, in exchange for prolonged life and youth.

Her eyes snapped open, pressing his memory back towards him.

"What a wonderful trade," said Mal, his head tilting to the side. "I got the Dread Spellbook, which has shown me more about my power than I ever imagined, and I get to keep you like a polished trophy forever."

Maeve scowled, not even bothering to hide her resentment.

"Have you felt the way at times it bleeds from you into Maxius?" he asked, his features sharpening. "Makes it truly impossible to know just how many times you fucked up. Just how long we've been at this. But I can assure you now, that this is the final destination, Sinclair."

The use of her last name burned. No affection. Nothing but the aim to hurt her. Just as she had hurt him.

The attire she'd once cherished as Mal's second felt like a costume. Perfectly sculpted to her body, but otherwise unfitting. Her entire reflection in the clouded windows of the great hall at Castle Morana was like a distant version of herself, the bruise on her cheek from his fist still evident, healing at a Human pace.

Someone, Astrea she assumed, had healed her broken arm. There was no trace of soreness there. The suspicion that Mal had instructed Astrea not to heal her face swelled inside her. She pressed down on the feeling.

A large throne-like chair was positioned at the head of the table that dominated the space. Once a place for dinners and music, this was now a meeting hall. She walked silently behind Mal, observing that every seat was full. Roswyn and Mumford, always tailing Roswyn like a dog, other officials and high-ranking Bellator were there, enduring the silence of Mal's approach. Alphard was nowhere to be seen.

Maeve's throat tightened as her eyes landed on Abraxas sitting to the left of the oversized chair. She steadied her breathing. He was alive.

Maeve took her seat at Mal's right.

"Show her," Mal ordered Abraxas.

Abraxas' throat bobbed. He hesitantly opened his mouth. Maeve prepared herself to see the result of Mal's mutilation. To her surprise, Abraxas' tongue was now bright silver. Mal's Magic, no, Shadow's Magic radiated from his mouth.

"Lovely adjustments to my most trusted," said Mal. "Maeve can no longer disobey me, and Abraxas can no longer speak against me."

Abraxas met Maeve's eyes across the table. Neither of them spoke.

"A matter of the utmost importance is at hand today," said Mal. "It seems with a recent break in Magic thanks to my cunning and selfish Dread Viper, that the whiff of a rebellion on Hiems has taken root."

Mal's eyes moved to Abraxas. He spoke at once. His voice caused Maeve's chest to tighten. Her cousin, previously so full of life and mischief, now spoke with reserved fear.

"Mordred made us aware of the situation early this morning," he said. "He's been overseeing Hiems under Mal's rule for months, squashing small rebellions and maintaining order. But this. . .incident was different."

"What happened?" asked Roswyn. There was no fear in his voice. He had not betrayed their king. He had nothing to fear.

"Some of Mordred's wolves joined with a pack of wild wolves," answered Abraxas. "This particular group had been giving Mordred and his Guard some trouble. They killed at least a dozen Bellator, and

Astrea is seeing to a handful more who are in critical condition. Even a Dread Knight is among them. Somehow, they have an Alpha with quite explosive Magic. Roswyn, you'll head to Hiems and aid Mordred. Take as many Dread Knights as you see fit."

Roswyn nodded and shared a sickening grin with Mumford.

Maeve dared a glance at him fully, wondering if he thought of Antony, too. And if he was commanded to kill those wolves, who were likely only protecting themselves from the tyranny reigning down upon them all, would he feel Antony's disapproving stare as he did it?

Magic drifted under her chin, bringing her attention back to Mal. His eyes were already on her.

"I'm sure you're wondering what good you are to me now that you sacrificed the only useful parts of yourself," he said.

"Yeah," drawled Maeve, "that's exactly what I was thinking."

Abraxas' eyes flashed to her. A beg. A warning. She ignored it. Mal's cool demeanor didn't change, despite her lack of manners.

His head cocked to the side. "I thought you wanted to go to Hiems? Remember? I said I'd take you when you were lying naked in my bed?"

Reason drained from her as that warm kindling in her stomach grew. The thread of Magic bonding her to another pulled tight. She yanked on it, setting her chest ablaze.

"Is that meant to be a blow?" she asked. "If I recall, you found release twice."

Warmth spread through the base of her stomach, settling like ash.

Careful, kitten. Don't piss him off so badly there's nothing left of you for me to scrape up off the floor.

It took everything in her not to react as Reeve's voice echoed across her mind. She swallowed slowly, watching Mal with careful interest. He showed no indication he knew Reeve had just spoken to her.

Mal stared at her, unaffected by her bold comments.

Dead eyes. Dead fucking eyes.

"Maeve," said Abraxas, pulling her from her thoughts and directing her attention to him. He hesitated, chewing on his words, his lips twitching as he avoided eye contact with her. "This evening, the High Lord of Aterna will join us here."

Mal clicked his tongue. Abraxas tensed. "Apologies, my King," he said. "Reeve will join us here."

Mal's chin landed on his fist, propped on the arm of his chair. "There's not much point in calling him the High Lord anymore, is there?"

"No, my King," answered Abraxas swiftly.

"Especially not now that I understand it was he who granted the Elven Lands power." Mal's eyes landed on Maeve. "Some things are worth overlooking, though, when I stand to gain so much more."

Maeve shook her head at her cousin in disbelief. "Why would he come here?"

Mal's words carried through her. She looked over at him sharply. There was no way. Her mouth fell slightly open. "To bend the knee?"

Mal smiled, his brows pulling together as if it was obvious. And when he spoke, her stomach plummeted to the floor. "To take you."

Her voice shook as she said, "What are you talking about?"

"Don't you remember?" said Mal, his fingers running along the table between them. "His armies for a bride."

Maeve grabbed that ridiculous thread of Magic deep in her stomach and yanked on it.

What are you doing? she hissed towards Reeve.

His reply was delayed. *Just breathe.*

This is exactly why she couldn't stand this arrogant man. She was always in the dark. Always ten steps behind him.

Mal continued, a smooth satisfaction in his voice. "It seems after all this time, he still desires his mate above all. You should celebrate, today you are worth an entire army of trained and broken soldiers."

Maeve swallowed, a sickening feeling replacing that warmth in her stomach.

"Oh, Maeve," said Mal, feigning pity as she exhaled sharply. "Did you think you'd stay at my side when you can no longer fight? Your new duty as my right hand will be in Aterna, finding out who Reeve's Inheritor is."

She leaned towards him. "How could that possibly matter

anymore? You have everything. *She* has everything."

Mal leaned towards her, accepting her challenge. "If you think I have everything, you couldn't be more ignorant. I have only just begun." Mal gave one final thought, his voice laced with the unspoken threat that she wouldn't continue to question him. "It's imperative Reeve's power remains with him. You will ensure that. Of course, you could stay here. All it would take is the surrendering of your spell."

Maeve leaned back, shaking her head.

"That's fine," said Mal. "We have forever together, you and I. Pour toujours, a tout jamais, right?"

Forever. And always.

To hear those words twisted on her was hearing a death sentence.

Chapter 22

Malachite

Sinclair Estates, sometime. . . before.

Ambrose appeared at Mal's side, narrowly missing a drunken guest stumbling onto the balcony at Sinclair Estates.

"Alright, my boy?" asked Ambrose, following Mal's gaze to Maeve, where she sat with Abraxas out on the balcony.

"Reeve and her," said Mal, softly, something bordering on defeat in his voice. "Their Magic is. . .bonded."

"Hmm," said Ambrose, looking over his shoulder where Reeve stood, a glass of dark liquid in his hand.

Mal didn't look over at Ambrose. "You don't sound surprised."

"Magic is tricky. Some Magic is deceitful even."

"I know what I feel," said Mal.

Maeve laughed at Abraxas, covering her smile with the crystal goblet in her hand. Something she did often. And each time, it made him want to smash his lips into hers.

"I am not arguing you don't," said Ambrose, taking a puff of his cigar. "You'll learn, Maeve, too, that the definitions and rules we apply to Magic, well, let's just say it seeks to break them. I call it deceit, but maybe that just means your Magic is trying to show you something else."

"You speak of it as a living thing."

Ambrose chuckled. "You'll come to understand that, too. We are but Vexkari ourselves. Given power from something entirely not Human."

Mal was speechless for the first time in his recent memory. He finally peeled his gaze away from Maeve.

"You never wondered why we can bleed out like Humans unless Magic intervenes? Why, aside from whatever special energy that courses through our veins, we are utterly Human?"

"You know about Vexkari?"

Ambrose looked over at him at last. "You are not the first to seek such knowledge."

Mal was silent for a moment. "Reeve."

Ambrose hummed. "What about him?"

"Those marks on his face and neck. Those scars."

They were Vexkari.

Ambrose nodded slowly. "You've a keen sense of Magic, Mal."

He pressed his cigar into the tray and turned towards him fully. "What do you feel in my daughter?"

Mal hesitated, reflecting on the one and only time he'd felt her Magic fully, shortly after she nearly drowned. "She's a fortress of resistance."

Ambrose smiled. "Good."

Mal didn't return it. His mind was on the thread of Magic that connected his Little Viper to another powerful being. And how it grew stronger with each moment they shared space.

Chapter 23

Maeve

The earth beneath Castle Morana trembled at Reeve's presence.

Maeve watched from a balcony, high in Castle Morana, as Shadow's newest addition to her army emptied into The Dread Lands, pouring from massive Portals in perfect formation.

"You need to get dressed," said Abraxas, his voice clipped.

"Why does he need them?" she asked, her eyes still on the thousands of Warriors below.

"To take Earth," answered Abraxas.

Snow brushed her exposed shoulders as it fell from the sky, settling across the balcony in sheets of ice. She returned to Abraxas' suite, twisting her wrist at her side to gently pull the doors closed behind her.

The doors to the balcony remained open. Maeve stilled. She didn't let the pang in her chest linger as she turned and closed them by hand.

"Still no word about Zim?" she asked quietly, crossing towards Abraxas.

Abraxas shook his head once.

A long silence fell between them.

The gown Maeve was meant to wear lay draped over the sofa, pooling to the dark floors like white water. It was exquisite. And under different circumstances, perhaps she would have been over the moon to wear such a finely crafted gown. But being traded. . .wearing a wedding dress just for the purpose of cruelty, was far from a dream come true.

"How can I leave you here, Brax?" she uttered, her voice at a loss.

"Because it is our duty," he replied swiftly, his silver tongue talking for him.

Duty. The word's meaning had changed so quickly, in just a matter of minutes. But she knew what it was that kept her breathing. That kept her heart beating.

She had failed time and time again, it seemed.

"I meant what I said," she whispered softly. "I failed him before. I will not fail him again."

"Good. You are needed in Aterna."

She couldn't look at her cousin as words that weren't his spilled from his lips. How could she tell him that wasn't what she meant at all? How could she express that she didn't give a damn about Reeve's Inheritor or what lands Mal claimed and conquered?

His destiny was written in prophetic Magic.

Her's wasn't. But that didn't matter. She would save him from Shadow.

Maeve ran her hands over her face and looked back at the gown. A mockery of something she'd once envisioned for herself. She'd known she and Mal would change the world. She had felt that so deep in her soul.

This wasn't ever what she imagined.

She stepped towards Abraxas. As she placed her arms around his waist, his arms moved across her back and shoulders in tandem.

There was no look of satisfaction on Reeve's face as he entered the filled Throne Room. Not even a hint of that usually present, playful gleam in his eyes. No, Maeve had seen this look of pure disgust on him before. His expression was cold and unyielding, just as it had been that day he refused to kneel, and now she would face the consequence of his resentment.

This was the face of war.

Eryx moved behind Reeve, several paces back, as they strode towards the throne in similar armor.

Maeve stood beside Mal, where he sat on the throne, the Dread Crown sat perfectly in his dark hair, and she in the white gown she'd almost rebelled against wearing.

Eryx stopped, stepping to the side as Reeve ventured a few more paces towards them. Reeve stood in perfect opposition to Mal. His glowing skin, broad shoulders, and muscled body screamed that he was a Senshi Warrior, not just the Immortal holding all of Aterna's Magic. His long, black hair fell gracefully to his shoulders, half of it tied neatly at the top of his head. He'd shaved and faded one side, the side bearing his dark, scar-like Magic, and it had two lines completely shaven running through it, following the pattern of his scars.

Reeve's eyes landed on her at last. The thread of warm Magic connecting them flared. Maeve pressed down on it, determined not to let it grow.

"Don't you want to run to him?" asked Mal. "Have him sweep you away from your torment here?"

Maeve remained where she stood. She had not been instructed to move.

Mal laughed. It was dark. Nothing playful about it. "I trade you and you learn obedience?"

She looked over at him. His green eyes were already on her.

"Go to him," he said, impatience in his tone.

Maeve stepped forward, gathering her dress in her fists as she stepped down the dais. Her heels echoed twice across the hall before Mal called out.

"Stop."

She halted at once.

He Obscured, suddenly behind her. He circled her and brought his lips to her ear. Together, their eyes locked on Reeve.

Mal whispered, with his arm snaked around her, so softly she had to concentrate to hear every word. "I don't want to hear a single word of your rebellious resistance. Is that clear? You find out who his Inheritor is and put a stop to the Inheritance. All your traitorous thoughts are best kept to yourself. If you cost me this army, and the allegiance of the man that leads them, then it will cost you every last one in The Dread Lands you care for."

Maeve understood then. She was the bargaining chip between Shadow and Reeve. He was here to bend the knee in exchange for *her*. He offered his armies for her. He saved Maxius again and again for her. Another Inheritor, someone who wasn't in a fated bond with Maeve, might not care to lay down their sword and let Shadow reign.

They might fight.

The thought made her sick. Reeve couldn't possibly be so reckless.

Mal dropped his arm and stood at his full height, passing by her and examining Reeve.

He looked back at Maeve. "Crawl to him."

The spark of rebellion he had just warned her against kicked inside her. She couldn't contain her cry as a whip of Magic slashed across her, bringing her to her knees. Her eyes burned as they squeezed tightly shut. The white gown pooled at her waist as her palms made harsh contact with the floor.

She pressed her knees into the cold tiles, her hands moving forward at once, crawling as she was commanded. Reeve didn't spare her a glance. With each of her movements, his eyes remained on Mal.

"Is this necessary?" drawled Reeve.

"If you had just bent the knee the first time I gave you the opportunity," replied Mal smoothly, "perhaps you could have spared her the embarrassment."

Magic crackled like electricity down her spine, the residuals of her refusing to follow his command. She whimpered against the weight of it, forcing herself to keep moving forward. Palms then knees.

"You didn't want to give her to me the first time," Reeve reminded him.

When she reached Reeve's feet, her breathing was tight and labored. He dropped into a crouch, his face inches above hers. His fiery eyes scanned hers and then locked on the lingering bruise from her duel with Mal. His brows pulled together in annoyance.

Without asking or offering, he stood and pulled her to her feet, his eyes still locked on hers. He placed her behind him and turned back to Mal.

"I don't intend to draw this out," said Mal.

Reeve nodded once.

Magic snapped between them, harsh and sharp, a whip hitting its mark. Maeve gasped as she felt the exchange between them. The Enslavement Curse Mal placed on her shifted into Reeve's possession. Her stomach turned over, but the chain she'd felt pressing against her mind was gone.

Completely gone.

"It is done. Amaranthine Maeve Sinclair is yours."

"It is done. The Senshi Warriors, yours to command."

Mal moved towards the empty throne. Reeve's eyes found Maeve.

Eryx appeared at Maeve's side. He did not look at her. It was only his duty to Reeve, who now controlled her, that brought him to her side. She knew the hatred he felt for her.

The firelights in the Throne Room flickered. Shadow's oppressive blanket of weight filled the air, pressing down on them. Maeve pitched forward. The room spun violently, blurring in one perfect loop. Without her Magic, Maeve could barely stand in her presence. If this was the evil meant to ascend upon Earth, she could wipe out the entire race of Humans with ease.

"You'd come across the Black Deep and not bow to your Queen?"

Shadow appeared on the throne, black, misting Magic barely concealing her naked body. Her long white hair draped across her front. Reeve turned from Maeve, his eyes locking with Shadow's.

Mal joined her, standing at her side.

"You look different, Shadow," said Reeve, his head cocking to the side. "Those blue eyes don't suit you, my Queen." His voice was almost flirtatious, but his face remained stoic. "Perhaps, you can give them back to their owner as a sign of good faith."

Shadow's lips pursed, and her legs spread. Reeve's eyes never left her face. "Still so brave, I see," she remarked.

Reeve made a small motion, something like that of a shrug. "I offered to surrender my crown and my armies for Maeve. You accepted that offer. That means all of her."

Shadow giggled. Maeve would never become accustomed to the sound. She steadied her breath, begging her body not to vomit as rolls of cursed Magic ripped through her.

"I never thought I'd see the great Dragon of Aterna begging for scraps," she said. "Your Magic is clever, much more so than when it resided in your father. You Immortals, always so specific in your Magic and how you use language. But it doesn't matter. She gave them to me willingly." Shadow's voice dipped into something far less patient than when she first appeared. "That makes them mine. Not hers. And you still have not kneeled."

Reeve stepped towards her.

Shadow smiled, getting her way at last. "I told you that you'd be bowing before me soon enough."

Maeve anticipated his quick and clever return.

As suspected, Reeve said, "Three hundred years is quite a blink when you've been alive as long as we have."

And then the bastard returned her smile.

"I have waited far longer than three centuries to rule the seven realms," said Shadow.

Reeve didn't reply. He drew his sword, where it was sheathed at his side, and held it out in both his broad, tattooed hands, a symbol of his dedication, and kneeled, fully kneeled before Shadow.

The sight dropped Maeve's jaw as he fixed his stare on the marbled floor. Red flashed in Maeve's eyes. So much blood against the deep-green tiles, she wondered how it wasn't stained crimson.

Beside her, Eryx's face remained perfectly poised, but the words he whispered held a horrible weight.

"Aterna has fallen."

Chapter 24

Maeve

Reeve's Portal to the Celestian Palace closed in a swirl of Magic behind her. She heaved a loud sigh, finally out from beneath Shadow's blanket of Magic. As they stepped across the pale crystal floor, the amethyst banners along the walls shifted, turning a deep emerald green. The Aterna coat of arms vanished, replaced by the Dread Mark. Maeve stilled.

A skull and two serpents, one ferociously baring its fangs, shone in gold against the deep green fabric. Reeve stepped beside her, his gaze also fixed on the changed insignias.

Maeve pulled her arms to her back, locating the lacing of the white gown. She began to pull, loosening the bodice, until it slipped free from her back. She pulled her arms from the shimmering sleeves and threw it to the floor, leaving her in just a fitted undergarment. Reeve didn't look over at her. His eyes remained on the changed banners. His face was unreadable. Her fingers moved to the skirt next, letting it fall to the ground like a large deflated balloon.

He shrugged off his overcoat and extended it to her. She stepped out of the skirt and snatched his coat from him, sliding it over her body. It was laughably large, but it was better than that tainted pile on the floor and better than remaining exposed.

"Take me to him," said Maeve softly.

Reeve nodded, and she followed him silently across the Celestian Palace. Not a single word was spoken as they walked. Maeve's white boots were the only sound as Reeve guided her through the massive palace.

With every step, Maeve felt them growing closer.

"I can feel it," she said, breaking their silence at last.

"Of course you can," replied Reeve as two crystal doors opened at their approach. "It's your Magic."

Maeve's pace quickened as her eyes saw it. The room opened up into a vast cathedral-like space. Pale-blue crystals, in varying shades and intensities, shot up like deadly swords from an altar. The solid stones, jagged and massive, thrummed with her power. Beneath Maeve's crystalized Magic lay Maxius, perfectly sleeping with the Dread Locket around his neck.

She found it difficult to be relieved. This would just be another part of his life taken from him. And for how long this time?

Spinel lay curled asleep at the foot of the altar.

Maeve stepped towards Maxius, placing her hand on one of the stones and looking down at her son. She wanted nothing more than to feel the warmth of his skin. To run her fingers through his soft hair. To see his face light up as Spinel massaged his paws against him.

"Will they remain, you think, after I am dead?"

"Of course they would," Reeve replied. "Your body is merely a vessel for this power."

"What if I die before it's safe for him to be released?"

Reeve hesitated. "At some point, the Magic in him will awaken. Besides, you plan on dying anytime soon?"

She ignored the question. The answer was obvious. "My sister and her children are on Earth? Agatha?"

"Yes," answered Reeve. "Alphard as well."

Her throat tightened at the thought of Zimsy, her blood coating the floors of the Throne Room at Castle Morana. She hadn't been able to get her to safety.

Nor Abraxas. How could she have just left him there? She should have forced him, found a way.

"Mal can be saved," she said, her eyes still on Maxius.

Maeve expected a snappy reply, something about how delusional she was. It never came.

"And how do you think that's going to happen?" was all Reeve replied.

"I don't know," she admitted, running her fingers over the crystal casing. "I don't know the path. But I know the prophecy. He will vanquish her. That means. . . he'll be saved. Right?"

Reeve crossed to the other side of Maxius.

"This must have been brutal," he commented, his eyes on the crystals, ignoring her question completely.

"It was," she answered.

"Let me heal your face," he said.

She looked over at him, tearing her eyes away from Maxius at last. The crystals cast pale-blue light across his face. His eyes lingered on the bruise across her cheek.

"No," she answered softly. The thought of his hands on her was out of the question.

Her eyes widened. He commanded. She disobeyed.

No pain sliced through her. No stinging of Magic whipped down her back.

"I broke that Curse the moment it shifted into my possession," he answered her unasked question. "Disgusting Magic."

Reeve looked down at Maxius. A small smile pulled at the corner of his lips. One that looked like regret and acceptance all bundled together.

"He's so big now," breathed Reeve. "The last time he was here, he was so small."

Maeve remembered it all now. How it had been Reeve she'd hid Maxius with the first time. She hadn't meant to erase her own mind of Maxius then. That was the first time she cast her spell, and judging by how quickly it broke and Maxius was back at Castle Morana, she had cast it poorly.

"I remembered the most beautiful thing this morning," she said, looking down at Maxius as she twisted her Sinclair family ring. "My father knew I was pregnant before he died. He was the second to know. Mal and I knew almost immediately. But getting to see my father's face for the first time again when we told him. . .was remarkable."

They sat in the moment together, enduring the silence, until Reeve spoke.

"Do you think you've broken all the times you used the spell?"

Maeve thought for a moment. "How would I ever know?" she answered truthfully. "I think I have, but it's like a bunch of timelines crossing and lapping over. It's all real, even the parts I made up in my head. It's not like I forgot them. Just. . .now there's even more life added back in."

Another long silence.

"Why did you do it?" asked Maeve. "Why the fuck did you give them that army? Earth stands at risk now."

"We are all at risk now. I did what I think will lessen casualties until a greater plan can unfold. It would have only been a matter of time before The Dreaded Dead crossed the Black Deep and slaughtered my people."

"A greater plan," repeated Maeve. "You have one of those?" She looked back over at him.

He held his tongue.

Maeve laughed darkly. "Of course."

"I'm sorry, Maeve," said Reeve, an edge in his voice. "This is all happening rather quickly, and you are somewhat of a loose cannon."

She shook her head, a smile at her lips that was far from happy.

"I can tell you more when the time is right," he said.

"For you. When the time is right for you."

He fell silent.

"I'm grateful for your protection of Maxius," she said. "But you can go now."

She felt his eyes burn into the side of her face for a moment longer before disappearing from her periphery.

"Mely is looking for Zimsy. I do not know if she's alive," he said, and then his footsteps retreated, plunging her into complete silence save for the soft, vibrating thrum of her crystalized Magic.

She slid down the side of the altar, back pressing against it, and pulled her legs in. She buried her face down, forehead resting against her knees. Smooth fur rubbed against her hand as Spinel forced his way into what little space was accessible in her lap. His damp nose rubbed against hers as small purrs began to vibrate through him.

Each day in Aterna brought less sunlight. Sunlight Maeve couldn't even find joy in. Another warmth stolen. The frozen tundra crept across the Black Deep like vines. Soon, snow would begin falling in Aterna, coating the land just like it had in the Dread Lands.

It had taken a week of sleeping on the floor with Spinel next to Maxius for Maeve to relent and move to a chamber. The entire palace sat high on the north mountain cliffs overlooking Crystalmore. With a balcony spanning down the side of the palace, she had a firsthand view of the brewing dark clouds across the Black Deep. It was visible even from the plush bed, as the west walls of her chambers were made of high arching windows.

Tempting as it was to close the drapes and forget about the evil lurking in the mountains across the sea, she left them open. No servant visited her. Nor did Reeve. Food appeared and vanished for each meal on a gold tray by the desk in her chambers.

Adjusting to a body without Magic was tedious. Sleep was endless and all-consuming. She lost track of time, and no matter how long she slumbered, it was never enough. Food tasted different; nothing was the same on her tongue. Not even bread. Even if it tasted good, her appetite was absent.

She only ate when the lining in her stomach became so desperate that she stuffed a cold roll or pastry in her mouth, and then retreated into the comfort of her four-poster bed. Her chambers were close enough to Maxius that she could feel the steady beat of his safety. Spinel slept with her sometimes, but most nights, he remained curled at the foot of Maxius' altar, waiting for Maeve to join him each morning.

She had given up on trying to wash her skin clean in the ensuite bathroom. She would be tainted and dirty forever. The water was never scorching enough to burn away the feeling of his Magic hurting her. Each pass with soap and water across her arm was a relived memory of the bone snapping. And his fury.

She'd never imagined his hands inflicting such pain.

She tried, manically, to scrub her body free of the dark, inky veins that ran along her body. It was illogical. But she scrubbed until her skin tingled with a red coat. Where once in those veins there had been a life, a second heartbeat almost, there was only a void of connection.

A tap on the door. Maeve ignored it. A louder tap with more persistence had her pulling the covers back and stalking towards the door. She slowly pulled open one of the smooth white doors and peered outside.

A girl bowed at the neck and didn't meet Maeve's gaze.

"The High Lord of Aterna requests your presence at breakfast."

Maeve surveyed her, wondering if the downward look at the crystal floors was a sign of respect or fear.

Something deep inside her laughed emptily.

"Requests?" asked Maeve.

The girl nodded. "The High Lord says if you don't feel up to it, he will try again next week—"

That was enough for Maeve to close the door quickly with a snap. She turned on her heel, the cold floors guiding her back to the bed, and sleep claimed her swiftly.

As promised, a week later, another knock came at her door.

"The High Lord requests your presence at lunch," said the girl.

She was an Immortal. Maeve looked up at her, where she towered over Maeve, as all Immortals did.

"Tell him to try again next week," was all she said.

The Immortal raised her brows, but Maeve closed the door without another word.

Sunlight, pure, golden sunlight poured into the room. Maeve groaned and rolled over, attempting to hide under a pillow.

The covers were swiftly drawn back, and the pillow vanished. Maeve sat up and squinted as an older Magical with grey spiraling hair was finishing snapping back the curtains with the palm of her hand. With Dread Magic.

Maeve rubbed her face and sat up at once. Confusion at the audacity of this woman.

"Afternoon, dear," said the Witch without turning to Maeve.

The woman snapped her fingers, and Maeve's dressing gown appeared next to her on the bed, and Maeve snatched it up, throwing it around her.

"And you are?" said Maeve with a yawn as she stood from the bed.

"Name's Gelsey," said the Witch. "Head of the High Lord's household."

Gelsey snapped her fingers, and a duster appeared. She began cleaning each surface of the room.

The bedding behind Maeve snapped new. Clean, fresh sheets appeared from nowhere, smooth and fluffed.

"You don't have to do that," said Maeve uncomfortably.

"I do actually," said Gelsey with a smile, the wrinkles in her face spreading. "It's my job and it pays quite well." She laughed.

Maeve stood awkwardly, avoiding looking out those giant windows.

"Besides," said Gelsey. "You need to get dressed for dinner with the High Lord."

"I won't be going to any dinner," said Maeve.

"Of course you will," said Gelsey happily. "I laid out fresh clothes for you."

Gelsey jerked her head towards the closet Maeve had not even entered since her arrival. A fresh set of clothes in the morning and pajamas in the evening had appeared every day on the bed; now she understood that was Gelsey's doing.

"You know, technically, you should all be calling him a King or something. That title doesn't make any sense."

"The High Lord refused the title of King after his father before him," she stated. "Oh—A few of the members of the house staff would like to place flowers around Maxius. If that would be alright with you?"

Maeve rubbed her eyes, speechless. With a small shake of her head, not understanding, she said. "Why?"

Gelsey twirled her fingers across the tray of barely touched food, and it vanished at once. Maeve's stomach tightened with something like envy. Gelsey turned towards her.

Something shifted across the old woman's face. She smiled with a gentle understanding. "Because we adore him."

Maeve's mouth opened and then closed as she stammered a response.

"You didn't think the High Lord kept him all to himself, did you?" she asked with a smile. Without waiting for a reply, she said, "So no to the dinner then?"

Maeve shook her head. Gelsey didn't argue and merely said she'd send something up. As the old Magical made for the door, Maeve called after her.

"You're of Dread Magic. And yet, you reside here in Aterna."

Gelsey nodded. "One of the many Magical families that made it into Aterna before the Shadow War."

Maeve couldn't understand.

"You've never been to the capital city, Crystalmore, have you?" asked Gelsey.

Maeve shook her head. Even when Mal had attacked the city, shortly before Reeve erased Aterna from their minds, she wasn't there.

"Oh!" She laughed sweetly. "You'll be in for a surprise then."

Just before Gelsey closed the door on her way out, Maeve stopped her once more.

"Flowers would be fine," she said. "Thank you for asking."

Chapter 25

Maeve

She yanked open the door to the hall where Maxius lay, mouth open and prepared to tell Gelsey to go away. Her mouth snapped shut as she took in Reeve, standing on the other side with one arm behind his back. She kept her hand on the door, prepared to close it in his face. He spoke before she even had the chance.

"I have a single proposition."

Maeve's brows raised, hiding half her frame behind the door. "Oh, suddenly I'm to be included in the plans?"

Reeve talked over her. "You eat with me every meal, and we can begin conversations towards a mutual trust."

Maeve's eyes narrowed. She frowned, disliking the idea she was the one undeserving of his trust when he was the one piling up lies and always keeping things from her.

"Every meal, meaning?" she asked hesitantly.

"Breakfast, lunch, and dinner," said Reeve casually. "And you must actually eat."

Maeve looked away from him, annoyed.

"I haven't come empty-handed," said Reeve.

Maeve looked back at him. He pulled from behind his back a single book, newly bound. He held it on display for her.

The Witch of Whitehaven Manor by Evelyn Starbound. Reeve flipped open the inside cover, where a sparkling signature swirled across the page in blue ink. Maeve's face relaxed instantly.

"Where did you get that?" she asked with awe. "I've never seen that title."

"She wrote it just for me as a special request," said Reeve with a smile.

Maeve's mouth fell open.

Reeve flipped open the pages and said, "Did I neglect to mention even your favorite author isn't immune to the effects of such a handsome Immortal such as myself?"

Maeve rolled her eyes.

"Do you want it?" he asked.

Of course, she wanted it. "Obviously," she snapped. "A single book in exchange for spending three meals a day with you doesn't sound like a fair trade."

"But it's not just the book, is it?" said Reeve. "It's the beginning of our ally-ship."

Maeve hesitated. "I will consider it."

She held out her hand, and Reeve laughed.

"You don't get the book until you come to breakfast in the morning," he said, his arrogant grin blown wide across his face.

Maeve huffed a small sigh of aggravation as he turned and began walking away from her.

"Reeve," called Maeve.

The High Lord of Aterna turned back towards her.

She didn't know why it mattered, why she cared, but the question spilled from her lips all the same. "Did you offer your allegiance in exchange for me, or did he seek you out with such a proposal?"

Reeve hesitated. "I sought him out," he answered, his voice dull, and that grin gone.

What little food lay in her stomach threatened to lurch forward at his words.

"You could have run further from all of this. You could have taken your people anywhere and remained hidden," said Maeve.

"Just as your spell was breaking, mine was too," replied Reeve.

"I don't believe you," she said with a shake of her head. "I was remembering my lies. Never you."

Reeve's eyes narrowed. "Not once, huh?"

Maeve shook her head.

"Now who's lying?" he said, no trace of a smile.

She closed the door with a soft click and without another word.

Reeve

Maeve's breakfast spread with Reeve was double what had been brought to her chamber each morning, but her fingers drummed happily on the cover of her new book. He fought a smile at how easily she caved with just a little bribe. How could he forget how deeply she loved gifts?

"Has Aterna ever experienced a winter like the one coming?" asked Maeve, her voice bleak.

Reeve waited to see if she would eat before beginning his breakfast, but Maeve merely looked out the amethyst-and-crimson stained glass along the hall they dined in. Still, he waited for her.

Magic hummed across her body; it was so weak and untouched he was certain she didn't feel it at all. He nearly doubted its existence. All the things he wanted to say remained bound behind his teeth. Besides all of that, he knew the real death was within her mind, not her Magic.

Shadow hadn't hesitated to show him the events of that night in the Throne Room at Castle Morana when he met with her, agreeing to trade his allegiance for Maeve. How Maeve still clung to the idea of saving Mal after watching him mutilate her closest friends and break her body, he didn't understand. But it wasn't his to understand.

She'd grieve Mal in the coming days. Weeks. Months.

However long this took.

And he remembered his promise to himself: this time, he wouldn't let her go.

Her eyes slid to him. Even though they were no longer dark-blue, shimmering beauties, her gaze still held every bit of power over him as it had since the first moment she laid eyes on him.

Her hand fell into her lap.

"Allies," she said, as though she were tasting the word.

"I'm sure I'm not your first choice," he replied.

"Far from it," she said smoothly. "But as my grandmother Agatha would say, 'beggars can't be choosers'."

"I've yet to see you do any begging," he replied. "That would be a treat."

She didn't smile. "Always a game to you," she muttered. "Allies is a joke. We'll both just be waiting for the other to stab us in the back."

"But we'll have so much fun at each other's throats."

He could tell she didn't have it in her to argue or engage. Her eyes didn't light up with desire for a fight, not like they used to.

"Answer me this at least," she began. "Is saving Mal part of your plan?"

"No," he answered honestly, watching his words sting her. "But I know it's part of yours. So if we are to become *allies*, then I suppose that makes it part of *our* plan."

She shook her head. "None of this is his fault."

"That is a dangerous delusion at best," he argued back.

"I was the one who released her."

"I was there."

"Then you know I am to blame. I started this."

"This began," he said in a correcting tone, "centuries ago."

"Well, it didn't for me," she snapped.

"Damn. How could I forget just how center-minded you are?"

"Me? That's rich considering you stole my spell and went into hiding with it."

"I prefer to think of it as self-preservation, and I did not run for merely my preservation."

"Nor did I. And that's a shit excuse, and you know it. You handed over your army, your precious and sacred Warriors, to two of the most powerful Magicals because you still feel as though you are owed me."

Reeve looked up at the ceiling, fighting a scowl, and chose his words carefully in response to such a ridiculous statement. "Why does everyone call you clever?"

Maeve stood from the table, her chair scraping backwards across the shimmering stone floor. He could see it on her face—fury raced through her with nowhere to go. No escape from her fingertips as she was so used to resorting to.

"Say it," said Reeve, his eyes locked on hers, giving her permission to release her anger.

"I fucking hate you," she whispered without hesitation.

Reeve nodded. "Anything else?"

"I think that about sums it up."

Reeve watched her for a moment and then nodded. "Good. Now, sit down."

Maeve's breathing kicked audibly at the command.

"You agreed to one thing, Maeve," said Reeve, holding up a single finger. "I know you to be a woman of your word. And you have not actually eaten like you agreed to."

She stood a moment longer, each of her breaths slower and more controlled than the last.

"You know about my mother," she said. Not a question. A statement. "When will I have those answers?"

Such an unanswerable question from the beautiful obstacle who stood before him. If he could have answered it, he would have. If it would buy her trust, he'd have told her everything.

But there was Magic holding Reeve's tongue that didn't negotiate.

Reeve smiled in a bitter way. "If only it were that easy."

"All Magic is breakable."

"At a great cost," he agreed.

"I am not afraid of the cost," she replied, with her chin held high.

Reeve's eyes scanned the black lines that ran the length of her veins. "No," he said softly. "You are not."

Maeve didn't tug at her sleeves. She didn't attempt to conceal the marks as he'd witnessed her do in the past.

"Tell me what to do," said Maeve, "and I will see it done."

"I—" he began, his head rolling back against his seat and his throat closing. His elbows landed sharply on the table, shaking the plates and cups. "Enough."

Maeve was silent for a moment, watching him reel under unseen Magic. "That's some spell." She pulled her chair back towards the table and took her seat. "So what is *your* plan?"

Reeve looked down at her untouched food and then back up at her. She huffed a breath and then picked up her knife and fork, cutting her omelet, which had surely gone cold. She placed the tiniest bite she could in her mouth, swallowed, and then looked back up at Reeve.

There, in her eyes, was the smallest flicker of the flame he fully intended to re-ignite.

"Shadow cannot move on Hiems yet," he began. "She cannot move to Earth yet. Her form is weak, even I saw it, unless she's fully possessing Mal. The more she drains him, the stronger her form gets."

"What does that mean to you?"

"We move on Hiems and stoke the fires of the rebellion already building there."

"Are you insane?" She pointed at the banners that ran the length of the hall, now bearing The Dread Mark. "Look around."

"Then what do you propose?"

His brows raised, and he waited. And waited. When no reply came, he spoke.

"My plan requires your complete cooperation, Maeve," he said sharply. "You want me to be able to give you honesty? To understand the things you are in the dark about? Then you must act for once without ulterior motives. You will not move behind my back with other intentions. And that begins with telling me what purpose Malachite gave you here."

She remained silent, chewing her lip. An action that forced him to look away from her. He allowed her to debate answering in complete silence, and when she finally responded, he was surprised.

"I'm to stop the Inheritance."

Her confession sounded bored almost. She had no idea the weight of such a statement. She cut up more of her omelet and shook her head.

"Starting a rebellion," she muttered. "Ridiculous."

Chapter 26

Maeve

Maeve.

She wanted more than anything to walk away. To leave the balcony of her chambers and crash into the warm, silken sheets of her canopy bed.

Maeve.

She cursed under her breath. Thunder that rumbled across the sea in the Dread Lands sounded unmistakably like laughter. Giggling, horrible laughter. Mal's voice continued to call to her.

Maeve.

Maeve.

Her knees pressed into the cool stone of the balcony. Her cheek pressed against the railing. Her body ached for rest. For sleep. His voice plagued her.

Maeve.

Please stop, she begged that distant thunder.

Another laugh echoed across the sea.

Maeve.

"Mal, please, wake up," she whispered.

The thunder settled for a moment, still and quiet, and Mal's voice faded. A swell of hope rose in her chest. But distant laughter rang across the Black Deep.

Maeve.

Maeve.

Maeve.

She felt Reeve move behind her. She still didn't know if it was purely his raw, lethal power that resonated through his body, or because she was not much of a Witch without her own Magic, that he had such an effect on her now.

"I can't look away," she uttered.

"From the mountains?"

Maeve.

"He calls to me," was all she replied.

Reeve moved closer, watching The Dark Peaks with contempt in his eyes. But his voice was a soft hum. "You hear it often?" he said.

He ran his fingers through his hair.

Maeve.

Reeve kneeled at her side, slowly bringing himself to her level.

"I can't tell if he's calling my name in a prayer or a curse," she confessed softly, wiping her eyes pridefully before more tears fell. "I'm not sure which is worse."

She stood tall and faced him, forcing down the remaining tears.

"Can you hear it?" she asked.

He shook his head.

Maeve.

"Then why are you here?" she asked sharply.

Reeve studied her face for a moment. "Because I can feel you."

"Right," she said with a nod. "Our lovely little bond."

There was nothing lovely in her tone.

Reeve hummed. "You've pleaded for my help many times through that lovely little bond."

Maeve.

She sighed, accepting Mal's voice would remain in her head. That it would likely keep her from sleep.

"You're so stubborn," commented Reeve, but his tone was laced with something like a compliment. "I could help you sleep. My Magic, there are potions—"

"No," she said plainly.

She turned towards the doors to her chamber, dismissing the idea entirely and leaving him on the balcony.

Green firelights flickered in the darkness, illuminating the walls of the North Tower in Castle Morana. Maeve's heart raced, jumping out of her chest.

No. She couldn't be back there. She tried to move, frozen in place.

Mal's bed came into focus, and it was occupied.

Shadow pulled her long white hair to the side, exposing her breasts. She tossed her head back in pleasure as Mal lay beneath her. His hands gripped her hips, pulling and pushing her in a steady rhythm.

A sick and draining feeling dripped through her at the sight.

Shadow's blue eyes appeared almost black in the dim light. A serpent's tongue slipped from her mouth, long and unnatural. She arched her back, leaning towards Mal's face as she continued to ride him. The tongue slid across his neck, his jaw, his lips—

Maeve's body moved at once, but the North Tower at Castle Morana disappeared, her gaze now fixed on the muraled ceiling above her bed in the Celestian Palace. Chills covered her arms and legs as she gripped the sheets beneath her. Her stomach threatened to empty itself with every replay of what she had seen.

Not a nightmare. No. That was real. If he could speak into her mind from such a distance, then she supposed he and Shadow could torture her further. But she had the strangest inclination she couldn't quite explain, the feeling that neither Shadow nor Mal had been aware she was watching.

She kicked the covers off and pushed out of the bed, quickly pushing her hair from her face and discarding her nightgown as she walked to the ensuite bathroom. She turned the golden knobs of the sink with haste and splashed her face with cold water, letting it drip down her bare chest. She placed a cold, wet hand on the back of her neck and gripped the edge of the sink with the other.

Maeve let out a jagged breath. *Why* had she seen that, of all things? Her stomach rolled at the thought of his hands on another. Of his body being used without his consent.

That horrible creature. . .

She let go of the sink and lay down on the cool tiles, letting the cold lower her body temperature. She wouldn't be able to sleep, just as the past few nights had been sleepless. The intimate moment she witnessed played on repeat in her mind.

Breakfasts, and lunches, and dinners with Reeve blurred. She lost count of how many mundane meals they shared, Meals where she hated the taste of food and ate just enough that he wouldn't comment on it. He never told her much of the moves he was making, but she still refused to help him stoke the fires of rebellion on Hiems.

Sleep was rare. The more she watched Shadow and Mal together in her mind, the further from a rebel she felt.

"I've been seeing them when I sleep," said Maeve, pushing around part of her meal. "They're not dreams, though."

"What are they?"

"I guess. . .visions. But not like the future. It's like I'm somewhere else in my mind, watching, but I can't move. I've had them before. I saw. . ."

"What?" he pressed.

It was a long time ago, but she'd seen it somehow.

Maeve didn't look at him. "You on the battlefield. With Shadow."

Reeve didn't dwell on the comment. "What have you seen most recently?"

"I see them fucking," she admitted, the words tasting like filth in her mouth. "I watch that gaunt, slimy woman begging for his heir inside her." Maeve stabbed the meat on her plate with enough force to rattle the table. "It makes me want to vomit."

Reeve's face faltered, and the color in his eyes drained slightly.

"She wants to bear his children?"

"Yes," said Maeve. "Not incredibly enjoyable to see."

He was silent for a moment, then spoke after a long exhale.

"Do you know what happened to Mal's ancestors? Orion the Dread and all his children?"

Maeve shook her head.

"She absorbed their Dread Magic."

Maeve's grip on her knife and fork slid loose.

"Just as she's doing to Malachite. Just as she will do to the children he may give her."

She really would be sick at any moment. She was speechless. Completely speechless. Reeve ran his tattooed fingers over his face and closed his eyes. Only after a moment did Maeve offer a small piece of information back to Reeve.

"She made a vow with me," she said, causing his eyes to snap back open. "She will not kill him."

Chapter 27

Maeve

"Miss Gelsey said you weren't feeling well."

"Miss?" Maeve questioned, straining to open her eyes and look at Reeve, where he stood in her doorway. She hadn't heard him knock. Or come in. She rolled over in her bed, putting her back to him. "What are you, twelve?"

She closed her eyes, hoping he'd take the hint and leave.

"You were missed this morning and at lunch, so I figured you were dying if it meant you were breaking our agreement." A pause, then, "You do look like hell."

Maeve didn't even have the energy to scowl at him. His boots clicked across the floor until he was beside her bed.

"Don't touch me," she said, putting all her energy into inching across the bed, away from his outstretched arm.

"How else will I know if you have a fever?" he asked calmly.

"A what?" she snapped.

Reeve's arm dropped to his side as he muttered. "I didn't even think of that."

"Think of what?" she groaned. "It's always riddles and half-stated information with you."

He was too close. The fire radiating from his body made her ill.

"You have a cold," he said solemnly.

"A cold?"

At last, that fire-filled hand pressed against her forehead. The heat was so unbearable, she jerked away from him at once.

"You're burning up," he muttered.

"*I'm* burning up?" she asked incredulously. "You're a walking furnace."

Reeve made a contemplative sound. "Your Magic was protecting you from minor illness."

"Minor?" she sighed, each breath feeling like it wasn't enough.

He grabbed the decanter of water on the bedside table and poured a glass. He offered it to her. The command, or suggestion, she wasn't sure which, was silent, but she didn't have it in her to argue.

She took the glass in shaking hands and sipped the water.

She held the cool glass to her cheek and sighed. "How long is this illness going to last?"

"A day or two," he answered. "You need rest."

Rest was impossible. Not with the aches running through her body. When she did manage to land a moment of unconscious slumber, there was nothing peaceful about it. Her body fluctuated from freezing to cold. Her throat burned with each swallow.

Maeve waited for Reeve to offer his assistance, but it never came. She sighed.

"Could you possibly help me sleep?" she relented, rolling towards him.

Reeve smiled, his tongue lifting beneath one of his canines. "Oh," he said with a purr. "She's desperate."

"Never mind," she muttered, placing the glass of water back on her side table.

Reeve laughed, and it was the last sound she heard before a soft blanket of Magic consumed her, drawing her eyes closed and settling her mind into nothing.

The Crown's Quarters, Maeve's old rooms at Castle Morana, looked just as she remembered them. Beautiful, deep shades of blue and plum decorated the space. Memories of sleeping there with Mal as he held her back against his chest, their legs a tangled mess.

Now tainted by the presence of a demon.

Shadow's hand crept up her breast, playing with herself as Mal moved between her legs, spreading them wider—

"Stop it," she cried, her fingers bracing herself against the edge of the bath.

Reeve's assistance had worn off, putting her mind at the mercy of watching such heartbreaking things. But she couldn't even think about Mal at that moment.

Fire raged through her.

Maeve had never felt anything like it. The cool water should have offered her some relief, but she may as well have been sitting in a hot spring. She sank deeper into the bath, just that small movement draining her.

A muffled voice echoed across the bathroom. At her side, a figure appeared. Maeve opened her eyes groggily as someone leaned over the tub, eyes shifting between Maeve's half-conscious ones.

"Oh dear," they said. "Come on, child. Let's get you up before you accidentally drown."

The figure moved to help her out of the bath, reaching an arm around her back.

Maeve.

Mal's voice sounded out, so clear that it had to be his touch against her back, lifting her. Panic raced through Maeve. Electricity crackled down Maeve's arm and across her chest, wild and violent. The figure recoiled quickly, dropping Maeve. Water sloshed over the edge as they gasped and jumped back.

The room darkened, only for a moment, and Maeve felt his presence as he appeared from the mist in the bathroom.

"The fever, My Lord," said the voice softly. "It's too high for her."

Reeve inhaled stiffly and moved towards Maeve. He did not look down at her exposed body.

"Don't," she started weakly, barely able to open her eyes, but knowing it was him, "touch me."

Reeve didn't break her gaze. He nodded and kneeled beside the bath.

"Who can touch you?" he asked gently.

Maeve didn't answer.

"Someone has to, Maeve. You have to get to the healing waters. Your fever is too high."

"How far away is it?" she asked.

"If I can Obscure us, it's instant. Otherwise," he looked up at the blurry figure, "perhaps sedation for the journey there."

Maeve surged forward, water shifting beneath her momentary strength. She reached towards him, gripping the collar of his shirt, forcing his attention back on her. His eyes slid to her hands.

"No," she said weakly, her grip already faltering as her body threatened to slide fully into the water. "Please don't do that. Please don't—"

Reeve didn't move to touch her. His face was pained as he said, "No one is going to sedate you. I'm sorry I said that."

She looked back and forth between his saddened eyes. "Obscure me."

"Hand me a robe, please, Miss Gelsey," he said.

Gelsey. Not Mal.

Gelsey stepped towards them, placing the robe in Reeve's outstretched arm. "Thank you," he said. "You may go."

Gelsey took her leave at once. Reeve's eyes returned to hers as her body gave her a clear warning: it was going to be lights out in just a few moments.

"Can you stand?" he asked, his voice low.

She shook her head in defeat.

With each movement, Reeve's eyes never left her wavering ones. His hand moved to the back of her neck, supporting her head. Fire surged from his fingertips, but she barely had the energy to register it. Her grip on his shirt loosened at once, and her arms fell slack into the water. His other arm wrapped around her waist like a ribbon of fire, his broad hand gently gripping beneath her hip. He stood, pulling her out of the water and soaking the front of his clothes as he supported her.

Her head rolled forward, settling against his chest with a shallow breath. She was too drowsy to understand how he managed to wrap her in the robe, but as he slid her arms through the smooth fabric, the feeling of being smothered crashed over her instantly.

She found the strength to lift her eyes up at him, completely pliant and soft against him as he towered over her. The breath that left him was calm, his focus on dressing her. She met his eyes, dark and swirling with molten, violet fire. They bore into hers with such gentle intensity that her knees took it as permission to buckle, but he held her perfectly still.

A bolt of electricity raced up her arm and crawled over his shoulder. It affected him less than a small breeze would have, but his eyes followed the bright blue path of light until it dissipated.

His eyes returned to hers. "Full of surprises, kitten."

Her top half barely moved as he scooped up the back of her legs. Her body compressed against his as they moved through space. The lighting changed as he stepped forward.

New voices appeared, but her fever drowned them all out.

The water was ice as it hit her skin. Terrifying and smooth. It smelled of lavender and eucalyptus, and swirled with a thick purple color, rendering her unconscious in the white, oversized pool of water only moments after being placed in it.

Now minutes or hours later, she didn't know, her fully conscious eyes were on Reeve, who sat in a chair at the far end of the pool.

She sank deeper into the water, which was now pleasant. Her body was wrapped in a white gauze-like material that clung to her skin. She relaxed as she realized she wasn't completely exposed to him.

Though she already had been. And he'd kept those devastating eyes up.

Her hair felt clean, washed, and dried atop her head.

"How do you feel?" he asked in a low hum.

His eyes were tired.

"I feel. . .rested. That fever is gone."

Reeve nodded. "I can feel that."

"You can feel my body temperature?"

"I can."

Maeve leaned her head against the tiled wall behind her. "Is that because you are so great, or because of some other reason?"

Reeve didn't smile. "All Immortals have heightened senses, should we want or need them. Smells, heartbeats. But with you. . . I haven't got a choice."

Maeve shifted in the water, letting it reach her back fully. She changed the subject.

"How long did it take for my fever to break?"

"Mere minutes. But the Healers worked on you for hours. Your arm had some residual issues they addressed. And their water did its part."

Maeve brought her hand to the surface, and the deep violet waters glistened around her fingers.

"The famous waters of Aterna," she said softly.

The place that she wanted Mal to come to before she'd altered reality, before he'd been lost to Shadow.

"How old do you think I am now?" she asked, a question she'd been wondering for a while. Wondering just exactly how much time had passed since she first began messing with her, and everyone's, perception of time.

"You don't look a day over forty," said Reeve.

Maeve's mouth fell open. Reeve smiled triumphantly.

"Easy," he said. "I wouldn't want to evoke more of that lightning from you."

Her eyes narrowed. Then widened as she remembered. She looked away from Reeve, down at her hands.

"How?" she asked, shaking her head. "I put all my Magic into those crystals. All of it. That lightning. . .it's Dread Magic. I know it is."

Reeve nodded. "It's *unheard* of Dread Magic," he corrected her. "Magic, your sister can also produce."

She dropped her hands back beneath the water and looked up at him, at a loss for any explanation.

"My father couldn't do that," she said, partially a statement and somewhat of a question.

"No," Reeve assured her. "He couldn't. The first time you used it was the night he died. Is that correct?"

She nodded. "I think so."

"Has Maxius ever?"

Her thoughts drifted to the little Magic her son had been able to produce. How Mal was helping him grow stronger and find that inaccessible and dormant power inside of him. But that was before.

She shook her head and then asked, "How long was Maxius here?" She braved the question, her own sense of time completely ruined.

"Which time?"

Maeve's head hit the wall behind her. Reeve's words dug deep, a reminder of her failure. Of relying on him again and again. Of how he didn't trust her, shouldn't trust her, and yet he came every time she called.

Likely sensing the guilt running through her, Reeve spoke.

"You trusting me with his life may, strangely, be the greatest honor anyone has bestowed me."

"You took him without question."

"What question was there?" asked Reeve quietly.

Maeve held his gaze for a moment and then slipped deeper into the water until it covered her lips. Pride kept her from expressing gratitude. Gratitude she'd never be able to repay.

"You have to eat," said Reeve with a sigh. "You have to eat and actually sleep. Your body doesn't have the things it once relied on to keep you well. And I think," he hesitated, "that you need to do more than sit around the palace and read."

She rose, only an inch, in order to reply. "I'm just so weak in your eyes, aren't I?"

Reeve's head moved to each side. "You're so strong, it makes me feel sick. So resilient. You've been forced to build armor that didn't exist on you years ago." He nearly smiled as he said. "I have no doubt you'll be the last one standing."

Chapter 28

Maeve

Sleep was a thing of the past. A foreign notion and a dream itself. *Maeve*.

Thunder cracked far across The Black Deep, always sounding like his approach. The rumbling of a distant footstep, always angry. Always seeking pain. Always seeking to break her further.

It banged louder and louder. He was coming closer and closer.

Down the hall.

Maeve.

He was already here. He'd made his way across the Black Deep to finally put an end to her. To break the crystalized Magic protecting Maxius and fulfill the prophecy.

Maeve.

Broad, warm hands grabbed her shoulders.

But Mal's hands were cold and slender. Not like these. He had surely sent another to claim her. To break her like he'd broken Zimsy

—

"Maeve!"

She bolted up with a scream. Her breathing was too rapid and too strained to see clearly. She gripped at her chest, her heart slamming against her bones. The room spun, shapes and colors twisting in and out of focus. Electric Magic ran down her arm, collecting at her palm and firing out of her fingers in sporadic bursts of lightning.

"Breathe," said the voice again.

She couldn't. Her heartbeat hammered out of time. Energy surged through her. She squeezed her eyes shut just as the loud, high-pitched sound of glass shattering boomed.

Those unfamiliar hands moved to her face, warmth spreading through her shaking body.

"Breathe," he said again, ignoring her destruction.

She sucked in sharply, the warm air sedating the electric force running through her. Another breath and she opened her eyes.

Reeve kneeled in her bed, his hair down, framing his face.

"Good," he said lowly. "Keep breathing."

Maeve nodded in his hands.

"You're not in danger," he hummed.

Thunder rolled in the distance, and Maeve's breathing kicked, accelerating quickly. Blue lightning danced at her fingertips. He gripped her face, forcing her eyes back to his. His stunning firelight eyes.

"No," he growled this time. A primal command that caused every bit of her to still. "You are not in any danger," he repeated.

She nodded again, her rigid spine relaxing vertebra by vertebra beneath his attention. Her eyes slid down the Vexkari marking the side of his face and neck. The scarred Magic pulsed with power she'd never felt, but it boasted itself as something ancient. Something unlike Reeve.

Her eyes dipped lower to his shirtless chest, and the Vexkari markings that were carved into his skin there, too. Healed in solid-black color, like tattoos. Her eyes trailed lower, to the way his loose-fitting pants hung low on his hips. The dark room shadowed his muscles and darkened his tan skin. It was enough of a distraction that her panic faded.

His fingers moved along the back of her head, spreading in and out. Her eyes fluttered shut immediately at the motion. Her head reeled back, instinctively begging for more.

A satisfied and throaty chuckle hummed in the space between them. "Good, kitten."

He lowered her back onto her pillows and ran his fingers freely across her hair, massaging into her scalp. Reeve's Magic gracefully resonated across her entire body like a warm blanket. She took one last deep breath, and the smell of earth and smoke drifted her to a silent and dreamless sleep.

Hazy morning sunlight poured into her room. The pale-blue-toned stained-glass shot beams of light across the white floors. She was fully submerged in layers of fluffy sheets. It was completely silent in her mind.

She waited for Mal's voice to fill her head.

Nothing.

She waited another moment, swallowing hard in anticipation, but Mal's voice never called to her.

She sat up quickly, remembering the night. Reeve was gone.

But the feeling of his hands on her face lingered, infuriatingly so, like small, warm beads of Magic.

She was certain she remembered glass shattering. The sound had been so deafening, it must have been all the windows that ran the length of her room. But they were back in place, and they hadn't been that light-blue color before.

The new windows drenched her room in soft jewel tones, reminiscent of her room at Sinclair Estates. She held up her hand, examining the blue sapphire stone in the ring her father gave her and twisting her wrist to let it refract the morning light.

The lightning she produced, something she'd always assumed was part of her Dread Magic, had been triggered twice now when she was distressed. She looked back up at the new windows. She'd owe Reeve an apology for that.

Light was still fading every day as the darkness across The Black Deep grew. She slid from the bed and stretched, pushing down on how eager she felt to get to breakfast.

Reeve wasn't there when she arrived in the small hall where they met for meals. She rounded the corner and stopped at the sight of the empty table. No tableware, no drinks or food. Maeve crossed the hall, her footsteps echoing off the crystal walls.

"Hello?" she called out hesitantly.

When no reply came, she ventured farther into the palace, walking in silence.

"Does no one live here?" she muttered, realizing that besides her chambers, the hall where Maxius lay, and eating her meals with Reeve, she hadn't explored the palace at all. It was the size of a small city itself.

"Many once roamed these halls and called them home."

Her shoulders jumped as she turned back quickly.

Eryx stood with his arms folded across his chest. He was dressed casually, and his long white hair was pulled back in a sleek ponytail behind his pointed ears.

"Why's it so empty now?" she asked.

Eryx's eyes narrowed.

"This was once the home of the Senshi."

Maeve's throat tightened.

"And now that they are no longer here, there is no longer a large staff of cooks, cleaners, maintenance, and so on. Not only did you successfully manage to run Aterna dry of its army, you also unemployed hundreds."

Maeve sighed, remembering the last time she and Eryx fought. Now, in a rematch, she'd be at quite the disadvantage.

"Reeve wouldn't let hundreds go without their pay," she argued back.

Eryx shook his head, but didn't deny she was right. "I'm just waiting for the moment this act of yours falters."

She hated that those words burned. She hated even more that they were warranted. "Thinking so lowly of me?"

"It comes easy with a record like yours."

Another justified blow.

If her Magic had once been fresh air in her lungs, she was choking. Anger, resentment, grief, and so many other things she didn't want to name rolled through her with nowhere to go. No way to expel them.

"Where's Reeve?" she asked, keeping her voice calm.

A new voice answered. "In his quarters."

Maeve and Eryx looked to the side. Melione, or Mely as Reeve introduced her, stood leaning against a large arch.

"You're late," snapped Eryx.

And Maeve could see why. Mely's skin was flushed with a sickly green color. The skin beneath her eyes was dark. She stood clutching herself as though she might topple over any moment.

She smiled, as best she could, at Maeve. "I'm alright," she said. "I have an. . .affliction that makes times of war quite difficult when it's nearly on our doorstep."

Maeve nodded. She remembered her.

"You can sense death," said Maeve, more of a statement than anything else.

Eryx snorted. "If by sense it, you mean vomit and whine," he remarked, and then walked past Mely.

Mely took a steadying breath and prepared to follow him.

"Reeve's in the northern wing, past the sculpture garden," said Mely.

"The sculpture garden?"

Mely turned back towards her. "Oh, you haven't been? You must go, truly. Quite lovely." Her voice was light and kind, despite the way she looked like she'd pass out at any second as she gripped the wall. "Follow the carvings in the crystal walls." She pointed up.

Maeve looked up as Eryx's annoyed call for Mely carried down the hall. Sure enough, beautiful carvings of directions sat high on the crystal walls. Maeve looked back at Mely.

"Thank you," she said.

Mely nodded, already chasing after Eryx. "Gods, you're in a foul mood!" hissed Mely as they disappeared.

Maeve followed the arrows, pointing up a long staircase, and passed the sculpture garden, just as Mely said. It extended farther than she had imagined, wrapping out of sight. Maeve continued for far too long down the open-air halls until she reached another large carving, high on the walls: NORTHERN WING.

Another wrapping staircase, and she felt him. The thread of Magic that connected them thrummed in warm delight as she approached the partially opened door at the end of the corridor.

Maeve rapped her knuckles against the smooth white door.

A sound of approval came from the other side. She pushed open the door. Despite its monumental and solid stone build, it slid gracefully across the floor with little force.

Reeve sat in a large chair by an empty fireplace with letters sprawled across a table before him. In his hand was a single roll of parchment. Maeve remained planted in the doorway. Reeve looked up.

"What's wrong?" he asked with a partial shrug.

Maeve's brows pulled together. She gestured behind herself as she said. "We are meant to eat breakfast together."

Reeve laughed. "Maeve," he said, amusement in his tone. "It's after noon."

Her head whipped to the open windows of his study. It didn't look like midday.

"But," she began, cutting her own thought short as she realized her mistake. Less and less sunlight meant the days themselves were changing.

"Why didn't you wake me?" she asked, looking back at him.

Reeve leaned back in the chair, pure satisfaction radiating from him. "Because you were sleeping so soundly. I couldn't bring myself to."

Sleeping soundly with his help.

He tossed the parchment onto the table. "You've kept me up for weeks now, and I couldn't take it any longer."

Maeve chewed her lip, ignoring the reference to their bond. "Always so gracious."

Reeve's brows flicked up in something like agreement. "You should know I placed a new spell on the perimeter of Aterna. One neither Malachite nor that thing can see." Reeve's head tilted to the side. "You won't hear his voice again."

She inhaled a small, quick breath at the words. They were an unwelcome relief. She'd never imagined feeling grateful to stop hearing Mal's voice.

She'd never imagined any of this.

Reeve's eyes didn't leave hers.

Long moments of silence passed between them.

"I will help you on Hiems," said Maeve. "But I'll need new shoes."

"What? Can't go traipsing through the winter woods on Hiems in those lovely slingbacks?" he teased, bringing his tongue to the tip of one of his canines.

The act made her stomach tighten.

The corners of Maeve's mouth turned up ever so slightly. Reeve loosed a hefty breath. She forced her lips down into a frown, but Reeve's smile only widened.

"Are you hungry?" he asked, his tone telling her he already knew the answer.

She nodded and then quickly said, "I'm just hungry. It has nothing to do with your sleep aid."

"Sure," said Reeve lightheartedly. He snapped his fingers, Magic pulsing from them gently. "Food will arrive shortly. Now for business talk."

Reeve waved his hand, and with a small twinkle of light, a letter appeared before her in the air. Her fingers snagged it, pulling it closer for inspection as she crossed towards him. The emerald green seal was already broken on the letter. Her heart turned heavy.

She didn't move to open it, despite recognizing the handwriting as belonging to Abraxas.

"What's it say?" she asked, her voice dry.

"They are coming here in two days."

Maeve looked away from him and the letter, not having expected a visit. The thought of seeing Abraxas overjoyed her. To ensure his well-being, as well as he could be, was a gift.

But that meant having to see Mal. No. That meant having to see Shadow's version of Mal.

Reeve contemplated his words carefully before he spoke. "I hate what I am about to say, Maeve. I want to tell you, you have a choice. I want to lie and say you have the freedom to choose if you attend this display of power."

"But I don't," she said softly.

Reeve nodded. "If we are going to right the world, it will require us to play the game.”

Maeve let out a cynical laugh, but there was no disagreeing. He was right. She couldn’t escape facing it. If she was going to try and save Mal, hiding wasn’t an option.

“You couldn’t defeat her the first time,” said Maeve reflectively, no condemnation or judgment in her voice. No, she kept that resentment buried. “And with Mal in this state. . .what plan do you truly have? Beyond a rebellion with some creatures on Hiems?”

“The first time I faced Shadow, there wasn’t a prophecy.”

Maeve’s eyes narrowed, her voice growing darker with each word. “A prophecy? Which one? The one that says Mal is the one to defeat her, or the one that says in order to do so, he has to become one with my son? Absorbing his Magic? His life force?”

“Maeve,” said Reeve calmly, “I only meant—”

“I know,” she said tensely. “I’m sure you think at some point I need to accept Maxius’ fate. That I should think of it as some honor only he can carry. But I don’t. I’ll do whatever I can to protect him.”

“Have you considered that if Shadow is removed from Mal’s mind, perhaps Malachite could control—”

“Stop it. Do you hear yourself?” Maeve shook her head. “I can’t imagine how buried beneath her he is for him to. . . regard me the way he does under her possession. She told him to kill his son, and he did not hesitate.”

The words, the truth of them, and their infinite weight hung between them. Reeve’s face showed every emotion she hated in an opponent: pity, consideration, and a light annoyance. His voice held all of those things as he spoke.

“Do you know what drove Shadow to manifest her body? Do you know why she wanted your eyes?”

Maeve refused to answer.

“You are the only one who can draw him out of this.”

She recalled the way the green in his eyes faded beneath her touch. No. Not that.

“You want me to throw myself at him?” she asked, her voice barely audible, as though just speaking the words would taint her.

“No,” said Reeve. “I want you to be mine when he comes here.”

Maeve's eyes shot up to his as he finished his thought.

"And I want it to strike him so strongly, so violently at his core, that the Malachite you know surfaces."

"And Shadow? You think she will fall for something so pathetic?"

"If Shadow is present, you can let me handle her."

Maeve rolled her eyes. "So that's your grand plan? We whore out our bodies?"

"Don't be crass, Maeve," said Reeve, but his voice dripped with something sensual. She still hadn't figured out if he did it on purpose or was even aware of the way he spoke to her. "I have an arsenal of traits to distract with. Shadow, for example, loves to hear her own voice. I intend to let her remind me of all my failures while you use those pretty lips to drain the green from Malachite's eyes."

Pretty lips.

She pushed down on those words and bit back her reply as footsteps entered the room. Reeve's eyes left hers and regarded the Immortal man with two plates of food.

"Thank you, Venn," said Reeve, his voice genuine, holding that powerful humility he seemed to only have towards others. Never her.

Her stomach growled quietly at the smell, giving away just how eager she was to eat. Venn dismissed himself silently after placing the food before her.

And with that, Maeve picked up her fork and began to eat without reservation.

"Eryx told me the Senshi lived here," she stated between bites.

"They did," he answered plainly.

"He also told me that because the palace is now empty that it meant hundreds of citizens lost their jobs, their livelihood."

She chewed on a perfectly steamed vegetable and swallowed, her eyes on him. His attention dipped down slightly, watching her throat bob as she swallowed.

"But I know you're too righteous to ever do that," she finished.

Reeve's eyes were back on hers. "You talked to Eryx?"

She nodded. Reeve's eyes narrowed slightly, his mouth pinching at the corner. Maeve paused her eating to observe him.

"What else did he say?" asked Reeve.

Maeve looked down at her plate and shrugged. The action was a lie. Of course, she remembered his harsh words.

I'm just waiting for the moment this act of yours falters.

Reeve accepted the lie, but something on his face told her he was fully aware of Eryx's opinion of her, and that Eryx had made it clear to her as well.

"He will go with us to Hiems," said Reeve, as though preparing her for his company. "And tomorrow morning we will meet to go over everything during breakfast."

Maeve merely nodded, her mind far from the plan for Hiems. She was more concerned with their guest in two nights' time. She sighed, not realizing just how quickly she'd eaten everything she'd been served.

When she set her fork down, her eyes met Reeve's. Maeve took in the satisfied expression on his face and scowled, but she couldn't deny the positive difference a full meal made. She lowered her pride, reflecting on just how foreign her body now felt without her Dread Magic.

She shifted in her chair, propping her arms along the sides. "If I asked you to help me control this lightning, is that something you could do?"

Reeve's smirk dropped into something more sincere. She wanted the smirk back the moment his eyes sparked with something more than just arrogance.

"Yes," was all he said.

She knew two days wasn't enough time to perfect the technique, but it was better than nothing.

"Now?" she asked.

Reeve nodded.

Chapter 20

Maeve

Aterna's main armory lay near the Celestian Palace, but the armory Maeve stood in was part of the palace, just off of Reeve's own private quarters. The smooth crystal walls held an assortment of weapons, mostly swords. They were all unique, with hilts and ornamentations each their own, no two matching. Some had engravings she could read, like a smaller, thin blade that had a date carved in it. A date from nearly three hundred years prior. Some had carvings and markings that pulsed with Magic Maeve could understand.

This was no average royalty's stash of weapons. This was an arsenal that reflected time, wealth, and divine rule.

"What's the significance of this date?" she asked, pointing at the skinny sword as she walked along the display.

"My seventh birthday," replied Reeve.

Maeve observed the weapons a moment longer. "These are all yours?"

When no reply came, she looked over her shoulder. He stood at the center of the room, his eyes on her. He nodded.

She placed the wall of weapons to her back and faced him fully. "I am going to assume these swords bear purpose in today's lesson."

Reeve's eyes trailed down the wall behind her.

"It's likely your control came from your Magic," said Reeve. "It offered strength and stability for the lightning to flow through you, just as your Magic did. Now those currents are empty, and conducting such power isn't easy. But lucky for you, I'm an expert at such things, having once been without inherent Magic myself."

She'd never considered that. Before Reeve Inherited the power of Aterna from his father, he'd only used weapons forged with Magic. Just as all the Senshi Warriors did. Her eyes drifted to the wall of the armory.

As if reading her thoughts, he said, "My Magic is imbued in the weapon, and the body must learn to use it."

"That sounds easy enough," she said, feeling confident and hopeful as she turned back towards the wall.

"Why don't you pick one up and see?" he asked, smiling softly. Encouragingly.

Maeve wrapped her fingers around the hilt of one in reach, noticing they all had varying-sized stones in them that glowed like violet fire. The sword she grabbed had a small stone inside its hilt, barely larger than a small pea. She pulled up on the blade, removing it from its display on the wall.

All hope and confidence faded as she faltered beneath the sword's power, swaying sideways as the steel blade made contact with the floor with a bang. Reeve moved in silent swiftness and appeared at her side, correcting her wobble as the sword brought her to the floor with its magnetic pull. Magic swarmed from the hilt, wrapping her arm possessively in a dizzying way.

"What kind of Magic is this?" she asked, blinking a few times beneath the blanket of power.

"That is the minimum amount of Aterna Magic required to be a Senshi Warrior."

Maeve's mouth fell open.

"If one cannot wield that by age nine," he continued, "they cannot enlist."

It occurred to Maeve that perhaps she hadn't fully understood just how devastatingly different the Senshi Warriors were from that of another Magical army. A roll of power whipped through her, radiating from the sword. Reeve laughed through his nose as his fingers wrapped the hilt of the blade she was still clinging to.

"Though," he began, taking the sword from her grip as she let loose a strained exhale, "nine-year-old Immortals are still very different from you. An Immortal is designed to carry Aterna Magic. You are not."

He effortlessly placed the sword back in its proper place on the wall and turned towards her, their shoulders squared with one another.

"How'd your Dread Magic flow?" he asked.

Maeve inhaled deeply, as if she were about to use said Magic she no longer had at her disposal, and exhaled to see what feelings she anticipated.

"It moves from my center, up my spine, then back down my arms."

Reeve made a quiet sound of interest. "And the lightning always felt the same?"

She shook her head. "No. The lightning backflows to my center, then shoots back down the path it came up, and out my fingers."

Reeve's head tilted. "From the hand," he said, both a question and a statement. "That is different, then."

Maeve held out her right hand, her dominant one, the one that earned her a Supreme title, and the hand where lightning could be conjured. She turned over her palm, acutely aware of Reeve's eyes on the line of raised tissue scarring her palm.

"Arianna can produce it too," said Maeve, more question in her tone than Reeve's.

"Arianna has a more potent amount of Dread Magic than you."

Maeve's eyes lifted to him at the comment.

"That wasn't an insult. She's—"

"A Pureblood," finished Maeve. "I know."

"Your Magic is very different than hers, though. Your ability to manipulate it, bend it to your will, is far greater."

Her eyes returned to her scarred palm. "Is understanding why I can produce it critical for learning to control it?"

Reeve made a pleased sound deep in his throat. "Now you're thinking like a clever girl with little time."

She let her hand fall back to her side and lifted her chin.

His hand slid into his pocket, and he retrieved a smooth, round ball, made of solid crystal, barely larger than a marble. He extended his arm to her and dropped it into Maeve's outstretched open palm. She anticipated the pulse of warm Aterna Magic, but it never came.

"What is it?"

"For our purposes, it's a siphon. One for you to channel your lightning through. It's small, so it can't handle much. Which is perfect because the last time you pumped out a bunch of uncontrolled lightning, I had to replace thousand-year-old glass."

Maeve chewed the inside of her lip.

"This will help you understand the energy. It's how our swords and arrows are imbued with Magic. Crystals like these."

Maeve looked back at the wall of swords, each one with a glowing amethyst stone set inside the hilt. She looked back down at the dull crystal in her palm.

"But this one looks dead."

"They would all look dead," corrected Reeve as he placed a single finger on the small marble, "if my Magic wasn't in them."

The crystal marble shot to life, spreading warmth through her hand and up her wrist as it illuminated just like the rest. Reeve's finger withdrew, taking his Magic and warmth with him, and the crystal turned flat and dull once more.

"Care to try?" he asked.

"With the lightning?"

Reeve nodded. Maeve curled her fingers around the marble.

"Maybe you should step back," she said.

Reeve's head lowered in pity as he fought that cocky grin. "Kitten."

Maeve's fist tightened around the crystal marble. "Don't," she hissed, "call me that."

"Or what?" he said smoothly, flashing his teeth. "You don't stand a chance against me. I could will it, and you'd be a pile of ash."

Heat burned in her stomach, the meal she'd enjoyed turning over in acid. Her brows pulled together as a flicker of electric energy pulsed beneath her skin, coiling down the white knuckles that curled into a tight fist.

Reeve's grin only widened. "There's that pretty hatred."

Maeve inhaled slowly and with agonizing control, tightening every muscle in her core as Magic from her hand back flowed up her arm.

"Into the crystal," he reminded her, his eyes tracking her fist.

Fine. If he wanted her to force her Magic into that stupid little ball, she'd do it. But the swell inside her wasn't electric as she released the energy running through her. No, it was a feeling she was quite familiar with. The sensation of being submerged in water crashed over her. All the weight, distortion, and pressure in her head, with the wetness against her skin.

Suddenly, Maeve kneeled before the occupied throne at Castle Morana. Crimson red caught her vision. Her front was stained with red blood, dripping from a sizeable wound at the base of her neck. Her head hung low as her breathing tried to maintain a steady pace.

She looked up.

Mal sat on the throne with his legs spread enough to make room for a barely clothed Shadow to lounge between them. Shadow hummed quietly in the otherwise vacant hall with her head kicked back against Mal's shoulder. Her humming stopped abruptly.

Mal's face was vacant. Devoid of any emotion she could see.

Shadow's head lifted from his shoulder and slowly placed her gaze on Maeve.

"I asked you a question, Emerie," said Shadow, her eyes narrowing more with each word.

Maeve's stomach plummeted. She was in Emerie's mind. Emerie, who was alone on the Throne Room floor, wounded, and being questioned by Mal and Shadow without an audience.

"Have you gone deaf?" asked Shadow icily.

Shadow's eyes widened with a dangerous realization, in synch with Maeve's own sudden understanding. "She is learning to move through minds without jumping."

Maeve had to retreat. She had to pull back, for Emerie's safety. Maeve yanked herself out of Emerie's mind, as she had done in many minds while jumping. It was so small, so fractional, but Maeve could have sworn something like fear split across Shadow's face.

Reeve's armory in Aterna slammed back into Maeve's view.

Reeve's face, hovering just above her, held a firm expression of shock, a look she wasn't sure she'd ever seen him wear.

"I jumped," she said, but judging by the look on his face, he knew that.

Her eyes fixated on a spot on the floor as the weight of her words took root. But jumped wasn't the right word for it, not for what she had just done. In the past, she'd used others to travel through paths of the mind, connections, and memories.

She had moved from her mind to occupying Emeries. And that was it.

She looked back up at Reeve. "How is that possible? I jumped into Emerie's mind. She was with Mal and Shadow."

Reeve's lips turned under in a thin line, and he stepped away from her, giving her his back. "Holy shit," he muttered to himself more than her.

Her jumping abilities were her own. Truly her own. Not part of her Dread Magic, as she always assumed and was told. No, this, like the lightning running freely in her arm, was *special.*

Reeve laughed. "Yet another ability that makes you just that much more of a pain in my ass."

"I always figured I'd reach that eventually," she said defensively.

Black Magic swirled like fire around him, creeping higher and higher in solid form, expanding like wings—

"Oh," he turned back on her, "did you? You didn't even mean to do that. You were suppose to put lightning in the fucking crystal." The Vexkari running the side of his face and neck flared, pulsing with ancient Magic she didn't understand.

Rage.

She *did* understand.

That beast takes rage kitten. Do I look enraged to you?

His old words slammed across her mind. From when, she couldn't particularly remember. But he said it all the same. And Gods, did that rage call to her. She desired to touch those markings, to see what it would show her. It pulsed again, louder this time, drawing an audible breath through her. She desired to feel that rage.

Firm fingers pressed against her wrist, forcing her eyes away from the Magical scarring on Reeve's face. Her gaze slid to where he held her wrist in the space between them, just inches from his face. She tensed, not even realizing she had reached towards him.

His eyes were already on hers when she looked up at him, an apology on the tip of her tongue. It was swallowed by his grip, remaining one moment longer than truly necessary.

Two moments, and the pulsing from his Vexkari lessened. His eyes remained steadily on hers.

Three moments, and it retreated further.

Four moments, and it was gone completely.

But as five, six, and seven silent moments passed between them, Maeve's shoulders relaxed and her fingers uncoiled from her fist in his tight grip. A small relent.

His attention became too much. Too close to forcing her to face the emotions she worked each day to repress. Guilt, above them all. Guilt that she could possibly crave his protection when she deserved nothing close to it.

She swallowed hard as his eyes tracked the movement. Twice now he'd done that. His pupils dilated slightly.

And he let her go. She yielded a small step back, desperate for space she should have demanded as soon as he grabbed her.

"Practice with the crystal today," he said.

"And if I accidentally jump again?" she asked, her mind flashing to Emerie's bloodied chest and wondering if her previous visions of Mal and Shadow were accidental jumps as well. But reason fought that argument, for there had been no one else there.

"Then practice that too," he said. He smiled softly. "I'll make Eryx volunteer to help you."

Maeve grimaced.

Reeve chuckled. "That'll be the same face he'll make."

She bit back the urge to ask him why he was abandoning training her himself, but as a rough sigh slipped from him, she didn't need to. And she realized she, too, wanted space from the man before her, who was breaking past barriers that only one other had managed before.

"I noticed Shadow Slayer is not among these weapons you display so proudly," she said, hoping he understood the question.

Reeve contemplated her words a moment, his eyes on the wall of weapons fit for a king. But he wasn't a king. He had refused that title hundreds of years ago, when, according to her father, he had been forced to Inherit his father's power. To take.

To drain his life force.

What a cruel world.

"No," said Reeve after a moment, "that sword isn't worthy to hang alongside these."

"And yet, that is the sword you keep at your side," said Maeve.

Reeve smiled, but it hardly touched his eyes. "I haven't been worthy to wield a blade on these walls in centuries."

Maeve's eyes grew large at the raw honesty in his voice, but Reeve's playful smile appeared on his face before she could push him any further.

"Best of luck with Eryx. It's more a punishment for him than you," he said with a grin as he turned to leave the armory. "I hope you understand."

Maeve laughed softly. "A punishment for him?"

Reeve nodded. "I told him not to talk to you if I wasn't present."

He turned the corner of the doors, and Maeve's mouth fell open as she rushed after him. But on the other side of the armory doors, the dragon-shifting High Lord was nowhere to be seen.

Chapter 30

Maeve

Reeve and Eryx were the last to enter the intimate dining area, where breakfast was already prepared and spread. Eryx stalked behind Reeve, his long hair unstyled, and his face held a cold expression that didn't match Reeve's. Mely and Drystan were already seated with Maeve, having offered her polite "good mornings."

Eryx offered no such pleasantry. She was acutely aware that his body turned from hers purposely at the breakfast table.

Reeve's head tilted to the side as he took his seat. "Where's your siphon?"

The smooth crystal marble rolled beneath her fingers, where it sat hidden in her lap.

Reeve tapped a single tattooed finger on the breakfast table twice. "Out," he said, a gentle command that she obeyed without question.

Her hand moved to the tabletop, rolling the lifeless crystal ball beneath her fingers across the smooth wood.

"What's this about, Reeve?" asked Mely as she poured herself a glass of juice with twitchy fingers.

Maeve resisted the instinctive urge to ask her if she was alright, because it seemed the girl's nauseated and sickly demeanor was currently her natural state.

"We are going to Hiems," said Reeve, and then he looked at Mely. "Well, not you. You'll stay here."

"As if I want to go to that ice planet," she replied, her voice playful despite the fact that her hand moved to her stomach and she exhaled sharply.

"Who is 'we' then?" asked Eryx.

Maeve didn't miss the sharpness in his tone.

"The remaining four of us," answered Reeve.

"The wolves' rebellion on Hiems is your angle?" asked Drystan with a smile, as though the thought excited him.

"The rebellion grows stronger," said Reeve with a nod. "But Hiems is just the first step. One that must be made in complete secret."

"So that's why I'll be staying here," said Mely in a statement, not a question.

"Our favorite spy," said Drystan.

Mely toasted him with her glass of juice and smiled.

Spy. The word made something swell up in Maeve. It made her feel vulnerable, wondering how often Mely's unique abilities had aided Reeve in checking on Maeve's own well-being. Then she nearly laughed audibly. Reeve didn't need Mely.

He could sense her every emotion, every move, every drop of blood that flowed through her.

Before Reeve could continue expanding upon his plans, however, Eryx spoke again, his voice cutting through the comfortable atmosphere, turning it tense.

"I'm not going anywhere with her," said Eryx.

Maeve watched him carefully, despite his determination to not look at her. Reeve remained still as he spoke of Maeve. Then he nodded, not in approval, but in acceptance.

"You made it twenty-six seconds," said Reeve. "Twenty-six seconds when I just told you, two minutes ago, to hold your tongue at this table."

"Yeah," said Eryx, his nostrils flaring, "and I should have told you to fuck off one minute ago. Since when am I, your second in command, ordered not to speak my mind?"

Reeve remained casually leaning in his chair, not touching his breakfast. No one touched their breakfast.

"Since your resentment made you forget to speak with consideration," said Reeve smoothly.

Eryx laughed lowly, the sound threatening, like the noise a desperate and cornered man would make. His hostility, Maeve knew, she deserved. But his anger towards Reeve surprised her.

"Consideration," repeated Eryx, sounding the word out slowly. "You expect me to offer such a grace to one who has never *considered* anyone but herself?"

So faint she almost missed it, the crystal ball at her fingertips sparkled.

"Yes."

Maeve's brows pulled together. That was the best defense of her Reeve could offer? She swiftly realized waiting on someone else to speak for her had never been a problem before. So why now was her voice buried beneath shame?

Electric energy coiled up her arm, a teasing temptation. She rolled the crystal beneath two fingers, as it thrummed with one single thought: Damn that shame and damn Eryx too.

"You have no idea the things I've done to protect the ones I love," she said carefully, still rolling the crystal between her fingers.

Eryx's head angled to the side, still not looking at her, as though her very voice ate at his skin. "And I bet she'll continue to do such things where her Prince is concerned."

Her fingers stilled, but the Magic crawling up her arm did not.

"King," said Maeve, hating the ferocity with which she corrected him.

Hating that she corrected him at all, that she felt the need to defend the title Mal ordained himself, while under said title he had done such horrible and dishonorable things. But what she would not feel guilty for, however, was the truth of Eryx's words. She affirmed them with her next breath.

"And yes," she said, resuming her slow roll of the crystal, "I have every intention of saving Mal."

Eryx raised his hands, sneering, his eyes still drilling into Reeve, in a sign of "see I told you so," but Reeve didn't react, of course, already knowing Maeve's desire to redeem Mal.

It drove her mad that Eryx still would not address her, despite sitting not three feet from her. So she fixed her stare on him and said, "You're allowed to talk to me. Reeve's here," she added, gesturing to where *their* Lord sat.

Eryx's eyes nearly popped out of his head as he fumed at Reeve, who merely raised his eyebrows, daring Eryx to continue down this path. Eryx shook his head, his spiteful expression darkening.

"Have you told her yet, Reeve?" he asked. "Have you told her why Mely is literally green with the effects of death?"

"Stop," warned Reeve, his voice so low with command, Maeve stopped breathing for a moment.

Then her mind raced up to speed. More secrets. The electric Magic surged back, flooding towards her hand. More fucking secrets. "What haven't you told me?" she pressed.

The crystal siphon glowed, small tendrils of electricity cracking across the table. Reeve's attention was fixed on it.

"Oh, she doesn't know," said Eryx, satisfaction of knowing something Maeve didn't dripping from his tone.

"Eryx," muttered Reeve, his eyes closing.

But Eryx didn't, couldn't, heed Reeve's warnings. He appeared set on crushing Maeve with any blow possible. "Mely here has quite the strange disposition, as you know," began Eryx.

"Eryx, you are being cruel," muttered Mely, but it was washed out by Reeve's annoyed growl.

"Gods fucking damnit, Eryx," said Reeve, with a laugh that was hardly filled with joy. "Do not make me silence you."

"Why am I the only one looking at *this* clearly?" bellowed Eryx, pointing directly at Maeve. His hand jerked back towards his empty glass, the glass he hadn't even bothered to fill for breakfast. "Gods be damned," snarled Eryx as the glass made contact with the wall, shattering under his rage.

Maeve jumped in her seat and gripped the crystal tightly in all five fingers, electric energy swirling hotly against her palm, pulsing against the smooth siphon. Her reflexes were so infuriatingly dull now. Reeve didn't move from his relaxed position in his seat, but his eyes slid to Maeve quicker than a blink.

"You believe you are the one thinking critically?" responded Reeve. "You think inflicting more pain onto Maeve will save our people?"

"More pain?" spat Eryx. "She has—"

"She has endured," said Reeve, his voice musical and quiet, like a small praise slipping from his lips. "She will continue to endure, which is more than you are currently offering."

Eryx leaned forward against the table. "When you told me you were going to trade the Senshi for her, Reeve, I thought you had more planned than this. You actually see potential for redemption when you look at her? As she sits here and openly claims that her goal is to save the sadistic ruler we all knew should have never stepped foot in that cursed land across that fucking lake."

Her palm was on fire. She was too flustered, too spread bare to let it go. Her fist only tightened around the crystal siphon.

Reeve's answer cut through her. "Redemption isn't relevant when we are talking about the fall of civilization." His eyes moved to her. "Open your palm."

She twisted her fist and opened her palm to the ceiling. The blazing crystal ball glowed with bright blue Magic, tiny bolts of lightning scattering across the inside like a stormy sky. She lifted her eyes to Reeve. His head tilted in acknowledgment of her small accomplishment.

Praise in his eyes was a dangerous thing. Her fingers clamped back down on the crystal, hiding it from view.

"So I am to trust her?" asked Eryx, paying no attention to them, his voice still climbing in anger, in perfect opposition to Reeve's resigned behavior. "I am to trust that she will choose—"

"You are to trust me," said Reeve plainly with a sigh as he looked away from Maeve.

Eryx braced his fists on the table. "Why do you still cling to this notion that she is yours to save? It will cost us everything."

Reeve's eyes narrowed in understanding. "You think Shadow and her new Dread King won't come here if we stay out of it? It was on a whim I cast that spell years ago. I had no idea if it would last ten minutes or ten centuries. We are lucky it lasted the time it did."

"Then do it again and let it last until death is at our door," Eryx fired back.

"It is here, Eryx," said Reeve, impressively calm still despite his Second in Command's heavy breathing. "Look at Mely," continued Reeve. "She is beside herself. She cannot sleep. She cannot eat. It lurks around us."

"This girl will not protect us from that lurking death!" argued

Eryx.

"Stop talking about me as though I am not here," said Maeve, continuing to pour all her electric energy into the crystal, despite how badly it wanted freedom.

Reeve's eyes closed. When they opened, they remained on Eryx, who now looked to Drystan, his eyes begging him to speak up. But the small-framed and young-looking man did not. His eyes met Eryx's, but all he offered him was an encouraging expression.

Eryx rolled his eyes and looked back at Reeve. "She was not the one prophesied to end Shadow," Eryx reminded him.

"No," agreed Reeve. "But I believe she's the only one who can save the one who was."

Eryx continued to shake his head, and another expletive slipped from his lips as his fists slammed down on the table, shaking the glassware and untouched plates of food.

It hit Maeve then. The root of his anger. She remembered the times Eryx joined Reeve at Castle Morana. She remembered who occupied his attention, his gaze. . . his hands. Cold guilt surfaced in her stomach. Images she'd spent weeks trying to forget flashed before her eyes.

Her control buckled, and bright blue lightning danced across her knuckles. "You were in love with Zimsy," she blurted out, barely above a whisper.

With a flash of swirling mist, in a single blink, Maeve's point of view shifted. She looked down the long table now from Reeve's seat, and Reeve sat in hers. Eryx stood, his sword in his grip. The long blade pointed perfectly where Maeve's face had been only moments ago. Now, it lingered a fraction from Reeve's chest, with Reeve's hand gripping the blade in effortless strength.

Blood seeped out against his hand, coating the shining silver blade with slick and shimmering crimson. The blade that would have pierced her skull.

She loosed a hefty breath, and her neck rolled involuntarily as lightning charged down her arm. It spiked into the small crystal siphon in her fist, shattering it completely and sending a few sharp lines of electric Magic out across the table.

But none looked her way. Mely and Drystan's eyes were locked on the feuding friends, just as Maeve's were.

The silent tension was oppressive as the two men stared at one another. Reeve wore an expression Maeve hadn't seen, or hadn't cared to notice if she had, on his handsome features before. He looked wounded and disappointed all at the same time.

"Sit down, Eryx," commanded Reeve, lowering his bloodied hand.

Eryx's eyes moved down the table towards Maeve, his sword following his gaze. "The moment you falter, it will be me who ensures your eyes close and never open again." With a wildly controlled motion, he shoved his sword back in its sheath and returned his attention to Reeve. "She may have you fooled because of some useless bond that runs between you, but you know deep down you should have snapped her neck the moment that Enslavement Curse shifted into your hands."

The thought, the reality that he could have, was a sickening one.

Eryx turned from the table and left the hall.

Reeve didn't call after him. He watched him silently, and once he was finally gone, he looked across the table at Drystan.

"We leave in one week," he said.

Drystan nodded.

"Keep him away from the palace tomorrow night," said Reeve.

Tomorrow night. Maeve's stomach tightened. She would see Mal tomorrow night. She reached forward over the table and opened her fist. The shattered bits of crystal clinked to the table. One by one, falling loose from her palm.

"That's all," said Reeve, his voice quiet as he leaned back.

Mely and Drystan stood with empty bellies and left. Maeve didn't move. No, she stayed silent until just she and Reeve remained, picking out small bits of sharp and shattered crystal from her palm.

He did not look at her.

"What aren't you telling me about Mely?"

Reeve's head hung, but he did not hesitate to answer. "She is experiencing more trauma from death than she ever has. A single death at that. Because it is a great force that is dying. Slowly, day by day."

If she could have taken back asking, she would have. Reeve's truths were, it seemed, nothing more than added burdens.

Mal was dying.

Maeve's voice shook when she found the courage to speak. "She swore. She swore in Magic she wouldn't kill him."

Reeve's words may as well have been Eryx's long sword straight through her skull. "There are worse fates than death."

Heat flooded Maeve's body. Her eyes burned, becoming wet. But she would not let tears fall. Not in front of this man who already had so much to hold over her. She turned and left him, fighting off tears until she reached Maxius. She leaned over the cool crystals encasing him, placed her forehead against her forearm, and let herself mourn.

Even if she managed to save Mal, would such an act be a mercy or a punishment?

Chapter 31

Maeve

A package arrived just as Maeve finished her breakfast the morning of Mal's visit. A long, rectangular, thick black box sat on the table between her and Reeve. Maeve knew what it was at once. Something that should, and did once upon a time, thrill her. But as she suspected, the gown that lay in the dress box was just a punishment wrapped up like a gift. She found no joy in a new garment.

She rolled a new crystal siphon, a larger one Reeve gave her to replace the first one she shattered, beneath her palm on the table, pushing and pulling a small amount of electricity through the smooth ball with her eyes locked on the dress box.

Reeve sat across the table from her, a table that somehow got smaller with each meal they shared, forcing them closer, with one foot propped in his chair, hiking his knee up as he finished an apple.

He watched Maeve reluctantly stand and glide her fingers beneath the lid. With a sigh, she pulled up, revealing just a part of the glittering green gown nestled on white satin. She closed the box at once, shielding it from view, and looked at Reeve.

"It's a dress for this evening," she said rigidly.

"I can see that," was his casual reply.

Maeve rolled her neck. The crystal siphon, still gripped in her palm, shot a few small static bursts of lightning across her knuckles.

"I don't want to wear green," she whispered, stepping back from the box and retaking her seat. "I don't want to wear anything."

Reeve grinned. "Thank the heavens."

She frowned at him. At his carefree position. Unconcerned and unworried that in just a few hours, Mal would be at the Celestian Palace. He'd have her cornered again. Would he torture her further? Or would he not even glance her way?

She wasn't sure which was worse. His cruel attention or his

apathy.

Mal's Magic seeped from the box on the table, and her throat turned to ice. The message was clear. She would wear the dress he desired to see her in, or there would be consequences.

The sound of her bones snapping, then Zimsy's bones snapping, popped in her ears.

Her disobedience. Her defiance.

Consequences.

Her arrogance released Shadow. It was her fault Mal had fallen.

She was the catalyst for all the horrible things that happened that night in the Throne Room. What if she had just given him the spell? Could she have spared Zimsy the torture she'd endured? Her life, which Maeve was still uncertain of—

Her heart kicked, no, shot into a race, as though she was suddenly being hunted for sport. Her palms turned slick, and her mouth dried. She shook her head. Then shook it harder, as though she could simply whip out the feeling of his lethal hands on her by squeezing her eyes shut.

They'd be back on her tonight, relishing in breaking more of her bones.

You think I'd stand by and let him hurt you?

Reeve's voice didn't sound out in the room. He spoke directly into her mind, something he had not done since she arrived. His words, the velvety smooth way they caressed her scattered mind, were like a dousing of warm water. The thread of Magic connecting them swelled to life, calming her heart with flowing wafts of assurance, drowning out the snapping of bones.

I am weak. If he managed to break me before, when I had my Magic, imagine what he could do now.

Maeve opened her eyes, her gaze cast down at the table, as tears streaked her cheeks.

"Look at me."

She raised her palm to wipe the proof of her weakness from her skin, but a second command from Reeve stopped her.

"Leave them, and look at me."

She faced him and lifted her chin, clinging to the warmth the bond between them offered, allowing it to bloom in her chest. Reeve's face was set in stone. Before her was the wartime High Lord she'd seen on rare occasions.

"I will ask you again," he said. "Do you think I will stand by and allow him to hurt you?"

She shook her head, silent and swift tears falling across her cheeks.

"Words."

The answer was so obvious. She knew he'd let the entire palace crumble before harm came to her. He answered the call every single time, despite the positions it put him in.

"No," she choked out. "You wouldn't."

Reeve let out a shuddering breath. The scarring on his face writhed, as though it were in agony. Darkness swirled behind him, shadowing the entire room.

She's seen it before, that beast he rarely became.

Reeve smiled, but it was laced with agony. "That's the third time I've had to witness him break your arm," said Reeve. "And it is truly a testament to my control."

His eyes locked on hers, and his expression melted back into one of leisurely control as the giant shadow of a beast behind him shrank to nothing, bringing what little light the morning offered cascading back over the table.

"Cheer up, Maeve," said Reeve, rolling out his shoulders. "We're going to have a delightful time this evening. And no, you won't be wearing emerald."

The gown that hung in her room was certainly not emerald. Reeve sat on the edge of her bed, watching her expression. She frowned.

"So I just don't get a say in my own attire for the evening?" she asked sharply, her attention fixed on the iridescent violet and amethyst dress.

She had to act insulted, but she'd never seen a gown so lovely. It was exquisite, fit for not a queen, but *the* queen. The sleeves were long and sheer, sparkling like a pale galaxy. The train billowed to the floor like clouds. Silver embellishments, not a single thread or bead out of place, defined the shape of the gown.

But the jewel that was set at the center of the breast was the true marvel. It danced in its own light, even though there were no beams or rays presently hitting it. Deep within its fiery core, it moved like a constant, spiraling, shooting star.

"I've never worn purple," she said, still clinging to her pride despite the fact that in her mind she longed to feel the radiance she knew this garment would provide her.

Reeve chuckled, deep in his throat, allowing her the blow, as though he knew just how much she loved it. Maeve shook her head. Of course, he knew. He could feel it all.

She never let herself wonder why she couldn't feel him the way he felt her.

"Quit stalling and try it on," groaned Reeve.

Maeve turned towards him, pride festering further inside her. "What's the point in going when I'm no longer the weapon I once was?" she asked.

Reeve shook his head. "A weapon? You've got plenty of those. And you only need one weapon tonight, and it's buried so deep in your very existence, no one can take it from you."

Maeve raised a brow. "That so?"

He hummed his agreement. Then said, "You do not need a weapon when you were born one. Do not forget there is Magic you possess that is inherently yours, the uncontrolled lightning aside. Though you seem to be doing much better in such a short time. Annoyingly adaptable." His eyes praised her despite his words. "Anyway, the Magic I speak of is in your smile. In your voice. In that cunning way you look up at a man through the corner of your eyes. The delicate and yet purposeful placement of your hand on a woman to trick her into thinking you pose no threat."

Maeve grinned.

"I watched you play the game the summer before everything went to shit," he answered her unspoken question.

Her smile faltered completely.

"And look where playing games has gotten me," said Maeve, her voice dry.

Reeve watched her for a moment, and his eyes softened. "Wear the dress, show him that warrior's smile, show him he has not broken you—"

She turned and made for the door.

"Stop," he said coolly.

She obeyed, annoyed.

"Show them you are not broken, even if you think you are, show them you are not. Show him, with those pretty lips and the gown you are pretending to hate, that he should desire you above all. Remind him it is you he should bow to."

Maeve's chest moved up. And then down. Up and then down.

"Please," he added with a mischievous grin.

"Fine," was all she said, but she was already grabbing the hanger and heading into her dressing room.

Minutes later, when she reappeared, Reeve's eyes widened, and an audible exhale slid from his nose. He bent forward, where he still lounged on the bed, crossing his arms and covering his mouth with one hand.

"Where'd you get this?" she asked, suspicion in her tone.

Nothing this luxurious had ever hugged her so flawlessly. Even the length was just right, no alterations needed. She crossed her chamber towards a large pointed mirror, Reeve's eyes following her every step of the way. The train slid across the floor in a light hiss.

"I fucking hate this whole thing," said Maeve, arms folded over her chest as she observed herself in the mirror.

"Yeah," said Reeve with a controlled sigh behind her. "And you look hideous, too."

Maeve's eyes snapped to his in their reflection. He was already smirking. She fixed her face quickly, showing no sign of concern for his opinion, and rolled her eyes.

"Well, my hair isn't done," she muttered, absently touching the messy way it was clipped at the top of her head.

He stood and crossed towards the mirror, coming to a stop behind her. His hands moved without hesitancy, his fingers connecting with her skin at the base of her scalp. She froze, her fingers still on the sleek clip holding her hair, and her breath caught tightly in her chest. His fingers carded up her hair until they brushed over hers.

Electricity zapped between them, rolling Maeve's head back. She released a tight breath, hating that he heard it. He bent, placing his mouth near her cheek as he observed her in the mirror.

"Will you wear it up?" he asked, his breath ghosting across her skin. His fingers tightened around hers fractionally, forcing the clip open. "Or will you wear it down?" he asked, his voice a soft hum, as her hair cascaded down her back. "Like this."

The sleek metal that had been holding her hair clattered to the floor, forgotten. Her eyes were locked on his scrutiny of her in the mirror. His fingers dipped through her hair, brushing against her exposed spine.

Her skin shot to attention, betraying her completely.

She forced words out, anything to distract her own thoughts from how he watched her with locked interest.

"Do you think he'll be mad I'm not wearing the emerald?" she asked, thankful her voice remained steady despite the fact that Reeve's fingers now trailed the fabric at the base of her spine.

He stood to his full height, watching his fingers glide between her skin and the dark beads lining the low-cut back. "Of course he will."

Maeve turned towards him, slow and steady, but as she turned, his fingers were already on the move. He took the back of her neck, palming her head in his broad hand.

"Remember that tonight is a game. And that our goal is to incite a jealous possession." His eyes slid down her chest, where the intricate and beautiful beadwork shaped her waist. "Wearing *my* colors is so much more. . . provocative."

Maeve swallowed. "And how far are you willing to go to provoke him?"

Reeve clicked his tongue. "We," he corrected. "How far are we willing to go, you mean."

Maeve hesitated slightly before responding, her eyes cast down, studying the dress. "I will do whatever it takes to save Mal."

Reeve's brows lifted, his hand still splayed at the back of her head. "Anything?"

Maeve's eyes narrowed reproachfully.

"So if I," he began, ignoring her dagger-like gaze and sliding his free hand over her stomach, touching where his eyes kept lingering, "touch you in front of him. . . like this. . .you won't shoot me with lightning?"

Maeve watched his tattooed fingers lift up across the fabric of her gown, as though he was drawing the very air she breathed through her lungs. "No," she answered, eyes cast down. "It's part of the game."

Reeve hummed. His fingers still on the move, now above the dress, they slid between her exposed cleavage and prickled between her collarbones. "And if I pressed my lips here?" he asked, his voice darker.

The rise and fall of her chest became heavy. Still, she would not meet his eyes. In pitiful and pathetic defiance, because whatever reason she told herself she did not stop him wasn't enough, she closed her eyes.

"No," she surrendered another answer of compliance.

His fingers continued, his attention tracking every chill, every minute flutter of her pulse, as his fingers grazed across her skin. They tucked beneath her jaw, craning her neck back and deepening her head into his palm. Her eyes opened, but she was still a coward. She cast her gaze to the side.

With his pinky and ring finger still hooked beneath her jaw, his thumb trailed over her lips. "What about here?"

Maeve's eyes closed once more as his thumb pulled her bottom lip down.

When she didn't answer, he spoke. "Because I am determined to bring him to his knees with my performance. And I wouldn't want you to be surprised by my commitment to my role."

Maeve scoffed and opened her eyes at the ceiling.

"Is this your way of telling me not to get attached to your

attention? A little reminder, it isn't real and you are just pretending?"

His grip tightened. "Would you prefer I not pretend?"

She nearly laughed and met his gaze at last. Her tongue was prepared to mock him until his parted lips and heavy-lidded eyes settled over her, halting her words. There was nothing else in the world designed so perfectly as his face. Not even the gown. His violet fire-filled eyes harbored an edge of sin, of wickedness that caused a burning deep in her belly.

Because he was a paradox.

He was a rogue, a six-foot something God of power, with a face designed to corrupt. But the Aterna Magic pumping through him offered her something entirely different. Something pure. Something of promises that could be kept. Something that ensured pain was a foreign idea. Something that. . .

Reeve hummed, the sound pulling her closer to him, to that something she refused to name, to give further weight to.

His fingers moved from her lips and jaw, gliding up her cheek as he softly carded them through her hair. His voice mirrored that sinful look in his eyes. "If you look at me like that, he'll come unglued at once."

His fingers repeated the motion with a tenderness that contradicted the way his tongue briefly slipped forward and coated his bottom lip. The way his breathing sang to her in warning.

His top lip pulled wide, revealing his pointed canines.

She hated those perfect teeth. She hated how they painted him as the apex predator he was. She hated that they were pearly white. She hated that she wondered what they'd feel like pressed into her skin, just where her neck bled into her shoulder, if they could bite through skin and tear her apart the way she deserved—

Reeve's satisfaction only blossomed. "My, my," he purred. "You're giving me so many ideas for this evening."

This evening.

A game.

As she always was to him: a game.

Maeve huffed, blinking and breaking the trance he held over her. She brought her arm between them, forcing him away. He didn't fight her and let his hold on her fall. She moved away from him, breathing fully at last.

"You really do enjoy getting under my skin," she muttered.

"It's so difficult now, with someone else crawling through it."

Her shoulders lowered. She turned back towards him, refusing to be ashamed of the darkened veins running across her body. He offered her a weak smile and a look that expressed a half-apology.

"How about this?" she said, chewing the inside of her lip. "The first one to make that disgusting green possession in his eyes fade wins."

Reeve's smile returned. "And what will I get when I win, kitten?"

Maeve shook her head, ignoring the term she'd told him many times not to call her. "*If* you win," she corrected. "If you win, you can choose your prize. And if I win, I can choose mine."

Reeve's eyes sparkled. "No exceptions?"

Maeve shook her head, already plotting her own prize he'd be forced to give her. "None."

Reeve tipped his head back and laughed. It was disarming, filled with pure joy. "Oh, perfect!" When his eyes landed on her, that divine face, that paradox, that challenge in his eyes, made her brain fire off a multitude of signals.

All of them meant trouble.

Chapter 32

Reeve

Hours seemed like a long time for Reeve to wait to see her in that gown again. But he passed the time swiftly, plotting and planning his behavior for the evening. It had always come easily for him to flirt, steal attention, bring the party to him, ensure he was seen and heard. Not that tonight would be any different.

Except it was different. Tonight, the balance of Maeve's own psyche hung between him and Malachite. Her own emotional convictions were on the line like never before. Breaking the Dread King would be so easy if her own sanity weren't a concern he held.

So fucking easy.

He'd taste her lips before Malachite's very eyes, wrapping his fingers around her throat and pressing his claws against her pulse point, something he knew would draw a sweet sound from her throat. He'd shove his tongue so far down her throat it would mark her permanently.

But she wasn't ready for that. Despite her bluff that she'd do whatever it took, Maeve was not ready for his kiss. For his hands to bring her pleasure, or for his attention to be more than a war game.

Temptation was a brat, much like the girl he'd watch like a hawk all evening, keeping in tune with every breath she took. At her first sharp inhale, he was prepared to bring out the nastiest version of himself to ensure Malachite didn't see fit to take her back in a cruel power play.

A binding Magical vow. Reeve scoffed. He could take her back so easily, force Reeve's hand. But something told him that gaunt demon wouldn't let Maeve return to Morana. That perhaps Shadow was the only reason Maeve was here at all.

What a strange twist of fate, to be grateful for that wretched creature.

The creature that stood before him now was far from wretched. Her milky skin glowed in the moonlight that reflected off the Black Deep. The pale light danced across her gown, the one that he'd had made for her long ago.

Selfishly, he couldn't wait any longer to see her in it.

Realistically, he didn't know if he'd ever get the chance in the future.

Any lesser woman couldn't wear such a gown. It would wear her. But not this woman. Not Maeve. She stood with her spine tall and her gaze fixed on the horizon, focused on The Dread Lands, wearing an expression of soft defiance. Her hair was up, much to Reeve's joy, giving him a perfect view of the curve of her back, the subtle dip of her spine that ran from the nape of her neck and disappeared beneath the smooth fabric.

She was without fault.

Nearly without fault, he corrected himself as his fingers brushed over the ring in his palm.

"Have you given any thought to what you'll claim as your prize should the heavens shift and I lose tonight?" he asked.

She didn't startle as he spoke from his watching place. Reeve knew this because, since that morning, she had kept a loose hold on the thread between them, ensuring she felt his presence. Normally, when that bond presented itself or she called upon it, she pushed it back down as soon as she was no longer in need of it.

"I have options," she replied diplomatically, her eyes remaining forward.

He smiled at her response. She kept her cards close, a trait Ambrose instilled in her, no doubt. His chest tightened at the loss. His fingers tightened on the ring.

He joined her and stood abreast of her, his right shoulder to her left as he too watched the calm horizon, patiently awaiting the storm.

"Do I look good enough to evoke envious desire?"

"Almost," answered Reeve. "You're missing something."

Maeve sighed, nearly scoffing as she began to peel her eyes away from the dark horizon. "Of course. How could I ever achieve perfection next to such—"

Her words halted sharply as she took in the jewel raised between his fingers. The thin band of the ring was balanced in his large hand, like it were floating midair. A sparkling pale tanzanite stone sat at its center, shaped like a bursting star.

Reeve felt her pulse quicken. Her pupils dilated, blackening her snowy white eyes.

My armies for a bride.

Those words he'd spoken long ago, when he was desperate to get her out of Castle Morana. They tasted bitter on his tongue then, and they felt like filth running through his mind now. She couldn't be bartered or traded. If she desired to flee from him in her next breath, he'd let her. . .

No. Not this time.

He would not lose her.

The conflict raged inside him. His desire to claim her, to take her for himself, clashed with how he craved for her to choose him. Not because of some bond, or even because she felt fated to him. But because she wanted him.

"That's beautiful," she noted, her voice soft. "Will it fit?"

The answer that rose in Reeve's throat was silenced at once. So, with a sigh, he merely nodded his reply. Maeve's left hand rose between them, her empty ring finger beckoning him in silent approval. He obliged, silently taking her hand in his. Her fingers sat over his, so small, so fragile in appearance, drawing some primal desire to the surface.

But he knew better than to believe Maeve was anything but strong, even as she relinquished her dignity and allowed him to slip the one-of-a-kind ring on her finger, something that marked her as his, all for a ruse. This was the girl Eryx refused to see. The girl who persisted.

At last, she noticed the twin band to her ring on his left hand. No dazzling stone, just a matching band that physically designated them as a pair. A set.

If she hated the notion, she did not say it. If she felt repulsed, she hid it well. All Reeve felt through her loose grip on their bonded Magic was her contrition.

Her breath sharpened. Reeve's eyes shot to the veins running down her chest as they darkened.

The Dread King had arrived in Aterna.

Reeve looked down at her as she looked up at him at last.

"If you want me to stop," he began, but then his voice became silent, exclusive just for her as he spoke into her mind, *I'll need more than a "stop." I want a designated word.*

She chewed this inside of her lip, her gaze drifting somewhere distant.

Foxglove? she asked.

A villainous smile spread across Reeve's face. *Perfect.*

Maeve nodded.

Satisfied with her mind-to-mind acknowledgment and their agreement of a "safe word," he pulled her close, closer than was necessary since they were still all alone, and gave her one final thought before they stepped into the bright lights of the crystal palace.

When I win, you're going to want to remember that safe word.

Chapter 33

Maeve

Mal stood in all black, funeral black, at the center of the largest hall in the Celestian Palace. With one long wall completely open to the west, it allowed a breeze from the Black Deep to glide across the hall through its pale crystal pillars.

He stood alone, save for the white wolf Mordred, who traced the perimeter of the hall. Somehow, in the months since she had last seen Mal, his face had changed even more. And Gods be damned, he was intoxicatingly vicious. A perfect feline smile curved up between the shadowed bones of his cheeks and jawline as their eyes met. His raven hair sat in elegant ease, making him look approachable in a brilliant predator's trap.

But his eyes were more dead than they were that night in the Throne Room. Merlin, Primus, and all the seven fucking realms. She didn't know eyes could be so. . .void. So nothing.

So lost.

But the way his eyes tracked her every step across the hall. . .the way they narrowed in on Reeve's fingers pressed around her waist. . . the way his head tilted to the side as if he was ready to strike, all told her she hadn't truly considered the stakes of the game she agreed to play to send Mal over the edge.

Because Maeve was terrified of that edge. What if it didn't look like sweet hazel eyes, and instead it looked like shattered bones and blood pooling across crystal tiles?

She halted when Reeve did, a lengthy distance from Mal. His hand dropped from around her waist, and together they bowed before their King.

"What a welcome."

Mal's smooth voice sounded out, not in a call or in an exclamation, but in a pointed tone that felt like it was just for her. She lifted her gaze to him.

Reeve stood as Mal crossed the hall towards them.

"My King," said Reeve, reverence in his tone, as he gestured towards the table set with goblets and trays of food.

The intimate table near the open-air wall, or lack thereof, was set for four, but one guest, who had been presented as attending, was not present.

"Where's Abraxas?" Maeve asked, daring to speak to him at last.

Mal looked her up and down, slowly, soaking up every inch of her gown. And his lip curled. "Where is the gown I sent you?"

"Emerald is not my color anymore," replied Maeve, surprised at the steadiness of her voice. "You sold me to one who prefers shades of violet."

"Green is still your color," argued Mal, his tone dripping with boredom. "Just as I am still your King."

Maeve hummed in agreement. "Then my apologies are in order."

Mal's eyes shifted to Reeve, then he turned, crossing towards the table and placing himself at one of the four seats. He sat without waiting for any formalities or instructions. Maeve and Reeve followed suit. She looked to her right as Mal surveyed Reeve across the table. Reeve, also to her right, poured himself a shot of amber-brown liquid.

"I suppose with Abraxas not attending, I'll be drinking alone," he said, downing the shot in one go. When he set the glass back on the table, he looked up at Mal and spoke casually, as though the apex predator wasn't sitting six feet from him, tense and on edge. "How can I be of service?"

Mal's eyes moved from the empty shot glass up to Reeve. "Hiems has become troublesome."

"Are the Senshi not able to get it under control?"

"I haven't sent them in."

Reeve hummed. Maeve wondered if anyone was actually going to eat. Food seemed frivolous, but as Reeve grabbed a bite, she couldn't help but wonder how he was so at ease.

Reeve looked away in thought. "You want the rebellion to die quietly."

Maeve's mind snapped up to speed as she looked away from both of them. Why was Mal being so transparent? Her eyes slid back to him, but he watched Reeve and merely nodded in reply.

"There is a variety of life on Hiems," said Mal, crossing one leg over the other, "though it remains small in comparison to us. Many creatures, some that possess Magic and some that don't, Humans, Magicals, Elves, and even ones like your second. Half breeds."

Mordred continued pacing the large hall, his gleaming red eyes on the three of them as Mal continued.

"I don't intend to rule ashes."

Reeve nodded slowly. "Do you know where the wolves in question are?"

Maeve's brows pulled together softly. Mal was practically leading Reeve straight to the very rebellion he sought to light a fire under.

"Mordred will accompany you on Hiems," answered Mal, swiftly dampening any upper hand Reeve might have had.

Reeve hardly reacted. "Dead or imprisoned?"

"Dead," answered Mal swiftly. "Save for the alpha. I have promised him to Mordred."

"How many?"

"The pack is twenty-two strong," said Mal.

Reeve looked over at Mordred, where he paced. "His company will pose an issue."

Mordred growled, baring his teeth at Reeve.

"I'm aware," said Mal. "Which is why he will be hidden during your journey."

"They'll still smell him," said Reeve. "I can smell him."

It wasn't an insult. It was stated factually, a byproduct of Reeve's heightened Immortal senses.

Mal paused, contemplating. Mordred spoke at last, his gravelly voice sounding across the hall. "They shouldn't go alone, my King."

The corner of Mal's mouth pulled up ever so slightly. "Mordred doesn't trust you."

Reeve looked at the wolf, matching Mal's smile. "Was it the comment about the smell?"

Mordred growled, widening Reeve's smile. He looked back at

Mal.

"I'll do whatever you command," he said, his smile fading, "but, if I am to assume Mordred himself has not found them yet, but I am expected to. . . perhaps that won't happen if he is present."

Mordred made a noise like he was about to argue once more. Mal clicked his tongue, and the wolf fell silent and resumed his pacing. Mal's eyes remained on Reeve, narrowed slightly.

"Just get it done silently and swiftly," voiced Mal at last.

"Why aren't you doing it?" Maeve asked, her eyes on Mal.

Mal didn't look at her. "Does spending endless time on a freezing planet looking for a bunch of dogs sound like something a King should spend his time doing?" His attention landed on her at last, unwelcome and distant. "Have you ever jumped into the mind of something that wasn't Human?"

Her stomach plummeted.

"You can still jump, can't you?" he asked.

The debate of whether or not to lie battled silently in her mind. That is, until Mal sighed and looked back at Reeve. "Have her jump once you are on Hiems, until you pick up something useful."

Mal's slender finger traced the rim of his empty goblet.

"Since I'm denying Mordred the hunt, I'll be careful not to kill your alpha," said Reeve. "How will I know which one it is?"

"He wears a chain around his neck, with a ring on it." He looked to Maeve, his eyes on her new ring yet again. "A stone more substantial than that gaudy thing sitting on your finger."

"I am quite taken with it," she replied smoothly.

"Your vanity prevails," he sneered. "Though," he continued, his expression becoming cold as his finger continued running circles across the glass' rim. "There isn't a trace of him on you, despite that ring on your finger."

"You almost sound jealous," she stated boldly.

Too boldly, and with too much hope in her voice.

Mal's finger stilled, and his eyes set on her, plunging them into silence as he forced her to look into his all-too-green eyes. He studied her with such intensity, with Magic creeping between them, casing her in thorny vines, that she thought if he blinked, she'd simply cease to exist under his will.

"I come here graciously," he said lowly, "just for you to think the nostalgia of you means something to me?"

"Doesn't it?" she challenged, the game and her prize long forgotten. Her words were her own, desperate and weak.

Mal smiled without teeth, an image of pure and malevolent chaos as he enunciated each word like she was the dumbest prey ever caught. "Oh, Sinclair." Her stomach rolled at the implications of him using her last name. "Let me show you just how nostalgic I am."

With a lift of his hand, his previously empty goblet filled with wine. He lifted it from the table.

"A toast is in order," said Mal, the corners of his mouth turned down. "To my former Dread Viper and the former High Lord of Aterna."

Maeve didn't reach for her glass, not that Mal noticed or cared, seeing as his toast was far from genuine. He paused, faking confusion with his eyes still on Maeve.

"Strange. It seems I'm remembering another time when a toast was made and you lost something very special. I can't quite place it, though." He turned to Reeve. "You were there, do you recall?"

Maeve swallowed, aware of the scowl plastered on her face.

"Ambrose's death," said Reeve softly.

Mal snapped his fingers, raising his goblet slightly. "That was it." He looked back at Maeve. "Oh, I have an even better one. This one, too terribly sinful not to commemorate. Your aunt's birthday dinner, before I was crowned. You remember that toast Leslie Loxerman made? That was before you shattered her mind, of course. I remember it. I remember that it was so boring and exaggerated that you couldn't keep your hands off me under the table. Or perhaps when I returned to Castle Morana after fighting to secure the Elven Lands for months on end, only to find the most traitorous thing of all with her eyes on me during my Hand's toast of my return, as if she wasn't responsible for manipulating and erasing my memories all along."

Mal set his goblet down, and his hands returned to his lap. "Was that enough nostalgia for you?"

"Why are you here?" she seethed, cutting off his words.

Easy, do not let that lightning surface, Reeve's voice warned across her mind. *Keep that trick up your sleeve.*

"I'm here, because that," Mal pointed a single finger at Reeve, "is a valuable weapon. One that is now mine, thanks to whatever he seems to value in you. Personally, the thought is unfathomable."

Reeve took her hand into his own on top of the table, holding her shiny new ring on display, and the game began.

"I'm not sure how anyone could let such a gem slip from their fingers," said Reeve.

Maeve remained calm, holding tight to that warm thread of Magic between herself and Reeve that helped her heartbeat remain reasonable. Mal maintained his unaffected expression.

Reeve's lips pressed down on her fingers, kissing them gently, but his eyes swirled wildly. Wickedly.

He was already doing his damndest to make Mal come unglued. And when Reeve's mouth slipped around her thumb, her mouth fell open and she realized he hadn't been bluffing when he said he intended to win.

Reeve's fingers slid to her wrist, wrapping it completely. He yanked her sideways, with little concern on his face, as she toppled out of her seat. He guided her perfectly onto his thigh, his other arm snapping around her waist, forcing their noses just an inch apart.

Maeve swallowed hard. Fear was a complex emotion when she was held in the arms of someone like Reeve. Someone who never showed the holy power that dwelled inside him. Whose stare told you he could turn you to mist with a blink. Someone who had all the ability to be nasty, vindictive, and cruel at his disposal, but who never let any of it touch her.

The contradiction blurred her line of reason, giving her a false sense of safety. She reckoned even Reeve could admit to that. He'd been patient, but beneath it all was still a man with his own agenda, desires, thoughts, and goals. Still a man with secrets he held against her. He proved her right immediately as he pulled her false sense of safety right from under her.

Reeve's fingers pressed into her spine, arching her towards him.

"Tell me, Malachite, how will she like it best?"

Maeve's eyes widened. She stared at him in horror.

"On her back? On her knees?" Reeve continued, his fingers trailing up her spine.

Her mouth fell open, and her eyes narrowed, hatred boiling deep in her belly as his vulgarity put her on bare display. She may as well have been naked, spread across the table.

That thought may have been a bit too loud.

Reeve growled lowly, the vibration from his chest seeped into her own.

"Why don't you find out for yourself, Reeve?" asked Mal, his scowl deepening. "Waiting won't make her any less of a snake in your sheets."

"I like to play with my quarry, Malachite," said Reeve with a grin. His free hand grabbed his goblet, and he tossed the entire contents of the liquor back and sighed, satisfied. "I'm certain you can understand that."

Reeve's hand moved to her face, trapping her jaw in his large hand. He fixed his gaze on her now forcefully puckered lips. "I like that she doesn't know when I'm going to snap and take her." His grip tightened, drawing a whimper from her. "I enjoy watching how completely wrecked she is, with nowhere else to turn but to me."

Maeve's brows pulled together, her eyes frantically searching his for any sign his words were part of the lie. But her stomach tightened the longer he held her trapped. His voice was too genuine and too smooth with desire to be an act. When his eyes lifted from her lips to her pale eyes, a smile developed across his face in pure devilish pleasure.

"Just look at her," he purred, angling her head back and forth in his iron grip. "It's like she forgets part of me isn't man. Like she doesn't know the fear seeping from her pores fills my mouth with saliva. That the more she runs. . . the more I want to make it hurt when I catch her." Reeve's hand on her back braced, hitching her hips directly against him. "You'll look so pretty covered in my sin, won't you, kitten?"

The word "foxglove" was at the forefront of Maeve's mind as she fought the urge to push her palms against Reeve's chest in protest.

But she froze, the word never traveling down her bond with Reeve, because something else, no, *someone* else's Magic, slammed between them in invisible power, attempting to separate them.

Maeve's eyes widened. Reeve angled her head towards Mal, forcing her to look at him at the other end of the table. Mal sat, one elbow on the table, propping up his cheek with his other hand coiled in a fist.

The air in Maeve's lungs tightened. The Magic pressed between her body and Reeve's was indeed Mal's. Distinctly Mal's. Not Shadow's.

Reeve's fingers heated, nearly turning an uncomfortable temperature against her skin. His voice carried too much sincerity, too much venom, as he said to Mal, "She's still infuriatingly yours, though, isn't she?"

Too much jealousy; not enough lie.

Reeve gripped her hip, adjusting her until she faced Mal fully. His broad hand remained at her jaw, dominating her throat. Mal's Magic swelled between them as Reeve settled her between his spread legs, forcing icy cold beams of possessive rage between them and keeping him from pressing her against himself fully.

Mal's face was so cold, she wasn't sure if he even knew what resonated from him was his own Magic. But his eyes were locked on hers.

She hated them. She hated their color. She hated the way they were an unavoidable reminder of her failure. Her defiance. And the costly errors of her own ego. Even the scar, running down his beautiful face, was hers to carry.

She was to blame.

She was the catalyst of his fall.

Only when wetness pooled between her skin and Reeve's fingers did she realize that silent and angry tears streamed from her eyes and coated her cheeks. Electric Magic trickled down her arm, scattered and unstable.

"Mal," she cried, unable to keep silent any longer. The words spilled from her lips like a broken and begging prayer, soft and defeated. "I'm so sorry."

Her words landed like a physical blow.

Mal recoiled, his eyes closed sharply, and his face twisted in agony as his fist raised and slammed against the table. Magic rippled in multiple pulsing waves as he stood. Reeve kept them all from landing on himself and Maeve, pulling her flush against him at last.

Mal's arms raised, and he hunched violently over the table, palms slamming flat against the surface. His fingers retracted in torment, scraping as they clawed into the wood. His eyes were feral as he looked up at them.

But they were not green.

They were dark as night.

Maeve's chest swelled. Reeve had been right. She had been right. Mal, her Mal, was buried beneath Shadow's possession, and her Mal's desire for her was alive, furiously fighting.

Maeve didn't hesitate. "She'll drain you dead if you don't wake up, Mal. Break free of this—of her!"

Mal's Magic burst from him, encasing the room in a vortex of swirling death. The crystal walls splintered beneath the weight. The force of the winds pinned her to Reeve and dried her mouth as she tried to call out to him once more. Mordred tried to advance to Mal's side, but was pushed outside the swirling tornado of Magic.

Her arms gripped at Reeve's, desperate to escape his hold, to comfort Mal, this Mal that finally surfaced. To take his face in her hands and aid him in expelling Shadow's talons from his mind. She'd slice her palm again and again, she'd bleed out all over again for him

—

"My blood," she rasped, freezing. "My blood," she repeated, now frantic to slip from Reeve's grasp. "You can drink my blood, Mal! Take all of it!"

The violent winds of untamed Magic drowned out her desperate cries, but Reeve tensed behind her, his hold tightening, as though he had no intention of letting her do such a thing. His devilish smile had vanished, replaced by the face of a diplomatic warrior, ready to protect.

"Then you could end her! You could unleash Maxius' power without her influence over you!"

Her pleas, if he heard them, were futile.

Mal's head dipped back, shielding his face from view. A horrifying call blasted from his lips, overtaking the continuous rumble of wind. A scream so furious that Maeve's darkened veins hissed in approval. A scream so violent that when his head tipped forward again, and his cold expression returned, his green eyes were more catastrophic than ever.

The room plunged into silence as Mal's furious outburst contracted back into him. The temperature dropped so significantly that ice cracked across the table towards them, freezing the decanters and pitchers of drinks. Maeve's exposed skin shot to life. Her lungs burned in the intense freeze. Her bones shook beneath her chilled skin. Reeve's heat flared against her, attempting to warm her.

The silence broke as Mal made a singular sound: one of amusement. It slowly grew louder, like it was occurring to him what had just happened, until it bubbled into a hysterical, all-knowing laugh. The unsettling sound continued as he lifted his hands from the table and ran them through his dark hair, pushing it back from his forehead.

He stood tall. "You want my obsession, my possession, so badly, Maeve?" he asked, still amused. He pointed a single finger at her, palm up, and beckoned her. "Then come."

She shook her head, pressing back into Reeve.

To her horror, Reeve's hold lifted. "Go to him."

I will not let him hurt you. But you must go to him, he spoke into her mind.

She shook her head again, her eyes locked on Mal's deadly ones.

Reeve's hand palmed her exposed back and pushed her into a standing position. The betrayal of his supposed protection stung as he forced her into Mal's certain cruelty. Still, she did not move towards Mal.

Dark swirls of Magic appeared before her, blackening her view. Icy fingers pressed against her chest, sending her back onto Reeve's lap. He grabbed her hips, softening the blow as her only free hand gripped the arm of their shared chair. As the mist cleared, Mal stood over her, leaned against the table with ease, and held her left wrist in his grasp.

His eyes were on the crystal ring on her finger as she remained trapped between the two of them. Mal's fingers constricted, and he gripped her wrist with bruising force.

Please stop him, she begged Reeve.

I can't, he said back. *Not without him hurting you.*

Tendrils of Magic wrapped her hand, trailing up her ring finger, not piercing her skin, but threatening to. She tensed beneath him, pressing back into Reeve in a useless attempt to escape. She twisted her wrist beneath his icy Magic.

Foxglove.

She sent the word straight to Reeve. A safe word they'd only just established if things became too much for her. But that word only had power over Reeve as he sucked in sharply behind her. She could feel, even with her back to him, the Vexkari on his face calling to her. Calling for Reeve to tear, and rip, and—

Maeve, darling, don't fight him, Reeve replied, tense and fighting against the rage boiling through him.

Magic, too dark and perilous to be purely Mal's, swarmed over the ring she'd only worn for show, for an act, and showed her just how little it cared about her pathetic attempts to save the one it possessed. The ring shattered with an audible bolt of energy into absolutely nothing.

Not a shard or fragment of its existence remained.

And in its place sat a ring familiar to her. The Dread Ring gleamed with dark intent as it thrummed with ancient and intimate power. Her head tossed back against Reeve's chest as her eyes fluttered closed.

Dread Magic.

It tasted so fucking sweet infiltrating her. She didn't care that it was meant as a punishment. She relished the familiar scent, the cool feeling dancing across her fingers, up her arms, and down her center. It transported her back to a different time, a time when she and Mal dueled freely at Sinclair Estates. When he'd first placed the ring on her finger and she'd felt part of him merge with her—

Maeve's eyes shot open, her pupils blown wide, as she looked up at Mal, a slight hope blossoming in her heart. But there wasn't a single pigment of his eyes that lacked that sickening green. She waited, her head resting against Reeve, but they remained unchanged.

Despite their green color, she wasn't convinced the ring was entirely punishment after all.

Mal's voice was devastatingly calm as he said, "Consider it an upgrade. Hope you don't mind, Reeve. I'm sure she remembers what happens when she takes it off."

Mal released her wrist, and it fell into her lap at once beneath the heavy strength of the Dread Ring.

"If you ever do slide beneath the sheets with her," continued Mal, "know every black mark along her body is a result of my stealing her purity, and doing such wicked things with the remains."

"Enough," snarled Reeve, shadows of his Dragon form swirling behind him and his grip on her hips tightening.

Mal looked upon him slowly. Then, with the ease and fluidity of a serpent, he hinged at the waist, bringing both his hands to rest on the arms of their shared seat, and brought himself face-to-face with the Immortal Senshi Warrior.

"Finally, the beast threatens to appear," he said lazily.

Maeve's head spun as the Dread Ring continued to work through her.

"She is yours, because I will it," continued Mal. "But do not forget that you are mine. And in this hierarchy in which I wear the singular crown, where everything in this realm belongs to me, your King. . . she is still mine just as much as she is yours."

The two deadly forces stared at one another, one at the mercy of Maeve's love for the other, and one at the mercy of an allegiance that granted him an army capable of taking Earth.

"Is that clear?" finished Mal.

The surging beastly shadow behind Reeve retreated in long, drawn-out seconds. And with it, the rage resonating from him dissipated.

"Yes, my King," answered Reeve, delivering him the proper, submissive, and obedient answer.

Mal's eyes dropped to Maeve and lingered over her for a fractional moment. Then a swirl of black mist encompassed him, and he was across the hall, Mordred at his heels. Without looking back at them, he addressed Reeve as he exited. "See to Hiems at once."

Neither of them watched him leave. They remained stuck in the chair until Mal's Magic lifted, and Maeve's darkened veins paled, signifying his departure from the palace. Her chest shook, practically quaking. Her bones rattled so violently, the muscles in her arms seized up. Maeve pushed off Reeve, wobbling into the table. Her body reeled from his Dread Magic without her own to balance and counter it.

Reeve stood and pushed out of the chair, stabilizing her with both his hands before she tumbled to the ground. She slapped away at his hold and found her footing through her own stubborn will, moving towards the open space overlooking the Black Deep.

Darkness coated the water below; no moonlight in sight.

"Did you win?" she asked, her voice clipped between staggering breaths.

Reeve joined her at her side, the breeze shifting his hair. "I'm afraid we both lost, kitten."

She turned towards him with unsteady steps. Her fist made contact with his stomach in three consecutive punches. "Don't fucking call me that."

She raised her fist above her shoulder and slammed it into him once more, bits of lightning traveling across his chest. Again and again, exhausting herself further. Reeve didn't move once.

"Aren't you going to stop me?" she said, panting, in a moment of reprieve.

His fingers tucked beneath her jaw. "No," he hummed. "I'll stand here all night if that's what you desire."

Maeve gripped his hand and peeled his fingers from her skin, shocking him with a purposeful bolt of electricity. He didn't even recoil beneath the surge. He merely dropped his hand in surrender.

"'How will she like it best?'" she quoted, each word enunciated by another punch to his chest.

"It worked."

"You're vile," she hissed, stepping away from him and running her hands across her face.

"Yes," he said, his voice laced with dangerous disappointment. "I am. And now you know he's in there."

"You don't sound happy—"

"I'm not!" he roared, causing her to whip back towards him. "I haven't been happy since I watched him stick his tongue down your throat in your father's ballroom."

The Vexkari markings along his neck and face screamed with ancient Magic. Giant dragon wings unfurled from his back, more substantial than she'd ever seen them manifest from his anger, completely disproportionate to his body. They were part mist and part glimmering scales of skin. His arms darkened and thickened, his fingers dipping into long, dripping Magic that would soon enlarge and become claws. He was changing—

Violet streams of fire swirled around him, forging his alternate form.

"Do you know how long it had been since I transformed before I met you?" he asked, his eyes alive with fury. Without waiting for her to answer, he revealed it to her. "Two hundred years, Maeve." He rolled his neck, his body darkening and bulging beneath his rage.

"Spare me your blame," she said. "I did not ask for this."

Reeve laughed, dark and empty. "How convenient it must be to make the bed, and then claim it isn't to your liking."

His fire surged, and the hall fell into shadow as the makings of a dragon burst into being, forming from flames that rose as high as the towering ceiling itself. He shot out over the Black Deep in a swirling mass of fire. She rushed to the ledge, gripping a crystal pillar, desperate to see his beastly form, but dark mist covered his wake as his faint outline shot into the sky.

Chapter 34

Maeve

Breakfast and lunch were canceled in an unspoken agreement between Maeve and Reeve. Unspoken being that neither of them entered the room where they customarily met for meals the following day. Maeve sulked all morning, barely able to read any of the books that kept appearing in her rooms. Books she assumed were from the library in Aterna, the largest in all seven realms. She also assumed they were from Reeve, which made them even more difficult to enjoy.

Despite his display before Mal, and despite the Dread Ring now on her finger, Maeve felt revitalized. She had been tempted in her fury to release and sever her hold on the thread of Magic connecting her to Reeve, but somehow that bond ran stronger in the hours after Mal's departure.

"Spinel," she groaned, resting her head against the crystal altar where Maxius lay and lamenting to her cat. "Why does he have to make it so hard? Why couldn't he have prepared me?" She ran her fingers down his shining coat, answering her own question. "Because then your reaction wouldn't have been genuine and wouldn't have truly provoked Mal," she said in her best impression of Reeve's casually arrogant voice.

Spinel chirped an unhelpful reply.

Her thumb traced the underside of the band on the Dread Ring as she stood and made her way through the palace absentmindedly. Foolishly, the feeling of Dread Magic back in her grasp steadied her. She spent the morning in Reeve's personal armory, alone, and able to hold smaller swords pumped full of his Magic that she'd previously not been able to lift. Her lightning, mixed with the Dread Magic the ring provided her, gave her strength. It wasn't close to what her own Dread Magic provided her, but still. . . it felt like a gift.

Hope was a dangerous emotion in such dark times.

As the future became the daunting present, she questioned what the aftereffect looked like. Who would be there, and who would be changed? So many, herself included, would never be the same. Abraxas would need to heal after Mal's cruelty. Zimsy, if they ever found her, would be different after such horrible trauma.

Maxius.

She pushed down on that one. The guilt was too heavy. Rivaled only by her guilt for Mal. To understand Shadow's possession, his slow death, according to Mely, was to accept that even if she removed him from the grips of that possession, what would remain?

She's still infuriatingly yours.

Reeve's words bounced across her mind. He was right, and he was wrong. Mal was hers to save. To honor. To redeem.

Past that, her mind remained blank of possibilities. Or desire.

She'd never been in a time like that, where tomorrow was so very unknown and unpredictable that there was little point in trying to picture it. Even the time after her father's death had given her some promise of the future, dismal though it was.

And so, after a roundabout journey through the palace and due to that crushing feeling of uncertainty in tomorrow, but certainty that a certain Immortal stood a chance at warming her cold and hollow insides, she stood in the open threshold of Reeve's palace wing.

She leaned against the large frame of the doorway. Reeve sat, not at his desk, but at a large dining-like table, writing with quick purpose. He kept his attention on his work, but she had no doubt he was aware of her presence.

"Who was she?" asked Maeve softly, her mind lingering on the statue of a goddess-like woman that sat prominently at the entrance to the Celestian Palace.

"Who was who?" he replied without looking up at her.

"Your first love."

Though he tried not to act caught off guard by her bold questioning, the quill in his hand scratched to a halt, and then quickly resumed.

"The statue. It's her, is it not?" Maeve asked.

"It's her," was all Reeve offered her, an edge in his normally casual tone.

"An Immortal?"

Reeve looked up from the papers sprawled across the large table, but Maeve met his frustration with her soft expression.

"Why do you want to know?" he asked with a forced calm.

She looked around the room, the portraits of Immortal Royalty from hundreds of generations ago staring down at her.

"You know me. Startlingly well. You know everything. And I. . .don't know you. Not really."

Reeve stared at her, unblinking, his expression one of uncustomary exhaustion.

"This place has so much history, so much of you," she continued. "I feel left out." She offered him a small smile, the closest thing he'd get to her saying, "I'm sorry I make you so mad that you turn into a monster."

He held her gaze for a moment more and then studied the vast space between them. His brows pulled inward, and she felt him tug gently on the bond that ran between them. It jolted her stomach, nearly bringing her to the tips of her toes.

A small sound of acceptance hummed in his throat, as though he, too, could feel its expansion.

"Can I give you a tour of the palace tomorrow?" he asked, his voice still distant and drained. "I'll answer all your questions with great patience. Patience, I unfortunately lack currently."

The corner of Maeve's mouth turned up, only for a moment. She nodded.

As promised, Reeve was in a much better mood when he met her at the entrance to the palace the following day. Their journey to

Hiems was in just a few days, and Maeve had many questions about that as well. But she swallowed them and prioritized the, realistically, unimportant questions that coursed through her. Reeve had promised his honesty, as much as he could, given that some of his secrets were sealed in Magic, in exchange for one veto.

The first, "What was her name?" Maeve asked as together they looked up at the statue of the woman Maeve had assumed was Reeve's mate. She was sculpted in shining white marble, ensuring her tall and goddess-like figure was preserved forever. A fountain of clear blue water surrounded her, flowing gently.

Behind them, the skies remained darkened despite the early morning hour as Shadow's reach moved over Aterna day by day. Maeve kept her back to it.

"Leandra," answered Reeve.

"And how old were you when she died?"

"Fifty-five."

She hadn't been expecting an answer that reflected a time so long ago for him. She allowed Reeve to guide her through the palace as her questioning continued. He kept his normally long strides short, keeping pace with her.

"And how many have there been since then? Did they get statues?"

Reeve's eyes sparkled, back to his usual self. "Why? Are you wondering if you'll get one?"

Maeve chewed the inside of her lip and shook her head. "That doesn't answer my question."

"Does it bother you that many beautiful women have shared my bed, kitten?"

"It wasn't even a sexual question, you complete ass," she shot back, but Reeve only grinned.

"Ah," he responded, looking straight ahead. "Then you were asking how many women I've loved? Married? What?"

"I don't know," she offered softly.

"Yes, you do," he said with an all-knowing chuckle. "And the answer is once. I've been in love once after Leandra."

Maeve recalled the beautiful Immortal women he'd brought to

Sinclair Estates and Castle Morana. Their glowing skin and long legs.

Maeve glanced up and over at him. "And what happened then?"

Reeve looked down at her. "She forgot about me."

Maeve couldn't resist a light tease. "How could anyone forget about *the* Reeve of Aterna?"

Reeve smiled down at her, but it didn't match his eyes. "I failed," he said plainly. "I didn't fight for her."

The way you fight for Mal, she felt like he meant.

"The things you said to Mal, to me. About me. About us." She rambled on, "And you said you haven't been happy since that Summer Solstice party."

Her words plunged them into dangerous territory.

"Are you asking me if I desire you?"

Heat smeared across her cheeks, blushing them. Reeve's lips pulled back, revealing the way the tip of his tongue played with his sharpened canine.

"You're insufferable," she stated with a shake of her head, annoyed by his carefree satisfaction, but all the while fighting her own smile.

"If you're hoping my words were solely an act to shake Malachite, I'll give you a chance to retract this particular line of questioning."

Maeve bit her lip, completely aware that was an answer in and of itself.

"Stop that," he ordered, his eyes on her lips.

They turned a corner, and Maeve stilled, a whisper of a gasp on her lips as she took in the view before her. Above the smooth crystal floors, towering high into the magnificent ceiling, was a mural painted with vibrant colors of violet fire, surging high above black rock and ash. It performed in drastic juxtaposition to the bright crystal architecture surrounding it. At the center was a monster she'd seen only a handful of times. But he was depicted in a grotesque light, an image she disagreed with. The dragon she'd seen undulated with glittering, holy scales. The markings, which mirrored the very ones scarred onto the side of Reeve's face, jet across its oversized body in jagged lines. Its eyes blazed with violet fury.

So many questions burned at the tip of her tongue, but she halted them all. They felt too personal. Too raw. Too intimate to ask. How? When? *Why?*

"The last dragon," she said softly, noting the reality that although he wasn't fully dragon, he was the last of the kind. "Is this how you picture yourself?"

Reeve stood still as she walked the length of the massive mural.

"I did at a time, yes."

She continued pacing the mural. "You want to know something that makes me feel sick?" Without waiting for his approval to continue, she confessed, "I used to brag at Vaukore how my Uncle killed the last dragon. How he traveled all the way to the Dark Planet and slew the final beast. 'The last Ironclad'." She halted. "I was so stupid. Content believing the things I was told were right and good weren't worth comparing to my own instincts. A perfect contradiction sitting in my own home. The skull of a dragon, claimed like a trophy, while judging the ones who killed my brother for being part wolf." She looked back at him, shame present on her face. "Not just judged. I had them killed. Their entire family. And by that logic, if any dragons remained who loved the one my uncle killed, they should kill me."

Reeve crossed towards her until he stood before her, their shoulders squared with one another. "An endless cycle of death and destruction," said Reeve softly. "Which benefits no one."

Maeve looked away from him, as he was suddenly too good, too pure, and too holy for her stained and dirty attention. Reeve's hand moved in her periphery, brushing her hair off her shoulder and exposing the side of her neck. His fingers trailed up to the side of her jaw, tucking beneath it and drawing her attention back to him.

Their eyes met, and that thread of Magic between them pulled her one step closer.

"You're not responsible for the sins of those who came before you," said Reeve. "Your own will suffice when your judgment time comes," he added, his voice lighthearted. "And your list is long, kitten."

"And who will deliver my judgment?"

"A god, of course," he purred, sin alive and raging through his voice and his half-lidded eyes.

"I hope you aren't referring to yourself," she challenged as his fingers slid up, running through her hair and across her scalp.

"I imagine you'll want to seek judgment from a different god," said Reeve. "One who hasn't already decided your punishment."

Heat pooled low, *low,* inside her, pulsing between her legs. Reeve inhaled deeply through his nose, his chest expanding as his lungs filled with air. And when he exhaled, his fingers tightened, gripping her hair as his eyes rolled back to a close.

"Please, ask me another question," he said, his voice strained.

Maeve's mouth was suddenly dry, and her mind was blank. All she saw was a man trying his hardest to deny himself his trapped prey. Because she was. Signals fired off in her brain telling her to let herself fall apart beneath his desire, completely trapped by his hands, his eyes, his voice, and his words.

Reeve straightened his arm, his elbow locking in place as he put distance between them. His hungry eyes landed back on her with a sharp exhale.

"Another question," he commanded, raw desperation dominating his tone.

Maeve swallowed, trailing back to the list of questions she'd prepared. She stumbled across forming words, until at last she asked, "What about your mother?"

Reeve's hold on her hair loosened, as if her voice had broken some spell, and he pulled back from her, running his fingers through his own hair as he continued past the mural and ventured deeper into the palace. "She was good and kind. She died just after. . . She passed on a few years ago."

"Died?" asked Maeve gently, quickening her pace to catch up to him. "She was Immortal?"

"She was," he answered.

"And so was Leandra?"

Reeve nodded.

Maeve stayed in step with him. "I'm sorry, I guess in my mind

Immortals don't die. I never thought about it."

"Immortals bleed like any living thing."

Maeve didn't press him further. He had witnessed the most horrible death in her life, something she hated that he'd seen. Stood there and watched. Didn't move to help until—

She stopped the spiraling thoughts and moved to another topic as they walked.

"How did you know you'd inherit the power of Aterna?"

"Veto," said Reeve without missing a beat.

Maeve's mouth fell open in protest. "You don't trust me?"

"It has nothing to do with that, Maeve. I don't talk about inheriting my father's power on my best day, so I won't be discussing those dark days today."

Maeve was speechless. That was the most he'd ever spoken of his past to her. Or of his father. He offered her one last bit of himself.

"You have no understanding of what it's like to be forced against your father. Ambrose honored you. And you honored him."

They had brought to light three out of the four of their combined parentage. Only one remained unspoken of.

"Is there truly a chance that someday you'll be able to tell me about my mother?"

Magic whipped across Reeve, so potent, Maeve could feel it. He closed his eyes and let out a singular, small groan. With gritted teeth, Reeve nodded once.

The sound of birds and running water met her ears as they stepped from the palace into one of its many contained gardens. A wide bridge arched over sparkling water, feeding various forms of plant life in the lush environment. She stopped along the bridge, her fingers trailing the ornate railing.

It was so serene, so peaceful, so reminiscent of a time when her biggest problems were exams and one-upping her sister. Her sister, who regularly occupied her thoughts and worries, like so many she'd failed to protect the day she freed Shadow.

"All out of questions?" asked Reeve, pulling her out of her thoughts.

"Hardly," she said with a soft smile.

Reeve leaned against the opposite railing, a perfect picture of male ease. The places on her neck and scalp where his fingers had been, lingered with warmth, like little pockets of his mark. His essence.

"C'mon," he encouraged. "I know you've got one eating away at you. You wanted to ask it earlier and wouldn't let yourself."

Maeve frowned. "If you can read me so easily, then why don't you just answer it?"

"Because someone's got to teach you how to communicate with words."

She frowned deeper.

"Ask me."

She huffed a sigh, hating that she cared, that she was curious about him at all in that way. "How many have you been with?"

Reeve pretended like the question completely blindsided him.

"Quit that," she whined, turning her back on him once more to look over the water. "You knew what it was."

He moved behind her in a flash that her senses didn't register until his chest brushed against her shoulders.

"Why do you want to know?" he asked, his voice dropping.

She whipped around, pressing back into the railing. "It's just I would assume the total is much greater than mine."

Reeve nodded, placing his hands on either side of the railing and caging her in. "I have been in this world for three hundred years, of course it is."

Maeve swallowed. "And?"

Reeve shook his head and clicked his tongue three times. "You want the answer? You won't like it."

"I want the answer," she confirmed, keeping her voice casual.

Reeve sighed and hung his head.

"You've promised to be honest with me," she reminded him.

He nodded in agreement that indeed he had. "I've lost count."

Maeve's shoulders fell, and she let out a sound of complete disbelief. "That's not possible."

"I've been alive a long time," he hummed. "It's no different than losing count of how many times I've done countless other things."

"It's very different," she argued.

"It's very different to you because you're brand new," he said, offering her a dazzling smile.

Maeve smiled back at the sentiment.

"We can have this conversation again in a hundred years, and then you can tell me if you remember how many times you ate dessert in the past eighty of them."

Maeve laughed, truly laughed, content and warmth spreading through her body, forgetting Mal's immortal promise that he had forever to lord over her. "Fair enough."

"I felt you this morning," he said, changing the subject matter completely, "in my armory. You can handle a larger siphon with the Dread Ring on your finger."

Maeve nodded and noted that there was both gratitude and regret in his voice as she looked back and forth between his eyes.

"That's good," he said. "You're going to need all the help you can get."

He pushed off the railing and continued across the bridge, Maeve following soon after as he continued their tour.

Chapter 35

Maeve

"Your braids," said Eryx tensely, as they stood just outside the Celestian Palace, preparing for their journey to Hiems. "They're Elven."

"Well," said Maeve with a small shrug, absently touching her hair, "Zimsy taught me."

She and Eryx hadn't spoken since he nearly put a sword through her at the last mention of Zimsy. Neither of them needed to ask if there was an update. There wasn't. No news from someone with a gift like Mely's was good news.

"Zimsy told me a story once of your childhood," said Eryx as they remained waiting for Drystan and Reeve to bring the horses.

"Oh?" asked Maeve.

Eryx nodded. "She said you were rebelliously independent, and she herself was always being punished for it."

Acid churned in Maeve's chest. She didn't look at Eryx as he continued.

"You wanted to make your own bed, run your own bath, do your own hair. But one day, your mother struck both of you as punishment. And Zimsy said from that day on, you had a common enemy. And you swore to her that she would pay for her sins."

It was clear to Maeve her friend had spent a decent amount of time with Eryx before Reeve hid him away in self-preservation. And even clearer, as he continued to speak, that he'd paid astute attention to Zimsy."

Eryx was silent for a moment. "I've seen the scars on the backs of her arms. So my question is. . . Did you make her pay?"

The thought of Zimsy's scars and her horrible stand-in mother. . . Clarrissa Sinclair.

She thought often about her, about her cruelty. Mal had asked

Maeve numerous times if she wanted her handled, brought to the court at Castle Morana and added to Maeve's list. But as much as Maeve hated her, there were two distinct factors that stopped her from shattering her fake mother's mind.

The first was that Maeve wondered what such infidelity would feel like. What the physical reminder that your husband chose to sleep with another woman would do to you, let alone having to pretend you created, carried, and birthed said child. None of it was an excuse for her mistreatment. But it was enough to stop and make her think.

The second, and strongest reason she didn't kill Clarissa was Arianna. She wouldn't suffer her sister the loss of another parent.

So all Maeve said was, "I have no idea where she is."

"How old were you when you swore that?"

"I was eight. It was a Thursday. Zimsy and I played cards afterwards. Then I showed her the spot where Arianna hid her diary." She paused a moment and smiled, reflecting on that day. "I refused to let Zimsy make my bed. It wasn't the first time, but it was the last time I allowed her to be punished in that house by a choice I made. My mother struck her across the face with the back of her hand. No Magic. Just the physical manifestation of her hatred. That wasn't the first time I had seen her hurt Zimsy, but I hadn't cared. Zimsy was always trailing me, wanting to help me, annoying me, and I didn't understand then. . . After my mother struck Zimsy, she turned to me and hit me so hard across the face, my head spun. She had never hit me before. And suddenly I understood two things. The first was that I would never allow Zimsy to be hurt again at my fault. And the second was that I had made a friend through our mutual hatred of my mother."

"And you failed."

Despite Eryx's temper being much more in check than it was at their last breakfast, his words still cut deep. For indeed, she had failed. Eryx scoffed as if speaking to her was so beneath him. Maeve smiled, a wicked thought occurring to her.

"You know," she began, "you should be nicer to me if you want to be with her."

Eryx frowned.

"Couple bad words from me and who knows," she continued, sucking in through her teeth, "my best friend might not find you so worthy of her companionship."

Before Eryx could tell her off, Reeve and Drystan appeared with the horses.

Reeve's gaze locked on her at once. His eyes traveled from her turtleneck, down the fashionable coat, to the boots at her feet, and back up to her eyes. He wrestled with the smile twisting at his lips.

"You look. . .nice," he said, fishing for her gratitude.

Gratitude, she wouldn't give him so early in the morning. For all Maeve knew, the head-to-toe matching luxury winter set just appeared in her room. She held her chin high and remained silent.

"There's only three horses," said Eryx.

Maeve's head whipped to where Drystan stood, with indeed only three horses' reins in his hands. She looked back up at Reeve.

"Something to say?" he asked with false concern as Eryx and Drystan mounted two of the three horses with ease.

"You just think you're so clever," she said up at him.

Reeve bent until his nose nearly brushed hers. "What if I just want to feel those clothes I bought you up close?"

"In that case, I'll take them off," she quipped, before she realized her mistake.

Reeve's nose scrunched, exposing all his teeth in a sharp smile. "Even better."

"I don't need help riding a horse," she argued.

"No, I'm certain you ride with a perfected gait," said Reeve with a mischievous shake of his head. "It's your inability to protect yourself currently that dictates you'll be riding with me."

"I can protect myself fine," she muttered coolly, knowing it wasn't true.

Reeve shrugged. "Alright," he flicked his hand up, and across the crystal courtyard, at a decent distance from them, a glowing symbol appeared. "Hit that with lightning and you can have your own horse."

Maeve rolled her eyes and stepped towards the remaining horse, knowing she couldn't do as he instructed, not without proper stimulation.

The Gods must have had pity on her in that moment, because Eryx grinned and said, "Damn. She's not even going to try," with far too much satisfaction.

Power sparked to life beneath her skin. She whipped around and pointed two fingers at the symbol Reeve conjured, firing on it with a singular electric bolt of bright blue lightning.

Static clung to the air like glue in the aftermath, erasing Eryx's smug expression.

But Maeve's brows pulled together and her lips parted in confusion. She had not hit the target. She missed by mere inches. She looked over her shoulder at Reeve. His arm was raised, Magic still lingering on his fingertips.

"That's not fair," said Maeve, her outstretched arm dropping to her side.

"Why did you assume your target couldn't move?" he questioned. "Do you think out there if someone aims to hurt you, they'll stand perfectly still and wait for someone to piss you off?"

Maeve wanted to punch him for acting like she'd never been in a fight.

Reeve reached for her arm.

"I don't need help getting on a fucking—"she began, but the words died in her throat as Magic pressed against her, contorting her body against his as her stomach flipped over.

In her next blink, she was straddling the largest of the three horses, and Reeve was flush behind her. Her back straightened at once.

With a sigh, she said, "Can I at least have the reins?"

Reeve reached beneath her arm as a Portal swirled into existence before them, painting a blurry picture of distorted blues and greens, and snow and ice on the other side. He took the reins in one broad, tattooed hand and pressed his nose against the tip of her ear, his warm breath fanning down her neck.

"No," he hummed.

His other hand slid flat across her stomach. The bond of Magic between them swirled in warm approval. Slowly and with immense hesitation, she placed her hand over his and relaxed against him.

Hiems was colder than she remembered. The freezing assault on her face didn't last long, though, as Reeve put up a warm shield around them as his Portal swirled closed behind them. Drystan and Eryx flanked her and Reeve on either side, turning in circles to get a full view of the forest surrounding them.

Thick sheets of snow coated the ground in pure white. Evergreen fans of branches and leaves peeked out from beneath shelves of snow, shooting into the sky. The air itself flurried with drops of ice, which bounced off the shield Reeve kept around them.

There was no path. Reeve maneuvered them between trees and around the underbrush as Drystan and Eryx spread a bit farther from them, expanding their line. The expanse of the forest stretched as far as she could see in all directions. And judging by how silent the atmosphere was, she knew they must have been deep in the woodlands of Hiems.

"How do you know where they are?" asked Eryx.

"I don't," said Reeve. "But they should have felt me the moment we crossed into their lands in the forest."

"So they are coming to us?" asked Maeve.

"They are," he answered.

They traveled in silence for so long, venturing deeper and deeper beneath the snowy canopy that when Reeve spoke into her mind, she startled.

See if Mordred is tailing us.

She nodded. "Can I use your mind to jump?" she asked, looking up at him as best she could.

He shook his head.

"Then how?" she asked.

"Jump straight to him," Reeve answered.

Maeve let out a frustrated sound as they moved between two massive trees. "You're just set on watching me fail today, aren't you?"

"You've done it before."

"On accident."

"Now do it on purpose."

"If you'd known you were going to have me do this, you could have prepared me. I could have been practicing yesterday instead of listening to you ramble on about yourself—"

The hand splayed on her stomach compressed, bringing her impossibly closer to him. "Quit whining," he said, but she could hear the smile in his voice, "and do it."

He released his tightened grip, but his hold on her remained.

Jumping to Mordred, without already being inside a mind, without having access to the pathways between memories and those who shared them, seemed impossible.

Her free hand slid over Reeve's, where he held the reins, a silent command. As instructed, he stopped their horse, and the soft sound of its hooves crunching into packed snow fell away.

Magic, she reminded herself, was merely the will of the mind.

With an exaggerated sigh, she tossed her head back against Reeve and looked up at the white canopy above them. It was terrifyingly serene. So soft and beautiful, but so deadly in its frozen nature. She let her eyes drift closed.

Mordred. How could she jump to Mordred without a connection, a shared memory? She thought of their first meeting, when she confessed the fate her brother faced as a wolf. Then, how his coat was smeared red from the blood of all those men he and his wolves slaughtered. She could still smell the metallic sting in the air—

Her eyes shot open, and she straightened.

Perhaps she didn't need another's memories to find Mordred; he was in her memories. They shared paths of the mind. Her eyes drifted closed once more as she brought herself back to her interpreted memory. Her skin prickled, and she clung to that metallic taste in the air, breathing it in fully as the feeling of Reeve behind her, and the saddle beneath her dripped away into nothing.

She allowed her mind to fall into the memory of his bared teeth and the sounds of flesh ripping.

Her vision flashed with a burst of bright colors and shifted into a long room at Castle Morana. Abraxas and Mal sat at a wide table, their voices hushed. Maeve's heart jolted at the sight of her cousin. He'd lost weight, but he was alive.

She wanted to call out to him, ask him to verify his safety, to tell her where Zimsy was, if she was alright, but the only sound that made it out was a high-pitched whine. At last, Maeve realized she wasn't observing them through her own body. She looked down, taking in the bright white mass of fur. Her attention shot back to Abraxas and Mal. Neither of them looked her way, or rather, neither of them looked Mordred's way.

She yanked herself out of the wolf's mind, knowing she didn't need to risk giving herself away. Like moving through a current of water, she slid back into the bright white forest on Hiems, back into Reeve's gentle hold.

She did it. She did it with ease. The possibilities were endless for where she could jump, who she could see. She could jump to Zimsy!

If she'd ever acted faster, she couldn't remember a time. She didn't slowly dip into her memories with Zimsy. No. She let the world fall out from beneath her and plunged herself into endless falling darkness. Memories and time spiraled around her, twisting her body in every direction and way. She pulled, no, sucked them all towards her until she was drenched in the feeling of her ally, her best friend. The sound of her laugh, the smell of her cooking, the color of her eyes bled into the darkness, replaced with an infinite warmth of sisterhood that sat deep in Maeve's chest. Irreplaceable and unmistakable.

She twisted her body, perfectly timed as her feet slammed into solid matter. At the same time, her eyes opened, and before her was a vast expanse of earth. Long dead and dark, blurred and fuzzy. Violent winds assaulted her at once. She could barely open Zimsy's eyes to take in her surroundings, but she got enough of a look to understand.

Zimsy's vision faltered beneath Maeve's intrusion. Maeve looked down, Zimsy's body barely strong enough to obey the motion, where she lay on rocky terrain. Her bones were still exposed, her skin torn. But, confirmed by the small rise and fall of her chest, she was alive.

"Zimsy," she said, forcing the words out of the Elf's mouth. Her voice was raw, cracked, and barely audible. "I am coming."

She yanked herself back to the forest at Hiems, twisting her torso and looking up at Reeve, triumph blown wide across her features. "He's at Morana," she said with certainty. "And Zimsy is on the Dark

Planet."

Reeve's face was completely unreadable. She couldn't tell if his shock held praise or terror. Maybe it was both. The sound of Eryx's fast approaching horse flooded her ears.

"What did you just say?" he asked tensely.

Reeve held Maeve's stare for a moment more, then the light of a Portal reflected on his face. "Go," he said to Eryx, who didn't need to be told. The man was already hurtling towards a Portal Reeve made for him.

"I'm going too," said Maeve, but Eryx was already through the Portal, and Reeve's hold on her tightened fractionally.

She glared up at him.

"You found her, Maeve. Let Eryx get her to the waters in Aterna, and she will be waiting for you when we return."

Maeve opened her mouth to speak, but Reeve spoke first, his voice so bare and unmasked, the thread between them tightened.

"I need you here."

"No," she said, her voice stern. "I want to go to her."

Reeve's eyes were devastatingly soft. His head lowered until his forehead touched down at the crown of her head. With closed eyes, he begged her. "Please, Maeve. I need you here."

The absence of a command for her to stay or expected obedience was more infuriating than if he'd forced her. Because the soft torment in his voice was so filled with need, she quieted.

Reeve inhaled shakily and lifted his head. Their eyes only met for a moment before Drystan's voice broke their silence.

"We are surrounded."

Maeve turned, facing forward in the saddle once more as wolves, all sizes and coats, stepped from behind trees and bushes, from shadows of low-hanging foliage.

But her eyes were captured by one, the largest of them all, who stalked down a small clearing towards them. He stopped just a few yards from her as Reeve became uncharacteristically tense behind her. She didn't look back at him as he took yet another steadying breath. Her gaze was fixed on the solid black wolf with blazing blue eyes before her.

The Alpha. With a chain and a ring around his neck, just as Mal had said. Her eyes locked on the jewel. Her hands tingled, and her shoulders slackened. Her lips parted at the deep sapphire stone set in the band that was not unfamiliar to her.

It was not possible!

She swung her leg around the saddle, ripping Reeve's fingers from her front, and dropped to the snowy ground with a soft crunch. He did not attempt to stop her.

"I have seen you in my dreams," she began with a shaking voice, stepping towards the creature. "It cannot be."

He was massive. The widest among them, and with a towering height that nearly put him eye to eye with Maeve. He stepped towards her, finishing the gap between them, his paws silent atop the snow. He lowered his head until his forehead and Maeve's were one. A spark of Magic, barely more than a swift whisper, fluttered through her.

It was *known*. It was like *hers*.

Like Arianna's.

Like her father's.

"It can't be," she repeated.

A small whine slipped from the wolf's throat. His mental shields slipped open, a silent and bursting invitation for her to see.

And it was all there.

Their childhood.

Antony smiled down at her in the foyer of Sinclair Estates before leaving for his first year at Vaukore.

"Don't frown like that," he said with a chuckle. "I have agreed to meet you in London for tea once a month."

The memory shifted.

Antony and Alphard stood on the lawn in sunglasses, drinks in their hands, as the summer sun beat down on them. Alphard teased Maeve about how bad her game of bocce was. Antony's arm swung around her neck, pulling her into a loose chokehold.

"Careful, Al," said Antony with pride, "she's more venomous than she looks."

Maeve remembered that day, too. It was the first day of summer, and Antony had just turned fourteen.

The lawn glittered against the sunlight and shifted into a darkened bedroom.

Antony's bedroom, based on all the sports magazines sprawled across his bed. They were strictly a secret mother couldn't know about. She hated that Antony loved American sports.

He was maybe twelve, holding up his palm, casting light so he could look through the magazines. Maeve slept soundly next to him.

Another memory flashed across her mind. And another. Each tender and full of life and joy, memories Maeve herself cherished, and proof that the wolf before her was unquestionably Antony Sinclair.

When she withdrew from his mind, her cheeks were slick with tears. His snout sat along her shoulder, tucked inwards and cradling her head, and her arms were wrapped tightly around his broad frame. She lowered her own mental shields for him, and his voice was like a swelling chord in a symphony.

Maeve.

Her fingers twisted into his soft fur. Antony's nose brushed against her neck.

How how how? she asked.

Steel ripped inside her, crumbling beneath the weight of his heartbeat, his Magic, and the impossible reality that he was alive. She'd felt it before, the gut-wrenching tear of Magic as a false reality shattered. She knew this one was hers as soon as it began to rip through her.

The truth, something unexplained in her Magic that had been gnawing at her for years, begged for acknowledgment. It wasn't just the false memory of Antony's death that tapped against her mind. It was something more. Something that until she'd purged herself of her Dread Magic, she hadn't realized stood separately.

She pressed down on the thought as her own memories surrounding Antony flooded her mind, toppling over her lies and contorting what was new and what was old.

She sniffled. "I remember now, just barely," she said, looking back at Reeve, who had dismounted his horse, her grip on Antony remaining steadfast. "You were there. What did you do?"

"I only did what your father asked of me, Maeve," he said. "I owed him a debt. He called it in."

"What did you do?" she repeated forcefully, as more confusion flooded her mind.

"Before I tell you—"

Maeve's chin lowered, and she released Antony, turning towards Reeve fully. Electric Magic surged down her arm, spiraling into a deadly ball of energy at her fingertips. "Stop! Just answer!"

Reeve barreled over her words with his own.

"Come and look."

Maeve hesitated. He nodded encouragingly.

"My shields are down. I will show you everything."

"I can't," she said, her voice shaking as reality continued to split inside her. "It's too much."

The lightning, ready to strike at her fingertips, dissipated. She groaned and ran her hands over her face.

She can slip through minds.

She is learning to move through minds without jumping. Shadow's words.

Shadow Magic is deceit so natural that when faced with it, I cannot tell if reality is my own. Reeve's words.

The fear that had become increasingly prevalent in her mind for longer than she wanted to admit, the Magic tracing unapologetically just beneath her skin, forced its way to the forefront of her mind, begging at last to be acknowledged.

"It is not me that is special. I am merely part Shadow Magic. Aren't I?"

Magic shattered between her and Reeve, sparking across the snow in a single beam, and echoing across the forest like two boulders colliding. He heaved a painfully relieved sigh and fell to his knees, shaking, as though he'd just been flogged.

"The Magic holding your tongue is broken," she remarked, confirming at last, Reeve had known all along what she was.

Reeve pushed up, his hands buried in the snow, and looked at her. He spoke with such urgency that she was certain she missed half of every other word he uttered.

"That horrible day, I showed you that with your Shadow Magic, you could alter memories. I showed you that power, and per your father's command, you did exactly as he told you. You didn't hesitate to not only use it on yourself, not just your family, but the entire reality surrounding Antony. Just as he told you to do. Everyone but me. And I kept this burdensome secret because that is the job of a Sentinel."

Maeve's knees sank into the snow. The act was silent. Her ears simply rejected the sound. She had been altering reality long before Mal.

"I wanted so badly for it to not be true," she said in defeat.

Antony pressed closer to her, a low whine building in his throat at her distress. The sound wasn't comforting. It was merely a reminder of all the things she still hadn't sorted out in her head: did Antony choose this? Or did she force it upon him like she'd forced reality to alter the last time?

"Shadow," she repeated. "Shadow Magic runs in my veins."

A nauseating numbness slipped across her arms, around her stomach, and down her legs, holding her immobile. No thoughts ran through her mind except that one word. Over and over.

Shadow.

She disregarded the discovery that her beloved father had known, kept it from her, and encouraged her to erase the truth from all their minds.

Shadow.

That Reeve had known what she was.

Shadow.

That Antony was alive.

Shadow.

That her mother must have been—

Shadow.

She was. . .of Shadow Magic.

"I am like that horrible creature?" Her question slipped out as it trailed across her mind.

She hadn't realized Antony retreated and Reeve kneeled before her until his knuckle tucked under her chin, bringing her gaze from the icy snow—

. . . the color of her hair, her skin, her nails, her lips. . .

—and gently pulled her eyes to his own.

Reeve was solemn. Knightly. Sincere. "You are nothing like her."

Maeve's jaw tightened as fear rippled through her. "Not yet."

Reeve pushed her chin up further, a darker, more regal light in his eyes. "Not ever."

Her mind was on fire, overloaded with information.

She shook her head, desperation in her eyes as she said. "What's rippling across my mind where you are concerned is. . ." She couldn't finish the thought. She sucked in sharply. "I don't understand." His fingers slid to one cheek, his other hand raised, and he cupped her face gently. She leaned into one of his warm palms. Tears of confusion, denial, anxiety, and devastation poured from the corners of her eyes. "What am I seeing, Reeve?"

And then her vision flooded as Reeve poured his memories into her mind.

Chapter 36

Reeve

The bar at Sinclair Estates, Earth, 1943

"I have told your father it is not the same as my own beastly transformation," said Reeve. "But I am willing to try as much as you are."

"I'll drink to that," said Antony as their crystal goblets clinked together, his sapphire Sinclair family ring gleaming on his finger.

"Drink to what?"

Maeve appeared at the bar beside Antony, placing her elbows on the smooth wood. She was dressed casually in comfortable clothes.

"Trying to control my transformation," said Antony plainly.

Maeve looked from her brother to Reeve. His head tilted to the side as he surveyed her. Her eyes narrowed slightly under his scrutiny.

"This is my sister, Maeve," said Antony.

Reeve was well aware of the name of the creature before him. Her existence had plagued him for all nineteen years of her life, despite never having met her.

"Maeve," continued Antony, "this—"

"I know who you are," said Maeve, her eyes still on Reeve.

"Then you know I am a friend to your father and brother," said Reeve, speaking to her at last. "No need to scowl."

"That's just her face," said Antony with a smile. He reached out and pinched her cheek. "She's moody."

Maeve batted his hand away as the corner of her mouth ticked up.

"You're in high spirits," she remarked at Antony, eyeing down his glass. She looked back at Reeve, no care or concern for his title or his power in her voice. "You're here to help my brother?"

"As best as I can," he replied.

She eyed him once more, a lack of belief prevalent across her expression, and smiled softly at her brother. She grabbed his wrist, twisting it towards her to view the time on his golden watch with an emerald inlay and twin serpents for hands.

"I'm going to bed," she said. "Enjoy your evening."

Reeve returned to Sinclair Estates many times that summer at Ambrose's request. Despite nineteen years of not speaking to his old friend, he did not ignore Ambrose's desperate plea for help. As he grew close to Antony and attempted to manipulate the unfortunate Magic that demanded Antony's body mutate into something completely inHuman, he found an unexpected joy in toying with his old friend's youngest daughter, who learned that after each lesson with Antony, Reeve and her brother shared a drink at the bar. She began to frequent their late-night wind-downs, never pouring herself anything more than water.

Antony, who was understandably exhausted, began retiring for the evening before Maeve, leaving the High Lord of Aterna sitting at the bar with a dangerous weapon, who looked at him more and more each time they met like she wanted to fight, to see what he was made of, to see if she stood a chance against him in a battle of words.

They sat on two tall barstools, Maeve swiveling hers slowly with her foot.

"How old are you?" he asked. It was rhetorical, of course, as he knew the answer. But it was aimed as an insult after she'd thrown one his way.

"I'll be twenty at the end of summer," answered Maeve, leaning her cheek against her fist on the bar, the movement drawing up a desire Reeve quickly pushed down on.

"Old enough to know better than to be so disrespectful, then," he said.

"Have you earned my respect?" she asked, bringing her nails to her teeth and biting on them gently as the corners of her lips curled upward.

His voice dropped. "You are just begging for someone to put you in your place, aren't you?"

"Are you up for the job?"

"You'll be the one doing the job."

Maeve's teeth sank into her bottom lip as she fought harder not to smile. "How dare you speak to a lady in such a way."

"Yes, I can tell you're quite repulsed by the way your heartbeat accelerates with every moment that I hold your gaze."

She faltered for a moment. "You can feel my heartbeat?" The question was genuine, even somewhat awe-struck.

"I can sense it," he answered. "Immortals have far more advanced senses than you Magicals."

She took a sip of her water and made a mocking motion with her hand. "Does the arrogance work well on Immortal women with far more advanced senses than me? Or do they find you as annoying as I do?"

Reeve chuckled. "They don't find me annoying." He slid off the barstool and closed the gap between them. A single finger tucked beneath her chin. "And neither do you."

He dropped his hand at once and left her with flushed cheeks and wide eyes.

Reeve watched her from a distance, where she and her friends sat on the main balcony, sipping his drink as party guests moved around him. He was certain Ambrose was talking. Then the Orator, then Ambrose again, but whatever they had to say had stopped mattering to him the moment he spotted her.

She tossed her head back in laughter as Alphard Mavros scooted closer to her on the settee. She didn't notice his advance. She never did. Antony and Abraxas were seeing who could drink the most Dragon Whiskey at once while Astrea monitored them.

Antony yanked his bottle from his lips and clutched his stomach. After a groan, he said, "Damnit, Rosethorn."

Reeve would have to get on him about drinking so much at their next lesson. Lessons that yielded nothing for the young man. Reeve told himself he kept returning that summer for Antony, but he knew that was a lie.

Abraxas finished his bottle and then raised his arms in a celebratory cheer. Maeve and Alphard applauded. Astrea and Abraxas exchanged a whisper.

Antony gasped. "You cheated, didn't you, Brax?"

Abraxas' mouth fell open in hurt, but he didn't deny it.

"My sister made you a little potion to help you win, didn't she?" asked Alphard.

"Mind your own business, Al," said Astrea.

Abraxas slapped her on the arm. "Shut up," he said through his teeth.

The rest of their conversation vanished from Reeve's ears as Maeve's eyes landed on his. Her smile didn't falter.

It blossomed.

His chest tightened.

Ambrose's voice pulled him away from the beauty with her eyes latched on his.

"Come, Reeve," said Ambrose with a smile. A smile, Reeve knew, he reserved for politics.

Ambrose didn't speak again until they were both seated in his study. Reeve knew what was coming.

"Don't lay a hand on her."

Reeve anticipated the crack of Magic that would normally

accompany such a command, but it never came. Ambrose's Magic lay calm and still.

Reeve looked up at his friend. The Premier stared at him with unwavering resolve. Reeve maintained his poker face.

"You might be the most powerful of us all," continued Ambrose, "but when it comes to my daughter, there isn't a man alive that can slip past me."

Reeve shook his head. "I don't want to slip past you."

"It doesn't matter. You don't have my blessing. Make no mistake, I am aware that there is likely no safer place for her than at your side."

Reeve relaxed in the chair. "Then what is your reservation?" he asked with a small shrug.

"Is there Magic that grants her everlasting youth and life like you have?"

Reeve was silent. Ambrose pressed further.

"Is there some incredible spell Magicals have forgotten that would grant us the years an Immortal is blessed with?"

"No," answered Reeve quietly.

"What happens when she out-ages you? When her body begins to decline, and you are just as you appear now? What happens when she no longer looks like the beautiful young Witch she is, and you desire something fresh—"

"Enough," said Reeve, an edge in his voice, insulted at the insinuation.

"Act indignant all you want, old friend," said Ambrose. "It's a valid concern."

"I think you're acting a little prematurely, Premier," said Reeve with a half-hearted grin, trying to dissuade his friend from worry.

But worry racked Reeve himself. He hadn't felt a pull in his chest like Maeve in two hundred years.

Ambrose was so rarely without a cigar that the lack of one in the Premier's hand unsettled Reeve. After a moment, he spoke at last.

"I mean it," said Ambrose quietly. "Stay away from my daughter."

"Are you asking as the Premier of Magicals or as my friend?"

"I am not asking." Ambrose turned in his dark leather chair, now facing the enchanted window of his study. Behind the glass was a dark, cloudy evening sky. "She deserves to grow old with someone. She deserves youth before that. She will be cast into the fire of the adult world harshly enough as it is." He turned back towards Reeve. "She is too young to understand. And so you will be the one to sever whatever this is before it begins."

"She is not a child, Ambrose."

"She is my child, Reeve. And will always be."

"I am certain it is not proper for you to be on my balcony unannounced," said Maeve as a Portal closed behind Reeve. He stood with one hand behind his back, looking down at where she sat reading in the setting sun.

"First thing you need to know about me is that I don't particularly love rules. Which reminds me. I got you something."

Her gaze traveled to his hand behind his back. She bit her lip. "I told you to stop," she said, no trace of disappointment in her voice. "I can't keep lying about where the gifts are coming from. My father thinks the bouquets of foxgloves are from my distant great aunt Merrilyn. Who will, by the way, be sour I used her in a lie."

Reeve rolled his eyes and brought his concealed arm towards her. In his large palm, he carefully cupped an all black kitten with wide-set eyes.

Joy spread across Maeve's face. She tossed her book aside and stood. She joined her hands with his and brought her face close to the tiny creature's nose.

Reeve relished the look on her face and the feeling of her hands over his. "It can't be more than a few weeks old," he said, "and he's already bitten a chunk of my finger off. Made me think of you."

She looked up at him, her eyes sparkling with appreciation. "Can I hold him?"

Reeve nodded. "He's yours."

She scooped up the kitten and held him close to her chest. He began purring at once.

Reeve continued to visit Maeve in secret, only when Ambrose was away. Maeve remained unaware that her father had directly commanded Reeve not to touch her. And yet, as his fingers moved through her hair, he couldn't find it in him to care about the order. Especially when she wore soft sweaters and ribbons in her hair, like the way she was before him on her bed.

She leaned back against his chest as the all black kitten chased a trail of Magic she made with her fingers, rolling across the sheets in fits of clawed mania.

"What did you name him?" Reeve asked, his fingers still carding through her dark hair.

"Spinel," she said softly. "For his eyes."

Spinel jumped suddenly, puffing up and swiping at the ribbon-like Magic Maeve controlled with her elegant fingers. She laughed softly. The sound was euphoric.

"How's Antony?" asked Reeve, his mind drifting to the rough few weeks her brother had been through.

"No better," she answered.

"He's irritable almost all the time. Quick to snap. To destroy. He tries to control the urges, but they are strong. Stronger than he is most days."

"The shift isn't easy for all werewolves to control."

"Well, if he doesn't get it under control, he won't even be able to live a normal life. The Double O could find out at any minute, and then he'd be in true danger."

Knowing he failed to help her brother stung. But truthfully, Reeve hadn't had hope from the start. Antony's transformation wasn't like his own.

"I can't stay for much longer, kitten."

"Kitten?" she asked uncertainly at the new nickname as she angled her head and looked up at him.

He smiled. "You're just so. . .feisty." His eyes moved to Spinel. "Like your new friend here."

When he looked back down at her, her expression had shifted. He, too, realized their lips' close proximity. He bargained with himself, as he had been doing for weeks now, that denying himself her taste would keep him safe. That if he just saw her one more time, he could cut it off. If he just brought her one more gift, he could say goodbye. If he brushed his fingers across her cheek one final time, he could walk away with closure.

"Is it true what my father says?" she asked, breaking their silence, still looking up at him. "You can turn into a winged beast?"

He nodded, bringing his palm to her cheek.

"So right now, you could just turn?" she asked with a snap of her fingers.

"No. It takes a great deal of rage for me to transform. And right now, I feel completely content."

A small chuckle left her throat, but her eyes still begged with innocence that made him speechless.

"Let down your walls," she said. "I want to talk to you."

"We're talking right now," he said lowly.

"I want to hear you in my head."

Reeve pulled back, leaning far enough away from her to take in her whole face, still stroking her cheek with ease. The snake was asking to sink its teeth into him, unaware it had venom. Letting down his mental shields for her, a girl with Shadow Magic buried in her blood, was idiotic.

But her eyes made him brainless.

And so he did.

She bit her lip and took a steadying breath as he opened his mind for her. He understood at once why she wanted to hear his voice in her head. Because her voice in his was heavenly. It was visceral, soaring through his insides as she said.

I want to see you in that magnificent dragon form one day.

He could smell her from across the ballroom, where she danced with Abraxas. It was so overwhelmingly sweet, he couldn't even pinpoint it. He just knew that it was her. It was she who drove him mad. It was she who had him coming back to this damn realm.

Ambrose had joined him at his side moments ago, remaining silent as Reeve unashamedly watched his daughter.

"You know what she is," said Ambrose finally. "You know it, and yet nothing I say keeps your gaze from her."

Reeve didn't answer right away, despite just how correct Ambrose was. He knew that Maeve harbored Magic that should send him running. He knew just how delicate that Magic was.

Ambrose continued. "Not even a direct command to keep away from her it seems."

"Do not act as though it is me who you aim to protect," muttered Reeve.

He turned towards Ambrose, pulling his gaze from Maeve. Ambrose's eyes narrowed ever so slightly.

Reeve spoke casually. "It was you who came to be terrified of her mother. Not me."

Ambrose's Magic flared. "Don't you dare talk about her so effortlessly."

"Don't you dare forget what I did for you that day, Ambrose. It is because of me she lived to birth Maeve at all."

Reeve turned, feeling far too heated to be around so many people. Ambrose was quick on his heels, the voice of The Premier oozing from his tone.

"The relevance of that day is nonexistent," said Ambrose.

A few heads turned their way as they continued their argument out of the ballroom. Reeve ignored them all. A tall, rounded door slammed open in the corridor, inviting him in. Ambrose joined him in a flash.

"You think it matters what you did for the woman I loved? As my best friend?"

Reeve turned on him. Black and deadly Magic flared at his back in the shape of a beast.

"It matters because I allowed her to live! I allowed her to live, and I allowed Maeve to be born, despite the horrifying Shadow Magic that pulses through her veins."

"As if I would have allowed you to kill my daughter."

"You wouldn't have had a say, Ambrose," snarled Reeve. "No one alive, not the Double O, not the Order in Aterna, not Queen Lithandrian herself would have given one second of a thought to it. She would have been dead on the floor in a blink, and Maeve would have died inside her. Maeve would be dead right now if anyone outside of the two of us knew what she is."

Ambrose's Magic whipped out, rattling the windows and giving way to the floor beneath them.

"That may infuriate you, and it should," continued Reeve. "This is a cruel world. But I alone am the one who permitted the perpetuation of Shadow Magic to exist, when I swore an oath to do just the opposite after the Shadow War."

"And because of that, I am to look aside as you desire my daughter in ways I cannot allow you to have her?"

Reeve shook his head. "Do you think I want to be so consumed by her? When her eyes lock on mine, I am reminded of all that she is capable of. All that she could destroy and deceive, and manipulate in a blink. I am *terrified* of her."

Ambrose took a long inhale, and his hands ran across his face.

"Fear is the absence of Magic."

"I do not wish to fight you, Ambrose. You are one of my closest allies and one of my longest living friends. I am sorry."

"Sorry for what?" asked Ambrose with a huff, crossing the small smoking lounge and taking up in one of the chairs. "Throwing her life in my face or the fact that you have no intention of obeying my wishes?"

Reeve sat opposite him in a large tufted chair. "I came here to help Antony. I have not been able to do so. All I have done is driven another wedge between you and I."

Ambrose was silent for a long moment.

Just one more touch, he thought.

No.

"I will leave tonight," said Reeve, the words pouring from him before he could talk himself out of them, "and I will not return."

"Your word," said Ambrose at once.

"No," replied Reeve, even quicker. "I will not swear upon such unbreakable Magic without knowing what the future holds."

Ambrose nodded in acceptance and sighed. "Thank you, my friend."

Reeve stood. The walk to the foyer dragged. Sounds from the party where he knew she laughed and danced, stuck in his skin like needles. He didn't need to use the exit. He could Obscure right there, overriding all of Ambrose's far weaker Magical enchantments.

But he dared fate to let him see her one last time.

He skipped the last few stairs and was nearly to the door when her presence slammed into him from behind. She stepped into the moonlight, the winding stairs above shadowing half of her.

Her hands slid behind her back innocently, the action driving something through him. Something he was certain he'd never felt. Maybe something close once, with Leandra.

But not like this.

Not like her. Never anything like Maeve.

"You're leaving?" she asked.

He turned back towards the door, grasping desperately at his resolve, and replied, "Yes."

"Does that have anything to do with whatever you and my father were arguing about?"

He stopped. He didn't answer. She crossed the darkened entryway towards him, running her fingers along the marble side of the stairs.

"There are no secrets in this estate," she elaborated.

Reeve turned towards her, pushing down and down and down on the way her Magic called to him.

She leaned against the large pillar at the foot of the stairs and looked up at him. "Could it be me you were arguing over?" she asked with a wicked grin.

Reeve groaned at her position. How inviting and carefree it was. His heightened senses caught the slight smell of sweet green apples, which lingered on her lips. "Don't do this to me, please."

"A high lord of Aterna, using such begging words."

"The High Lord," he corrected her.

"High Lords have Ladys," she said boldly at last.

Reeve laughed. "Not Human ones."

She pouted at once. He smiled in satisfaction. Their dance of dominance was addictive.

"I'm not a Human," she said.

"Well, you aren't Immortal."

Her arrogance faltered, and the courage she'd come before him with withered.

"You'll be back for Antony?" she asked.

"No," he replied. "I won't be back here for quite some time, I imagine."

The playful way she'd approached him was long gone. They stood at the foot of the stairs as distant music filled the painful silence between them.

"Why?" she asked softly.

Reeve looked at her and spoke without hesitation. "Because I cannot help Antony. And this is not my war. Not my home."

Her brows raised, expecting him to say something more, something real. Something with courage. About her.

"That's it? That's my goodbye?"

Reeve didn't answer.

She scoffed. "I guess I'm beginning to understand why you're three hundred years old and not married."

She was a wicked creature.

He closed the gap between them faster than she could register his move. His fingers slid across her throat as he pushed her against the glittering marble wall of the stairs. She had only a moment to gasp before the sound was stifled by his lips. Her body tensed beneath him at once, and she moaned softly against him.

Ownership surged through him as his tongue tasted her sweet mouth at last. The desire to claim, to provide for, to honor, to multiply

—

She relaxed beneath him, and with a long inhale, her hands slid across his chest, winding their way to the back of his neck. His fingers twisted up through her hair, gripping just enough to force her mouth open farther. His free arm wrapped around her waist, holding her up. Her feet dangled as he stood to his full height, never releasing her lips as he lifted her.

He licked across her tongue, frantic and forceful. Her lips allowed him whatever he wanted. She responded to him with supple submission and soft, throaty whines he was certain would be burned into his memory for a thousand years.

Her fingers spread, grazing his exposed skin on the back of his neck and coiling up through his hair as she kissed him back. Red sirens of warning blazed through him as the deadly creature in his arms said his name against his lips.

Sense, something he hadn't had in two months, appeared, as though it had never departed. Reeve dropped her with a growl, letting her lips rip away from his. She wobbled as she landed, bracing herself on a marble pillar. His back was already to her, making for the door.

Maeve's fingers moved to her slightly swollen lips as his departure, as the desperation in his touch, clearly washed over her. "That wasn't a first kiss. That was a last kiss."

He did not stop. Just a few more steps and he'd Obscure away from her. Just one more step and he'd force himself to do it.

"Reeve."

He halted. How could he not when she called his name? He

turned on her, ready to fire whatever insult or cocky bullshit at her was necessary for her to accept their circumstances.

"We come from different worlds, Maeve. You live here on Earth, and have duties here on Earth. You should uphold them."

Magic zapped across his mind. He nearly recoiled as she tried to slip through his thoughts in one quick motion. He laughed in amazement and horror. She'd nearly succeeded.

But his voice was mocking as he said, "Surely you can do better than that."

"Kiss me again," she said, stepping towards him.

"No," he breathed and shook his head. "I have tasted all I can handle without losing control."

It was a dream, a fleeting one at best.

Maeve Sinclair was part Dread Magic and part Shadow Magic.

A fact he could not and would not escape.

Her Dread, he could handle, dominate, and understand.

Her Shadow Magic was another dilemma completely.

Shadow Magic, she didn't even understand. Everyone was convinced that her ability to traverse minds was unique. But he knew better. He knew to fear her unclaimed Magic.

But her smile created a void of emotions, negating anything that wasn't one singular thought that lingered in Reeve's mind:

He had to have her.

But he could not, and would not. . .let himself have someone with the same power as Shadow.

Incoming footsteps drew both their attention.

With inHuman speed, he was on her, his hands transporting them to them far from the house, down the jagged cliff-side and onto the rocky beach. His hands gripped the sides of her face, forcing her an arm's distance away as water crashed around them, thickening the hazy air.

"There is no future for us," he said harshly, a low growl slipping into his voice.

Maeve shook her head in his grip, her own temper flaring. "You are a god. There is any future you desire."

"You speak as though you could possibly know what it is I

desire."

She yanked herself free from his grip. "You're unbelievable."

Reeve didn't hesitate to wound her further, to create a barrier between them.

"I hope the best for you, Maeve," he began, his voice reserved.

The tone caused genuine hurt to flash across her face. "Fuck you."

Reeve smiled softly. He couldn't help it. She was so perfectly fierce. He had been denied many things in life. What was one more? Fair was an illusion to him.

Reeve stepped back from her. Her heart rate skyrocketed. It took all his strength not to place his hand over her chest and slow her frantic breathing as her eyes liquified.

"Please, Reeve," were the last words he heard before darkness surrounded him, and he Obscured away from her.

Ambrose beckoned him back to Sinclair Estates one final time that summer. Reeve, the noble and worthy High Lord he was, answered the call. But when the quick ordeal was over, he wished he had never returned.

Antony lay on the floor of the dining hall, in his pitch black wolf form, sedated under Ambrose's Magic. His snout and paws twitched, writhing despite being unconscious.

Clarissa escorted a sobbing Arianna from the room, leaving only Maeve sitting at the table, watching in horror as her brother had just tried to attack Arianna. She did not look at Reeve.

Ambrose was muttering to himself, "It's because he's repressing it. He's repressing his true desires."

"I know," said Reeve, kneeling beside the father and son. "How can I help you, Ambrose? I've already failed to help Antony."

Ambrose's attention shifted to Maeve. He looked at his youngest daughter with sorrow and closed his eyes.

"Show her," he whispered.

Reeve's insides plummeted. "No," he said coldly.

Ambrose's eyes opened, his gaze still on Maeve. "You have a very special gift, Maeve."

"Ambrose," snarled Reeve. "I will not let you."

"You've told me— I know that," she said, her voice devoid of any emotion, just as her face was.

Ambrose ignored Reeve. "More than jumping minds. You have a unique gift. And you must use it to help your brother."

"Ambrose," said Reeve. "Do not—"

Ambrose's eyes were on Reeve now. Gone was the face of his friend. This was the face of the Premier. "You owe me," was all he said. "Come here, Maeve. There isn't time."

She obeyed with haste, pushing up from the table at once. She stood at her father's side, her fingers twitching anxiously.

"Under different circumstances," began Ambrose, "I would never have burdened you with something like this. But there is no time. Antony needs our help. So when I tell you what I am about to tell you, I need you to understand that you are my daughter, and you are capable of great things."

"You're scaring me," she said, a slight shake in her voice.

"You should be fucking terrified," said Reeve.

She still did not look at him, but as she chewed the inside of her cheek, he knew it was taking everything in her not to.

Ambrose lifted one hand from Antony, the other still enveloped in his fur, and beckoned Maeve down to the floor. Her knees folded as he instructed, and his hand cupped the side of her face.

"You have Shadow Magic."

Maeve's lips parted. Her skin, if it was possible, paled ever further.

"Antony has known about your abilities for a while now," began Ambrose, and Reeve's eyes widened, "and I have waited and tried to do everything I could to avoid this last resort. Antony has begged me for weeks now to talk to you. . .and I admit I have foolishly held onto hope that there is some other way—"

"I have what?" she interrupted, her voice quiet.

Ambrose sighed. "Shadow Magic."

Maeve shook her head, slowly at first, then more frantically.

"Why, why, why do I possess Shadow Magic? It is banned. It is illegal. It is not spoken of anymore. It is gone. It was eradicated."

Ambrose did not answer her question. "Antony has asked that you alter things, so that he may go and live a peaceful life on Hiems with other wolves. A realm where he can allow himself to be what he truly is. But Hiems does not allow wolves from Earth on their planet. So you'll have to ensure you alter that as well—"

"I don't understand," she said, her voice cracking. "I'm—what?"

Ambrose's eyes shifted to Reeve, who looked on in complete disbelief.

"Show her," said Ambrose. "I know you understand the Magic you've been face-to-face with on the battlefield. And you will be the Sentinel."

"The what?" asked Maeve.

"When you alter reality with your Shadow Magic, there must be an anchor to reality. The Magic will demand it. You do not have a say over that. Reeve will be that anchor today."

"Ambrose," began Reeve hesitantly.

"How do you know all this?" asked Maeve, but her father ignored her questioning a second time.

"You will do this, Reeve," said Ambrose. "You will do this for my son."

"I'm certain I will," replied Reeve gently. "But she is not ready. That is advanced and complex Magic she has no grasp of."

Antony stirred. His paws twitched as a low groan reverberated through his body.

"There is no alternative! Not a single Magical alive is capable of producing this Magic," argued Ambrose.

"We'll be lucky if Maeve inherently pulls it off. And why aren't you the Sentinel?"

"Because you are the Immortal one!" he hissed.

"Stop it," snapped Maeve, her eyes on Antony as he writhed in pain. "I'll do it just. . ." She looked up at Reeve at last. "Help me."

And so Reeve did. He told her what she was capable of. That she could easily alter the mind of every living thing. He showed her, with his own Holy power, what ran through her blood, forced her to feel its ability at her fingertips. And when he was done, and she understood what she was about to do, tears streamed down her face.

"Maeve," said Ambrose sweetly. "It's alright."

"But I'll never see him again," she cried.

"He's in pain, my love," answered Ambrose, holding her tighter, as his voice caught. "We have to let him go. He wants this."

Watching Maeve alter reality on the first try was humbling for Reeve. She endured every bit of the Shadow Magic that wrapped around her as it twisted her own mind. She held an understanding of her Magic that, to his knowledge, was unprecedented.

And for Reeve to be impressed meant that he hadn't been nearly scared enough of this woman.

Reeve moved Antony's limp body to Hiems with ease, fulfilling his agreement to deliver him there, but with every intention of turning right back around and making sure Maeve hadn't accidentally shattered her own mind in the process.

When he returned to the Dining Hall at Sinclair Estates and closed the Portal to Hiems behind him, Maeve was laid out across the rug. Ambrose kneeled before her, his mind empty and his eyes blown wide in a vast expanse of white. Golden orbs of light swarmed his body as Maeve's Magic took hold, rewriting reality.

But Maeve herself was barely breathing. Reeve moved one arm beneath her back, lifting her off the floor. Her Magic was scattered, unstable and. . .breaking. She'd done too much, pushed too far, just as he feared. Learning her limitations appeared to not be so natural for her.

But it didn't matter if she was on the verge of death. The Immortal who cradled her close to his chest loved her, and death was easily defeated by one who held the power of the Gods.

A tiny glowing star burst from his chest and slowly lowered into hers. Her lungs filled with air instantly, and her Magic stabilized. A small thread of Magic materialized between his soul and hers. It was warm, fluttering like a heartbeat.

Her eyes shot open, just as veiled and white as her father's. Reeve released her as Ambrose stood. He helped her to her feet as Reeve himself stood and stepped back from them. Together, the father and daughter blinked, and their blue orbs returned.

Maeve looked up at her father, then her gaze flicked to Reeve, only for a moment. The look of a stranger, quickly holding another stranger's gaze. Realizing she'd been crying, she wiped her tears.

"Ah, Reeve," said Ambrose. "Let's go and have a cigar, shall we?"

But Reeve's eyes were still set on Maeve.

"Oh," said Ambrose casually, "terribly rude of me. This is my youngest, Maeve. Maeve, this is Reeve, the High Lord of Aterna."

"Hi," she said softly, then smiled up at Ambrose. "Enjoy your evening, daddy. I'm off to bed."

He kissed her quickly on the cheek and then stepped towards Reeve, heading for his study as she turned her back to them.

"Maeve," Reeve called her name as she turned from them both.

She looked over her shoulder, and his heart froze.

From just the look in her eyes, Reeve knew at once what she had done. Her Magic didn't move towards his. She hadn't merely altered reality where Antony was concerned. She hadn't just fabricated his death in everyone's mind except his own.

As she looked up at Reeve with uncertainty and curiosity, he knew without a shadow of a doubt that she remembered none of their time together. Not a single stolen glance or kiss.

She'd erased them completely.

Chapter 37

Maeve

The snow beneath her should have soaked her shins in a freezing grip. She should have been shivering, shaking. Her bones should have seized up, prevented her from breathing.

But she was warm. So warm.

Reeve's hold on her face remained, keeping her from collapsing completely, but he did not force her gaze up at him. His thumbs moved in slow, caressing motions across her cheeks.

But she hardly felt it. His presence before her was distant and fuzzy. Comprehending the overload of information she had just received was impossible, even for a Witch as clever and instinctual as Maeve. As Reeve's memories settled over her, as her mind verified them as real and as matching the ones she was now remembering, she concluded that she was, indeed, mad. Only a madwoman would have done this to herself more than once.

"How many times?" she asked, in a hushed voice meant only for Reeve, as if he had the answer. As if the answer could ever be in her grasp.

She searched her mind for any trace of her previous knowledge of her Shadow Magic. For any understanding of why her. There was nothing besides the argument she'd witnessed between her father and Reeve.

It was you who came to be terrified of her mother.

It was too heavy. All too much.

"Let go, please," she muttered.

A queasy sensation settled in her stomach, further blurring all thought. Reeve obeyed her request and dropped his hands from her face. She looked to her side until her eyes found Antony. She reached for him, and the black wolf stepped towards her, towering over her kneeled form. Maeve wrapped her arms around his thick neck once more, burying her head in his smooth fur.

Reeve stood from the snowy ground and turned to one of the wolves, one of many that had transformed into Humans again. It was a painful sight.

"You can't change freely, can you?" she mumbled into Antony's neck.

The sound was small, but it confirmed her words were true.

She wanted to judge him for giving up, for abandoning her and their family. But as her own repressed memories surfaced and showed her the agony Antony endured for so long, the half-life he lived, she couldn't find it within her to be so selfish.

His decision to choose the life that was best for him wasn't about her. And so she just held him tighter as his head tucked into hers in a comforting manner.

She allowed Antony entry into her mind. His voice was so much like their father's as he said, *I've missed you so much.*

She didn't pay much attention to the conversations that happened next. Even if she had wanted to soak in the plan that developed between Reeve and Antony's pack, she couldn't have. Her mind drifted through thoughts almost sleepily, and she was certain at one point she had drifted off against Antony's warm body.

Ambrose's voice drifted into her senses, as though he stood before her.

"Please, calm down, Maeve," he said lovingly from behind his desk.

"You told him to stay away from me, didn't you?" Her accusation came with an edge.

"What makes you think that?"

"Because there's only one loyalty I can think of that would keep the most powerful being alive away from me. And that's to you."

"There's so much you don't understand, my darling. We are in the middle of a war, and Reeve is—"

"Are we? Are we the ones dying? I believe the Humans are in the middle of a war, and the Double O has done nothing. You have done nothing."

"My Militia shields Human cities and homes every day, Maeve. Just because we move in the shadows doesn't mean we aren't moving. Give it twenty more years, and you, too, will understand Humans will wage war with or without Magicals' assistance. They are addicted to the notion, the instability, and the power it brings."

"What do Reeve or I have to do with any of that?"

"He is an Immortal ruler of a different realm. He is hundreds of years your senior, and you have obligations to another."

"I do not want to marry some boy I hardly know."

"And you want to marry Reeve? You don't know a damn thing about him."

"I didn't say I wanted to marry him. I only want the freedom to choose if I do or don't. The freedom to know him."

"Reeve is out of the question, regardless of who the Committee wants for you. He is not on the list. That's final. He will not be returning here."

"Then it was you!" she shouted. "You told him to keep away."

"And he listened," argued Ambrose. "Perhaps you overestimate his affection."

She *turned on her heel and stormed towards the door of his study.* *"That isn't fair, and you know it."*

With a flick of her wrist, his office door slammed shut behind her

—

Maeve's eyes popped open. She groaned immediately as she registered the aching pound in her head. She ran her hands across her face, forcing her body upright as silken covers pooled at her waist. Her chamber in the Celestian Palace was quiet, calm, and dark. What felt like late-night or early morning sky filtered through her tall windows.

"Hey," said a musical and delicate voice at her side.

Maeve turned. Next to her in the sheets was the greatest sight she'd seen in months. Zimsy sat up, no sleep prevalent on her face, as though she'd been awake for some time.

Maeve took in the sight of her, eyes scanning her with caution. Was she another memory? Another lie? She looked down at Zimsy's arms and fingers. No blood. No protruding bones. No broken skin. She glowed like she was meant to, perfectly pieced back together.

"Are you real?" asked Maeve, the pounding in her head persisting.

Zimsy nodded and opened her arms. It didn't take much effort for Maeve to fall into them. Their embrace was grounding, solid.

"You found me," said Zimsy, her voice strained as she tried to be strong.

Maeve gripped the back of her head. "I'm so sorry. I'm so, so sorry."

Zimsy held her tightly as they tried to stifle their tears. "Are you alright?"

Maeve shook her head. "No. I've ruined everything."

"No, you didn't, Maeve," said Zimsy, tears slipping down her cheeks and pooling along her jaw.

"You knew," said Maeve, guilt wrecking her voice. "You were the Sentinel for me when I last altered everything."

Zimsy hugged her tighter. "I was. And I didn't keep you from him like I should have. I hoped things could be changed."

It wasn't her fault.

They stayed that way until they'd sufficiently cried out their tears, and when Maeve pulled away and they wiped their cheeks with their palms, Zimsy said, "Let's go make some tea."

It was days before Maeve was ready to talk to Reeve. Even then, ready was a bold word for what she was, how she felt. She hated that she'd give anything to down a bottle, a whole cauldron full, of Astrea's potions and forget everything. All of it. She'd drown in the swirling liquid if she could.

But as her father had raised her under his own strength, she did not perish beneath the weight of her mistakes and the unfair hands she had been dealt. She persisted.

She tucked her legs beneath her by the blazing fire in Reeve's quarters, finding some comfort in the way the chair was soft beneath her, even though the conversation she was about to have would be anything but easy.

Snow clung to the windows as the first drops of Shadow's freezing reign reached Aterna. Reeve had already added barriers to the Celestian Palace to keep it warm. The open-air halls and rooms that once kissed her skin with sunlight fell dark. The soft sounds of the Black Deep no longer echoed through the palace as the lake stilled.

Maeve pulled the sleeves of her pajama robe down over her hands as Reeve threw on a shirt, concealing most of the Vexkari tattoos across his chest that called to her, asking for her touch. The hour was late when she had knocked on his door. He ran his fingers through his hair, exposing his undercut, a gesture that always had Maeve forgetting he was three hundred years old.

When he was seated on the other side of the fireplace, she realized his eyes were heavy with exhaustion. The thread of Magic between them hung with new weight.

The tension between them was thick, nauseatingly dense.

She shifted her knees in front of her in an attempt to shield how anxious she was. "I am going to ask you questions and you are going to answer them all without argument."

Reeve nodded.

"My mother was of Shadow Magic?" she asked finally, beginning her interrogation.

Reeve nodded. "She is why you are part Shadow."

"Why did you know? And why couldn't you tell me? Why have you known everything all along while I have been in the dark?"

"Because your parents wanted you to live a different life than your mother did. Free of the mental slavery that Shadow Magic can create. Free of the persecution you would have faced beneath the Orator's Office."

"That doesn't explain why you know."

"Your father was my best friend then. When your mother began struggling beneath the Magic she didn't understand, he asked for my help."

"And were you able to help her?"

Reeve looked at the fire. "No."

Maeve asked her next question carefully, acid turning deep in her core. "How did she die?"

"She shattered her own mind."

Maeve exhaled loudly, dipping her head back and closing her eyes. She remained there as more questions spilled from her.

"How old was I?"

"You were barely a week old."

"Where did they meet?"

"At Vaukore."

Maeve looked up at him, their eyes meeting like magnets snapping into place.

"And he loved her?"

Reeve smiled, softly. "Very much."

"What was her name?"

"Maeven."

Maeve couldn't smile, despite the sentiment of her given name.

Her own memories ran wild, forcing things to the forefront of her mind that felt like a past life reincarnated. Every quiet and quick moment she and Reeve shared. The way he kissed her with bruising force, like he wanted to consume her whole.

His tattooed hands, much larger than hers, as she hooked her fingers around his pinky alone. His grin, and those perfectly pointed canines the tip of his tongue loved to press against.

"It's all coming back to me," she blurted out, her voice small.

Reeve's reply came with brutal honesty as their eyes remained locked together. "I never forgot."

"Why didn't you tell me?" she asked breathily.

"Tell you? Tell you what?" he asked gently. "That in your heartbreak, you'd erased me completely? Or tell you I was the one who broke it? When I returned to Sinclair Estates, it had been two years, and you were already in love with another and remembered nothing of what you and I once were."

"We are not fated mates. The bond we share is the part of your Aterna Magic you placed in me in order to save my life."

"That is correct," he said.

She laughed softly, her shoulders dropping. "I told you that was all a ridiculous notion."

Reeve watched her closely, smiling as she began to relax. "Fated or not, I do not know," he continued. "I suppose it depends on how you view fate. The connection we share was a choice on my part to give you life. Just as those lines that run your body are traces of Malachite's Magic."

"Why is there no physical marking of your Magic on me?"

"It is only Dark Magic like Dread Magic that leaves traces, demands an exchange. Aterna Magic is pure. Given freely. It's small, but it's there. I can feel it. You can feel it. And it connects us in a way that differs from most spells."

"Small?" said Maeve with a shocked scoff. "It feels like it's bearing down on me."

"Small to me, then," he corrected, showing teeth now.

"Must be so hard holding that much power," she muttered. "Is that how Zimsy is alive? Do I owe you her life now, too?"

"No," said Reeve. "That little bit of Magic you gave her kept her alive."

If anything was fate, it was that. Fate that she had accidentally shifted some of her own Magic into Zimsy while breaking her Enslavement Curse.

Reeve's smile faded slightly as he contemplated their exchange. "I have never lied to you to wound you, Maeve. The Magic that held my tongue from presenting the truth led you to create the beliefs you had. I could not correct them. When you placed a hold on my tongue, just as your mother had before you, you no longer trusted me. The both of you ensured I could never share your secrets, and what you were, with you, or anyone else."

"But you speak freely now," she pressed.

"Because you realized the truth. It is no longer a secret between us nor anyone else you may tell."

"How were you able to use Shadow Magic if you are not of Shadow? How were you able to do what you did and erase you and your people from all our minds?"

"Because you manifested Shadow Magic into a spell. Your understanding of it, your comprehension, enabled it to be tangible Magic. It is not mere flattery when I tell you your ability to assimilate Magic, to dissect it and grasp it at its very core, is unprecedented."

"Not even Shadow could do such a thing?" she dared.

"Shadow is a leech. She can move into minds, and has a skill for taking them over, infiltrating and filling them with her desires, but she never altered reality like you. And I think that if she could, she would have by now."

Maeve shifted in her seat, rearranging her legs beneath her. "How will Mal react now that you have not obeyed? Now that Mordred hasn't killed my brother, as promised?"

"Easy," said Reeve. "You're going to make them both think I slaughtered them all, and that I delivered the white Alpha to Castle Morana myself."

Maeve's stomach turned, but she nodded, grateful to be of use at last.

"Mal may break through the spell, as he did before," she said.

"That's fine," said Reeve. "We just need to stall."

Maeve looked at the fire and wondered if the ornate fireplace had ever been used. Maybe during the first Shadow War? Did Shadow's cold domain make it to Aterna then as well?

"They are willing to fight with you, then?" she asked.

When Reeve didn't answer right away, she pulled her attention from the fire and back to him.

"They are," he answered. "But I didn't take you to Hiems to stoke a rebellion. I wanted you to find Antony. I wanted you to realize the truth. I wanted to be unburdened of the secrets that forced you not to trust me."

Honesty at last.

But she found no joy in his own relief.

Maeve didn't return the sentiment he displayed. She couldn't bring herself to smile or feel the weightlessness Reeve surely felt at the truth. She felt shackled by the truth.

Chapter 38

Maeve

To share even one singular quality, ability, or trait as the creature who possessed Mal's mind made Maeve sick. Physically sick. She knew it was time to get to work. She knew it was time to hone the gifts granted to her by Shadow Magic. But each time she tried, all she saw were long pale arms, with skin flapping off the bone, forcing Mal into submission.

And when she wasn't thinking about the state of mind and well-being of the man she'd sworn to protect, she was thinking, infuriatingly so, about Reeve.

Moments of soft laughter and hesitant touches in the darkened halls at Sinclair Estates.

Slowly remembering his hands, his lips—

She slammed the bottle of liquor down on the solid ground next to her, shattering it instantly. Her feet dangled off the edge of a high-sitting balcony at the topmost point of the Celestian Palace. The entire city of Crystalmore glowed effortlessly below her in the dark night.

Her fingers traced the railing above her, where she'd slid between a tiny arch to enjoy the Aternian Absenthine she'd stolen from Reeve's bar. She looked down at the broken bottle as liquid poured from it, coating the smooth surface beneath. It didn't matter. She had another.

She messily poured more of the numbing liquid into a small glass and groaned as Reeve appeared behind her.

"I did not invite you," she said without looking back at him.

She couldn't look at him. Not when every time their eyes met, she remembered something new. The memories weren't some foreign idea buried in the back of her head. When an image of Reeve lacing their fingers together with a wicked smile surfaced, she felt his warm hand on her own. When she watched him lick his bottom lip at her in her old home, her stomach actually flipped.

With a frustrated groan, she stood, holding her full glass in one hand and running her hand over her forehead with the other. She moved farther down the balcony in retreat.

"You're drunk," said Reeve plainly. "Very."

Maeve kept walking, ignoring him completely. He was in front of her in a mist of Magic before she could make a sharp remark about minding his own business.

He whisked the glass from her hand. "We're not doing *this*," he said, eyes on the glass.

"You said I could do whatever I wanted here—"

"I *said* we're not doing this," he repeated.

Maeve tried to snatch the glass of Aternian Absinthine back, but it vanished. She scowled up at him, prepared for a taunting remark. But his face was solemn.

She shook her head. "There is no we. You can't tell me what to do," said Maeve as she took a step towards him, wobbling slightly.

He didn't counter a step, but his eyes narrowed slightly. "Is that what you think?"

The warmth radiating from him was like nothing she'd ever felt. It seeped through his clothes, pulsating towards her. A welcome feeling after so long feeling cold. Carved out.

He stood to his full height, lording over her, forcing her neck to crane back to meet his stare. With their chests nearly pressed together, more memories flooded her system, and she had to admit they felt . . . good.

"It's not a punishment, Maeve. I want to help you," he said.

"I don't need your help," she said coolly.

A lie. A bold-faced lie.

"My mistake," he said, looking down at her.

He finally countered with a step towards her, catching her off guard, as she quickly attempted to step away. She lost her balance as one of his hands rolled gently off her chest, sending her backwards. His other hand swiftly cradled the back of her head before it collided with the crystal wall of the palace.

She sucked in tightly, and her breath halted in her throat at their contact. She was suddenly very aware that her skin was too dirty for his holy hands.

His hands moved to either side of her frame, blocking her in.

"Since you don't need my help, you can go stay elsewhere. I can recommend a lodging down on Svin Square. A rather shady part of the capital city, but they accept other forms of payment besides gold. Since you don't have access to any of your gold. And even if you did, they don't accept gold mined on Earth."

Maeve let out a laugh that didn't meet her eyes. "I suppose you expect me on my knees thanking you for your generosity in hosting me."

That damn smile blossomed across his face. "It would be an honor to see you on your knees, Maeve," purred Reeve.

A playful glimmer danced across his firelight eyes as his head cocked to the side.

Maeve wouldn't let herself think about those eyes.

"Move," she said.

"No."

"*Move.*"

"Make me."

Maeve rolled her eyes. She sighed and relaxed against the wall. Something shifted in Reeve's expression as her body softened. She closed her eyes for a moment and then looked up at the ornate ceiling overhanging the balcony. It was much like the painted ceilings at home. Plant life and fire-breathing creatures of lore decorated the landscape above. Swirling vines danced together in shades of green, intertwining much like the creatures.

She'd give anything to see the painted tapestries at Sinclair Estates. To push open those double doors and be greeted by soft-blue eyes.

"How do you do it?" she asked. "Why do you do it? Turn into one of them, I mean." She nodded up at the ceiling.

Reeve was silent for a moment, his arms still caging her in. Then, "You really want to know?"

"Mmhmm," she hummed.

Reeve's own eyes never left her until she returned her attention to him. His playful demeanor was gone, but his voice was calm.

"Then you're in luck. I am traveling to the very place I first transformed tomorrow."

Maeve's chest rose and fell. She squinted one eye as her vision of him blurred beneath the effects of alcohol. "And you'll take me with you?"

"I will on one condition," he answered, his brow raising.

"And what's that?"

"No complaining. Not about how heavy your body feels, or the pounding in your head, or how your body feels like someone rang it out like a rag—"

"I will be fine tomorrow," she argued, shifting on her feet.

A small chuckle vibrated in his throat. "You'll be hungover tomorrow," he corrected.

"You could fix that with a snap of your fingers," she said, tilting her chin up at him.

"But you don't need my help," he hummed. "Right?"

Maeve couldn't help the smile that pulled at her lips. She shook her head and looked away, her eyelids feeling heavy. Damn his charm.

He angled his head to the side, forcing her to meet his gaze once more. "No drinking yourself into nothing. That is not the path I intend to see you on."

The violet flames dancing along the walls rippled across his face, across the strong features that suited him as the warrior he was. One she knew didn't hide from the front lines in battle, and had very little interest in court affairs beyond protecting his home and his people.

Nothing quite so striking had ever shown her so much warmth. Mal had always been icy, cool, and refreshing. This was something begging, pleading, to be awakened in fire.

The darkness inside him lay a moment away, ready to snap to action at his call. The raw power of the Gods. A storm ready to be unleashed.

She wondered what his skin would feel like against hers. What her pale hands would look like against his tan cheeks. Would she at once feel shame and fear as their skin made contact? Would a hundred baths not be enough to erase the grime from her?

But still, even if it meant those things, she yearned to know what that scarred Vexkari felt like against her own. Her arm was heavy as she raised it boldly. Reeve didn't protest as she grazed her fingertips across his face.

He released a long breath that, had Maeve been sober, she would have caught.

His skin had truly been kissed by fire. It pulsed through her fingertips, down her arm, eventually spreading to her toes. She smiled. A small sound of shock escaped her lips at the feeling. Her smile faded as she spoke.

"I'm sorry."

The words came out, barely above a whisper, before she even realized she had said them. She didn't withdraw her fingers from his face.

Reeve's head tilted slowly, positioning his lips to her fingers, and pressed them against her soft skin. He watched her closely, ensuring that she remained relaxed despite his movements.

"Why are you sorry, Maeve?"

Honestly and vulnerability came quickly beneath her intoxicated state. "Because. . . everything I touch falls to ruin."

Another tender, slow kiss across her knuckles. . . his lips barely touching her skin.

His voice was smooth and dark. "I am still standing." Her fingers shook against his cheek. "I will stand by you until the end."

Maeve's arm grew weak and began to fall to her side. Too quick for her eyes to detect, Reeve grabbed her wrist. He held her gently, not with greedy force, and placed one last tender kiss on her fingertips, before lowering her arm smoothly to her side.

A long moment of silence passed.

"I won't drink anymore," she said.

"You can drink if you want, Maeve," said Reeve. "It's the lowering of your heart rate to a creeping pace I won't allow. If you want to drink, I need you to be responsible—"

She sighed hotly. "I don't want to drink. I hate feeling like this."

"I know you do," he said softly. Reeve pushed off the wall,

pulling away from her.

More honesty poured from her as she kept her gaze averted from his. "How am I going to master Shadow Magic when the only one like me alive wants me dead and is. . . possessing someone I love?"

If the admission wounded him, he did not show it.

"The same way you have overcome each and every obstacle this far."

She ran her hands across her face, her legs begging her to give them a break.

"Bed or bath?"

His question caught her off guard. Her cheeks flushed, and in her drunken state, she mistook his genuine question for another one of his flirtatious word games.

"I—" she stuttered. "With you?"

Reeve grinned and let out a low laugh.

"My, my. Your mind is in the gutter, it seems. But if you're offering—"

Maeve frowned as she pushed off the wall and made to shove him, quickly losing her footing as her head spun. A dark chuckle filled the air as she headed straight for the ground. Just before she planted face down, the smooth stone below wheeled out of view. Reeve held the back of her knees with one strong arm and her waist with the other. Warmth filled her bones once more, freely flowing. Pure white Magic rippled into her.

Maeve groaned as everything spiraled like she was trapped in a sphere.

"So which is it?" he asked as he carried her into the palace.

Maeve clamped her eyes shut, feeling a wave of nausea coming.

"Just take me to my chambers," she said weakly.

"Bet you'll never drink Aternian Absinthe again, will you, kitten?"

Maeve didn't answer. She draped her arm over her eyes and groaned.

It wasn't long before she felt the cool satin sheets of her bed. She didn't fight him as he set her down. She took a deep breath as her focus settled. Reeve stepped back, but Maeve's hand shot out towards him, gripping the hem of his shirt.

She shifted her knees beneath her on the edge of the bed and tugged him towards her. He yielded the step, but his hand moved slowly to her fingers and peeled them away from the fabric, holding them in his large hand. He caressed the tops of each knuckle. She looked up at him, her mouth parted and her eyes inviting.

He scanned her face for a moment and shook his head gently. "Not like this."

Maeve swallowed hard and tensed. The rejection slammed into her like a punch to the gut. She yanked her hand from his. Reeve's face was soft as he took her chin in his hand and held her firmly, forcing her gaze up at him.

"Do not misunderstand, Maeve. I want you to remember every little detail when I bed you."

His fingers pressed against her temple, and a warm night's breeze sent her to sleep.

Chapter 30

Maeve

Her morning was quiet. Reeve was not present in the dining hall, but there was a note by her breakfast spread that expressed she needed to be ready by noon for their journey. Upon reading his words and remembering his promise to take her with him, she realized the entire affair had certainly not been a dream or a hallucination.

She nursed the raging hangover that ached through her body, unaccustomed to such a feeling as her mind slipped into what might have been if he hadn't said no.

Immortals were different in every way. Their bodies were taller, their shoulders broader. They were physically stronger. Larger. If he could control his dragon shift—

She suddenly remembered all those books Lavinia had given her at Vaukore.

She scolded herself under her breath for thinking such unimportant thoughts.

But. . .

He had not rejected her, not totally.

"Are you hungover?" Zimsy's musical voice drew her away from her thoughts of Reeve. Thoughts that, if he could see, would have his head exploding with ego.

"Yes," said Maeve, not bothering to hide from Zimsy, not that she could.

Zimsy's eyes grew large.

"Zim, I've already been lectured. I don't need another one," said Maeve.

"I don't lecture you," she replied, stacking pancakes on her plate.

Maeve looked around, her brows pulling together. "Um. What?"

"There's a difference between telling you what I think you should do and lecturing you."

"No, there is not. The literal definition of lecture—"

"You really should eat your breakfast," said Zimsy casually, slicing her pancakes into triangles. "You need to regain your strength. The food here is so terrible, I don't know how you didn't starve."

While the food in Aterna wasn't as abysmal as Zimsy claimed, she was right about one thing: nothing compared to Zimsy's cooking. And so Maeve didn't argue. She ate her breakfast and met Reeve at the edge of the Black Deep, just outside the palace.

"You don't look nearly as bad as I was expecting."

Maeve frowned at Reeve. It didn't affect him. His hair was pulled back messily as he strode towards her. The under shave she, only hours ago, had visualized running her fingers across—

"Did you sleep well?" he asked wickedly.

She regretted ever taking a single sip of that vile drink she'd lifted from his stash.

"Where are we going?" she asked.

"The Dark Planet."

"That's where you first transformed? Why?"

Reeve lifted his hand, palm flat, and created a swirling Portal. "Patience," he said.

"Where's your sword?" she noted, slightly nervous at its absence on his hip.

"I won't need it today," he answered. "Well, I suppose I don't need it on any day, but I find it helps me control my Magic."

Maeve played absently with the band of the Dread Ring on her finger.

"Come," said Reeve, nodding towards the Portal. "We shouldn't keep them waiting." He stepped away from her, preparing to enter the Portal.

Maeve's brows pulled together. "Them?"

Reeve stopped and turned back towards her. He bent over, bringing his face to hers. "So distrusting today," he said, but there was no bite in his tone. "And here I thought we'd gotten past that. What with you practically dragging me into your bed last night and all."

Maeve's fingers shot out, lightning dancing across the tips. Reeve looked down at where the silent threat lingered, an arrogant grin on his face.

"I was drunk," she countered.

Reeve half rolled his eyes at her deflection and stood to his full height. He turned back towards the Portal and beckoned her over his shoulder. She trailed him through the swirling mass of color, where a faint blur of brown mixed in the center.

The atmosphere changed at once as she moved into a different realm. Though, courtesy of the bubble of soft warmth Reeve provided at all times, she didn't feel it. The Dark Planet was barren. It was a planet of rock and solid matter, long abandoned. But her mind shifted back to Reeve's words. Who would possibly be in this place?

Its desolate nature was why Zimsy was dumped there to die. The thought forced her to focus on her breathing.

The grey sky hung low, dipping into the thick fog all around them.

As the Portal closed behind her, Reeve spoke.

"I feel I should prepare you for what you are about to see." Reeve's eyes lifted to the sky, watching carefully, waiting for something. "Despite how much I enjoy hearing the affection in your voice when you refer to me as 'the last Dragon', I am not."

Lightning cracked across the grey sky in the distance, followed by a low rumble. Her eyes were drawn to it at once as she took a step closer to Reeve. The sky darkened further, and more bolts of bright golden lightning soared across the mountainscape.

"You're kidding," she breathed in awe.

A thundering clap, like a boulder cutting loose from the side of a cliff, slammed behind her. She whipped around as another shadow formed along the slope of the closest peak. She hadn't realized her fingers were wrapped around Reeve's forearm until he spoke.

"They won't hurt you, Maeve."

"Oh, I know," she said, a smile of anticipation at her lips. She hadn't grabbed him in fear. She had grabbed him in an expression of her awe. "I have lightning too."

Reeve chuckled and said lowly, "There's my girl."

The rumbling and light display grew closer and closer until the Earth beneath them rocked. Reeve's barrier, like an invisible shield around them at all times, kept them unimpacted. As rock and debris flew by them, not even a single hair on Maeve's head was blown out of place.

Steady, unhurried steps of a monster crept closer to them, casting them in complete darkness. Through the fog, a glimpse of shining and leathery gold became visible. The dense mist around them parted beneath a growling exhale.

"Reeve."

The voice was deep and booming with a menacing quality that made her question why Reeve didn't turn and run immediately. A few more earth-quaking steps and most of the creature's form was visible. Glittering, golden scales covered its massive form. It was larger than Reeve's dragon form, much larger. Its scales gleamed like polished metal.

The dragon held an air of grace as it twisted its humongous frame down towards the earth to level its slit-like eye with them.

"Demevirld," said Reeve.

More boulders slammed together all around them, circling them in.

Demevirld exhaled, shooting out more steam as his attention fixed on Maeve.

"A Sinclair," he said, his voice vibrating through her bones.

She loosed a breath of disbelief. A dragon stood before her. Ten dragons surrounded her. An impossible fact, yet her eyes, and the blood coursing through her, said otherwise.

"How do you know my name?" she asked politely.

"Your scent," he answered. "I have smelled it before." Demevirld inhaled loudly, a hum of approval vibrating in his giant neck. "You share blood with Alian Sinclair."

"You knew my Uncle?"

"Alian Sinclair was the last Magical to ever lay eyes on the Dragon. Before you."

Maeve stammered. "He. . ." Then she understood. "He said he killed the last of you. . . he lied to protect you."

Demevirld's head lowered. "The Sinclair boy brought to Earth the skull and skin of Varra, who died of old age when he was here."

"But why did he come here, if not to hunt you?"

"The Sinclair boy came here seeking knowledge. Knowledge of beastly afflictions." His eyes traveled to Reeve. "Like the one on your brother, Antony Sinclair. Like the one on the Aterna at your side."

A curse. Her father had told her, even back then: Reeve had been cursed. The Vexkari markings that traveled down his face made sense. He had been scarred by a curse.

"My Dragon form is not Aterna Magic, as I'm sure you're understanding. Nor is it part of the Magic I inherited from my father."

"No," said Demevirld. "I placed a curse on you, boy. And I placed it well, it seems. How many moons did it take you to control your rage?"

Reeve smiled. "Many." Reeve turned to Maeve.

Demevirld's snout raised. He sniffed deeply.

"That is why you cannot transform freely," said Maeve. "It was not a gift of power. It was a curse."

Reeve nodded. "If I wanted to be a man again, I had to learn to control my temper. My rage. After the Shadow War, after my father lost his mind, and Leandra died, I was so angry. More fury than one should know. I am ashamed of the beast I became. I just happened to come across Demevirld here on The Dark Planet, trying to escape the things that awaited me in Aterna. When I sought to take my fury out on him, he showed me just how pathetic I was."

"The lesson was necessary," said Demevirld. "Rage was consuming you."

Maeve looked up at Reeve. He looked upon the ancient and deadly creature with respect and admiration. Demevirld snarled and spoke directly to Maeve, pulling her attention back up at his magnificent size.

"You are of Shadow Magic," said Demevirld, and Maeve's stomach tightened in fear. "I thought my grandfather eradicated such a thing." The slits of his eyes narrowed and moved to Reeve. "You failed as well."

"I did," said Reeve. "Shadow lives."

"No," grumbled Demevirld. "You let the Sinclair with Shadow

Magic live."

Reeve hesitated. "I did."

"I advised you not to."

Reeve inhaled, long and slow, and then exhaled. "You did." He looked down at Maeve. "But look at her, Demevirld. Have you ever felt such Magic?"

A low growl built in Demevirld's throat, like fire swelling up. "It is a great source, a vessel like Human bodies have not seen, I would imagine. I sense no Dread Magic beyond what sits on its finger."

"She withdrew it all," said Reeve, his voice laced with pride.

Demevirld's pupils dilated. "Have you brought it here to defend your choices, Reeve?"

"No," answered Reeve with a laugh. "She got drunk and invited herself."

Maeve's mouth fell open. Reeve continued.

"I am here to ask you to help defend Aterna from Shadow and her Dreaded Dead army. If Aterna falls, Earth is next."

Demevirld snarled, the sound similar to a laugh. "Earth." He fell quiet for a moment, then the sound that erupted from him brought Maeve's hands straight over her ears. The shrill spikes, mixed with pulsing guttural booms of sound, danced across the mountains. When he quieted, a reply came from a nearby concealed shadowed creature. Then another. Demevirld continued to communicate with the other Dragon in their natural tongue. At last, he exhaled, the wake of it steamy and hot.

"We will consider your words."

Chapter 40

Maeve

"Why are you training with a blade?" asked Zimsy curiously as they walked to the Senshi Armory and arena.

"Because wielding one will grant me access to Aterna Magic."

Zimsy hummed.

"And since when do you watch me train?" asked Maeve with a knowing look.

Zimsy didn't look over at her. "We've been apart for some time," she said. "I thought you'd enjoy my company."

Maeve shook her head, fully aware it was not her company Zimsy sought. Eryx stood in clothes that were casual for an Immortal, similar to what Reeve wore on most days at the palace. It was rare she saw either of them in Aterna formal or in their armor.

It was clear Eryx's greeting was all for Zimsy. "Good morning," he said.

When Reeve told Maeve Eryx had offered to train her on a blade, Maeve had merely smiled.

"Making nice, then, I see," she had said.

Reeve had popped a single finger on her nose and said, "You be nice."

Until then, Maeve had been practicing siphoning the Magic in various swords and daggers, letting it flow through her and back out at her target. A target who, until then, had been a training simulation in the form of Reeve's Magic.

Eryx wrapped his hands in a long piece of linen as Maeve picked a small blade off the wall.

"Bigger," said Eryx. "I can't fight with something that small without shattering it."

Maeve's hand remained on the hilt of the sword she wanted. "Then control yourself and pull back. I don't do well with a larger blade. It throws off my balance."

Eryx didn't argue further. He picked a blade still more substantial than Maeve's, and they entered the Arena. Zimsy took a seat silently.

"Let's start slow," said Eryx. "I want to see how you move on your feet."

Maeve nodded as they took their positions opposite one another. Eryx gave her a quick nod and advanced. Maeve sidestepped him with ease, their blades not even making contact. She countered, raising her sword as he dodged her in return. Their pace quickened into a steady sound of metal on metal.

One particular shift, and Maeve's blade tapped against Eryx's shoulder.

She smiled. "What's got you so distracted?"

Eryx scowled, but Zimsy rocked forward in her seat and her lips curled into one another.

"How are you so arrogant?" he said, circling her. "Yet *again.*"

Maeve shrugged. "In my blood, I guess," she said coolly.

"Were you trained in the sword before?"

Maeve made a sound like that was partly true, then said, "I was quite good at fencing at Vaukore."

Eryx laughed. "And I took ballet in the Elven Lands."

Maeve's head cocked to one side as she surveyed him. "I bet you did."

Eryx's expression didn't change. "We'll see who is laughing soon enough."

Eryx advanced on her, done warming up. His moves were smooth and fluid, with the weaponry experience she lacked. The dance was similar to that of a duel with Magic, when she'd use only her hands, but the added weight and extension of her blade was still a challenge.

Just when she thought she'd settled into his rhythm, Eryx changed it. Again and again, ensuring she never had the upper hand. But adapting was a lesson in itself, she supposed. He changed quicker, knocking her off balance with a quick jab of his elbow. She tumbled to the stone, recovering quickly.

Maeve rolled as his blade slammed into the ground just where she had lain, flashing a spiraling color of violet light across the point of impact. She groaned, frustrated that he could Obscure and she could not. She scrambled to her feet and tossed the blade into her left hand, pointing two fingers at her side.

No lightning, Maeve.

Her mouth fell open as Reeve's voice shot across her mind. He was close. Not there watching, but she could feel he was close.

You're there to adapt to Aterna Magic, he continued. *Not to win.*

Maeve's fingers curled into a fist. *But then that means he wins.*

You could both win if you'd set aside your pride and take the lesson.

A small bit of warmth flickered through her, as if licking a wound.

Go away, she said, but there was no bite to it. *You're distracting me.*

Eryx laughed, charging towards her. "Trying to cheat?"

His exhilarated laughter continued, drawn from his love of a fight. Maeve's mind shifted to another sound.

Shadow and her wretched laugh. The way her fingers danced across Mal's chest without his consent. Without him being able to say no. Her fingers through his hair and her mouth moving in tandem with his—

A blow landed across her face, sending her sideways. The blade slipped from her hands as they instinctively moved to brace her falling body. But the landing never came. The smooth, crystal floor of the arena plummeted, sucking down into a thin line, and her line of sight shifted.

Vaukore.

The school was unmistakable.

Two students stood before her, their clothes ancient, a style she had never seen. On their breast pocket was a silver pin in the shape of two expanding, feathered wings. The boy was unfamiliar to her, but a nasty bruise was mid-healing across his face.

The girl was terrifyingly familiar.

Her long white hair cascaded down her back. Her pale skin was youthful, with a glow of adolescence. Her white lashes were long as she looked up at the boy before her. She was radiant.

"Stop it," she said as the boy stepped towards her, but there was longing on her face, not fear.

Maeve knew exactly where they were. The second floor, just outside a practice hall that was usually dominated by Combative Magic students.

"They'll take us away, Nevian," she whispered, her voice cracking. "We cannot touch."

"I don't care anymore, Judyth."

"I do," she hummed. "I can't carry your demise on my conscious."

"What does it matter? Haven't you heard?"

Shadow, then still just a girl named Judyth, shook her head.

Nevian laughed, a hollow and broken sound. He flicked the pin of feathered wings on her chest, "All the Shadows are being enlisted at dawn. Order of the Dread. We're done here."

Judyth's eyes liquified, glassing over. "No. No. They promised students would be safe from the war."

Nevian's hands moved towards her face, tentatively cupping her cheeks. "Please, Judyth," he begged. "We don't have much time left together."

"No," she argued once more, but didn't pull away from him. "They said we were accepted here to learn, to assimilate with a new society, a new world—"

Nevian hushed her gently. "We were allowed here to be trained," he said. "In chains. Like always. Coming here to perfect our Shadow Magic wasn't an act of graciousness by the Dread King. It was a lie."

The ground of the arena in Aterna made contact with Maeve's side, where bruises would surely form along her leg.

Eryx stood above her with a blade pointed at her forehead.

"Dead," he said plainly, but Maeve hardly heard him.

She pushed up, sitting on the smooth floor, her mind racing. She'd been in Shadow's mind, observing a memory from long ago. From a time when Shadow studied at Vaukore.

"I need to go," she said at once, pushing up and sprinting across the arena and into the palace.

Finding Reeve was easy. He appeared before her in just one

corner turn, his face a calm look of worry.

"What's got your heart so quick?"

"I know how I can perfect my Shadow Magic."

Reeve remained silent and waited for her to continue.

"If I can jump to her mind and view her time at Vaukore in her memories, then I can learn Shadow Magic from her classes and studies there."

Reeve fell silent. A long silence.

Maeve held her too-hot-to-drink-yet tea in one hand as Reeve came up with all the reasons why her plan was terrible.

"You entering her mind gives her direct access to target yours. Something she is not able to do right now."

Maeve didn't reply.

"If she finds out, she may attack us before we can attack her."

She blew on her tea.

"You don't even know that all the memories are there. What if they are unstable and you get trapped in her mind somehow?"

"I won't," she said.

"How do you know that?"

Maeve sighed gently. "Tell me another way to get this done?"

Reeve's mouth fell open, and he shook his head.

"There is no other way," she argued. "This is the way."

"No, it's not," said Reeve, disbelief in his voice. "You don't need to perfect it. You can perform it just fine right now."

Maeve frowned at him. "If I am to get inside her head, it will take more than some good-luck jumping."

"Then we scratch that plan—"

"No," she snapped, firmly this time.

His eyes bore into hers, a final silent plea to reconsider.

"I'm doing this," she concluded.

Arguing that Reeve not be there, watching her like a hawk, when she jumped into Shadow's mind and traversed her memories was futile, and so Maeve didn't protest.

Piecing together the world around Judyth and Nevian in her memories proved more difficult than observing her lessons at Vaukore. Though the familiar and nostalgic setting distracted Maeve often.

When she pulled herself from Shadow's memories, she grabbed her ink and quill at once, expelling her thoughts from the lesson.

"Any indication she can feel you in there?" asked Reeve.

"I don't think so," said Maeve. "I don't think even she recalls these memories because of how far back I am."

"It terrifies me when you go in there," admitted Reeve.

She looked up at him. "Because you think I'm going to become like her?" said Maeve, a little too much heat in her tone.

Reeve held her gaze. "I am not afraid of the darkness inside of you anymore, Maeve. I have seen you withstand its corruption."

Maeve looked back down at her notes, scribbling away as a burning confession slipped from her lips.

"That's why you left the first time, isn't it?" she asked softly. "Not because of my father. Because you were scared to care for someone like me."

Reeve moved, and the quill vanished from her hand, replaced by his own hand. He waited until she looked up at him to speak.

"Yes," he answered honestly.

"But you aren't anymore?" she challenged calmly, aware of the weight of her words.

He shook his head slowly, his voice as sure as a promise. "Not anymore."

She believed him. Her fingers moved beneath his, gliding across his palm. Reeve's chest swelled, and his grip tightened fractionally.

"So I can practice on you?" she said, deflecting from the very conversation she started, testing his conviction.

His response surprised her, and judging by the smirk on his face, he knew it would. His fingers brushed over her knuckles, and he withdrew his hand, placing the quill back in her grip. "Anytime."

It was clear Reeve wasn't expecting a confession from her and was content to continue their cat-and-mouse game. For that, she was grateful. Coming to terms with her desire for his protection and affection was entirely possible.

She just had to save Mal first.

She had to save Mal.

Chapter 41

Maeve

The capital city of Aterna was a marvel. Maeve had traveled all over Earth to cities like Paris and New York. They were nothing in comparison to Crystalmore, named for being like the light of dawn, which Maeve had resisted visiting since her arrival in Aterna. The metropolis was alive and warm, despite the winter at its doorstep.

Crystalmore didn't just house the people of Aterna. It was a diverse city of Elven people, Magicals boasting Dread Magic who were descended from those long ago, and even Humans. She questioned why such a place, where Magic roamed freely, had not been her home.

Why had the Sacred Seventeen, her father even, chosen a life in hiding on Earth?

As she watched the lives of strangers buying things, selling things, traveling, eating, and walking, she felt an understanding of Reeve's sacrifice. Kneeling before Shadow kept Crystalmore untouched.

For now.

She hated picturing the storefronts blown out, crawling with decay, the flower-lined pathway to the university nothing but rubble. Hundreds of thousands of lives uprooted, even destroyed completely.

It was a very possible future if she failed to save Mal.

If she didn't break Shadow's hold on his mind, there was no future at all.

She kept her hood up as she and Zimsy spent the morning in Crystalmore. It felt wrong to be shopping while across the Black Deep, Mal was drowning. Abraxas was. . .surviving. Each time her mind drifted back to her cousin, her stomach twisted. She wanted so badly to jump to him, to tell him everything would be fine, that she and Reeve had a plan.

But with his silver tongue, Maeve knew he wouldn't be able to lie to Mal, and so communicating with Abraxas was not an option.

And Maxius. Her regrets were multiple, but he fueled her determination to find the light at the other end of war. To have a future with her son.

The shame rolling in her belly for enjoying her time with Zimsy, doing frivolous things that made her happy, pulled tight and turned warm as she watched Zimsy enjoy sampling desserts from an Elven baker.

The resolution was coming no matter what she did, but it was not coming that day. And so she set aside her guilt and allowed herself to enjoy the day with her best friend.

When she returned to the Celestian Palace, she headed straight for Reeve. She hurried up the stairs of his wing, bags in hand, prepared to tell him just how amazed she was by the city.

She barreled through the open doors without invitation and halted when her eyes met his. They were warm and inviting, swirling with dark violet fire where he reclined in his chair, legs up on the table, and a drink of amber liquid in his large hand.

"Hello, Maeve," he hummed, his head tilting to the side.

"Zimsy and I went to the city," she replied, holding up her bags. "I found the loveliest tea shop off the main park square."

"Sereneteas?"

Maeve smiled softly. "Yes. They carry Earth brands. My favorite brand at that."

Reeve's smile grew. "I know."

"What are the chances? Isn't that so strange?"

Reeve crinkled his nose. "Not really."

Maeve's shoulders dropped as she understood the victorious look on his face. "You did that?"

Reeve didn't answer.

She pressed again, her voice soft. "You asked them to import Earl Grey?"

"Asked is a little demeaning, Maeve, I am their High Lord after all."

Maeve scoffed, a casual and appreciative laugh. "But you

couldn't possibly have known I would go to *that* tea shop."

"That is correct."

A silent moment fell between them as Maeve understood—

"You made sure every tea shop in the entire city, that massive city, carried Earl Grey?"

Reeve's smile faded, but his eyes remained glowing. "That seems like a waste of my time."

Maeve nodded. "Indeed." She swallowed hard.

The kindness of his action did not go unnoticed by her. The intimacy of it, of even knowing that was her favorite in the first place . . .

Reeve watched the forced breaths that rose and fell in her chest. His smile faded, dropping his triumphant expression into a hungry one. He raised his glass to his lips as he sipped the amber liquid, his eyes never leaving hers. "What else did you do?"

"I bought a book. And a dress."

"Tell me about them," he said.

Maeve crossed the room towards him, setting her velvet bags on the table carelessly. Reeve stood and stepped towards her in a gracefully fluid move.

She stopped. "The book is called *Crystalmore in Silk*. It's about fashion and style through different ages of Aterna." She knew she was rambling as he stepped closer to her. "The storekeeper recommended it to me based on my outfit."

"And the dress?" he asked.

Another step closer.

"It's blue," she replied, yielding a step towards him. "Though I don't have an occasion upon which to wear it."

He was just a step away now.

Reeve looked down at her. "I'm certain I can remedy that."

"You are the High Lord after all."

Reeve took the remaining step between them and brushed her hair behind her ear. Warm Magic flitted down her neck. She leaned into the sensation.

His fingers remained gently cupping her neck. "Have dinner with me tonight."

"I have dinner with you every night."

Reeve shook his head. "No. Not like that." His fingers brushed alongside her jaw. "Something special. I want to see you in that dress."

Maeve dared herself a fraction closer to him. "Dinner it is then."

They never ate in the formal great hall of the palace, and as Maeve stepped inside it, she couldn't understand why. The space was otherworldly, glowing with moonlight that had no source. The darkened night sky beyond the arches, where windows should be, created a stark visual.

Starlight refracted across the pale stone of the hall, moving as though she were traveling through space.

Reeve turned, standing in the middle of the hall, and faced her. He wore a dark suit with embroidered embellishments of silver fire. His hair was down, and his eyes were rimmed in the faintest smudge of black, almost indistinguishable from his lash line.

The sight of him was electrifying.

His eyes traveled down her body, taking his time as he watched her cross towards him. She glanced at the table behind him, already set with two chairs, one at each head of the table. She looked back up at Reeve.

"That," he said, "is your color."

"I know," she answered coolly.

Reeve's neck rolled, clearly invigorated by her confidence.

"Shall we?" he asked, gesturing to the table as starlight shifted in ease around them.

Maeve moved towards one of the chairs. He crossed behind, pulling it just slightly from the table, and extended his hand to her.

She took it without hesitation, with only the desire to feel their skin meet. He guided her closer, and as she sat, his lips touched down on the top of her hand.

From her seated position, his height should have been paralyzing. But the Immortal God was too busy tenderly kissing her skin with closed eyes to evoke any fear.

He flipped her hand over, touching his lips to her palm. Her palm, which was raised with a line of scars. Tainted with dark Magic where she had offered her blood countless times.

He kissed the scarring fully, opening his eyes to meet hers.

His hands remained holding hers in place as he withdrew his lips. He looked down the long table, where the only other seat was at the opposing head. With a snap of his fingers, the chair vanished and appeared at her side, Magically adjusting his plate setting and goblet as well.

"Shouldn't you be at the head and not me—" she started, gesturing to her own seat.

"I don't give a fuck," he said. "I just want to look at you."

Maeve bit the inside of her lip. His fingers brushed against hers as he let go of her hand at last and took his seat.

"Have you heard back from Demevirld?" she began.

Reeve poured them both sparkling water. "No," he said. "I have a request for this evening."

Maeve's brows raised. Reeve continued.

"No politics. No war. No remorse. Not tonight." He handed her one goblet and raised his own, until their rims touched midair. His eyes were heavy with steadfast, dark intensity. "Tonight, I want to fall in love with you again."

A positive charge shot through her. She smiled with a satisfied hum.

Maeve leaned towards him, their goblets still raised between them. "You already have."

Reeve grumbled a laugh, never breaking their eye contact. "If you think this is me being in love with you, you're in for a surprise."

"What's different than last time, then?" she challenged, enjoying every second of his eyes on her. "You buy me things. You can't keep your hands off me."

Reeve placed his goblet down, and his fingers wrapped around her wrist, tugging her closer to the edge of her seat. "You want to know what will be different this time, kitten?"

Maeve nodded in his hold.

"This time," he continued, bringing his free hand to hold her chin in his broad grasp, "will be very different. I need you to know that if we do this, you will be by my side until death. I will not give you up without a fight a second time. If redemption is what you seek for Malachite, then I can stand at your side. But if your goal is a life with him after this, you must tell me, and I will deny myself the dream." His thumb pressed into her bottom lip. "I'll repeat myself: If you become mine once more, I will not give you up a second time."

A reply caught in her throat. The answer was a betrayal she wasn't ready to voice.

Reeve's thumb bristled over her lip, swiping back and forth in a taunting movement. "This time," he said once more, "I want to cherish you boldly. Not in darkened corners or behind closed doors. I want to stand with you in the light." His hand slid up her face, sliding gently over her hair, ensuring not to mess it up. "I want to put a crown on your head."

The image, the thought, the words—*his* words had her nearly coming out of her seat and into his. He smiled, dark and devious, like he knew exactly that.

"This is dangerous," she said, her voice low and even. "You are dangerous."

Reeve nodded, accepting fully the truth of her words. "And that's why you like it, isn't it?" His eyes slid down to her lips. His thumb shifted, piercing the soft skin and causing a jolt to move through her. A sigh ran through him. "Such a pretty girl."

Before the confidence could leave her, she moved her mouth around his thumb, teeth barely pressing into his skin. He allowed her to hold him there.

"I bite," said Maeve lowly, her tongue flicking across the skin of his thumb.

Reeve nodded. "You'll beg, too."

Maeve's jaw loosened, and then she swallowed hard.

Satisfied, he pulled back, and she took a moment to compose herself. Food appeared before them, filling their places. Maeve knew at once it was Zimsy's cooking.

"Did you make Zimsy cook for us?" she asked.

"Firstly," he replied, "no one makes Zimsy do anything." He said it like he felt sorry for the soul who tried. Maeve held her chin proudly at the sentiment. "Secondly," continued Reeve, "she insisted."

"How did she even know?"

"She was in the kitchen baking when I went to speak to the chefs about it."

Maeve eyed him, uncertain if he was telling the truth. Either way, she was grateful it was Zimsy's cooking she was about to devour.

Chapter 42

Maeve

A square piece of parchment lay on top of Maeve's notes and writing on Shadow Magic. She read it with heavy breaths, exhausted from traversing Shadow's mind of her time at Vaukore, and then practicing her technique on Reeve. The lettering was unmistakably Abraxas', but the words read nothing like her cousin's hand.

"Earth," she said with a sigh. "The leader of the Magical Militia remaining on Earth has agreed to encourage the leaders of the Human world to stand down." She shook her head. "Not that it matters. Mal could take it all without a fight."

"From what I've gathered, 'leader' is a generous term. The Magical society and the militia on Earth are pure chaos."

She read over the words once more and shook her head. "Why doesn't he just use his Pathokenesis abilities and force the Magical Militia left on Earth to comply? I don't understand," she said bitterly and closed her eyes and sank further into her chair.

Reeve made a face between pity and agreement. "Do you remember how disruptive the bombs on Earth were to Magic?"

"Of course," said Maeve.

Reeve nodded. "I felt them here. In this very palace. Realms away. The pathways of energy and Magic transcend space and time."

"You think Earth's defenses stand a chance?"

Reeve shook his head. "No," he said. "I think their offense does."

Maeve remembered the impact of those atomic bombs, as they were called. She'd felt their power so deep in her core, her entire nervous system wanted to lie down and die.

"You fear Humans bringing their wars here," she said, understanding.

"I do," he admitted. "If they learned, or were given, the ability to

Portal. . .I fear Aterna would be the first to be conquered in the name of salvation. Ripped of all the power these lands offer a Human."

Maeve was silent a moment. "It sounds like you may fear them more than Shadow."

"Not more, just. . .differently."

"Shadow wants to conquer and absorb Dread Magic," said Maeve, her words feeling like dangerous unspoken territory. The pill was hard to swallow. "But. . .it was always Mal's desire to create a utopia under his Magic. It is his drive to rule all seven realms. She has merely corrupted his means of achieving said goal."

Reeve didn't answer, but she knew he agreed.

Spinel rubbed against Maeve impatiently, dissatisfied with her current position as she leaned against the altar where Maxius lay. Reeve stood in the doorway, watching her from across the hall. She didn't look up from her book, one hand petting Spinel absently in the late hour.

"How long are you going to just stand there?" she called, eyes still down.

"I wasn't sure you knew I was here," he replied.

"I can feel whenever you are near."

At last, she looked up from her book. He was dressed casually with a loose-fitting shirt that exposed a few of the black lines of Magic permanently marked across his tanned skin.

"I want to show you something," he said.

"I'm reading," she said.

"You've read that book before."

"The second read is always more enlightening than the first."

"Come on," he urged. "Or you'll miss it."

She chewed the inside of her cheek and caved, setting her book aside. She ran her fingers down the crystal casing holding Maxius and silently bid him goodnight. Each day, she wondered when it would be safe again for him.

When she reached Reeve, he offered her his hand. She slid her fingers over his, and before she could ask where they were going, he Obscured them. The dim crystal lights of the palace twisted and collapsed as they landed in darkness. Reeve's fingers remained holding hers.

The grass beneath their feet was dusted with a light snow, and the breeze was frigid. Only for a moment, of course, as Reeve ensured his invisible bubble expanded to cover her. He'd dropped them high in the Dark Peaks just above Crystalmore and the Celestian Palace. They were a soft dot of light down below them.

When she looked at Reeve, his eyes were up.

"The clouds have been blacking out the sky for weeks, but there's finally enough of a lull in the snowstorm."

Maeve followed his gaze to the starry night. Vivid constellations dotted across the canopy. With a wave of his hand, the snow beneath them cleared like a fresh blanket had been dropped. Reeve tugged her down gently, as they sat shoulder to shoulder.

He leaned back and placed his arms behind his head, suddenly looking younger.

"Do you know them?" he asked, looking up at the constellations.

Maeve looked away from him and back up at the sky. "Yes," was all she said.

They were different from Earth's, but she had learned them all the same.

A warm hand gently found the small of her back. She didn't look at Reeve as he gripped the fabric of her top ever so slightly and tugged her down to the ground beside him.

"What is that one?" he asked, pointing at a constellation, his voice casual.

"That one," said Maeve, scanning the sky to get her bearings, "That one is. . .wait."

"I thought you said you knew them," said Reeve with a chuckle.

"Shut up," said Maeve with a smile. "I do."

"Well, it seems like you would know Valahidi instantly. That's a major constellation."

Maeve turned her head towards him and raised a brow. "That is absolutely not a *major* constellation."

"It looks pretty big to me," he said, those firelight eyes swirled with mischief, and the corner of his mouth cocked up.

"If you knew it, why'd you ask?" said Maeve coolly, and she turned her gaze back towards the sky.

After a moment, Reeve asked, "Why haven't you pressed me about my Inheritor? Do you not wonder what will come of that?"

Maeve digested his words. Her eyes remained on the stars. "Must it happen?" she asked, her voice barely above a whisper.

Reeve's voice was cool and low. "It must."

Maeve chewed the inside of her lip. "When?"

"I don't know," said Reeve. "I didn't know when I would Inherit the power of Aterna until it was happening. Maybe, when I give up my life force, it will be the same."

She swallowed, feeling hollowed by the thought. "I don't want the Inheritance to happen," she said softly, too afraid to tell him what she really didn't want.

She blinked as a large, barely frozen snowflake slammed into her cheek. Followed quickly by more as the sky began to empty out above them. She waited for Reeve to shield them, but more snowflakes continued to assault her. Maeve wiped the melted water from her face and made to sit up.

"Absolutely not," said Reeve as he pushed up, rolling one leg over her and placing his left arm beside her face. He positioned his chest above her, blocking her escape.

Maeve's throat tightened as his body hovered inches from her own, suspended above her.

"It's just a little snow," purred Reeve. "There is no need to run."

Maeve's gaze moved down to his lips, and her own instincts betrayed her as she licked her bottom lip.

He hovered above her, watching every breath she took. He moved slowly, lowering his body into hers with careful control.

With one arm still at her side, his other hand glided up her arm, slowly dancing along her skin. His touch was sweetly and numbingly warm as always, washing a welcome calm over her. His touch made its way to her face, where the backs of his knuckles brushed along her cheek.

Reeve's face was relaxed, a portrait of ruggedly handsome ease. His eyes scanned her face as his thumb moved across her cheek.

"You're blocking the view," she said coolly, a small smirk tugging at her lips.

Reeve didn't smile. "My view is perfect."

Maeve's smile dropped, and her playfulness faded at the conviction in his voice.

Her eyes fluttered to a close as his warm lips touched down on her cheek. He moved tauntingly slow. His lips brushed down her jaw, dipping onto her neck. Maeve's hands gripped his arm as her breathing hitched loudly.

Reeve paused, his breath hot against her neck.

But Maeve didn't protest.

He took a deep breath and moved his lips to where her neck met her shoulder. And as his tongue licked across that soft place, she pushed her body up against his, and was unable to swallow the whimper that escaped her.

Reeve breathed deeply, the quiet rumble of a growl vibrated through her clothes and skin, and her very bones responded with shaking. She looked up at the stars as he kissed across her neck, the constellation he pointed to sparkling—

Maeve gasped and laughed as he tenderly bit a sweet spot on her neck. Reeve hummed in approval and pulled back, bringing their faces inches from one another.

He slowly traced his fingers down her arm. "How did I ever deny myself you?" His hand found her waist. "You aren't just perfection. You are the pursuit of it." His fingers moved beneath her shirt. Warm, broad fingers caressed the skin of her stomach on the other side of the light fabric. Reeve's eyes traced over her entire face before he spoke. "I try to give you time and space, but all I can see is you. I envision dying for you just to prove my worth. I see the rot of my grave giving birth to hydrangeas just to make you touch them."

"You have quite the worshipful imagination," said Maeve breathily, as her own hands moved up to his biceps.

"You have no idea," he groaned, as his forehead touched down on hers and their eyes closed in sync.

"If you deny me," he hummed, "I will understand."

Their noses brushed.

Maeve opened her eyes. "If thou dost seek to have what thou dost hide," she began, pulling a line from one of Shakespeare's sonnets, "by self-example mayst thou be denied."

She could feel and hear him smile at her declaration, at her acceptance. His fingers spread across her cheeks, and his mouth pressed into her own, lips already parted, encapsulating hers. Maeve moved in tandem with him, sliding her hands up his arms and into his hair. Victoriously, at last, her fingers felt the smooth undercut beneath his dark hair.

His kiss deepened, swallowing her as they shared breath. Her stomach tightened with need for more. More of his taste, more of his touch—

Ice scraped down her spine and flooded her lungs. Shooting shards of frozen knives slammed into each vertebra one by one. Her vision flashed white as she saw a swarming pile of Dreaded Dead, with brute weapons in their hands—weapons glowing green.

They gathered like an army. Like a horde of soldiers preparing for battle. A Portal, unmistakably at the southern territory of Aterna, spiraled open before the mass of reincarnated and necromanced dead.

They were moving to attack—

There are more important things happening than his lips, Little Viper.

Mal's voice shot across her mind like a backhand.

Chapter 43

Maeve

Maeve's hand moved across her throat. "Reeve," she started, wanting nothing more than to run from the reality she'd seen, to feel the warmth of his body on hers again.

It was soothing. It was solid.

It was safe.

Nothing like what was coming for them.

He hushed her soothingly. "What did you see?" he asked, his voice calm.

Maeve sat up slowly and steadied her breathing. "The southern cities."

"Are you certain?" his voice was low.

She nodded in earnest. "We have to go now."

Reeve nodded and extended his hand to her.

Maeve looked at it, the hand that moments ago was sending her further into the blissful ignorance she longed for. She knew if she took his hand, she'd be facing Shadow and more of her destruction.

But she took it, grasping hard, because the fight was hers.

In a fraction of a second, they were back at the Celestian Palace. Reeve placed his hands on her shoulders.

"Do you want to fight?"

"Of course I want to fight," she said, nearly insulted.

Reeve hesitated. "Do you feel ready to fight?" he asked, rephrasing his question.

"Readiness doesn't matter," she argued. "I will not stay here while you take all the glory."

His face relaxed, pride shifting into his previously worried eyes, and he looked like he wanted to kiss her again right there.

"Go to the armory, the Starsmith will meet you there," he said, dropping his hands, "then come and find me."

Maeve looked up at him, his face a perfect expression of preparedness. Like he was ready for the challenge, ready to finally let go.

Ready for war.

"What is it?" asked Maeve, looking down at the box.

"A gift from the High Lord," said the Starsmith.

Her name was Kaeren.

Maeve looked at her carefully for a moment before she removed the satin-wrapped lid. Pale-blue tissue covered what was beneath. Maeve delicately pulled back the wrappings. Her heart swelled.

A shining silver sword lay on bright sapphire velvet fabric. Its golden hilt was ornately carved with vines that resembled serpents. She ran her hands across the intricate carvings.

Her fingers moved up the blade. Something snapped inside her. Something that had been resting until that moment, something so instinctive she hadn't understood its absence until it crept up her spine.

Carved into the spine of the sword were words that caused her throat to tighten.

Usque ad Mortem, Sinclair.

She traced her fingers over the carvings, pride swelling deep in her stomach.

"How much did he place inside?" she asked quietly.

"More than any other weapon I have had the honor to forge, My lady," said Kaeren.

"My lady," repeated Maeve with a soft smile, unable to peel her eyes away from the blade thrumming with Reeve's power. "I am not your lady." She looked up at Kaeren, no bite or judgment in her tone.

"How soon can a horse be ready?"

"There is one ready for you," said Kaeren.

Maeve nodded. She gripped the hilt of the sword and pulled it from its box. It was lighter than she was expecting.

"Elven steel," said Kaeren, smiling. "Light as a feather and sharp as glass. Not much of it left in the world."

"How did you make this one?" she asked as she played with the blade, testing its movements.

Kaeren hesitated. "Forged from another sword."

Maeve stopped and looked at her. "Whose sword?"

Karen relented reluctantly. "The High Lord's."

"From Shadow-Slayer?" she asked in disbelief.

She nodded. "That is not all." She moved aside and gestured to a fully displayed set of armor. A sound of shock left Maeve's lips. It was beautiful, designed and made for a woman who valued her femininity in both its softness and its rage. The designs etched into the armor matched her new weapon. She smiled.

"The armor is similar to a Senshi's, similar to the High Lord's, plated in thin, flexible, crystalized Aterna Magic. Nearly indestructible."

"Nearly?" quipped Maeve.

"There are some exceptions," answered Kaeren, her voice hurried. "You just need to lay your hand on the jewel at the breast," she said, pointing to the centermost crystal of the armor.

Maeve reached out, her fingers barely bristling the smooth stone, and in a swirl of Magic, warm and inviting, she was transformed. The armor clung to her, perfectly fitted and lighter than a thin linen.

She made for the door of the armory and quickly addressed Kaeren. "You made all this? All the Aterna weapons and battle armor?"

Kaeren nodded proudly.

"Thank you," said Maeve.

Kaeren nodded again, following her into the open courtyard where Maeve's father's horse, Spitfire, was saddled and ready for her.

"May they keep you safe," said Kaeren, but Maeve barely heard her as gratitude swelled in her chest at the sight of Spitfire.

Maeve threw her leg over the dappled horse and muttered a greeting just for him. His mane was braided and woven with pale-blue ribbon. She rolled her eyes with a smile. Where did Reeve find the time to devote such attention to her?

Maeve took the reins. "Why are you called a Starsmith?"

Kaeren answered at once. "Because Aterna Magic was harvested from a star."

Maeve smiled softly. Of course it was. She straightened on Spitfire, withdrawing her hand from petting his neck.

Reeve, she called to him.

Magic swelled around her, tightening at her stomach.

Warmth spread into her bones. He was smiling, feeding off the electric energy her gifts of power gave her. She spoke to him again.

Bring me to you.

A Portal barreled open before her. Swirling violet fire and black stars grew and grew. She gently squeezed her legs together, and Spitfire stepped forward into the light.

Reeve and Eryx waited just on the other side, sitting atop their own horses. The late, cloudy sky provided little light across the snow-dusted valley below them. Small flecks of snow continued to fall from the sky.

Reeve looked her over, leaning forward casually on his saddle, triumph in his eyes. "Fits just like I hoped it would," he said.

"Your sword looks smaller, High Lord," said Maeve. "Peculiar."

Reeve shrugged. "It was over the top. Plus, I can't wait to tell Shadow I melted her blade and gave part of it to you."

Maeve looked over at him without a smile and spoke sincerely. "It's beautiful. Thank you."

His smirk faded, and he looked out over the calm valley. It wasn't the battle she was expecting to step into.

"Where are they?" asked Maeve.

"The Portal the Dreaded Dead are moving through is farther south. This is the southernmost village, and my lines of Magic are a ways from here for that purpose."

Maeve remembered breaking his old barrier, one that had existed for hundreds of years, and what that had done to her.

"What good are the barriers if they can just break them?" asked Maeve.

Reeve's head tilted to the side. His hand reached out and pinched her cheek. "Think of it as more of a light veil I lowered so a certain someone could get some sleep." He let go of her cheek. "Raising a full barrier wouldn't have pleased our Dread friends much, I don't imagine." Reeve smiled, his eyes on the horizon as a faint green glow appeared. "And I've quite enjoyed letting them think I was so easily broken."

Maeve followed his gaze, the Dread Ring on her finger alerting her to the incoming force. Her skin turned cold, each hair on her arms and neck rising.

All manner and matter of dark creatures in various stages of decay swarmed the valley below. An array of muted and cool greens, grey-blue, and white was their skin, their fur, their flesh, and their bones. They moved with haste in an unorganized manner. Maeve wondered if Eryx had experience in that sort of attack. So unplanned and uncivilized. A thousand mindless creatures barreling towards their men.

There was a distinct difference between these Dreaded Dead and the ones she'd faced previously. In the hand, or in some cases hands, of the creatures were savage weapons that glowed faintly green. It seemed Shadow had taken a page from Aterna's book as their weapons pulsed with Dread Magic.

She looked at Eryx as he scowled down at the creatures of the night.

"Filth," he spat. "Any day now, Reeve, they're getting dangerously close to the town below."

"Someone's pissy today," said Reeve playfully.

A prideful smile tugged at the corner of Eryx's mouth.

Reeve's arm swung wide, like he was welcoming the Dreaded Dead. A portal burst across the valley below them, like nothing she'd ever seen. It must have been a mile long. She watched the empty, swirling lights of the Portal, and then she smiled.

Antony stepped through the Portal, four massive black as night paws stalking across the patchy snow-covered ground. More wolves joined him, of all sizes and coloring, along the wide Portal, fanning out across the valley.

It was a beautiful sight, but Maeve's smile quickly faded. Despite the lethal ferocity of the wolves, they lacked a certain skill set required to kill a Dreaded Dead.

"How are they any match for the undead?" asked Maeve. "They must be burned or they'll regenerate."

Reeve's sharp smile was feral. "You can leave the burning to me. The shredding I'll leave to them."

Below them, Antony was already charging towards the line of Dreaded Dead, and the dozens of wolves behind him, still stepping through the Portal, also began to pick up speed. Eryx was already gone, barreling down the cliffside to claim his own quarry.

Maeve pulled on Spitfire's reins, readying herself to join them below, but Reeve's voice stopped her.

"The Aterna power in your blade yields fire. Use it well. I know you thirst for bloodshed, but keep your eye on your real battle. If Malachite appears, try to expel Shadow from his mind just like you've been studying to do."

Studying with no real practice. No hands-on training.

Reeve reached out and grabbed her chin, yanking her closer. His lips crashed into hers, and then vanished with a wet smacking sound.

"And hold onto that pretty new sword," he said with a grin, letting her chin go.

He Obscured away from her and dropped himself in the middle of the swarm. His massive horse reared back, kicking one of the Dreaded Dead so hard its head flew from its body. He drew Shadow Slayer, and the blade instantly ignited with violet flames. As the wolves tore through the Dreaded Dead at hyper speed, Reeve's sword set them ablaze.

A swirling mass of light caught her vision. A small Portal opened behind the continuous line of advancing Dreaded Dead. Two forms stepped through it: Roswyn and Mumford. More Portals opened up behind them, as more Bellator joined the line of Dreaded Dead.

Eryx's bellow of joy echoed across the valley, between sounds of bones ripping and shattering and rising plumes of smoke. He dismounted his horse, clearly eager for the combat. Roswyn and Mumford Obscured, sandwiching him at once.

Roswyn was too occupied with Eryx to see what charged towards him with raging intent.

Antony jumped, his massive frame turning sideways to knock into Roswyn. Roswyn pulled two fingers back, ready to strike as the air turned thick with static. Antony's side made brutal contact with Roswyn, but the bolt of lightning that expelled from him is what sent Roswyn flying.

His head hit the Earth, knocking the breath from him as remnants of lightning cracked across his body. He heaved, trying to upright himself in agony, but Antony's massive body stalked over him. Roswyn's eyes were impossibly large. His chest went limp as he fell back into the Earth.

He stared at Antony in realization, with much the same awe Maeve had. From the snarling behind his bared teeth, she thought for a moment Antony was going to kill him right there. His once friend. But he didn't. He stayed over him, both their bodies still in the chaos of battle.

A wail, the one a man utters as his last, sang from Mumford's lips as Eryx finished him. Eryx moved towards Antony and Roswyn, but with a single glance from the black wolf, Eryx knocked Roswyn unconscious, and they took him captive, alive and virtually unharmed. Antony rejoined the fight with barreling force as his teeth and claws shredded through Dreaded Dead after Dreaded Dead.

From the rising flames of burning corpses, the snow falling turned to black soot across the atmosphere. The Magic around her shifted.

A power signature entered the valley, one that triumphed over all the Dreaded Dead. The blackened veins running across her body darkened and hissed in welcome at Mal's arrival. The Morconis, slick black with tattered wings, flew down towards the earth with a screech, baring its razor-sharp teeth. Too many teeth. The creature slammed into the ground, revealing Mal atop it. It bent beneath him, crushing the ground and sending chunks of compacted earth spiraling.

Maeve squeezed her legs together and raced down towards him, swinging her sword with deadly aim at every Dreaded Dead she flew by. They burst apart beneath her power—beneath Reeve's power.

The Morconis shrieked a nausea-inducing sound, its eel-like neck snapping up a wolf in its jaws. Then another. Maeve recoiled at the sight, plunging her sword through the hollowed abdomen of a mindless corpse before her. The Dreaded Dead continued to swarm—there were simply too many.

No. There couldn't be. Not for Reeve. He could wipe them all out at once. So why hadn't he?

He was enjoying himself. She could feel it through their bond.

Mal's attention was not on Maeve, even as she hurled herself faster and faster towards him. A combination of swordplay and electric Magic destroyed each Dreaded Dead in her path. Mal's dead glare was on Reeve—Reeve, who kicked his horse back and smiled traitorously.

"What's the matter, Malachite?" said Reeve. "Why haven't the Senshi come alongside your Dreaded Dead?"

The darkness that flowed freely from Mal was stomach-churning. It was acidic. Unpleasant at best. Then Reeve's words struck her.

Why haven't the Senshi come?

The mile-long Portal Reeve had opened remained stretched across the valley, and from it filed the entire rank of Senshi Warriors. With their weapons pumped full of siphoned Aterna Magic, they immediately began destroying the undead creatures.

They were not under Shadow's control.

The Morconis gave another shriek, drawing Maeve's attention back to it as Spitfire raced towards it. Her eyes traveled up, but Mal no longer sat atop the great beast.

Her eyes snapped to Reeve, but it was too late.

Mal Obscured, appearing out of thin air, before her. Her heart sank. His body slammed into hers, knocking her sideways off Spitfire. Before they hit the ground, he Obscured them both.

The sound of battle vanished, replaced by complete silence aside from the chilling wind and the sound of soft moving water. The entire backside of her body hit cold, wet ground. She tried to turn, flip herself over, but Mal's frame above her locked her in place. His hand pressed against her throat, holding, not choking. Half-frozen, half-freezing water from the Black Deep pushed and pulled at her head, soaking her hair. She continued to squirm beneath him.

"Stop," he ordered, his voice colder than the ice clinging to her hair.

He was on the verge of breaking completely.

She fell still beneath his hold and allowed herself to look at him. His eyes, the whites, were a faded red. His skin was thin, exposing all the spots of deep purple muscle and blood vessels. His sharp cheekbones were hollowed further, getting dangerously close to starvation territory. His hair was oiled, dirty in a way he would never have allowed it to be.

Are you alright? Reeve voiced across her mind.

"You don't look so good, Mal," she whimpered, her voice filled with regret, not boastfulness, despite that such a thing meant breaking him from Shadow might be easier in this state.

She shivered, pushing down on the realization that it wasn't just the frozen ground that chilled her. His fingers were like ice against her throat. He stared down at her. Just stared.

Maeve, said Reeve.

"Strange," she whispered. "I can hardly feel your Dread Magic at all. Guess we both lost it, huh?"

Maeve, Reeve's voice snapped, dripping with fear at her lack of response.

"Why am I here, Mal?" she asked. "Why did you show me where the attack would be?"

His expression shifted at her words, like he debated between crushing her throat and bursting into tears.

"I don't know," he said at last, completely at war with himself.

"Let down your walls," she urged gently. "I want to see something."

Mal's fingers constricted fractionally, and his lips tightened, but her breathing hitched as he dropped his mental shields completely.

She remembered her teaching, drawing on the lessons she'd vicariously studied through Shadow's memory, and reached for the shackles that dug deep into his mind. The sharp chains of indestructible steel seeped out of his mind and into his nervous system. They clung to him like disease, and his body was far from immune. Each chain held more potency than the Enslavement Curse that had been on Zimsy, and Mal was covered in them.

At his center, his core, was his remaining Dread Magic, fluttering like the last of a flame desperate not to be extinguished.

Breaking Mal free. . . suddenly seemed impossible.

She pulled from his mind, letting her body sink fully into the frozen ground beneath her.

"Gods," she breathed, more to herself than him, "how am I going to do this? I don't stand a chance when she has taken so much of you —"

Her words were cut short by a flash of white light flooding her vision. The memory, Shadow's memory, appeared in an instant.

Judyth, as she was, then, stood with her long white hair gripped tightly in the hands of a masked individual. The memory was blurry and jumpy, but there were many masked men who appeared to be soldiers, part of a military of sorts. They wore deep emerald uniforms with a serpent crest on their breast pockets.

Judyth's neck, wrist, and ankles were bound in solid Elven steel, laced with all manner of stones meant to suppress her Magic. Judyth's face was wracked with horror as she watched the young man who was at her side in all of her memories of Vaukore, Nevian was his name, bleed out.

"Take a look, girl," said the man gripping Judyth's hair. "That's what happens when a filthy Shadow clings to the delusion they are stronger than the Dread."

His fingers tightened, drawing tears at the corners of her eyes, as his grip on her hair became unbearable. The soldier called out to the others as he heaved her to her feet. "Search the entire school," he ordered, "leave no Shadow filth alive. You'll know them by their silver wings pin." Jerking Judyth away from Nevian's dead body, he brought his lips to her ear. "All but you, of course. The Dread King is expecting you."

The memory shattered into darkness, propelling Maeve back to where she lay, still pinned beneath Mal. The memory had come and gone so quickly and had been so fragmented, she tried to recount it as accurately as possible.

"She has your eyes," blurted Mal, his expression vacant, his voice cold.

Maeve's heart raced faster.

"Those are your eyes, aren't they?" he continued. "I think about them all the time. They are the only part of her I think about." His fingers against her throat moved, dancing up her jaw with a hesitation Mal never had. "She never lets me think about you." His fingers moved back to her throat, and his other hand joined them. "Not even right now."

Magic pulsed in the Dread Ring on her finger in warning, sharpening her reflexes. As dirty and Dark Magic burst from his hands, her two fingers collided with his chest, sending a defensive blast of lightning through him at point-blank range. She twisted onto her knees and scrambled to her feet as her lightning knocked him backwards. She clutched her throat as her vision doubled, then tripled beneath the weight of his own attack.

At first, thinking it was a defect in her faltering vision, a great shadow cast over them, blocking what little moonlight drifted through the snow clouds. Mal's eyes shot up to the sky, his glowing green orbs filled with dissatisfaction.

Maeve looked over her shoulder as a great, black-and-amethyst dragon slammed into the earth with a snarl. Cracking the ground beneath it. Wind slammed into her, whipping her hair backwards. Her own heartbeat stilled at the sight of him. Glorious wings stretched across the open shore as he snarled, violet fire flared behind his teeth. Enormous black claws sunk into the ground as Reeve crawled towards her, his barbed tail snapping behind him.

He was almost to her—

A pinch of skin on her leg brought a gasp of surprise from her lips. A tingle that dripped through her spine. She looked down to her thigh, where the hilt of the Dread Dagger was buried. It sat splintered through her armor, perfectly centered on the top of her leg.

Her eyes lifted to Mal as the real pain began. His back was tall, his arm still extended from his throw.

Then ice, so cold it burned, set her skin ablaze.

"You shouldn't get so distracted in the middle of a duel," said Mal.

Maeve's arms disappeared from feeling, then her face, then her legs as she stumbled backwards. The only feeling remained deep in her stomach: sorrow. Cosmic night swirled behind her where Reeve's dragon form had once been. Warm tendrils of Magic wrapped her body, keeping her upright.

Reeve stepped forward from that black twister of night and grabbed her.

"I've got you," he whispered with one arm around her back, pulling her into his chest. Warm steel met her cheek as her head rolled against him. He never looked down at her. His eyes were set on Mal, but his words were directed at her. "Why the fuck didn't you answer me?" He was furious, rage and fear pulsed through him without control.

She fell more into that darkness, shivering in the burning cold, and Reeve's grip on her tightened as she became limp. Warmth slid through her body, caressing her skin. But it wasn't enough as the poisoned dagger seemed to sink deeper inside her.

"Look how she clings to you for dear life." Mal laughed, but he didn't smile. "You're welcome."

"You've lost this battle today," said Reeve, disregarding Mal's comments. "Run back to your Shadow master now and tell her the Dreaded Dead are ash, and the Senshi chose us."

Their voices faded in and out as Maeve fought for consciousness.

"There are more Dreaded Dead than you could possibly count," said Mal, a sneer developing on his sunken face. "How are the Senshi yours still?"

"You miscalculated," said Reeve. "Assumed. You traded me a sworn blood oath for free Magic."

"I felt the transfer. It's not possible you deceived me in such a way."

"You still don't get it, do you?" snapped Reeve, his breath quick and his furious temper still present. "I am a fucking God!"

Power rippled from him in all directions at lightning speed, shaking the earth. A barrier, like the line of Magic that had existed for centuries until recently, slammed up, spitting the ground between them and Mal. Even in her weakened and collapsing state, she felt the barrier rock across the Black Deep and into the Dark Peaks, once more separating the Dread Lands and Aterna.

Mal surveyed the wall of Magic, and then his eyes fell lazily to Reeve. Then, to the Dread Dagger buried in Maeve's thigh.

"Hmm," said Mal. "We'll see how that Godly power treats you once my Queen is fully restored."

Maeve's vision blackened, flickered, and Mal was gone.

"Reeve," she groaned.

An arm scooped behind her knees, and they Obscured. She'd barely felt the effects of transportation as Reeve stepped into a hall she'd only visited one time, when her body's temperature rose dangerously high. The smell of the lavender waters hit her nose, and hope swelled. She'd be in them soon, and she could remove the dagger and sink into the soft healing waters.

Without warning, she twisted in Reeve's arms and vomited. He continued towards the waters and called for one of the healers. He stepped them down into one of the pristine baths, carrying Maeve with him as the warm waters began to penetrate her armor, melting into her skin. He released her legs, letting them sink, and tapped the crystal jewel on her breastplate. Her armor vanished, and her clothes from earlier reappeared. The water clung to her skin now, but no relief came.

Reeve positioned himself behind her, holding her against his body with one hand as his other hand found her thigh, fingers wrapping around the hilt of the dagger.

"It hurts," whimpered Maeve as her whole body shook.

"I know," said Reeve, brushing his nose against her cheek. "I know, love."

Her stomach rolled. She'd vomit again at any moment.

Hands she didn't recognize, voices she didn't recognize moved before her, rippling the water around her.

"Gods, girl," said one. "You should be unconscious."

"Pull it out, High Lord," instructed another.

Reeve's hand braced across her front, tightened, then he ripped the Dread Dagger from her body smoothly. The pale waters turned crimson at once. Reeve tossed the dagger out of the waters. Its contact with the tiles of the hall echoed like a song.

"You're alright," said Reeve. "Healer Quintern works quickly. Don't you?"

Quintern looked up at her High Lord and nodded reverently.

Poison surged through her, sticky and heated but piercing like frozen needles. She groaned, wanting so badly to ask them all to please back away, that she felt like she'd vomit again at any moment.

Reeve's free hand moved to her cheek, tucking cold and clumped hair away from her face. He kissed her neck tenderly as the healer's hands moved over her thigh.

"The dagger," began Quintern. "It's laced with something."

Hope faded from Maeve as she realized she'd been a fool to think these waters or these hands could heal her. How could she forget what was inscribed on the dagger?

Forever wounded.

"No, no, no," managed Maeve.

"What?" said Reeve tensely. "What difference does that make?"

"It must heal naturally," Quintern said quietly. "I can stitch it up, High Lord, and stop the bleeding. But I cannot heal this. That is pure and ancient Dread Magic. It bends the laws of all other Magic."

Maeve let out a frustrated cry. Reeve gripped her tighter and nuzzled into her neck. She was drenched in sticky sweat, despite the moderate temperature of the ineffective waters and the remaining cold of her hair.

"Would you like to sleep, Maeve?"

She shook her head, terrified to fall into such darkness with such pain coursing through her, threatening death.

"Just through the night," he murmured into her neck. "I won't leave your side."

Promise, she said.

I promise, love.

Okay, she pressed into his mind, and then it was lights out.

Chapter 44

Maeve

Maeve was speaking, throwing out sentences before she even registered where she was or who she was addressing.

"Arianna and the twins—and—"

"They are all here now."

"Earth isn't safe for them now," she continued, "he'll find her."

"Your sister is here, Maeve. She is fine, as are your niece and nephew."

"Antony? Is he alright?" she asked quickly.

"Yes, he is. Back on Hiems."

"My grandmother? She's with Arianna?"

Reeve paused. "Maeve."

She met his eyes at last. His next words were delivered with grace.

"Agatha passed on Earth."

Another section of her insides began to chip away. Another hole that would need mending. Another goodbye forgotten. Denied. Maeve shook her head and swallowed painfully.

"Why?" she asked.

It was, of course, rhetorical, and she expected no answer from Reeve. She wasn't asking for the logical explanation of her ancient grandmother's natural death. She was asking why she had to suffer the loss of the closest thing to a mother in a time like this. She was asking why fate saw fit to deny her a chance to have one last tea.

Frustrated, she pushed up, sliding her back up the pillows, and warning signals fired off all across her body, each one narrowing down to a singular spot on her leg. Reeve's hands were on her instantly, wrapping her torso in careful strength. She let her body loosen as he aided her in sitting up against the headboard. His hands retreated, and he settled himself next to her.

They were alone in her chamber.

She pulled the thick velvet blankets to the side, exposing her bare leg. She pulled back the hem of the cream nightgown that brushed her thighs, exposing the bright red and black skin that peeked out from beneath thick stitchings, stitchings that almost glowed. The wound was swollen and raw, black at the center, with a red starburst shape surrounding it.

Maeve reeled, a wave of nausea crashed over her as shock splintered through her system.

Reeve reached for the decanter on the nightstand and began to pour her a glass of water. "Zimsy dressed you."

She didn't even care about that. She didn't care if all the healers saw her naked, and Reeve himself stared unashamed. She just wanted the pain gone. The Dread Dagger sat on her nightstand, gleaming and innocent with a clean tip. As though it wasn't the source of her agony.

"Your healers can't even numb the pain?" she asked weakly.

"They say nothing can subdue the effects of the dagger. It is darkness that is intended to hurt."

Maeve rested her head back. "That was far from the triumphant encounter I envisioned."

"It was your first."

Maeve raised her brows.

Reeve handed her the goblet of water. "You should never expect a victory during a first battle."

"This was not my first battle," said Maeve icily.

Reeve ignored her tone and remained casual. "Like this it was."

Maeve could feel her every heartbeat resonating from her thigh. Reeve watched her carefully.

"Drink, please," he said.

Maeve's eyes moved slowly back to him, and she sipped on the water. "I never imagined I'd be on the receiving end of such a weapon." She looked back down at her leg and sighed. "Yet another scar for me to bear. By the time this is over, my body will be nothing but flecks and lines of white flesh and black veins."

Reeve's eyes traveled down her neck and chest, where those darkened veins ran wild. "I don't see anything other than a warrior," he said softly. "One that has fought for her life, and for those she loves."

He took her hand in his, examining the bright-white scars across her palm from splitting it open again and again.

"A warrior does what they must in a moment's notice." He lowered his lips against the palm of her hand. "You have never been afraid to fight. That is what I see in your scars."

Maeve's eyes traveled to the thick white line across his own neck. The one she knew to be from an unsuccessful, but should have been fatal, blow from Shadow. She sipped the water once more.

"I saw something in Shadow's mind when I was with Mal," she began.

"Oh," said Reeve, "you mean when you weren't answering me?"

Maeve sighed, a sigh that took too much energy, and said, "I'm in pain, I don't want to be lectured like a child."

Reeve shook his head, no trace of his playful or flirtatious demeanor. "When I ask if you are alright, I expect an answer."

"I'm sorry," she said softly. "I didn't mean to scare you."

Reeve's hand lifted, his fingers brushing up her arm in a caressing motion. "Tell me what you saw."

"I saw her at Vaukore, like the other memories, but this was. . . different. There was an army of Magicals, Dread Magicals, that were there to kill all the students who possessed Shadow Magic. All except her. The soldier holding her captive said the king wanted her alive."

They sat in silence, mulling over Maeve's words. She looked away from him and put her attention back on her leg. She spoke first. "She had to watch the boy she loved die by order of the Dread King."

"Careful," said Reeve, "there's sympathy slipping into your tone."

"Not sympathy, Reeve," she argued. "Understanding. From what I've gathered, she went to Vaukore at a time when Shadow Magic wasn't permitted to be used freely. She and Nevian and the others were there with special permission to learn Shadow Magic. But, even in her memories of Vaukore, they weren't wholly welcomed. They ate in a different hall. They didn't sleep in the dorms like I did. I don't think they were there to study Magic. I think they were there to be studied." Maeve shifted her leg, groaning. "I've been so preoccupied shifting through her memories in classes and lessons, I never thought it would be helpful to. . . look at her life." She paused, her mind on the day she'd released Shadow onto Mal. "Why was it my blood that released her?"

"She was sealed with blood Magic of my own. Foolish Magic. The spell I placed sealed her away unless an offering of Shadow blood was made. I believed her to be the last of Shadow Magic, just as we all believed. Until I came face to face with it once more."

"When did you learn that I was of Shadow Magic?"

A sorrowful look overcame him. "When I met your mother," he said softly. "When she was carrying you."

Maeve stared down at the space between them.

"I prayed you'd never come to be," he continued. "And yet here you are," he smiled. "Defying my will with your mere existence wasn't enough, it seems. You had to become bonded to me and restart the very war I ended once already."

Maeve met his eyes. "Well, you did a terrible job ending it."

Reeve laughed lightly. "That I did." Then he asked, "Did you get into Malachite's mind?"

Maeve nodded gently. "A fortress. One it's unlikely I can break."

A long breath rose through Reeve.

"That doesn't mean I've given up," she continued.

A soft smile pulled at the corner of Reeve's lips. "You never do."

She found it impossible not to find comfort in his praise. Her mind traveled back over the battle.

"How is it the Senshi are still yours? You traded them."

"No," said Reeve. "I didn't."

"Yes, you did," she pressed. "I felt the transfer of Magic. I felt the Enslavement Curse move into your Magic's hold. I felt the Senshi Warriors move into his."

"What you felt," said Reeve gently, "was the same Magic that they have been under for over three hundred years. Which is my Magic, in their blades, their arrows. But their allegiance to me was never bound in Magic. It will never be bound in Magic. Not as it was before."

"Before?"

Reeve hesitated. "Before," he repeated, his words careful, like he was testing them, "the Senshi were under a sort of Enslavement Curse to my father, to Aterna's ruler before him, and the rest."

"Why did the Inheritor process begin?"

"I don't have a perfect answer," said Reeve, "just that thousands of years ago, the people of Aterna placed all their Magic in one ruler, chosen by the Gods to protect Aterna Magic. And each Inheritor that is picked is chosen by them as well. A god's power, handed down by the mercy of even greater Gods."

"And who is yours? When will they come and take you from me?" she asked, suddenly feeling groggy.

Reeve smiled, but Maeve's heart ached when it didn't meet his eyes. "No one's going to take me from you."

"So you'll leave me willingly? Because some other god decided your time was up?" she asked, her eyes heavy.

Reeve's hand cupped her face, his fingers sliding across the nape of her neck and through her hair. "Never willingly. Not again." His forehead pressed against hers. He sighed. "You need to rest and heal. Now is not the time for this conversation."

Maeve didn't argue, not because she didn't want to, but because her mouth wouldn't listen to her mind. Her body wouldn't obey her command to speak. Reeve shifted beside her, placing her head against him. As he pressed a kiss to her hair, sleep found her.

Chapter 45

Maeve

The Dread Dagger's infliction on Maeve's leg healed agonizingly slowly. With nothing but time on her hands, her mind was so unoccupied, all it could do was slowly draw up memories. Memories she'd long forgotten. Some of Antony, some of Reeve, Maxius when he was just a baby, and some of Mal.

She wondered, in the endless time she had, if Reeve had never rejected her, if she had never come to be at Mal's side, would she have freed Shadow? Would she have unleashed that evil upon Mal?

It was pointless to think such things. Because she couldn't imagine a life without Maxius. She wouldn't imagine such a thing. Prophecies and ancient laws of Magic be damned. She wouldn't take any more life from her son. She would see that his future was brighter than hers.

After all, wasn't that the duty of a parent? To plant seeds they may never get to cherish as flowers of their own?

She learned, as she had nothing but time in her mind, that Shadow's childhood was a barren garden. There were no flowers. No sunlight. If she'd had parents, Shadow herself didn't remember them.

The earliest memories she had were of steel chains wrapped around her adolescent body. Torture and pain. Torture for answers to questions a little girl named Judyth couldn't possibly have known.

From the time of her first memories, until she was in her early twenties, Judyth knew nothing but enslavement. She received no warmth, not even from her fellow prisoners of Shadow Magic. She was cursed, they said. Her pale skin, her bright-white lashes, and eyes were a bad omen.

When she arrived at Vaukore, to study and understand her Shadow Magic, the presence of those Dread Magicals around her grew. Maeve had never given much weight to her observations that Judyth soared ahead of her classmates, even those with Dread Magic. She mastered Shadow Magic in a way that had professors glancing nervously.

The Dread King is expecting you.

They picked her. The strongest.

Judyth became the then Dread King's favorite weapon. Her submission, beaten into her from birth, held strong as he used her ability to absorb another's Magic, to possess minds for his own reign.

Until the king's hold on her faltered, and trust filled the gap where chains once were. A grave mistake on his part. Judyth never forgot Nevian. She made certain that as she took the king's Dread Magic for herself, her hatred was known.

She'd go on to take the lives and Magic of all the royal Dread line.

Just as she was doing with Mal.

Attacks on Earth began, which meant that Reeve was intervening at all hours of the day and night, when Dreaded Dead slipped through realms, targeting only the Magicals that remained on Earth, the ones who had refused to come to The Dread Lands. He wasn't just killing Dreaded Dead. He was now taking the lives of her former comrades. Magical Militia, Bellator. Mal's soldiers.

Blood coated his armor and smeared across one cheek as he stood with a tight set jaw and tense shoulders in her darkened chamber. Maeve hadn't been sleeping. She never slept when he was gone.

She set aside her notes and writing on Judyth—no—on Shadow, and stood for him.

Adrenaline coursed through him. Maeve could feel it, like it always did after he fought. Like a cat, shifting its weight backwards, ready to pounce. Or the opening of a serpent's jaws as venom fills its fangs. Like the thick static in the air before thunder.

She walked towards him with hardly any limp in the pre-dawn morning, nearly fully healed. Her robe whispered softly against the floor behind her.

"You alright?" she asked.

He didn't exactly answer. "I've never had to fight like this. Even in the Shadow War, it was the Dreaded Dead who took my sword. Rarely, other men and women." He loosed a laugh. "I am ashamed that it makes me feel. . . unstoppable."

Maeve reached him, his tattooed hands finding her face at once. He looked over her, scrutinizing her with precision. The feral beast he had every ability to let gain control was in his eyes and the hard line of his mouth. It was in his loud and heavy breaths. He tilted her head to the side, his eyes shifting to her throat. To her pulse point.

His eyes blew wide, darkness casting out their swirling violet fire.

He lowered his mouth to it and licked, slowly, raking his tongue across her quickening pulse.

His nose brushed beneath her jaw, the ghost of his warm breath at the soft skin where her neck met her shoulder. His voice was needy, like a stifled groan. "I want you."

Without adjusting her head, his other hand trailed down her front, landing low on her stomach. A quick breath snapped out of her nose as his fingers danced along the band of her pajamas. She could feel the pressure building through him, still not satisfied despite expelling and exerting himself in battle.

"Gods, I want you," he murmured again, nuzzling further into her neck.

She slid her hands up his neck, ignoring the blood staining his front, and wrapped her fingers through his hair.

"Why do you wait?" she whispered. "What do you stall for?"

Reeve's breaths grew hungrier as he placed his forehead on her shoulder, his hold on her tightening. A small, anguished sound reverberated from him. "I don't even know anymore."

His control snapped. The cat pounced. The serpent's jaw snapped down, and thunder boomed. Reeve's mouth slammed into hers, already open and ready to feast. The power undulating from him was intoxicating, wrapped in the feeling that, as he said, he was unstoppable. That this unstoppable, feral god growled with desire for *her.* To be one with her in all the places their skin could meet. Electrifying flames rose in her chest, and she kissed him back, lifting onto the tips of her toes.

His plated armor vanished, leaving him shirtless with loose-fitting pants that hung low on his hips.

His hands dropped from her head as he bent, his lips and tongue dominating over hers, and gripped the back of her thighs. He hoisted her up as her legs spread and wrapped around him. She winced slightly from the soreness still lingering in the top of her thigh, but Reeve was too occupied with moving them to her bed to notice.

The lack of poise, the feral sound rumbling in his chest, and the way his hands slid to her ass had her melting into him. He licked and pulled at her bottom lip, his teeth breaking the skin, and then licking the wound. Again and again. Pain and then apology. Pain and then pleasure.

Her altitude changed as he dropped to the bed, his hands moving to her hips as gravity forced her down onto his hardened length. She rocked her hips instantly, and Reeve's grip tightened. She broke their kiss, panting, and pressed her hand to his muscled chest and pushed him back. His eyes were like molten lava, swirling in rich golden flecks of violet light. Her force wasn't necessary, as Reeve obliged and lay back onto the bedding. With fire still thrumming deep in her stomach, she remained straddling him, but bent down and licked across his front, her tongue sliding from the waistband of his pants, up his center, across each of his chiseled abdominal muscles.

The noise he made brought a smile instantly to her lips.

"It is dangerous to tease me," he said huskily.

"I have no intention of being a tease," she replied darkly.

He flipped her faster than she could blink, switching their positions. He shook his head with a wicked grin. His lips were nearly back on hers when Magic flew through both of them: an alert they shared. The Magic was Dread, belonging to two, but neither of the signatures were Mal's. It was close, on their side of the barrier, but it did not seek to hurt. The desperate Magic that had suddenly appeared was known to her. Unmistakable. Familiar.

Reeve's eyes were wide as they stared at one another in shock. Maeve's hands clasped over her mouth, and after a few more breaths, her body kicked into gear. They each fled the bed, Maeve running for the door, prepared to fly down the palace to their intruder.

Reeve silently snagged her wrist and pulled her close. He Obscured them just outside the palace. She took off from him at once, running towards the arches where large tiers of smooth crystal steps sank into the Black Deep. Drystan stood atop the stairs already, his bow drawn and his calm attack directed at their uninvited guest.

Eryx bolted into her periphery as she bounded past Drystan.

Water splashed around the unexpected visitor, the current lapping against the stone steps. But even in the shadowed early morning, that silver blond hair was unmistakable.

Abraxas kneeled, bloody and bruised.

Chapter 46

Maeve

Eryx took a step towards where Abraxas kneeled with bloodstained clothes. Drystan wouldn't fire unless ordered.

But Eryx. Maeve wasn't certain Eryx answered to Reeve fully. She anticipated his rash movements as he made to step towards Abraxas. Maeve moved to place herself between Eryx and Abraxas as Reeve's Magic flared, a silent command, and Eryx halted.

Maeve walked steadily to her cousin and kneeled in front of him. Water splashed at her feet, soaking her robe and pants and freezing her bare feet.

The blood was fresh and still dripping down his chin. She didn't hesitate to take his face in her hands. Blood squished between her fingers. Hot tears flowed down his cheeks.

"Brax," cried Maeve.

As her cousin inhaled sharply, his mouth parted enough for Maeve to see the bloody, mangled mess of his mutilated tongue. Abraxas had cut out his silver tongue, escaped, and somehow managed to make it to her. He straightened, revealing the second Magical signature she detected.

Lyrux was tucked securely in his arms, covered by his billowing black cloak.

The child was barely breathing.

Reeve was at her side a moment later, kneeling. Abraxas offered his only son to the High Lord of Aterna without hesitation. Her cousin collapsed into her arms. Reeve placed a hand on her shoulder, and the four of them were before several healers in their next breaths.

Juliet Rosethorn was dead.

Abraxas spoke little on it. Maeve didn't push him.

Lyrux lay sprawled against Abraxas, wrapped beneath both of his father's arms. The child, who now wore a small necklace filled with Reeve's Magic to help him heal, was afflicted with the same dark and deadly disease that began killing Magicals who occupied the Dread Lands three hundred years ago. Their presence there, as it now was for Magicals living in the Dread Lands, was a poison to themselves.

Refugees were taken into Aterna each day. The Barrier Reeve placed on the now frozen-solid Black Deep was a war zone. Citizens braved the Dreaded Dead that lingered beneath the ice, in the Greywood and the Dark Peaks, all for a chance to escape the toxic air forming over The Beryl City and the world Mal tried so hard to rebuild.

Abraxas' voice was soft with his healed and regenerated tongue, as he held Lyrux close and spoke without Magical restraint. She'd never seen her cousin so worn down, so utterly exhausted. His vibrant and sparkling eyes were dulled. Dimmer than felt appropriate for her vivacious cousin. Even his bright hair appeared wilted.

Like he, too, was having the life sucked from him.

Magic was dying beneath Shadow's reign once more.

"I remained at his side for as long as it was safe for Lyrux," he said, his eyes not on Maeve where they sat in two oversized chairs by the fire in her chamber. "I stayed by him as long as I could. . . I never wanted to leave him."

"I know," she replied softly.

Painful silence lingered between them. Silence had never been uncomfortable between Maeve and Abraxas. Now, after so long apart, Maeve had to force herself to ask him about his time at Mal's side these past few months. It had been weeks since she'd seen him, when he looked so broken.

"How is he?" she asked carefully. "When I saw him last. . . he was struggling."

Abraxas' eyes remained distant. "The decline in the past few weeks has been dramatic. Accelerated." His words were worse than a poisoned-tipped dagger penetrating her flesh and muscle. "He's dying."

Maeve looked away from him, her gaze shooting to her hands in her lap.

"And I stood by and watched as he was abused. Assaulted. As his body and mind were taken without his consent. Knowing if he had control of himself, if his own mental and bodily autonomy remained his, then she'd have been killed twenty times over."

Maeve's shoulders crumbled, and her hands covered her face as her chest tightened.

"I'm sorry, Maeve," said Abraxas, his own voice short of breaking. "I shouldn't have—"

Maeve stifled a sob and wiped the monsoon of tears pouring from her bottom lashes. "It's not your fault, Brax. It's all my fault."

"It's her fault, Maeve. No one's but hers."

When she continued to hide her face with her hands, Abraxas called her name softly. She looked up at her cousin, his own silent tears falling.

"No one is responsible for the evil she has committed. No one but her."

Maeve wiped her eyes roughly. "I have to get him out of there."

Abraxas fell silent. When he didn't immediately encourage her, Maeve locked eyes with him once more. His expression was apprehensive, hesitant even.

"You don't think I can?" she asked.

A swelling breath rose through him, and his hold on Lyrux tightened. "I just. . .don't want to lose you, too."

"Mal is not lost," she fired. "I can feel him in my very veins, Abraxas. I feel him in the ring on my finger. He is still fighting her possession. He has not given up. And so we cannot give up."

He nodded, his eyes on the Dread Ring, then on the darkened veins that dipped down her fingers.

"He lives within you," he muttered.

"If I don't do this, Brax. We lose him forever. And it doesn't end with him. Our children. . ."

She couldn't bear to finish the thought. Abraxas looked like he didn't want her to. His lips pressed down on Lyrux's head of silky blond hair.

"I'll help you in any way I can." The conviction in his voice was finally reminiscent of her Brax. "I want nothing more than to bring Shadow down."

Maeve didn't know what propelled her to Reeve's wing of the palace when she left her cousin to rest, only that she was desperate to see his eyes reassure her she wasn't going to break completely. She didn't care if it was stupid and shallow to seek comfort from him when she was crying over the loss of another man.

And to lose him in such a devastating way.

Even if it was for no other reason, no other purpose than for the sake of Mal's dignity—she would restore his honor.

The hallways and turns through the Celestian palace seemed longer than possible. The large arched doors to his wing barely inched closer as her heartbeat kicked faster and faster. Painting after painting blurred by. None of their vivid colors and purposeful brush strokes mattered to her when all else was lost.

But the way Reeve looked at her every day. The sword and the armor. Zimsy. Maxius. He loved that boy. She'd find him next to the crystals encasing him, reading to him or telling him stories. She couldn't get the image of his Dragon form stalking towards her out of her mind, that power. His kiss. His hands on her hips. He was otherworldly, and she was far from deserving such grace and protection.

The soft but strong way he spoke to her. His lighthearted humor and arrogance. His warm skin. . .

That is what kept her feet moving.

The double doors flew open before she was even upon them. Reeve stood waiting for her, his face calm, but with anguish glistening across his eyes.

Maeve didn't care that Eryx and Drystan stood behind him. She didn't care that she was interrupting their meeting. She didn't care that Eryx didn't trust her or Abraxas.

She didn't care what any of them thought.

She ran towards Reeve, faster now, propelling herself off the floor and into his outstretched arms. She threw her arms around him and buried her head into the crook of his neck and wept.

The sound slammed off the corridor walls, ringing out her sobs.

He pulled her tight against himself, his fingers dancing up and down her spine, until they found her hair. But not even such a familiar gesture could halt Maeve's sobs.

I have to talk to Mal, Reeve. I have to get him, I have to go get him—

His reply came quickly, his voice soothing. *I know.*

I know you'll say it's too dangerous, and I shouldn't go—

No, he replied. *I only ask that you let me help you.*

Maeve lifted her head to look at his face. He reached out and wiped the tear streaking down her flushed cheeks.

I am probably signing my death certificate, she said.

Then put my name beside yours, he replied. *It seems I am overdue.*

He shifted his hold on her, one strong arm sliding beneath her thighs as her chin rested against his shoulder. He walked them away from Eryx and Drystan, down the stairs and across the palace. They were silent until they reached the tall cathedral-like hall where Maxius lay.

Reeve set her down, and she wiped the residuals of tears from her hot cheeks. His attention was on Maxius with an expression that bordered on sorrow.

"It's likely you could convince me of nearly anything, Maeve,

Shadow Magic aside, and I would reason that I didn't have a choice," he began, his voice calm. "But with Maxius, I don't even need to be coerced. Deceived. I would do anything for him, and I would proudly acknowledge that I chose it. Whatever the cost. Whatever the downfall."

Reeve sighed, and as the thread of Magic between them grew heavy, she could feel that his incoming words weighed down on him like chains.

"I haven't been honest with you," he said, his eyes still on Maxius. "When I know that's all you've wanted from me this whole time, was my honesty at last."

"That wasn't your fault," she said, pushing down on the adrenaline wanting to surge and spike through her, feeling the incoming of something massive. "Magic held your tongue."

Reeve sighed and turned towards her. "I have one last confession to make. One final truth. Because without it, you will not rescue Mal."

Her stomach twisted at the torn conviction on his face. She shifted back, suddenly feeling out of place so close to him. No, no, no, he was going to say something that changed everything—

"You are my Inheritor."

The heat in Maeve's cheeks drained. She was certain she misheard him. Fear, cold and paralyzing, dripped down her spine at the insinuation, at the implications of his words.

She had misheard him. Surely.

Maeve listened to his heightened breathing. The High Lord, typically so relaxed and carefree, stood in front of her with a pained expression.

"No," she managed, a shake evident in her voice.

"You are going to Inherit the power of Aterna from me."

He said it like it was already decided! Like she didn't have a say. And nothing pissed Maeve Sinclair off more than being told what she was going to do.

Maeve shook her head. "I said no," she repeated, now fully in denial. She stepped away from him, giving him her back as she looked down at Maxius. She expelled a breathy laugh that was the beginning of hysteria. "No." She laughed harder, her head dipping back. "Absolutely not." Her tongue licked across her teeth, and she rounded back on him, her eyes narrowing. "How long have you known?"

So many steps forward ruined by another lie!

Regret dripped from his eyes, from his frown. "Since you stood behind me with those delicately deadly fingers at my throat on the day Malachite instructed me to bend the knee."

My, my. What a surprise, he had said that night.

Reeve continued. "I felt it surge through every bit of my Magic."

"But that means—"

"Yes," said Reeve. "You will consume my life force."

She shook her head. "How fucking dare you. How fucking dare you keep this from me and drop it on me like a bomb when I've finally chosen to accept that I want you! That I want to be yours!" She ran her hands violently over her face as an angry cry barreled from her throat.

Another deception.

"Why," she said, voice dripping with devastation covered up in fury, "why have you done any of this? What point was there if it was going to end? If I am to lose you now, too?"

Reeve didn't answer.

"Why?" pressed Maeve.

"You know why," he said quietly.

"To manipulate me into fighting on your side of the war?" asked Maeve, a dark quality seeping into her voice.

"Because I love you."

She was acutely aware that those words had never been directly said to her. Not in that order. Not in *that* way. Mal's love was evident in many ways, but never in the form of a burning confession.

She bit back the return of her own confession, one that would complement and complete his, truthful as the words were.

"Love? You've lied to me endlessly," said Maeve, her temper rising. "You lied to me from the moment we met— or re-met, you knew about our bond, you knew about my mother, you knew about my Shadow Magic, you knew about Antony, you knew I once loved you, and you knew about the fucking goblet!"

His voice was quiet. "I had no idea the goblet still held poisonous Magic. When it was poisoned—"

"When *you* poisoned it," she corrected him hotly.

Reeve nodded, accepting his part of the blame. "When I poisoned the liquid inside the goblet, I would never have guessed the goblet itself would retain that poison for hundreds of years. Poison, I'll remind you, that didn't work on its intended target."

"You once told me that Shadow Magic was deception. That to be near it was to lose sight of reality. That is what you are to me. I cannot see clearly around you! I cannot trust you."

"And I take responsibility for it."

"Shut up!"

Reeve did, his eyes never leaving hers.

"I won't do it," she said, her eyes burning. "I won't do it, and you can't make me." She sucked in sharply with jagged breaths. She shuddered a blubbering cry, her words broken and muddled. "I hate you. I fucking hate you. I hate that I love you."

Something cracked open in her chest. Her mouth fell open in a silent, airless cry.

Her knees gave way, and she let them. Reeve's arms braced her as she fell limply into him, and he lowered them to the floor. He cradled her head against him, his fingers firm but gentle.

"I can't do this," she cried, her voice raw, her fist finding his chest and curling into the fabric. "I hate you for this, and I won't do it! I can't, I can't beat her, I can't save him or you or Maxius—"

Reeve held her tighter and tucked his head atop hers. "Scream and cry and hate, but don't you dare start giving up. Not now." He stroked her hair tenderly and spoke with soft intensity. "You've only just been thrust into the fire, only just begun being forged. Now the warrior is made. Now is your greatest hour, Maeve Sinclair."

She raised her head, not caring that she was a complete mess. Reeve looked down at her, bringing a hand to her face.

"I love you," he said a second time. "I never stopped loving you. And even after you Inherit from me, I will still be with you in that Magic, our Magic, and you will feel all of my love forever. That is a promise."

The Inheritance was not stoppable. It was written in Magic: she would take his life-force.

"Why did I have to fall for you?" she cried.

Reeve as he stroked her hair, and smiled softly down at her. "Why is that such a bad thing?"

"Because," she replied. "What point is there?"

Reeve's hand stilled. "What point is there? Life is the point, Maeve. Living is the point."

"But everything—"

"Always comes to an end, yes," he spoke with intensity. "That is the even flow of our universe. What always was cannot always be, and what will be cannot have always been. But that doesn't mean you shouldn't live." His broad hand brushed across her face, his fingers moving smoothly across her skin once more."Gods, Maeve, you should *live*."

She threw her arms around his center and sobbed in his protective hold.

Chapter 47

Maeve

Maeve waited in Reeve's massive study, Zimsy now seated at her side, for Abraxas and Eryx to arrive, where Reeve would tell his best friends and closest allies that she was his Inheritor, and that they were moving forward with a potentially suicidal mission to retrieve Mal and evacuate the Dread Lands.

Reeve was across the room, pretending that he couldn't feel Maeve's Magic studying him like a book. Her mind was racing, calculating, determining. So many factors. So little time.

"He could have easily killed you that night," said Zimsy softly. "He could have won. And then had a new Inheritor in the cycle. One he could control, possibly."

"Yes, I had already deduced that myself," said Maeve.

"Then why are you so angry at his honesty?"

His honesty.

Maeve's fingers on her biceps tensed as she realized she was sitting in the armchair like a petulant child.

"I'm not angry, Zim. I'm furious."

How could she voice that her outrage wasn't even with Reeve's actions, despite how hateful her words to him had been only an hour ago? Her fury, as she said, was directed at these so-called Gods. It was directed at fate.

How many times would she lose those she loved? How many times would she prove her loyalty, be the strongest, rise to the occasion, and still have them be taken?

"You're angry that he let you come to terms with your trauma on your own time, helped you train and practice your Shadow Magic, and waited until you were emotionally stable to tell you that you were his Inheritor?"

"Do I look remotely emotionally stable to you?" snapped Maeve.

Zimsy crossed her legs gracefully as Abraxas entered across the room with Lyrux in his arms. "You look better than I can recall seeing you in quite some time," she said.

Maeve chewed on her fingernail. "For once, can't you just side with me instead of being rational?"

Zimsy let out a musical laugh. Maeve smiled behind her hand. It quickly faded as the acid in her stomach made itself known once more. They stood and crossed towards the table at the center of the room.

Lyrux's face lit up at them. He leaned excitedly towards Zimsy. She held out her arms instantly to accept him, but Abraxas hesitated, anxiety clear across his face. But as his eyes met Zimsy's, and she nodded serenely at him, her cousin released his son, and Zimsy held him close.

Drystan and Eryx entered shortly after, joining them at the table.

Reeve was the last to settle into his seat next to Maeve. She didn't look at him as he began speaking. "I'm not going to beat around the bush. You need to evacuate the Dread Lands, save as many as you can, and that includes Malachite."

Eryx laughed. She wanted to punch him.

Drystan spoke. "The Senshi are still aiding those who are fleeing, but if we can get to The Beryl City and start Portaling large amounts of people—"

"You can't Portal them," said Reeve. "They have to be brought over the barrier naturally."

"Why?" asked Drystan.

Abraxas answered, "Because the air in the Dread Lands is alive, toxic, and ready to strike. A Portal is too risky."

Drystan didn't argue. "So we have to get them across the Black Deep?"

Reeve nodded. Drystan nodded in return.

Eryx's voice was sharp as he said, "You put us all in danger by allowing Malachite on this side of the Barrier now. What point is there? He has fallen."

Maeve stared at the table, her jaw tight.

Fallen. The word was so heavy on her mind. Mal hadn't fallen. He'd been shoved.

"There is no one else who can bring Shadow down, Eryx," said Reeve. "Malachite is the chosen one."

"You can," he argued. "You have done it once before."

"I cannot, and clearly I did not," replied Reeve, dismissing him. "Maeve will go to Castle Morana," said Reeve, "and distract Shadow, and retrieve Malachite."

Eryx's voice grew sharp as he continued to argue. "You're truly going to bring him here, Reeve?"

"Maeve is," he said simply.

"And where will you be?" asked Eryx.

Reeve hesitated.

Then, he said it. "My Inheritor has been chosen. And it's time."

Eryx's face dropped. The room grew eerily still.

Rage coiled up and down Maeve's arm like a purring cat. Insistent and demanding attention.

It wasn't fair.

"It's Maeve, isn't it?" said Abraxas, without missing a beat.

Every head turned to him. His expression was concerned. Zimsy's eyes were massive. Eryx's jaw dropped, tension pulling up his shoulders. Drystan looked down.

"You really do know everything," replied Reeve, solidifying his statement.

Abraxas tipped his head at Reeve, but his worried expression quickly shifted to Maeve. But she wasn't looking at him. She remained staring at the wood grain with spiraling thoughts.

Magic whispered in her ear. . .things she'd seen but had never understood. Power she'd felt, but never acknowledged.

"You're lying," said Eryx.

"No, Eryx," said Reeve. "She will Inherit the power of Aterna. I can feel the Inheritance picking at my skin. It's near."

"You're just going to lie down and let it happen? When we are all on the brink of extinction?"

"Yes," said Reeve, as Maeve said, "No."

Eryx looked at Maeve at last, and then at Zimsy. He appeared to hold back his next words to Maeve, which were no doubt fueled by anger.

"Reeve," began Eryx, "You are blinded by the bond you share with her. You cannot see that she is not worthy to possess the power of the Gods. You cannot place the duty of protecting Aterna and its holy Magic with her."

Reeve's voice was sympathetic. "You don't understand. You think our personal feelings should stop the Inheritance? A power ordained from life we cannot even comprehend? My personal feelings did not stop it last time."

Eryx's face softened. "I know that," he reminded his friend gently.

Maeve's fingers drummed against the table, electric Magic trickling across her hands. Reeve continued, so infuriatingly at peace with his noble decision to give up his life for her. For Mal. For all life.

"For Maeve to stand a chance in a battle against Shadow, which will be required in order to release Mal's mind from Shadow's grip, she must have all available strength possible. I believe her Shadow Magic to be superior to Shadow's own, but the Dread Magic that Shadow has absorbed over centuries will dominate her when it comes to pure strength."

Eryx's eyes were slits. "So you die? And she lives."

"No," Maeve repeated, her gaze still down and distant.

Eryx scoffed at her. "You think you can just deny what the Gods will? And if you think I will stand by you as you seek to bring that monster here—"

"I will not abandon him," said Maeve plainly.

Eryx looked down at the table. And then at Reeve. "How many times will it take? How many times will she choose him before we're all dead? He chose his path, now let him—"

"Eryx," said Zimsy softly, speaking at last.

Maeve entered his mind before she thought better of it. She presented one single emotion and visual to him. There was not a particular memory of Mal's possession that she showed him, but more, she made sure he felt the weight of it all. That ultimately, it had been her arrogance and cowardice that unsealed Shadow. Not Mal's.

That his deterioration into the broken and lost form he now resided in was far from deserved.

She showed him in a blink, and when she pulled from his mind, his eyes were not full of fury. Eryx's eyes were glassy as he averted his gaze to his lap.

"Would you like to feel more? I can oblige. I just recently discovered that Shadow Magic is so much more than twisted memories. I can make you *feel* more, too, if you'd like."

"No," said Eryx, his voice clipped.

The hairs on his arms stood at attention as he met her gaze.

Maeve nodded. "It's not just about him. It is about getting the Magicals safely out of the Dread Lands before they are lost completely. Before Dread Magic is truly extinguished."

Having at last decided her course of action, she sighed loudly.

Her father had not raised her, and Mal had not brought her to power, just to be controlled.

She turned to Reeve.

"I have two things to say. The first is, fuck your Gods," she said, and the fire in her stomach ignited as Reeve began to grin. "And second, I am so sick of being cornered into choices," she said coolly.

Reeve smiled at her. All teeth and pride.

Her eyes flared with Magic, ruthless and reckless as she said. "So, I'm going to take control now."

She pulled the Dread Dagger from its concealment on her body and sliced across her palm, offering her blood in exchange for guidance. And oh, did it guide her.

Her left hand surged with Dread Magic, but not just any Dread Magic: Mal's Dread Magic. Every drop, every molecule of it buried within the Dread Ring was hers to command, hers to absorb. And she did. She took it all.

With it, she placed her hand on Reeve's arm, and Obscured, Dread Magic at her disposal at last. The floor fell from beneath them, and they twisted together, landing a moment later beneath the white trees of the temple that sat high in the Dark Peaks.

Sanctum. The highest point on the planet. Maeve had been to the temple before, when she'd begged Reeve to allow her to bring Mal to

Aterna. She'd been so angry at him for his denial, but she knew now it wouldn't have mattered.

Mal could only be saved by her. Not Magical waters or hands of healers. And saved was a generous term.

She wouldn't let him die alone.

The temple had not changed. Three pale trees, their bark nearly white, twisted together, their limbs becoming one. Save for the gentle sound of trickling water from the small flow of a clear stream that snaked its way beneath the trees, Sanctum was silent.

She gripped the fabric of his shirt and brought him close. And though the almighty Reeve of Aterna towered over her and easily overpowered her, he fell to his knees willingly. His hands found her hips, and his fierce heartbeat pounded in her ears. So loud.

The face of a man welcoming death evoked something intrinsic. What irony. To be so full of life, at the door of death.

"Maeve—" he began.

But his words were cut short. She wouldn't let him utter goodbyes when they were meaningless, when she had no intention of hearing final confessions of adoration. She was immortal now, just as he was.

And she would make sure he spent eternity telling her just how beloved she was.

Magic erupted from Maeve, mighty and paramount. Bright-white light radiated from the single finger she pressed into Reeve's chest. He barely had time to register his shock as his firelight eyes collapsed into darkness, and the spell took hold. His hands slid from her hips.

The blood still dripping from her palm aided her, nurturing and encouraging her Shadow Magic to its full potential as she drained Aterna Magic from Reeve. It was nothing like Dread or Shadow. It was pure, untainted, and holy. It filled her body. Then again. Then again. When she was certain she'd overflow with it, it continued to amplify, merging with her blood.

There was nothing painful about it. No scraping hands, or piercing fangs.

Just. . .warm Magic.

She tugged on her bond with Reeve, feeling for how much Aterna

Magic he still held. Soon, she'd stop and leave him with plenty.

When at last the scales tipped, and then tipped further, she severed the drain.

Reeve's eyes flooded with color, wide and locked with hers.

Divine violence.

That's what Maeve felt with the god's power running through her. Remade and forged of something completely and effortlessly bound to her. It sat at the ready. No bargain or price need be paid. It sat sweetly beneath her skin, ready to be commanded.

She brushed her fingers beneath his chin, feeling his racing pulse.

"Are you alright?" she asked.

Reeve's mouth fell open. She couldn't recall ever having seen pure shock on the High Lord of Aterna.

"Am I alri—" stammered Reeve. "Are you?" he asked incredulously.

She beamed. "I am a star reborn," said Maeve, as she took his face in her hands.

It wasn't a far distance to close, even on his knees, and he was ready for her as she pressed her lips to his. The kiss was delicate, cherished. He smiled at her as she pulled away.

"How did you do that?"

She held up her palm, the fresh wound raw and red. "You need only ask and offer, Dark Magic does the rest."

Maeve sighed, rolling her spine as new and undefeatable energy ran through her. She laughed, high on the feeling of what they now shared.

"This temple is stained with Magic. And I could feel it the first time I came here."

"How did you know what to do?" asked Reeve, his hands back on her hips.

"Those traces want to be seen, felt again. This is the very temple where Shadow stole many's Dread power. I saw that too."

Reeve nodded, grinning like an unhinged maniac. "Clever girl."

"And I saw where the Inheritance forced you to accept your fathers's power." Reeve's smile faltered. "My father, the story you told him was a lie. You did not take the power of Aterna. You do not have the power to absorb Magic. Why did you lie?"

Reeve pulled her impossibly closer and rested his chin beneath her collarbones. "Because I was crowned in an era of chaos. There was no peace. My father had long lost his mind. I lied, so that no one doubted the lengths I was willing to go to for my people. So that Aterna might enter an era of harmony."

"What will the Gods think now that I have defied their will?" she asked, though little of her tone suggested she cared.

Reeve's smile returned. "Defied?" he laughed. "No, kitten, I don't think so. This was destiny. I think you were chosen for this very reason, defiance and all."

PART THREE

Chapter 48

Reeve

She'd Inherited the power of Aterna roughly six hours ago. She'd been gone for five-and-a-half of them. And for Reeve, that was five-and-a-half hours too long.

"There's something I have to go do," said Maeve. "Alone."

Reeve's eyes narrowed. "Why alone?"

"Because this is mine to do."

Reeve opened his mouth to speak, but Maeve placed a finger over his lips. "What did we agree upon? No coddling."

Reeve nipped at her finger as firelight shimmered across his eyes.

He drummed his fingers impatiently on the table, recalling their rushed conversation, the glass of amber liquid beside him a failed distraction. Eryx napped on one of the sofas across the room. The poor man barely slept through the night now, too afraid of letting his guard down completely.

Still, Reeve could search their bond, the deep Magic connecting them, and know she was alive. He knew she was safe, but weakened at the moment. Completely depleted of her new Magic, and resting while it replenished. Reeve shook his head and cursed under his breath. She had done something astronomical to be that wounded. It might take another week just for her to regain her full strength. And what Magic could possibly be worth that risk when Shadow could strike at any moment in full force? When Maeve had been so adamant that getting Mal out of Castle Morana as soon as possible was her number one priority?

What could possibly trump her vow to save him?

She hadn't told him where she was going, and he hadn't pressed her.

Eryx let out a soft snore, startling himself, and bolted up.

She was far. Too far. He told himself that if she didn't return in the next twenty minutes, he'd tug so hard on the string of Magic connecting them that he'd be ripped through time and space to get to her.

His gaze traveled out the windows, where the last remaining ray of sunlight managed to break through the dark and snowy clouds. Once it set completely, it would not rise again. Of that, Reeve was certain.

Eryx stretched and sat up, assuming a relaxed position. "Still gone?"

Reeve nodded.

"What if—"

"I dare you to finish that sentence," said Reeve lowly.

"It's a possibility that needs to be addressed."

Reeve leaned back, casually letting his arms rest on the sides of the chair. "You doubt me now?"

Eryx straightened and grimaced. "No."

"Could have fooled me."

"I doubt her. As I always have."

Her Magic shifted—his spine straightened. She changed realms, jumping to another.

Reeve shook his head in a brotherly way. "You're going to have to get over that."

Eryx sighed. "I know. She means so much to Zimsy."

Reeve's head cocked to one side. "I was referring to me."

Eryx stretched his arms out and crossed one leg over the other. His head bobbed back, adjusting his gaze to the ceiling. "You're set on her, then?"

Reeve smiled to himself. "Quite."

Eryx looked back at him. "And if she isn't?" he dared.

Reeve's eyes moved smoothly to his second in command. "If she isn't what?" he pushed back.

"If she isn't, as you've said, 'quite set' on you."

Reeve inhaled deeply, picturing it almost adoringly: her futile attempt to get away from him. Her resistance. It made him hungry for her.

He grinned. "She is."

A sharp tug on his bond with Maeve brought a deep inhale through his nose.

"Despite the fact that she still aims to honor him?"

Eryx's question hung heavy in the air between them as Reeve stood, feeling her Portal opening just outside the walls of the palace and prepared to go and see what could have been so personal to her he'd been excluded.

"One day you will understand," said Reeve. "Her loyalty isn't to be feared. It's her greatest strength."

He didn't wait for another reply, and moments later, he watched as Maeve moved through the swirling illumination of the Portal. She was still drained of her Aterna Magic, but it was quickly replenishing.

"Where have you been?" asked Reeve, a fake tone of disapproval in his voice.

"Oh, nowhere," said Maeve, tucking her hands behind her back and smiling coolly. "Just using the power of Aterna in ways you couldn't."

Reeve's playful expression fell, as she hadn't returned alone.

Through the blinding Portal stepped Antony Sinclair, looking like his father.

Reeve's chest tightened at the resemblance.

He was the spitting image of Ambrose Sinclair twenty years ago. No longer confined to his wolf form, he stood tall with a keen look of settled confidence in his bright-blue eyes. The same look all Ambrose Sinclair's children wore.

Reeve smiled. "Well, well, would you look at that."

Antony stood abreast of Maeve and dipped his head at Reeve.

"Hello, Reeve."

He cocked his head at Maeve. "I'd ask how, but I already know the answer."

Maeve smirked. "I'd like to hear you say it anyway."

Reeve's eyes narrowed playfully. "No need to continue to over-inflate that ego."

Another stepped through the Portal behind them, a familiar face he'd shared many a drink with, one whose presence next to Antony wasn't surprising at all.

Alphard Mavros stepped forward and addressed Reeve at once. "How could you have let her take all that power? She'll be truly insufferable now."

Maeve's eyes slid to him, a friendly warning that harbored no real threat. He flicked his brows back at her.

He turned back towards the Portal and held out his hand. A third figure entered, holding a small baby in her arms. Her bright-red hair stood vibrant against the cool-toned crystal palace.

The Portal cycloned to a close behind her.

"Hello, Alphard," said Reeve, grateful to see the man in solid condition. "And I suppose congratulations are in order," he said, addressing Victoria Damario and the infant in her arms.

Reeve stepped forward and offered his arm to Antony. As their hands joined and the forearms pressed against one another's, Reeve could feel just what his kitten had done. She hadn't merely altered Antony's Magic—the Magic that bound him to his wolf form—she had transfigured it. Now, Antony could move freely between his forms.

He shook his head in proud disbelief and let go of their embrace.

"How's two legs feel?" asked Reeve.

Antony laughed softly. The sound was Ambrose through and through. "Bit weird," he admitted.

Maeve watched them with casual triumph.

Antony tossed his head towards her. "This one just can't ever let things be, you know?" There was no bite to his tone.

Reeve's eyes widened. "Trust me. I do know."

Maeve rolled her eyes, never dropping her smile. "All of you quit complaining."

Another blissful moment passed between them. And while Reeve was certain Antony would want to see his other sister soon enough, he didn't hesitate to answer when Antony asked where Roswyn was being kept. Alphard's face dropped at the mention of his name.

Antony looked at Maeve. "I'll be back."

She nodded, and Alphard followed Antony at once.

Victoria's eyes met Maeve's as Zimsy appeared. Maeve sighed with relief at her appearance.

"Goodness," said Zimsy. "Look at this angel."

Victoria smiled at Zimsy, her chest heaving a sigh. "You look. . .well, Zimsy," offered Victoria.

"As do you and your precious child," said Zimsy, stepping closer and placing her arms beneath Victoria's. "May I?"

"Of course," she said at once.

As she transferred the swaddled infant into Zimsy's arms, she looked up at Maeve with gratitude in her eyes that Maeve wanted none of. Victoria's lips parted, but Zimsy saved her once again.

"Let's find you a room, Victoria," said Zimsy. "Little Lyrux will be so thrilled to meet this young babe as well."

Zimsy escorted her farther into the palace, leaving Maeve and Reeve alone.

"How are you feeling?" she asked, looking up at him.

Reeve stepped closer to her and disregarded her question.

"From now on, you tell me when you are planning to do something so reckless as draining yourself within an inch of your life. When you are putting yourself in such danger willingly, I want to be aware. I will never coddle you, and I will never control the choices you make where your Magic is concerned. But I want to be able to help you should you need it. You do not have to hide from me. What you did for your brother. . .even I couldn't achieve."

"I know," she said with a smile.

"Oh, Maeve," he replied. "You shouldn't boast. It's so unbecoming of a lady—"

He managed a laugh from her.

Chapter 49

Maeve

The evening sky dropped blankets of snow, but the endless snapping fire in Reeve's lounge provided warmth enough for them all. It was immortal itself. Maeve retreated from her siblings, Zimsy, Abraxas, and the little ones who couldn't stop asking their new Uncle Antony questions.

Antony didn't look bothered in the slightest as he told them stories of the grandfather they'd never meet. Alphard smiled, interjecting his own details here and there.

Maeve grabbed a quick bite from the table of food, satiating Zimsy's constant encouragement for her to please eat something. She wasn't sure she needed to eat anymore. She hadn't been hungry once since she'd taken the power of Aterna. But she popped a grape in her mouth nonetheless.

"I don't get you," said Eryx, appearing at her side, as she picked up another.

He spoke softly, his words meant just for her ears, but the elegant music kept their conversation private.

Maeve didn't look at him. "Is that meant to be some groundbreaking information?"

He pinched the bridge of his nose. "I am trying," he muttered.

"You're doing a wonderful job," she offered, being no help as she continued to chew the grape.

He opened his mouth to continue, but Maeve cut him off casually.

"You're confused," she said, then swallowed. "You don't understand how I could stand here and enjoy a party when, come sunrise, my view will look entirely different. You don't get how I smile, while Mal waits in torture and possession when I claim my priority is saving him."

Eryx didn't respond. Maeve's brows raised.

"Am I right?"

He nodded.

She looked across the hall, finding Antony and Alphard at once, as they laughed and drank like they'd never been apart. Arianna sat close by, smiling consistently. Maeve had never seen such a look of glee on her sister's face. Zimsy ate her plate of chocolate-covered sweets, her own recipe no doubt. Abraxas sat and sipped his drink, reserved and occasionally interjecting as Lyrux played at their feet with Arianna's twins.

The sight made her shoulders drop.

Her son was not free.

He was trapped beneath a spell of protection. A cage. A prison.

When would it be safe for him to live when she could feel every single Dreaded Dead on the other side of Reeve's barrier that clawed at that wall of Magic with the intent to harm him?

Maeve's chest ached. "It is not for me I celebrate. Nor for Mal."

She watched as her family reminisced and did their best to pretend like death wasn't at their doorstep. That the finite reality of conflict hadn't arrived.

"If I, alone, could evacuate the entire Dread Lands right now, I would," she said softly. "I'd leave them all here to laugh and remember an easier time. I'd pour you and Reeve a drink, and let you sit at the bar for hours while I shouldered the burden."

Eryx watched her with an intense desire to understand deep in his eyes.

"But even with this new power, I can't do it alone."

Eryx swallowed uncomfortably at her vulnerability. "And Reeve? Are you at his side because you can't do it alone?"

Maeve's face fell into a cold solemnity. She looked over at Eryx and nodded her head slightly towards Zimsy.

"She's standing over there just begging to be held and fed strawberries," drawled Maeve. "And for some reason, you're still standing here boring me."

Eryx scowled at her, but his eyes gave him away as he stepped away from her and moved towards Zimsy.

A brief moment passed, and Maeve anticipated Reeve's hands before they ever reached her. The power of Aterna that they now shared sharpened their connection, given that it had been forged in that very Magic. His broad hand rested at the small of her back, fingers pressing into her, rotating her body towards his. She looked up at him as their chests connected. His free hand slid down her arm and twisted their fingers together. Instinctively, they moved as one, swaying slowly to the ethereal music as Maeve placed her hand on his chest.

"Would you like to dance?" he asked lowly.

"I think we already are," she said softly.

Reeve hummed in agreement, his fingers moving absently over hers.

"I've always wanted to dance with you," he said.

"Why did you never ask?"

He smiled placatingly. "Many reasons."

Her eyebrows slid up, and he looked away from her as he answered, never ceasing their gentle movements in place.

"The most recent argument I made for myself was that Mal wouldn't like it. And I was afraid he would punish you for it. The second is that politically, it didn't look good. You were the daughter of an allied Premier. One who watched you like a hawk when you were with anyone but Malachite. And thirdly, because, at least back then, your father was furious with me for even looking at you."

"I've remembered so much from then," said Maeve. "He forbid you from pursuing me."

"Do you judge me for listening then? And for not listening now?"

She shook her head and moved her hand up to his neck. His breath stalled as her fingers traced over the Vexkari scarring he received from Demevirld, a product of his curse.

"I think the circumstances have changed now," she answered at last. "I think he'd understand this time."

Reeve's Magic curled beneath her chin, drawing her gaze away from his scars and to his eyes.

"This time," repeated Reeve, as if the words hurt.

As if he, too, wondered if his breaking her heart was the catalyst for everything that had built up and then collapsed. As though he knew if he hadn't pushed her away, that perhaps Shadow would have never been released.

And Mal wouldn't be the one suffering for their mistakes.

She wouldn't let herself think about it because ultimately, it didn't matter. The set of choices before her couldn't be altered by a what-if scenario, and so she didn't dwell on the thought. She wouldn't give meaning to something potentially destructive and damaging.

This evening was for life, choosing to live, as Reeve had said, despite the horrors that awaited her. Despite their next move and the darkness that lingered just beyond Reeve's barrier.

Maeve rested her head against his chest, and he drew her impossibly closer. Her eyes fell closed at his blanket of comfort. They swayed in serene silence, letting the laughter of their loved ones be their music.

When she looked up at Reeve, his content stare was already on her.

"Let's go and join them?" she offered.

Reeve nodded subtly, but he didn't release her back. He dropped their clasped hands and bent his head, capturing her lips against his as his fingers trailed through her hair, bracing the back of her head. His lips moved tenderly across hers, unhurried and free. Maeve responded with her own kiss, humming against his lips in appreciation.

Both his hands traveled to her face as their kiss broke naturally.

Do you love me, Reeve of Aterna? she asked across his mind, the thought tumbling forward without a care.

Reeve's thumb traced across her bottom lip as he replied.

"In the most maddening way."

Her chest swelled, and his fingers rolled under her jaw, kicking her neck back.

Maeve bit her lip. *I love you,* she said.

Reeve's thumbs slid up, tracing across her cheekbones.

I know, he purred as his grin widened and his tongue danced across the tip of his canine.

She rolled her eyes, desperately fighting her pleased smile, and tried to pull away from him. He didn't let her get far before he pulled her flush against himself once more.

"But I still want to hear it singing from those pretty lips," he said, his voice low.

Maeve shook her head devilishly.

Grinning ferally, he said, "I'll coax those words from you, kitten."

Her stomach flipped over, excited energy racing through her blood as she remembered their interrupted moment the previous night. When his armor vanished and she lay beneath him.

"Is that a threat?" asked Maeve, raising her brows and parting her lips.

"Consider it a promise," he said. "It's one of many things I plan to make you confess." His hands slid down her sides and gripped her hips with a jolt. "And just wait until you hear my confessions, Maeve."

Maeve laughed. A sound of pure, unbridled joy burst from her throat. The sound a woman makes when she feels completely worshipped. Her head kicked back, and her eyes closed as the sound poured from her.

Reeve bent over her, dipping her back and watching her face. "Absolutely fucking perfect," he muttered with a sly grin.

He drew her back up, never taking his eyes off her. When she stood straight once more, he released her. He tucked two fingers under her chin and pulled her to the tips of her toes. He planted a single, soft kiss against her lips, and once her head was fuzzy and filled with desire once more, he nodded his head towards their family and friends.

Her fingers found his as they crossed towards the pack of drinking and laughter. Abraxas scooted over, making room for them. He leaned forward and poured Reeve a stout drink. Reeve accepted it with a small nod of reverence. He settled back with Maeve, draping one long arm across the back of the plush sofa behind her.

"I'm just saying," said Alphard, his fingers over Victoria's in his lap, "it was because of me we got out of those summer classes."

"No, it wasn't," barked Antony in a half-laugh. "I told father to write Larliesl and tell him if we didn't come home for summer, that he'd pull his dueling club donations."

Alphard's face dropped.

Abraxas snorted. "You're both idiots."

Antony and Alphard looked his way.

He shook his head. "Uncle Ambrose didn't threaten Larliesl with pulling any donations. Larliesl was never even going to force you to attend summer school. They both just wanted to watch the pair of you stress and scramble." He sipped his drink in satisfaction.

Antony and Alphard stared at each other, both knowing that if Abraxas said it, it was likely the truth.

"Where is Larlisel?" asked Antony, his tone lighthearted, not knowing the question was a loaded one.

"He's at Morana," answered Abraxas.

"Not for long," said Maeve swiftly as Abraxas' face drifted into thoughts she couldn't bear to imagine.

Her cousin witnessed firsthand the decline of his life, his people, and his loved ones in the Dread Lands. He'd watched Shadow's darkness take over. He'd watched her defile the one she'd sworn to protect.

The one she'd failed to protect.

"When is that happening?" asked Zimsy.

Eryx stiffened beside her.

Maeve didn't answer right away, dreading having to tell her best friend just how soon they'd either salvage what was left of their world or watch it fall to ruin.

It sat at the back of Maeve's mind like an incessant reminder of what she faced. And based on the way it bore down on her shoulders, she knew facing Shadow was a breath away. Still, selfishly, she wanted to linger in that moment.

In the moment when her brother lived and told stories of their life before. She wanted to listen to Arianna speak of her children's father without crying, telling Antony how Arman died for Maeve, not with resentment in her voice, but with pride in her eyes. She wanted to cherish the way Eryx looked at Zimsy, certain no one had ever vowed to protect her in a way that triumphed over Maeve's promise except him. She wanted to bathe in Alphard and Victoria's forgiveness.

Abraxas, who watched Lyrux closely if he even disappeared behind a chair for too long, was just as tense as she was. She could feel it. The rest of them didn't carry the weight of consequence like Maeve and her cousin did.

"At dawn," said Maeve, answering at last.

Zimsy nodded. "I know that look on you well, Maeve. You don't need to worry about any of us. You need to ensure that Mal and Maxius are safe. Nothing else."

To Maeve's surprise, Eryx didn't recoil at her words.

"I would like to propose a toast," said Arianna, raising her glass of bubbling gold liquid towards Maeve.

Her throat caught tightly as her jaw tightened.

Zimsy's glass flew up without hesitation, a prideful look across her gorgeously delicate features.

One by one, her friends, her family, raised their glasses towards her—even Eryx.

"To my sister who, despite the horrors she has endured, remains fighting. My sister, who chose her blood, the blood of our father Ambrose Sinclair, the blood of our children, over her own desires. I am proud to be your sister, I am proud to fight alongside my family."

"Usque ad mortem, Sinclair," said Antony, his glass high, the Sinclair family ring once around his neck in his wolf form, glistened against the crystal, on his finger. The male twin to Maeve's and Arianna's, except his was set in a silver band.

Arianna's head lifted, her own matching gold ring dancing in the luminous candlelight just the same. "Usque ad mortem, Sinclair."

Maeve grabbed a crystal flute of water and raised it high, her eyes dancing over her own ring, the last of the set. The words engraved on the golden band were those they spoke, "Usque ad mortem, Sinclair."

She smiled at the impossible, that the three of them were together again, despite how much had changed, and despite their loss—

Maeve gasped, her grip on her glass nearly loosening completely as she looked from Antony's ring to Arianna's and at last back to her own.

Three were made and given away. Bound in gold and silver chains, the Magic lay.

Emerie's last prophecy echoed across her mind clearly as she stared at the three stones set in gold and silver bands. The lightning she produced, which Arianna, too, produced, unheard-of and ancient power, was no longer a mystery.

Reeve shifted in his seat, leaning forward to take in her expression.

"Three were made and given away. Bound in gold and silver chains, the Magic lay," recited Maeve.

Reeve's throat bobbed. "What?"

Her eyes moved back to the ring on her brother's hand. And then on her sister's.

Abraxas slammed his drink down on the table. "Holy hell," he said as he swiftly put together her words and her stare.

"Maeve?" Antony asked with concern.

Maeve looked back at Reeve, her heart beating fast. She pushed one single, simple thought into his mind.

We have the Dread Stone.

Abraxas recited the prophecy fully as they all stared at the three rings laid out on the table between them. "Three were made and given away. Bound in gold and silver chains, the Magic lay, buried beneath another, from the protection of the father. When the night devours the sun, when the holy three join one, the Dread Stone will stand alone."

"I can't believe I never knew," said Arianna as the three Sinclair siblings looked completely dumbfounded.

"How could you have?" asked Antony. "The Magic is sealed deep, buried just like the prophecy says."

Their father's Magic.

"If these are the Dread Stone," began Arianna, "how come Mal never felt the pull of them?"

"Because, like Emerie's prophecy said, they were laced with another's Magic," answered Abraxas.

"Father's," said Antony.

Arianna's eyes widened.

Maeve nodded. "Vexkari."

"Do you think Father intended to tell us?" asked Arianna, the question directed at Antony.

Antony ran his hand through his hair. He leaned back and shook his head. "I couldn't begin to guess."

"He didn't know this war was coming," said Arianna. "Or he would have equipped us with the knowledge that our protection was quite literally at our fingertips. Right?"

Reeve's hand took Maeve's smoothly, holding up her two striking fingers. "So if I put one on, I can produce some of that lightning that so easily slips from your fingers, can't I?"

Maeve glared at him, annoyed that it was simply a powerful object of the Dread Armor that granted her such abilities.

"Don't pout," said Reeve with a small laugh, "it's still incredible to be able to wield the power of something like this at all."

Antony laughed. "And here I thought I was special."

Alphard barked a laugh. "Oh Primus! That Sacred party where you got so mad at Kensing for beating you in the duels, the curtains in Mr. Iantrose's smoking room exploded. Everyone accused the old man of drunkenly starting the fire, but it was you! I knew it was you."

"It just sort of burst from me," said Antony apologetically.

Arianna looked down at the stones, lost in thought.

"They need to become one again," she said. "To give you a fighting chance."

"It's safer they remain in parts," chimed Abraxas. "Keeping it in parts is harder for Shadow to get her claws on. If the three of you can harness the power of these stones, I have no doubt she could. And she's been searching for this object herself and through Mal."

"But Maeve should still take all three of them," said Arianna.

"I don't disagree," said Reeve, "But you all have a part to play tomorrow."

"I'd feel better if they remained in your possession, and if you needed them, they'd be at your disposal."

"You are the one about to look Shadow in the eye," argued Antony. "You'll take all three."

Arianna nodded.

"See," said Antony, "you're outvoted."

"How nostalgic," said Maeve coolly.

Reeve's attention turned to the doorway, where Drystan and Mely appeared.

"Mely," said Reeve, his voice flooding with concern.

And rightfully so. She was corpse-like in appearance. Her skin was sallow, and her eyes were darkened by her flooded pupils. Drystan held her up with ease, despite his small frame.

She looked to be on the brink of death.

A hollowing feeling prickled across Maeve's skin.

She wasn't the one on the brink of death.

"Mal," whispered Maeve, as Mely's half-lidded eyes landed on her.

With just a few words, Mely solidified Maeve's claim:

"He is near his end."

Chapter 50

Maeve

With Aterna Magic forged against her bones, Maeve had never felt more certain of her place in the Magical world.

Her legs were tucked beneath her at the center of Sanctum. The smooth stone was neither cold nor warm against her skin, as though the temple maintained its neutrality through and through. The three white trees told her much without ever speaking.

"There is truly so much Magic in the air here," she observed.

Reeve hummed in agreement as he circled the trees.

"It almost feels similar to Vaukore," she said. "In the way that my home on Earth felt alive. Like it had its own thoughts. Its own feelings."

"Enough Vexkari will do that," answered Reeve. "This place is older than we can fathom. These trees were likely the first life here. At least," he said, his fingers brushing the smooth bark, "that's how they feel to me."

She recalled how strong she'd felt in the library at Sinclair Estates when she cast the brutal spell that removed Mal's Dread Mark from her chest. It must have been the same feeling Mal had when he relied on the strength of Vaukore to experiment with Vexkari.

Reeve turned towards her and seated himself on the steps leading down from the trees.

"You get out of there the moment something goes wrong, Maeve."

She nodded. "I will."

A few hours ago, it was only a theory she'd written down weeks ago when studying Shadow Magic in Judyth's memories of Vaukore. But she'd pulled it off successfully, twice. Once was good luck, twice was understanding, as her father would have said.

Afraid to attempt a third practice run and deplete her energy entirely, she now prepared to jump into two minds at once: Shadow's and Mal's. Shadow's first, to distract her, and Mal's second to speak to him without Shadow's interference.

One-hundred-and-thirty-two seconds.

That's how long she'd been able to hold on to two minds, separating herself between them.

She closed her eyes and, with a strong breath, jumped into Shadow's mind. She allowed the void, the darkness, to hold her, not calling Shadow's memory or current state forward. Just nothingness, until she sensed her enemy. With a youthful voice and a sinister signature of Magic, Shadow spoke.

I was wondering when you'd come talk to me.

Maeve didn't reply right away.

I've been waiting months for those jealous eyes to seek me out.

Jealous. Jealousy wasn't what she felt.

She felt **disgusted**.

How's your cousin and the boy? I was beginning to wonder if he'd ever leave my castle. I tried so hard to break him. She laughed. *Such loyalty to the Dread King.*

If Shadow wanted to listen to herself taunt and talk, then Maeve would let her. That would enable her to speak to Mal with greater ease.

"I want to help you," said Maeve, "if you'll let me."

Doubt filled the empty air.

"You haven't managed to become with child, yet," said Maeve.

That doubt turned to fury.

"I can help you."

And how, she hissed, *can you help me?*

"Because I've remembered now that conceiving Maxius was different than any of the other times Mal reached his climax."

The air shifted, and Maeve could smell desperation.

"Would you like to see—"

Why, why, why would you ever aid me—

"Because you got me to Reeve," she said plainly, perfectly hiding how painful the words were to voice, even though they were merely part of the deception. Her next words, however, were painful. "And I intend to stay with Reeve."

Shadow fell silent.

Maeve pulled out the oldest trick in her book: a singular, in real time, false memory that played out before them in hopes that the lie would occupy her attention long enough for her to speak to Mal.

"Is that a yes?" asked Maeve.

Yes, hissed Shadow.

She drew forth the perfected "memory," not a crack out of place, and let it manifest around them. It was fabricated, as Maeve would never show her the night she and Mal conceived Maxius.

Feeling Shadow's attention fully enveloped in her false memory, she grounded herself and prepared to move to Mal. It was like looking at two different things using both eyes, one as the focal point and one as a close periphery. She kept Shadow in her periphery and slid into Mal's mind with such ease her heart constricted at his weakened state.

Darkness swirled around her, spiraling up from the ground and swirling above her. Flecks of cosmic night flickered in the darkness. And he appeared before her. He was himself, nothing like the version she was certain occupied Castle Morana in the present. Nothing like the Mal she'd seen so utterly destroyed a few weeks ago.

This was her Mal. He was clean, his pale skin held a soft flush of life, his hair was perfectly placed, a small, soft ringlet brushing across his forehead. He stood tall, with a smile made for weakening knees.

And his eyes were a dark hazel dream once more.

His voice was like coming home.

"Is this my Little Viper, come to see me at last?"

Maeve returned his smile in earnest.

He was utterly himself in their joined consciousness. His eyes scanned down her body, slowly drinking her in, then snapped up to her eyes.

"You were his Inheritor?"

Mal had always had a keen sense of Magic. It came as no surprise to Maeve that he realized at once what power ran through her. Shadow, still occupied in her distant vision, made no notice of her entrance into Mal's mind.

Maeve nodded, answering his question. "I'm coming to get you," began Maeve, and Mal shook his head at once.

She searched his face, darting back and forth between his eyes.

"That's too dangerous," he said after a moment.

"I have a plan," she said. "Please listen."

After a moment of consideration, Mal nodded as Maeve told him about her gamble of an idea for facing Shadow and evacuating the Dread Lands. When she was finished, Mal did not argue.

He merely nodded and said, "Clever girl."

"Can you hang on just a bit longer?" she asked, her chest tightening at the words.

He nodded, just slightly, a small amount of disdain slipping into his features.

"I do not want to watch Maxius give up his Magic, Mal," she said, the vulnerable words slipping from her mouth. "I don't want to see his life ended before it's even had a chance to begin."

His face softened. "He won't die, Maeve. I promise you that."

"You will not defeat her until your Magic is one with Maxius'. That is written in Magic."

"So is your bond with Reeve." He smiled like the Mal she'd met at Vaukore. "I managed to work around that just fine."

"Good," she said shakily. "Then we are in agreement. Even if we can't destroy her right now, we circumvent the prophecy of Maxius and seal her away just as Reeve did three hundred years ago."

Mal's eyes left her for the first time. "So we're just prolonging both the prophecies?"

"Yes," she answered. "I know how to unlock Maxius' Magic. And once I can show him how to give you his Dread Magic while maintaining his Shadow Magic, then you'll be able to defeat her."

Mal's face fell, his eyes darkened. "She has my Magic, Maeve."

"You let me worry about that."

"And your Dread Magic? When are you going to take it back?"

"I'm not. I don't need it for this to work. He stays there, under protection, until she is defeated or I am."

"So he lives forever past our deaths in a crystal coffin of your

Magic?"

"He's safe there."

"He's the same as dead there."

Maeve didn't have a reply, despite just how painfully right he was. Mal watched her intently for a moment. His voice was smooth, void of any retribution.

"Do you love Reeve?"

Maeve couldn't bring herself to answer.

"Your silence is an answer unto itself."

"Mal," she said, her voice quivering.

"The thought of you finding happiness with another man is a distinct form of torture. And yet. . . I know you deserve it all the same."

"How am I supposed to do that without you? How do I live knowing that I failed?"

"Failed? We're not done yet, Maeve. We have time to ensure our son sees a future. If we can do that, I will consider our life a success."

"And if it destroys you to vanquish her?"

"Then my sacrifice for my family is given willingly."

My family. The words were just another blow. Another dream shattered.

"What redemption is there in such a sacrifice where your son grows up without the only person who understands his Magic?"

"Look at him, Maeve," he said. "He already is growing up without me."

"No," she began, shaking her head.

"We are holding on to something that no longer exists. We are not sinking. We have already drowned, Little Viper. You've spent your Magic creating worlds in which this is not our fate."

"And I can do it again," she cried. "I can save you."

"No," he said gently. "It is time. It's time for this reality, the true reality, to put an end to it all. I don't have much time left. Make me a promise—"

"I can create more time," she cried, ignoring his logic still. "I can give us whatever world we want until—"

"You already have. And she has found us in every alternate

reality you create within our minds."

"And so I'll do it again and again until we get it right."

Mal shook his head. "Maxius deserves what is *real*."

She couldn't argue.

After a moment, he repeated himself. "Make me a promise."

"Anything, Mal."

"I want you to remember me the way I was before Shadow. Before my fall. Don't remember me as I am now. Remember our summer at Sinclair Estates, not the winter we are in now."

Brutal words.

She would honor them.

She nodded. "I could never forget that summer."

"It was only you I desired, then. No legacy, no crown. Just your eyes on mine."

"They're not blue anymore," she said, suddenly feeling the weight of his restored appearance compared to her own.

Mal shook his head, the movement slow and small. "All I see is you." His head tilted to the side, watching her with newfound interest. "You look so beautiful, thrumming with the power of Aterna."

Her chest ached at his words.

He paused, looking at her. "I want to despise it, the fact that it's his, but I can't. Not when it means you are safe."

Shadow moved in her periphery. Her distraction was running up.

"She is slipping from my spell," said Maeve hastily. Her voice was broken, defeated as she said. "I have to let go."

"Do not forget your promise, Little Viper," said Mal as his fingers reached for her face. "Remember me, as I was."

Before his slender fingers could brush her cheek, they turned to mist. His entire body began to fade into nothing as the space around them collapsed.

"Pour toujours", he said, his voice fading.

Forever.

Maeve pulled from his mind and Shadows at once. The soft light of Sanctum flickered back into her eyes. Reeve leaned against the smooth stone silently, nothing but the quiet trickle of water running over the rough roots of the tree filling the space.

She pulled her knees up and buried her face in them, hiding her tears from him. Reeve's footsteps echoed across the temple.

A warm hand rested on the top of her head. The warmth faded as his footsteps retreated. Maeve held her legs close.

"A tout jamais", she cried softly.

And always.

Chapter 51

Maeve

Warmth brushed against her cheek. She moaned and settled into the feeling, not wanting to open her eyes. She needed less sleep now, but after so many nights without it, and the aftermath exhaustion of maintaining contact in both Mal and Shadow's minds, she'd gladly closed her eyes.

Reluctantly, she opened them.

Reeve moved one finger over his mouth and looked beside her, where Lyrux lay between her and Abraxas. Maeve followed his gaze to the sleeping little boy, his hair draped messily across his face, and then up at Abraxas. Her cousin sat reclined in the bed, awake and running his fingers through Lyrux's white blond hair.

She blinked sleepily.

Reeve wrapped his hand around her middle and gently pulled her from the bed, scooping her up like she was nothing more than a few pillows.

"Is it time?" she whispered, her eyes back on Reeve.

He nodded. Maeve looked back over at Abraxas. His gaze remained on Lyrux.

"You can change your mind, Brax," said Maeve softly as Reeve set her down. "We can evacuate the Dread Lands without you."

"Not efficiently, you can't," he answered, his fingers still wrapping his son's silken hair. "No one knows that place like I do." He paused. "Not even Mal."

Abraxas stood and lifted Lyrux with ease, gently placing his head on his shoulder. "I'll take him to Zimsy and meet you down there shortly."

His footsteps were soft as he left them. Maeve watched him go. Watched the tender way he held his son, and ached to hold hers. Maeve wrapped her arms around herself, feeling a cold that had nothing to do with the winter air seeping through the stained-glass windows of her chamber.

Reeve took her face in his hands, and her eyes instantly shut. He bent until their foreheads touched. Maeve smiled softly at the gesture.

"I wish I could have let you sleep," he said. "You looked so peaceful."

Maeve placed her hands on his chest. Her only reply was a hum as she nestled closer to him and his addicting warmth. When she pulled back and made to step away, Reeve protested at once.

"Not so fast," he said, holding her in place with warm hands pressed against her cheeks. He bent forward, his frame devouring hers, and brushed his lips across hers. "Not so fast," he mumbled again, against her lips.

Maeve melted into him. Their kiss was slow, sleepy almost, as she let herself drift into a final fleeting moment of bliss.

Castle Morana was a ghost. She and Reeve stood in the silent Entrance Hall. Their presence seemed meaningless. Minuscule and unnoteworthy. The grand staircase stood tall, climbing to the floor above, covered in a thick haze of toxic Magic.

Magic that no longer affected her.

She stepped forward, her footsteps silent in the thick atmosphere. The firelights were out, casting a look of abandonment over the emerald marble.

"I imagine this is what it looked like before Mal breathed life back into it," said Maeve, her voice low.

Reeve followed her without question.

Deeper into the castle they ventured, following the singular pull of Magic in the desolate space. Maeve knew where her feet led her.

She knew the room that awaited her.

She never wanted to set foot in it again.

She hated that room.

But as they crossed the dense air into the Throne Room, Maeve stopped.

Shadow sat at a small table, decorated with the finest place settings and silks Castle Morana could offer. A single candle floated at the center, and dripped wax accumulated in a hardened chunk beneath it.

Maeve's stomach sank.

The Dread Crown sat atop her head. The silver was dulled, but the emerald eyes of the winding snakes glowed, and the ruby tongues that flared from between their bared fangs pulsed with Magic.

She wasn't sure why the sight brought her blood to a boil. Perhaps it was many reasons. Shadow's unworthiness. The image of Mal wearing it.

Or perhaps it was the memories of what Maeve herself had done to ensure he reached the long-lost crown.

"Take that off," said Maeve, her voice low.

"I was worried you wouldn't come," said Shadow, ignoring her completely. "Sit."

The table was set for four. Maeve looked at the empty seat next to Shadow.

"Please," Shadow added, though there was little room for declining.

They crossed the Throne Room in silence and took the two seats opposite her. The singular flame cast a red glow, illuminating half of Shadow in the otherwise darkened room.

"As I said, I wasn't sure you'd come," she said, leaning forward to pour a large goblet of wine. Her pale white hair draped across the table, long and healthy.

"Funny thing," said Shadow after a long sip of her wine. "You were in my head." She wiped her mouth with the back of her hand, the movement slow and precise.

"I was," answered Maeve plainly.

"Please drink," said Shadow, suddenly alert. Then her expression twisted, and her eyes landed on Reeve. "I haven't poisoned any of the goblets." She smiled and brought her gaze back to Maeve expectantly. "Drink."

The second command was less inviting and more demanding. Maeve didn't move.

"I don't drink," she replied.

Shadow leaned back, bringing her wine glass back with her, nearly sloshing it carelessly over the rim. "How could I forget? The Dread Viper is so afraid to be out of control." She paused and looked to the empty seat beside her. Then her eyes snapped back to Maeve. "You weren't very helpful in my mind."

"No?" answered Maeve.

"No," repeated Shadow. "In fact, I'm worried I took things too far with our dear Mal. I don't think he's. . . capable anymore." Her lips puckered, and her nearly invisible white brows pulled together. "It's not fair he gave you the heir."

"Maxius will never wear that crown," said Maeve with certainty.

Shadow sipped her wine, a long silence falling between the three of them. "Aren't you hungry?"

Maeve shook her head casually. "No. Oh, that reminds me." She rested her head against the tall back of the chair and rolled her head towards Reeve. "Do we actually have to eat?"

"No," replied Reeve, a small smile on his lips as he took in just how effortlessly and fearlessly Maeve controlled the room. "In fact," he said, playing into her brazen display, "you can drink that wine and not feel a thing. Might as well be water."

The corners of Maeve's mouth pulled up, and together they returned their attention to Shadow.

She giggled. "So emboldened, isn't she, Mal, darling?"

As his name rolled off her tongue, the affectionate name reserved only for those he deemed worthy of calling him such, swirling black mist materialized in the empty chair at her side. In its wake sat Mal. Mordred appeared at his side, as he had been since nearly the moment they met.

If Mely's appearance had been corpse-like, then Mal was already six feet under.

His eyes were still a sharp green against his devastatingly pale skin, but they were dull. The glow they'd once carried under Shadow's possession was gone. His cheeks were hollowed, dipping into sunken shadows of decay. His fingers, once a deadly weapon, sat useless in his lap. Thin skin covered each knuckle and bone.

Maeve clung to the image of him in her mind when they'd last spoken. Just as she'd promised she would. But the sight of just how close to death Shadow had dragged him allowed wrath to root inside Maeve.

Her attention slid back to Shadow, unable to waste any more time now that Mal was before her.

"I'll make this quick today."

Her arm jetted forward, her Magic latching onto Shadow's mind. She dug deep, finding the claws of Shadow Magic latched in Mal's psyche, and began disintegrating them one by one. With lethal force, she ripped the connections of poison in his mind from the beast feeding off him.

Shadow's hands slammed onto the table between them, as she bent forward like a wounded animal. Her face of disbelief twisted into horror as Maeve successfully infiltrated her mind and controlled it. With a bang, one of the endless claws embedded in Mal's mind released.

A wave of negative energy surged through Maeve. It was vile and turned her insides to ice.

Mordred growled in uncertainty. Maeve almost admired his loyalty. Almost. Mordred had not protected Mal from the evil woman at his side any more than she had.

She glanced quickly at Mal and wondered if the version of him before her even recalled the conversation and the plans she'd laid out to him in their connected minds.

She returned her eyes to Shadow.

"How?" Shadow seethed, all teeth and breath, fury now radiating from her at Maeve's power. Her long, pale nails dug into the table.

BANG. Another claw triumphantly destroyed.

Maeve contracted her fingers, like choking the air in front of her, tightening her hold on Shadow's throat. "Because I am simply better than you." Her eyes narrowed. Then she said, "I freed you, remember? There is an Enslavement Curse on you still. Bound to me by the blood I traded for you." Maeve looked up at Mal. His eyes slid to Shadow. Maeve followed his gaze to the gaunt queen, who looked back at her with her own blue eyes. "Or were you hoping I wouldn't figure that out? That's it is my blood that chains you now."

More of Shadow's sharp claws lifted from Mal's mind.

Shadow smiled. "You think I won't have his mind if you break my hold? Go on then. See just how much life I took from him. See just how little is left of him now. There is but an ounce of Dread Magic left in him. Consider it a gift from your queen, Mal darling, that I allow you to keep it."

She truly had no idea, no understanding of what Maeve was capable of, or planning. Mal's Dread Magic no longer mattered. Sealing Shadow once more was the goal, and then once Mal was safe and free from her possessive enslavement, she'd give him the Dread Magic, his Dread Magic, that ran through her veins. She'd siphon out the part of him imbued in the Dread Ring on her finger and forge it with Mal's blood once more.

"So gracious," said Maeve sourly, groaning as she snapped two more points of hold.

Shadow swallowed hard. "I've absorbed the life of countless Dread Magicals, even more power than that Aterna Magic you now have offers you." Her teeth slid together. "Which makes me question how it is you hold my mind."

Another claw, embedded deep, shattered.

"It's taking everything I have," said Maeve shakily, "but my Shadow Magic is greater than yours. I understand Magic in a way none before me has, since King Primus himself. I see it down to its smallest particle. The way it molds and bends. I see your Shadow Magic, the way it flows and mixes with your stolen Dread Magic. And ironically, I learned it all through you. Through your studies." Maeve couldn't help but smirk, her eyes darkening. "Though you didn't grasp half the lessons. But I did. I was always top of the class, wasn't I, Mal?" she said, letting her eyes shift to him.

"Second place at best, Sinclair," he said, his voice breathy with relief as the dirty Magic eating his soul like maggots fell away bit by bit.

Another chain undone. Gods, she was so close. Her arm shook, her head was heavy, but his tone gave her renewed strength. Her Aterna Magic helped dull the poisonous effects of being so intertwined with Shadow's mind, but she still strained to keep a hold on Shadow as the white queen pushed Dread Magic against Maeve's Aterna.

Shadow shook, paralyzed beneath Maeve's hold, and the reaction to their Magic fighting for dominance. "I was chosen by the Dread King of old because I was the most powerful Shadow Magical."

If an artist of their age could have painted a portrait embodying Maeve Sinclair, they would have chosen the moment she said:

"You were the most powerful. Only for the single fact that I hadn't been born."

The final claw in Mal's mind snapped. His eyes darkened with a crack of Magic, and he collapsed, slumping forward in his seat. Maeve lunged forward as Reeve moved for Mal. She propelled herself across the table, sliding between Mal and Shadow with a speed unseen by even Shadow's sharpened senses. Mordred hollered, bounding towards Reeve, but Reeve understood his task, and no one would keep him from ensuring something entrusted to him as precious as securing Mal was a victory. In a single slice of Reeve's fingers, the wolf's throat slit wide. His legs buckled beneath him, and when he collapsed to the floor in a moving pool of red, he did not rise again.

With Mal at her back, Maeve's fist collided with Shadow's face, propelled by pure hatred as she ripped the Dread Crown from her head. Negative emotions were indeed required to harness the power of the Dread Stone, and Electric Magic barreled down her arm, faster than it ever had beneath the weight of her animosity. The hair draped across Maeve's shoulders lifted, dancing with static. The burst of lightning that erupted from her was catastrophic, with all three pieces of the Dread Stone at her will. Arianna's and Antony's rings hummed in approval around her neck, working in perfect synchronicity with the one on her finger. As the blow landed on Shadow, the subsequent explosion burst through the wall of the Throne Room, exposing the hazy green sky as she blew a hole in Castle Morana. The lightning jetted into the dark clouds, scattering them with bright blue illumination.

Shadow had been thrown from the castle through the now crumbled exterior wall. Smoke settled into the Throne Room as Maeve turned back towards Reeve.

Mal looked so frail in his arms. So gone.

Reeve's gaze lingered on hers for a moment longer than they had.

"Go," she said, urgency in her tone, tossing the crown back at him.

Reeve didn't disobey. He vanished in a swirl of violet fire just as his fingers closed around the silver and gold band of serpents, and Maeve heaved a sigh when she felt both his and Mal's Magic move to the other side of the barrier. She stepped across the rubble of the Throne Room, scattered marble and stone smoking, some still crackling with electricity, from the surge of energy.

She reached the edge of the floor, and below was a steep drop down to the unforgiving mountains below. No such fall could kill Shadow, but nor could it kill Maeve.

She stepped off the ledge with grace, falling from the Throne Room of the castle to face her enemy below. Icy particles of air attacked her face in her descent, but the warmth of her Aterna Magic disregarded them completely.

She'd never feel cold again.

Maeve slammed into the earth, a fall that would have broken her in the past. But now, with a body made new from the Gods themselves, she landed with a bolt of Magic that felt effortless.

Shadow waited for her with a look of interest, toxic air hovering between them. She jerked beneath the lingering electric Magic, wounded and down. Before she could open her vile mouth, Maeve pulled her into her mind at once, a particularly heartfelt moment between Nevian and Shadow ready for viewing. Shadow froze. Her big blue eyes held a disturbed look, like she was both uncomfortable and entranced.

Maeve's voice was smooth. "I understand a vow forged in revenge. Especially with what they did to Nevian."

Shadow's eyes widened only slightly, her attention locked on the memory before them.

"Though Mal does look like your precious Prince Darius, doesn't he?" She allowed Shadow a small moment of further shock before continuing. "I've seen the memories that linger in your mind. I've seen what they did to Nevian while you were forced to watch. And I've seen what you did to Darius."

Shadow smiled, but it was cracked and bleeding with disbelief. "It is but a life that once was."

"It is the life you were denied. That we have in common," said Maeve.

Maeve knew the corridor in Vaukore well, where Nevian pressed Judyth against the wall, his fingers trailing through her white hair as he looked down at her in worship.

"There's many of him," said Maeve, switching to something even more intimate between Shadow and Nevian.

Shadow's eyes remained glued on her past self, and the lover she was denied a life with. As Maeve flipped through the back corners of Shadow's mind like a picture book, they watched every tender memory, and then every tenacious one.

Right up until the moment she watched him bleed out.

And Maeve ensured Shadow felt it all.

She took her time. After all, this was merely a distraction while Abraxas, Eryx, Antony, and the rest evacuated the Dread Lands and Castle Morana without Shadow's intervention.

"I have more though," said Maeve, keeping her hold on Shadow's mind, "because he was the first love you lost, but he wasn't the last one."

As their view shifted from Vaukore to Castle Morana, Judyth aged by only a few years, and she glowed with Dread Magic that didn't belong to her. As she sat to the right of the Dread King, his face blurred since he wasn't the focus of her thoughts then, her pale eyes were on his middle son.

Prince Darius, who looked strikingly like Mal, stared back at her in silence, but their gaze was loud. Their memories were even louder.

"I spent a lot of time looking at these," said Maeve. "I think you loved him even more than you did Nevian."

Shadow watched, her face still struck with horror as Maeve reminded her of her time with a former Prince of the Dread Lands. Of just how wonderful he made her believe she was. Of how badly she wanted to be his.

But she was not his.

She belonged to his father in every meaning of the word.

Stolen glances and moments of weakness were all they shared. Conversations in the library, or quick moments at dinner before the Dread King arrived.

They watched as Prince Darius wed another. They watched as he gave her children. And they watched as Shadow slaughtered them, taking all their Dread Magic for herself.

Time dragged on as Shadow unfolded new memories, ones that had long been locked away, and the two Witches watched even more than Maeve was anticipating.

"In the end," said Maeve as they viewed her descent into darkness, "you remembered the vow you'd made when they took Nevian from you. You remembered that you'd promised yourself you'd take all the Dread Magic for yourself."

"Is that pity in your voice?" asked Shadow, her tone low.

"No," answered Maeve. "I haven't got any of that for you. I do not feel sorry for those who inflict their sufferings on others, just as the world has not felt sorry for me in my transgressions. But there is a difference between us, *Judyth*," she said, her voice dropping and Shadow tensing at the use of her given name. "You were all alone. I was not. The presence of those I care for gave me perspective, a chance to see my mistakes."

"Is that your way of telling me you intend to be merciful and let me live?"

"I'm not your executioner," said Maeve as the memories around them faded until they stood in a void.

"You think I can't feel what's happening?" asked Shadow. "I can feel the Dread Magic depleting from these lands as all your new allies usher everyone to safety."

"I'm sure you can," replied Maeve.

"You're nearly there," said Shadow, her voice shifting into something almost excited. "Thank you."

"What?" snapped Maeve.

"This is the war I always dreamed of." Her blue eyes landed back on Maeve. She smiled. "We both know those little prophecies are never coming true now. It'll be you and me. . .two Shadows. After all, no one rewrites reality quite like our blood can."

"My blood," argued Maeve. "You've never done it like I have. In one person at a time, sure, you've altered minds. But never like me. I'd wondered why you wanted my spell so badly. But I understand now that despite the abilities granted to you as a Shadow Magical, you lack the nerve required to pull off a mind wipe."

Shadow's smile fell.

"I hardly blame you, knowing now that the first time I did it, if Reeve hadn't given me life, I would have died. I still feel the damage I've done to my mind, to my Magic, from the countless times I've been forced to run from you."

"And now you face your reaper with a soldier's determination. Can't you see how beautiful our battle is?"

Time to let go.

Reeve's signal slid into her mind, a silent thought propelled through their bond, just for her.

Maeve released her hold on Shadow's mind, and together they plummeted back to reality. A warm, suffocating sensation wrapped her lungs as she passed through the barrier line of Aterna Magic. When she opened her eyes, the barrier separated her and Shadow at the center of the Black Deep. With solid ice beneath their feet, Reeve stood at Maeve's side, having just deposited them both on either side.

Shadow let out a small sound. "Always so clever." She reached forward, still reeling from Maeve's attack, one long, gaunt finger trailing against the wafting line of Magic. Black essence, dirty and contaminated Magic, shot up and out, towering above her, sticking to the barrier like slime. It dripped down, slowly streaking the barrier.

Shadow tapped the barrier between them three more times. It

rippled beneath her touch, and Maeve felt the change in her Magic then. She was drawing Dread Magic into herself. The scattered and roaming Dreaded Dead behind her collapsed, becoming nothing more than lifeless bodies once more.

She's taking back the Dread Magic she necromanced the Dreaded Dead with, said Maeve into Reeve's mind.

Reeve didn't reply.

Dark swirls of Magic encompassed Shadow's pale frame, and she disappeared on the wind.

"How long will that take her?" asked Maeve, finally tearing her eyes away from where Shadow had been.

Her eyes landed on Reeve at last. The blood on his face was already dried, mixed with sweat and dirt that glistened across his skin. A massive tear across his chest, which was slowly cauterizing itself, stained his front.

"Be a doll, will you?" he said with the cigarette between his lips.

Maeve's eyes narrowed, and her mouth fell open.

"Lecture-free," he added.

She snapped her fingers, and the tip ignited. Reeve held it between his tattooed fingers and inhaled deeply. His shoulders dropped at once. Another drag, and his eyes closed.

"Is that a cigarette?" she asked finally, in disbelief.

Reeve exhaled the toxic smoke. "I believe I said lecture-free." He enjoyed his cigarette another moment. "Small thing," he said, gesturing to the wound encompassing half his torso. "I'm healing at a fraction of the time I would have in the past. Not half."

"I never said I gave you *half* of the Aterna Magic," Maeve replied plainly.

Everything stilled. Maeve's head tilted as Reeve's jaw fell open, the cigarette lazily between his fingers.

"You didn't think you would be my equal, did you?" asked Maeve. "I had to tip the scales somehow."

Reeve took another drag and grinned. "Cruel little kitten."

"I did what was necessary to win this war and to keep you. We couldn't both share second place and turn the tide."

"Deceived by my own woman once again," he said.

"You couldn't feel it?"

"When you yield that much power, it is—"

"Incalculable," she finished for him. "Yes. I know."

Reeve's cigarette vanished, as if it had never existed. He lowered his chin. "So you think you are in first place now?"

Maeve allowed herself a small smirk. "I have, without a doubt, surpassed you."

Chapter 52

Maeve

Senshi Warriors and defected Bellator alike all contributed to the chaos around them as they secured refugees. Healers, both of Aterna Magic and Dread Magic, worked on reviving those terminally affected by Shadow's toxic presence. By the blight she'd become once more in their final days in the Dread Lands.

"Where is he?" asked Maeve as they entered the Celestian Palace.

"In the healing waters right now," said Zimsy. "Abraxas is with him. He's still not conscious."

"Where's Mely?"

Zimsy shook her head. "She's not well at all."

"Of course she's not," said Reeve plainly. "Death breathes at the nape of all our necks."

"I need to see her," said Maeve insistently.

Zimsy hadn't been exaggerating. Mely was both better and worse than before. While some of her coloring had returned, the obvious vertigo running through her had her reeling. And with nothing left to throw up, she dry heaved every other sentence from the chaise where she lounged.

"She's given me a wonderful concoction," said Mely shakily, gesturing to Astrea. "I feel able to sit up at the very least."

"Hello, Astrea," said Maeve curtly.

Astrea nodded in reply.

"Mal?" asked Maeve at once, turning her attention back to Mely.

Mely made a distressed sound as she threw up nothing at all.

"He's. . .no longer dying," she managed to gasp out.

Maeve's head tipped back as relief exhaled from her lips. She'd done it. She had successfully removed Shadow's contamination from him.

"But," said Mely, squirming beneath her nausea, "he's still in terrible shape."

Maeve nodded. She could fix that just as Reeve had gifted her with Aterna Magic long before it was hers to Inherit.

Maeve turned on her heel, prepared to head to the healing waters at once.

"Maeve," called Astrea, her voice strained.

She turned back, and Astrea began talking before she even had eyes on her.

"I'm sorry, Maeve. I failed. I couldn't—"

"You weren't capable," interrupted Maeve. "That isn't failure. Failure would mean you hadn't tried. And I know you tried."

Astrea nodded, her eyes thick with tears. "I really did."

"He'll be fine now," said Maeve with a nod. "I have him back now."

Astrea nodded, and Maeve turned on her heel. She paused and looked back at Astrea.

"Is Emerie here?"

Astrea swallowed. "Emerie's dead."

Another mother lost to her child. Another death on Maeve's tally of blame.

"And her girl?" she asked, almost afraid to hear the answer.

"She's here," said Astrea. "She's with the other children."

Except Maxius.

Maeve pushed down on that thought and assured herself that soon he'd be free. She moved swiftly from the room, darting across the palace and towards the healing waters. The icy air nipped at her skin as she crossed the open archways standing above the frozen Black Deep, hurrying to Mal.

A small jolt of Magic stalled Maeve mid-step.

"No," she breathed.

A rolling momentum of Magic violently shook through the palace. The ground itself seemed to ripple as a low grumbling noise undulated into a roar. Her footing shifted, and she gripped one of the crystal pillars, her eyes narrowed across the Black Deep.

Reeve appeared behind her as she stared across the darkened lake. His arms wrapped around her front, and he pulled her back against his chest. She allowed herself the short and fleeting moment. Reeve's lips pressed against her hair, finding her temple in a reverent way.

It was unspoken between them what they did in their next shared breath. Her head leaned back against his chest. Their arms moved as one, developing from their bodies and extending to either side. The bond of Magic between them tightened, humming in joyous harmony at their shared use of Magic. Reeve's fingers found her own, interlacing them with his.

As they erected a new line of holy Magic, one that separated the incoming Dreaded Dead from Crystalmore and the Celestian Palace, Maeve couldn't understand how the ability poured freely from her with no reserve. It was as easy as twisting two fingers to lift a feather. It had been the same with transfiguring Antony's Magic. She willed it. And Magic answered.

"I'm by your side, Maeve," said Reeve, his breath ghosting the side of her face.

Not enough time. There hadn't been enough time for Shadow to possibly absorb enough Dread Magic from the Dreaded Dead to breach the wall.

But as a distinct Magical signature and the distant pretense of toxic air pricked in warning in her Magic, and as the sounds of Senshi and Dread Magicals alike prepared for incoming, she knew a final battle was upon her. Seeing Mal would have to wait.

Chapter 53

Malachite

Abraxas stood in the darkened bedchamber of The Celestian Palace, his eyes on Mal. Not a cell. No chains bound him. The bedding behind him was cold, as all things were since *she* took him. Mal pressed his bony spine against the smooth headboard and held himself a little higher. Dozens of armed Senshi Warriors stood, surrounding the room, making no effort to move towards Abraxas. Only one barrier remained: the line of Magic Reeve himself cast around Mal.

It glimmered softly at the edges of the bed he didn't recall being placed in.

Had Reeve cast it to keep Mal in? Or to keep others out?

As the tips of Abraxas' fingers pressed against the wall of Magic, rendering him unable to pass, Mal knew at least one of them was certain.

"May we have the room?" asked Abraxas.

"No," said Drystan, drawing Mal's attention to the small framed archer in the corner.

He sat, relaxed in a chair, a book in hand, and answered politely.

Abraxas nodded and looked back at Mal as Drystan returned to his reading. The illusion of privacy was there, at least.

"Why are you here?" Mal's raspy voice asked.

"Surely you can feel what is happening, Mal."

The firelights flickered along the walls, casting a comforting warm glow on the bed. His fingers traced the fabric beneath him, and he felt her at once.

The soft floral, and clean scent of Maeve trickled into his senses, dulled. Like everything was. Like the forgotten feeling of soap and water. Like the distant feeling of water on his tongue, knowing it should refresh and revive him, but merely tasting like ash.

Abraxas kneeled beside the bed, getting as close to Mal as he could with the Magic that separated them.

Mal's head rolled against the headboard, slowly following his Hand's movement. "Mal? I suppose that is what you called me. I have only known another name for so long. Feels like decades since I've heard that name."

"I gave you that nickname," replied Abraxas with a small smile. "How could you forget?"

Mal inhaled deeply, searching for the memory. "Did you?" he asked fondly.

Abraxas nodded. "Stuck like glue. Of course, it was only for those of us who earned it. Otherwise, the use of such a familiar call had you glaring."

The corners of Mal's mouth pulled up. The feeling was strained, wrong even.

Abraxas hummed. "I remember the first time I heard Maeve call you Mal. You tried to hide it, though you hid nothing from me, but I don't think hearing that affection from any of us landed the way it did coming from her."

Mal looked down. After a moment of reflection, he spoke. "Nothing's ever come close to feeling like her."

And nothing had, indeed. Even in her absence, when she had erased them from each other's minds, he never looked at another. Even without the knowledge of her existence, Mal still never wanted another. The blue eyes of others meant nothing. Their gazes were filled with nothing but a desire to be his, as the wearer of the crown. Maeve had looked at him long before he wore a crown. Long before he understood just how powerful he was.

Was.

His body was drained, nearly depleted of his Magic. Shadow had left him but a drop, she said it was grace on her part, but Mal could feel the vow she'd made to Maeve.

She wouldn't kill him. And so there he lay, within an arm's length from death, because even as she ran from him, even as she took Maxius and erased his mind, she had still fought to protect him from

Shadow.

"Where's Maxius?" he asked, the question spilling from him at last.

"He's still under Maeve's crystalized Dread Magic," answered Abraxas,

"She's fighting," he said at last. "I can feel. . . her desperation."

"She's not trying to win," said Abraxas. "They are trying to seal Shadow again."

Yes, he remembered now. Maeve's plan.

She had taken him from Castle Morana. Or rather, Reeve had for her benefit.

"Maeve is going to give you her Dread Magic," said Abraxas. "As soon as Shadow is sealed."

Mal stared at the bedding between them. "Why does she persist after everything I have ruined?"

Abraxas cocked his head to one side, forcing Mal to meet his gaze.

"Oh, Mal," he said, his eyes sparkling, "it took all three of us in control to fuck things up this badly."

Something familiar to warmth simmered in Mal's chest, a long-forgotten sensation. He reached his hand forward, the action nearly taking all his energy, and placed it against the barrier that hung around him, wishing for the smallest touch of another. Of his Hand. His oldest friend.

Abraxas' hand met his, pressed on the other side of the invisible wall of Magic.

"I'm so tired, Abraxas," he said, the words mumbling out before he could care how weak he sounded.

His arm slid back down to his side.

"I know," said Abraxas kindly. "But you did so well. You stayed strong, and you didn't give up. Even when I know you wanted to."

"Would it be alright if I gave up now? Just for a while?"

Abraxas nodded. "You're safe now. You can rest, Mal. You can sleep for days if you need to. Let Maeve do her job as your second, as your Dread Viper. Let her handle Shadow. And we will be here when you wake."

Maeve

Shadow had indeed taken back a massive amount of Dread Magic from her army of the undead, but that didn't stop the tens of thousands that descended upon Aterna, scrambling their way into battle. Shadow was nowhere to be seen as Maeve fought alongside not just Reeve and the Senshi, dismembering and setting fire to the army of undead, but the Bellator and the Elven Army. Antony had gathered more than his pack from Hiems, but a great number of wolves to aid them in their battle.

Still, they were outnumbered. Maeve was hesitant, as was Reeve, to unload their power fully, effectively setting fire to their multitude of enemies that swarmed them all across the realm. Hesitant, and rightfully so, because Shadow's appearance was imminent.

The fleet of Morconis, their slick skin inky black against the starless sky, shrieked as they ascended like shadows of the night onto Crystalmore, their humongous claws breaching and penetrating the protective barriers. Some flew, their torn wings flapping vigorously, across the Senshi and the Dread Magicals who fought the Dreaded Dead, biting and clawing with rabid intent.

The Senshi continued to slice through their countless enemies with blades pumped full of Aterna Magic. The Bellator that made it out of the Dread Lands alive fought alongside them, Magic pouring from their hands in elite training. Maeve caught a glimpse of Larliesl, commanding and leading the less experienced in battle. But as the range of attack spanned across the realm, her sight of him was brief.

A black mass of fur whizzed past her, Antony, jaw wide as he ripped limbs and heads from torsos. She was certain that Antony and Alphard were competing, racing against a bottomless clock and thoroughly high on their bloodshed.

A piercing and sharp sound, followed by guttural snapping noises, sounded out across the sky. Maeve's eyes whipped to Reeve just as she sent a blast of lightning through a dozen undead. Together, their heads whipped towards the Dark Peaks, where flecks of shimmering starlight soared across the horizon.

Not starlight.

Scales.

Demevirld had answered Reeve's call. A hoard of Dragons with majestic bodies and regal forms lit up the distance with blue, red, and orange shades of fire, as they melted the creatures of the night below them. The Morconis shifted their attention at once, their wings flailing madly across the frigid air, in pursuit of the dragons with bone-chilling screams.

Maeve let out a frustrated sigh, heat barreling from her palms as she disintegrated the closest Dreaded Dead within a twenty-foot radius. Reeve sensed her, his eyes moving briefly to her as she stalled, Magic prickling up her spine.

What's wrong? Reeve's voice was clipped in her mind.

Before she could answer, Magic split wide across the realm. It settled deep in her stomach. It crawled beneath the ice at super-speed, heading straight for the Magical barrier they had erected protecting Crystalmore.

Not *it*.

They.

Thousands more Dreaded Dead swarmed beneath the frozen Black Deep, heading straight for the city.

"More," snapped Reeve, "beneath us and making for the wall!" he bellowed out at Eryx, at the Senshi and the Dread alike.

Maeve's eyes darted far across the ice, tracking them. "They're everywhere."

"How could she possibly have more?" spat Alphard, wiping blood from his neck, and then shooting his palm flat, setting fire to a horde of undead that fell from a newly formed Portal.

The Magical barriers they erected cracked as more undead burst from the ice, sinking their sharp-boned fingers into the wall, and began to climb. Blasts of fire blazed from the distance, illuminating the night as the dragons breathed down flames of destruction, each of them efficiently killing the Dreaded Dead by the hundreds at once.

Reeve could do that.

Reeve needed to transform—

Maeve's thoughts halted, her eyes shot to the Dark Peaks, near the highest point on the planet. Judging by the narrowing of Reeve's eyes, he felt it too.

Shadow entered the playing field at last.

Before Maeve could open her mouth, Reeve's hand was on her, Obscuring them. Magic compressed them tightly together as the world shifted, and the snow-covered mountains surrounding Shadow came into view.

Silence settled around them, leaving a hum in her ears from the distinct change in atmosphere. The battles raging below them all across the line that separated the Dread Lands from Aterna couldn't be seen or heard where Sanctum sat nestled high in the Dark Peaks.

Maeve stepped from Reeve, placing a few paces between them.

"I get both of you?" Shadow's voice sounded out. "My lucky day."

Maeve drew the sword Reeve had made for her, the one she'd scarcely used, but cherished all the same.

"You think a sword will do you any good at marking me?"

Maeve did not answer.

With a full and vocal inhale, she gathered every ounce of Aterna Magic that flowed through her, that obeyed her as its master, and poured it into the blade Reeve gifted her. She emptied herself completely, until not a drop of Aterna remained inside her.

Until it was only Shadow Magic, and the power of the Dread Stone at her disposal.

She turned her back to Shadow and gripped the hilt of her sword in both hands as she locked eyes with Reeve. His pupils dilated, and before he could successfully Obscure to her, she slammed the sharp end down, penetrating the snow-covered earth. Her Magic within the blade surged, creating a wall of pale-violet, almost blue, Magic. As it encapsulated only Maeve and Shadow, Reeve's eyes filled with anguish just on the other side.

"Maeve," he warned, his voice slipping into anger.

"She owes me a debt, Reeve," said Maeve calmly, releasing her fingers from the hilt of the sword. The ring of Magic she'd trapped herself inside remained. "And I will collect it."

She could feel the satisfaction radiating from Shadow behind her. Satisfaction she'd soon squash.

"You are needed elsewhere. I am needed here," she said.

You don't have to do this alone, he argued.

I won't be alone for long.

She gently pushed the image of the thousands of Dreaded Dead ascending upon Aterna, shattering their walls, his beautiful Capital City at risk of ruin. The feeling of his people's fear. The idea of Maxius' future on the line. The Vexkari markings of Reeve's dragon curse flickered as he filled with fury, and their eyes remained locked together. Maeve smiled softly, kindling the rage she felt surging through his breaths.

Burn them all, Reeve, she commanded, solidifying his animalistic desire.

Violet fire erupted from him as he allowed his transformation. It was different than the last time she'd seen the beast take over him. He didn't fight his rage. He used it.

With a screech and enough force to shake the side of the mountain, Reeve rocketed into the sky, his glorious wings spread wide as he conquered, not just controlled, his beastly form.

"What a wicked curse," remarked Shadow. "Though it seems he's learned to use his rage at last."

Maeve turned back to her.

"How do you expect to fight me with just Shadow Magic? I have gathered a force of Dread Magic greater than your Aterna into my veins once more, Little Vi—"

Maeve cut her words short, closing Shadow's throat with a pulse of her Aterna Magic that surrounded them, and ensuring she didn't utter the name that only one was allowed to call her ever again.

Two fingers extended at Maeve's side, lightning rippling across her knuckles, wrapping her wrist. "You talk too much."

Shadow's toothy grin faltered, and the lines on her face hardened.

The Aterna Magic surrounding them surged with Maeve's breath, warming her skin as small flecks of snow and ice began to gather in the air.

"I want to show you something," said Maeve, letting her mental shields down.

Intrigue flickered across Shadow's stolen eyes as Maeve made herself vulnerable.

"I found something of Prince Darius," continued Maeve. "I think you'll want to see it."

Shadow's reply came quickly and with a sharpened tone. "How could you possibly have a memory of his?"

"Because objects hold memory. Books, vases, paintings. . ." She held up the Dread Ring on her finger. "Jewelry."

Shadow's pupils widened as her eyes locked on the ring. The ring Maeve knew donned Darius' finger during Shadow's time with him.

"You've already shown me these memories," said Shadow, deflecting. "The trick is old."

Maeve hummed. "It's not a trick." A lie. "Don't you want to see a lost moment of his before either you are sealed or you defeat me? Because either way, you'll lose all chance at seeing him this way."

"What way?" she snapped, but Maeve could hear the resolve in her voice, wavering, like she'd already decided to fall for Maeve's cruelty.

And she had.

Maeve slid them both into a deception and savagery that would top the chart of her wrongdoings. As Castle Morana's Crown's Quarters manifested, reflecting across their shared mind-space like glass, Shadow's beloved Prince Darius was not alone.

If Shadow had been desperately naive enough to believe Maeve had something kind to share with her, she was quickly corrected. Shadow's Magic tensed, coiling around her protectively.

"That isn't real," she said darkly, her eyes trapped on Darius and the fictional woman Maeve inserted into the false memory.

"But it *feels* real," hummed Maeve. "Doesn't it?"

And she was certain, by Shadow's tightened throat, by the way her Magic weakened, by the unmistakable feeling of helplessness that Maeve forced upon her, that it all felt real to Shadow.

Maeve spoke softly, urging Shadow to view her precious Darius the way she'd been forced to watch Mal. "Until you dipped us further into your mind and I saw just how madly in love with Darius you were, I hadn't considered taking it a step further. Twisting it all, bending the reality in your mind to one of pure agony. You're right, the first time I held your memories captive, it was a trick, a distraction. But this is so much more. At least, it is for me. At first, I considered altering your memories in a way that made you feel the sting of his rejection, the weight of his unrequited love. But doesn't it burn so much more this way? To feel his anguish as he's forced into the arms of another? While she corrupts him and takes him in ways he doesn't want?"

Maeve had doubted whether this particular form of torture, inflicted on Shadow for purely selfish reasons, would work. But as actual drops of tears formed in the corners of the demented woman's eyes before her, she knew she had plunged Shadow into misery.

And she relished it.

"I'll admit this wasn't part of my plan until hours ago," continued Maeve, as visions of Darius, the literal feelings of his trauma, penetrated what was left of Shadow's soul. "I didn't tell Reeve or Mal I'd be forcing you to watch the way you forced me to watch. That I'd ensure you felt the helplessness I felt. To have to watch the soul who completes you be violated, mutilated, and degraded. To have his birthright of free will stripped from him. To watch as another, born Shadow just like you, chooses to torture and suffocate a man she'd never met. Simply because of the Magic that lies in his blood. Simply because she lost her Humanity." Maeve shook her head. "I have this desire, Shadow—and I hate it—to spare you. To end the never-ending cycle of death and destruction rooted in revenge, because if I don't, then who will?" Maeve paused. "But then I realized the most glorious thing. . .you're all alone. No one is coming to avenge your demise. And truthfully, that has set me free in my desire to hurt you. If someone must dirty their hands to end this, then I will take the stain of your blood like a trophy and wear it like a badge of honor."

She moved her physical body, the one outside of Sanctum, a fraction of a second before shattering the illusion, and collided with Shadow. Her bright white hair sprawled behind her on the snowy terrain as Maeve bared down on her. With a twist of her wrist, the

Dread Dagger appeared in Maeve's raised hand.

Shadow screamed, all throat and gut, as Maeve sliced the Dread Dagger through the stolen sapphire-blue iris. Blood, so crimson it was nearly black, spurted from her eye, from between the tissue Maeve carved away. Maeve pulled more of the Aterna towards her, holding Shadow down. Her body trembled beneath Maeve, unable to thrash fully away from her, forced to endure the dagger as Maeve carved out each of her eyes with jagged and haphazard force.

"Forever wounded," said Maeve hotly, her voice hissing between her teeth. "Though I don't think you'll have much longer to heal."

Maeve's grip on her Aterna Magic faltered as a surge of Shadow's own power knocked her backwards. Her back slammed into the icy ground as a blast of tainted Magic landed square in her chest.

It rippled through her like a shockwave.

She pulled Mal's Dread Magic from the ring on her finger and Obscured with haste, landing on her feet as Shadow advanced on her again. She blocked successfully, a wall of Magic, swirling between them.

"Damn," said Maeve, observing her bleeding eyes, "looks like I only got one eye fully out."

Shadow snarled, and they began a series of slices and blocks, slams of Magic and twisting in and out of mist, moving through space in quick blinks between advances.

Maeve released her Shadow Magic, latching onto her opponent and searching for Mal's own Magic, ready to reclaim it as she promised.

"You think I haven't learned all the tricks?" she asked hotly. "You think I don't know how to take back what you took from him?"

"Take it," said Shadow, licking across her teeth. Her shoulders slackened, and she stood tall. That heinous giggle bubbled in her throat. Magic moved towards Maeve, given freely.

Ice drained across Maeve's blood, alert and confused. Shadow offered Maeve Mal's Magic without deception. It was his, the distinct Magical signature was purely Mal.

Shadow smiled, dried blood coating her cheeks like melted tar.

Mal's Magic. . .it was shattered. Not usable. No longer viable.

Her heart ached. That wasn't part of the plan.

Mal needed that Magic back. He needed it to be strong to—

Silence filled her ears. No, not silence. A sharp ringing. The sound that comes after your head makes a hard impact.

Maeve lifted her head, the earth and her body spinning at once.

Another blow from above. Below? She didn't know. Shadow's Magic ripped through her, cold and relentless. Maeve's fingers curled under, refusing to abandon her plan, even if this demon of darkness had ruined part of it.

She slid into her son's mind, where he lay protected and asleep, and woke him with a single thought:

It's time, Maxius.

She groaned, squeezing her eyes shut, and prepared to make herself even more vulnerable to Shadow's attacks in order to show Maxius what must be done. To show him his Shadow Magic.

As she took hit after hit, her body becoming one with the snow beneath her, a beautiful male voice echoed clear across her mind, cool and low.

Get up, Little Viper. This isn't your time to die.

Chapter 54

Malachite

Get up, Little Viper. This isn't your time to die.

Maeve's Magic kicked back at Mal in response to his command, dousing his senses in her intoxicating presence through the bond they shared. He breathed heavily as she returned to her feet, her Magic slamming against Shadow's once more. His Little Viper was extraordinary. She'd freed him.

And now sealing Shadow was within her grasp.

But that only delayed the inevitable.

He pushed up, an involuntary groan sounding deep in his chest.

The soft sheets of Maeve's bed remained beneath him. Abraxas was gone, and the firelights were completely extinguished. The only source of light came from a small white glow before him. As his eyes focused, he saw the dozens of fully armed Senshi Warriors that previously lined the room lying unconscious on the floor. Drystan slumped over in his reading chair. Not dead. Asleep.

Reeve's line of Magic surrounding Mal remained. Steadfast and paramount.

But a new Magical signature had entered the space. One that called to him even greater than Maeve's.

Maxius stood at the foot of the bed with Spinel at his side, with every ounce of Maeve's Dread Magic inside him. The cat's long tail curled tightly around his body and draped across his feet. Mal didn't move as his only child peered at him across the darkened bedroom.

The Dread Locket around his neck glowed with Magic that called to Mal, ancient and of his blood. The Lux charm on Maxius' wrist illuminated the space between them with soft, white light.

The charm bracelet that had once been Maeve's.

"Hello, my boy," he said weakly, hearing his own heartache evident in his call.

You remember me? signed Maxius.

The words were a dagger to Mal's heart.

"I may only have a drop of my Magic left in me, but I'd recognize my son's anywhere."

The corners of Maxius' lips moved up.

I like your eyes now, signed Maxius. *I like them dark. Not green.*

Not green.

With a tiny single finger, Maxius tapped the invisible barrier holding Mal in. Emerald light sparked across the cell and dissipated into nothing as he effortlessly shattered Reeve's Magic.

At last, his son, the youngest to point a single finger, found his Magic.

Maxius climbed into the bed, Spinel close at heel, shifting on his knees across the bed. Mal's heart began a steady increase of rhythm as his breaths quickened, pouring quickly from him.

Maxius placed his hands on Mal's knees and crawled into his lap. Mal froze as Maxius rested his head against Mal's long and emaciated torso. He was a ball of warmth against Mal's cold skin. Mal's insides shook. Slowly, and with trepidation, Mal wrapped his arms around Maxius and settled him close. Maxius turned his head, nuzzling into Mal. His hold tightened reflexively, and he looked down at his son.

He didn't have any portraits or pictures of himself at Maxius' age, but that didn't stop him from knowing just how intricately replicated Maxius was of him. Right down to the curve of his eyelids.

Of course, Maeve was there, too. Just differently. In his soft expression and his fearless eyes.

Mal leaned back, resting against the headboard. He didn't tear his eyes away from Maxius.

It's time, Maxius signed, looking up at him.

How could it be time already? When, finally, at last, his mind was free of the blight, and he held his son.

He saw and felt what needed to be done.

"I know," he whispered, entangling his fingers through Maxius' hair. "She can hold out a bit longer. Just so I can hold you a bit longer. She's strong, you know."

Reeve says she's the strongest, his small hands signed.

Mal pressed his lips to the side of his temple. "She is."

To be denied a life with his child may have been the cruelest trick of fate bestowed upon Mal.

"You are strong too, Maxius," began Mal. "So strong that your mother and I knew the moment you came into existence."

How? signed Maxius.

Mal remembered it clearly. The way Maeve's hand moved over her stomach, the way she stared up at him in disbelief as they lay beside one another in a mass of sheets. The smile that blossomed on her face when his kiss was a silent confirmation that she was indeed pregnant with his child.

Maxius listened intently, a fondness in his gentle expression, as Mal continued.

"We saw a boy who would be the best parts of us both."

Maxius shook his head, his hands moving swiftly. I *still don't understand my Magic, or why I have access to it now.*

"I can't say I understand either," said Mal, fingers still trailing Maxius' impossibly soft hair. "Your grandfather once told me Magic was alive, something all to itself. So no, I don't understand why. But I do know what we must do now. And so do you, it seems."

Mal's fingers moved over Maxius' cheeks, grateful his son didn't recoil from his drained appearance, hoping that he, too, would remember what little time they'd had together as father and son.

Together they tensed as distantly Maeve took a harsh blow.

Maxius' eyes widened, pleadingly, silently begging for Mal to go and help his mother. How could Mal deny those eyes? Every moment that Shadow lived was a threat to his son's life. She would come for him and take him apart, strip him bare, just as she had Mal. She wouldn't stop until she'd consumed his heir. That had been made clear.

He wouldn't let her touch Maxius. He wouldn't let her abuse his son.

"Are you ready?" Mal asked.

Maxius nodded.

They shifted on the bed, and Maxius moved to his knees as they faced one another. He reached a single finger towards Mal's forehead, as Magic surged around them in anticipation. The pad of Maxius' fingers touched down, and Mal's blood instantly heated. It surged through him, transforming him as Maxius poured Maeve's Dread Magic into him. Where Shadow's absorption had been cruel, taking, unforgiving, and vile, this was pure.

And Gods above—it was *Maeve*.

He was regenerated and renewed beneath her beautiful essence.

Then came Maxius' own Dread Magic, the Magic required in prophetic certainty for Mal to defeat Shadow. It was heavy, and it was greater in volume and potency than Maeve's. It moved through him in thick waves as Maxius used his Shadow Magic to channel nearly all of his Magic.

As he finished, Maxius heaved a sigh, his eyes rolling back and his shoulders sliding sideways. Mal grabbed him gently at once, noticing then the color slowly returning to his long fingers, to his skin. Spinel rubbed against Maxius, purring loudly.

The boy opened his eyes, dazed only for a moment. His eyes scanned over Mal quickly, and he smiled.

You look better, he signed quickly, tucking his legs beneath him and petting Spinel.

Mal sighed, letting the weight of the Magic he'd been given settle over him. He touched his palm to his cheek, feeling a light flush, the return of his Humanity. He rolled his neck and shoulders, renewed strength coiling through him.

Mal's fingers tucked beneath Maxius' chin. "You truly are your mother's son. Extraordinary in every way."

Maxius' face lit up.

As Mal prepared to Obscure, Maxius' hands grabbed his.

"No," said Mal at once. "You must stay here."

Under no circumstances was he getting anywhere near Shadow. This battle was for him and his Little Viper.

Maxius withdrew his hands and looked up at Mal. He huffed a sigh.

"You must stay here," said Mal with a soft smile, running his fingers through his hair. "Who will protect Spinel if you are gone?"

Maxius looked over at the onyx cat, who chirped in approval, and covered his mouth with joy.

"Run and find Zimsy," said Mal, and the pair of them bounced off the bed at once.

Mal closed his eyes, and with a low sigh, he gathered Maeve's Magic, which would always be desperate to return to her, and used it to guide him to wherever she battled Shadow.

He Obscured, dark mist wrapping and transporting his body from her chamber, and landed directly behind her on the side of the mountain just as she took a substantial hit from Shadow's advance. Maeve spun, colliding into him.

The pale creature's hollowed and bloodied eye sockets landed on him, as though she could still see him, as her Magical signature spiked with fear. His fingers found her throat, and his turn at torture began.

Maeve found her footing as her fingers pressed into his exposed chest, steadying herself. Power surged through him at her skin on his. Her forehead touched down next, as she expelled a sigh at the momentary reprieve of battle.

Shadow remained locked in Mal's grip. Maeve had depleted her substantially, and now, with a prophecy fulfilled in his blood, and Dread Magic at his fingers once more, he stood above her in every meaning of the word.

"Tell me, Little Viper," began Mal, his voice dripping in lethal calm, his free hand at her waist. "Should we make it quick? Or have a little fun?"

A drained sound escaped Maeve, and her neck craned to look up at him. Mal's determination surged at her attention, but his gaze remained trained on Shadow, on the brutalized carvings at where her stolen eyes should have been.

"I see you already had some fun," noted Mal, praise seeping into his cold voice.

He looked down at her at last, soaking in his beloved Viper. Red scatterings of Magic that would yield bruises littered her face. Her bottom lip was swollen, a thin crimson slice decorating the pale-pink skin. Despite her battered appearance, it was the proud line of her mouth and slight narrowing of her eyes that made him crave her.

And Mal had never been one to deny himself something he wanted.

Never releasing Shadow, his grip on Maeve's waist lifted, drawing her up on her toes as his head tilted and he stole her mouth in a slam of fervor with parted lips. It wasn't gentle. It was fueled by the Magic soaring through him. It was the breaking of the horrors he'd endured for months beneath a monster. He didn't care that she'd chosen Reeve. He had no concern for the reality he faced.

She would always be his, to him.

And if this was the end of them, he'd finish it his way. No denial. No pretending he was someone he wasn't. Just her warm mouth after being deprived, denied, and starved of her.

As he stood tall and she lowered from him, her eyes fluttered open as a steady breath rolled through her.

"Take your Dread Magic from me," he said smoothly.

She obeyed.

The Dread Magic undulating through him swelled with approval at her immediate trust. Shadow began to thrash in his grip. She moved in vain, her efforts ineffective against his hold. Maeve's palms spread against Mal's torso, and with a lengthy inhale and the hum of an exhale, she got to work, gently pulling her Dread Magic back into her veins.

It slid from Mal with ease, bringing a sour smile of satisfaction to his lips, especially as Shadow's attempts to escape him became desperately violent. Maeve's shoulders rolled back as she stood tall, no longer leaning against him.

She placed a single finger at the center of his chest. Then three more. He felt a shift surge through him, lighter than her own Magic or Maxius'.

It was his.

His eyes shot down to her delicate fingers pressed against him. To the Dread Ring. The black, inky-like veins that ran across her skin writhed. She groaned beneath the strain of her gift as she siphoned his Dread Magic from the ring.

Like a tidal wave, it hit him. Not just his Dread Magic.

All the Dread Magic the ring harbored. His ancestors Vexkari.

It merged with him at once, blossoming beneath his skin. He tasted it on his tongue, metallic and cool. It wound through him in slick and easy paths, coiling like a serpent.

But his Dread Viper, his Little Viper, did not stop there.

He watched as her veins danced with Magic of their own. First flowing down her neck, draining of their darkened color, and down her arms, it emptied into him.

The Magic he'd accidentally scared her with. The Magic that bonded them.

She withdrew it from herself until the black lines running her skin looked like healed scars, pale and flesh colored. Until it was his once more.

"I wanted to give you more, Mal," she said, her eyes on her own pale fingers. "But your Magic, the Magic she stole, she. . .crushed it completely."

He already knew that.

"It doesn't matter now," he said. "I have what is needed to win. All I ask is that you indulge me and fight alongside me one last time."

Her chest rose and fell in response, and she nodded in earnest.

With a small returned nod, Mal's hand slipped from her waist. She stepped away from him, crossing the frozen ground to her sword, as he looked back down at his trapped prey.

At the vile creature clawing at his restored hands.

He raised a single finger, gathering his first strike in a swirling mass of Magic. The barrier of Aterna Magic that circled them collapsed as Maeve bled the weapon dry, seizing all the holy Magic she'd placed in it.

When she returned to Mal's side, they shared a single, silent glance and began their dance.

Mal was careful not to pour all his energy, all his fury, and ancient power into a single fatal blow, though he was certain that would come soon enough. He'd forgotten how seamlessly they moved as one. How Maeve anticipated his every move, how she Obscured just where he wanted her to, slamming Shadow with harrowing electric Magic as he blasted her from the other side.

The air was alive with their joined power as they moved across the slowly melting ice beneath their feet, cracking and oppressive. The ground shifted, plates of power scattering beneath each step they took as one force.

Again.

And again and again, Shadow buckled beneath their combined Magic.

Each time he glanced at his Viper's face of stone, he surged with more determination. She channeled the lightning of the Dread Stone with such ease, bending it to her intentions. He allowed himself a moment to admire her, the true-born fighter she was. How she'd grown from that girl he tutored at Vaukore, afraid to cast even a simple shield, to the woman before him. Who faced a threat as lethal as Shadow without a single accelerated pulse.

At last, when the Dread King and his Dread Viper had sufficiently wounded their quarry, Shadow kneeled before Mal.

Her head hung low, and her previously luscious hair was now stringy and faded. Her bony fingers pressed into the ground, skin barely clinging to them. She appeared shrunken in size.

Maeve stood at his right. Where she had sworn to be. Where he wanted her to be until his last breath.

"That little drop of my Magic that remains mine," uttered Mal, his gaze cast down at Shadow, "the bit you cannot take because you were foolish enough to agree not to kill me when I alone was prophesied to kill you. . . that drop was still enough to join with my son's. It *is* still enough to destroy you."

And so he did.

With a twist of his fingers, she rose, levitating. He lifted her until her gaunt-once-more face was level with his. He touched the filth that had ripped his world from him one last time, trapping one hand at the back of her head, and placed a single finger on her forehead.

Then he let the Magic of his blood, his family before him, guide his path to her termination. It sang through him in victory, eager to break its target. Despite being pumped full of stolen Magic she lacked the understanding to use, and being weakened from their attack, she remained a deadly force. It would take an equally deadly force to end her.

He called upon the Magic granted to him, and it answered, as it always did. Ready and pliant, though demanding of its own desires. The cost didn't matter to him. He'd pay it.

The air turned thick and oppressive, pressing down on them as his Magic charged the atmosphere. Shadow's form continued to decay as Mal overtook her fully. The exchange was swift as his power began depleting, shattering, vanishing rapidly as it did the same to Shadow. He was using all of himself against her, reckless and without restraint.

He *had* to use all of himself against her. Maeve may have been superior in her ability to understand Magic, but Mal could see what was required of him to make Shadow's death stick.

He'd suspected it for some time.

And as Maeve spoke, he knew she was realizing it too.

"Mal, stop."

But he couldn't stop. Not until Shadow was gone. Not until this Magic-thirsty blight was vanquished from the world his son occupied. He pressed harder, more, sharp cracks slicing across his front, manifesting in physical wounds. His teeth slid together, grinding in defiance as his senses told him to let go.

"Mal."

Her beautiful, panicked voice was closer now. Her hands moved over his wounds. Her sweet fingers pressed all of the Magic she'd Inherited from Reeve into the sliced skin.

"Mal, stop, now," she snapped. "I can't heal you at the rate you are going."

It wasn't going to heal even if he stopped.

Dread Magic came at a cost. There was always an exchange.

The exchange for Shadow's life was his life.

The swell of Magic around them grew impossibly still, breathing as one with Mal.

He pressed his limitations further, allowing himself to become fully washed with the darkness that thrummed through him with natural course. It tasted delicious, he had to admit, being a vessel for power beyond any of their comprehension.

It slid across his skin, burrowing into his bones, aiding his will to see Shadow's existence shatter.

The next blow cleaved across his face, icy and wet, but he endured.

Maeve's fingers dug deep against him, urging him to stop. He wanted to tell her it was for her that he persisted. That it was for their son, the perfect baby boy she'd given him, that he pushed himself to the edge willingly as the creature in his grip deteriorated further.

Not to the edge, he corrected himself as a warm dizziness settled over him. Over the edge. Another wave pressed down on him, cracking his insides, fracturing his bones, bursting his organs.

He tensed, his memory flooding and delivering him the feeling of snapping Maeve's arm clean in two. A stomach-churning sickness raced down his spine, further fueling his ripping, shredding, and complete destruction of Shadow.

With a zap of victorious energy that must have traveled for miles in all directions, Mal's fingers relaxed. And in that same instance, Shadow's life-force, though her body slid to the earth in a skeletal mass one would presume dead, snapped out of being.

She drew no breath; she sang no Magic.

The Magic propelling the Dreaded Dead across the realm shattered with her.

Mal's hands hovered where he'd previously held her. He couldn't help but feel disappointment at the sight of them. Ripped flesh clung to his exposed bones. His arms dropped, and only then did he realize Maeve was holding him up, with both her arms snugly around him. A shake began at his core, slowly taking over his body. His legs gave way, but Maeve was quicker.

She lowered him to the thawing ground with the ease of lowering a feather, cradling his shoulders in one arm with her focus on the lacerations he'd willingly taken. His head rolled against her warm body.

Finally, some mercy for him at last. It was she who would usher him from this life.

"Just hold on, I can heal you."

Slowly, too slowly, beneath her hands, his chest sewed shut and his blood regenerated. He placed his hand over hers as the wounds unsealed themselves—his debt of blood was still being collected by the Magic he'd used moments ago.

Her brows pulled together. "Stop," she commanded the blood, desperately trying to cover all the holes, the slices, the stabs of Magic.

"Eyes on me, Maeve," he muttered.

Her pale-blue eyes latched onto his at once. Her jaw shook.

"You keep those pretty eyes on course," he said, a strained gasp slipping from his throat. "You give Maxius the life he deserves."

She shook her head. In her determined silence, she continued to pour her Aterna Magic into him, but he knew. . .

It wasn't enough.

The ancient and holy Dread Magic he'd bartered with would not bend to such purity. Like the sting of the Dread Dagger, such wounds would have to heal naturally. But such fatal wounds would not.

Tension coiled through his body. He was fading quickly. These were his final moments, and he wouldn't spend them watching her futile attempts to bring him back to life.

"I told you I would die for you." He smiled weakly. His hand beneath hers slipped free, reaching, shaking, towards her face, desperate to feel her one last time. Warm blood slid between their skin. "And I will."

Tears fell, violently from her eyes, pouring across her face, dripping into his open wounds.

"I didn't want to fail you this time," she cried. "I promised I wouldn't this time."

"You didn't fail, Little Viper. You set me free. This was always my destiny. Written in Magic, remember?" His thumb brushed over her bottom lip.

"It isn't fair," she said, her bloodied and shaking hands moving to his face, abandoning her healing. Her thumbs moved over his cheeks, surging him with one final feeling of euphoria.

"What a beautiful last moment together," he said, his voice low and assuring. "To fight next to you with my final breaths to save our son. To see you, in all your glory, fight for me and Maxius. If I must go, I am happy it is next to you."

The assurance and acceptance in his voice shattered Magic between them. Something old and promised had come to completion: he would die before she did.

"Tell him the truth," said Mal, as the feeling of his lips and tongue drained. "Tell him what I did. Make sure he knows every detail. It is the only gift I can bestow in hopes that my mistakes are not repeated."

"Our son will know that his father gave his life for him. For me. And for all Magicals."

Mal's other hand joined at her face, trembling and cold knuckles brushed against her bruised and blood-smeared skin. "I love you, Little Viper. In another world, perhaps I will again."

A wailing cry barreled up her throat and ricocheted off the mountains. A divine final sound to his ears: his greatest love mourning him already.

Chapter 55

Maeve

She wept silently over him. The occasional sharp gasp slipped from her throat. She held him until all the snow melted, thawing Aterna. Until the skies were clear. Until sunlight beamed down upon the Dread Lands across the Dark Peaks.

She didn't know how long it had been since he drew breath. How long since she'd felt his heartbeat still. Each moment she waited for the miracle of his return, a rebirth, a second chance. For his eyes to slide back open and Magic to surge through him.

But he grew cold. His wounds no longer flowed with sacrifice. They were as still as he was limp.

Reeve's sudden presence on the mountainside sent a wave of warmth through her, an unwelcome comfort as she clutched Mal's broken and bloodied body. He stood, just a few feet from them.

Maeve lashed out, throwing all her despair on him, her nostrils flaring as she looked up at Reeve. "Don't touch him."

Her heart squeezed tight at the sight of him.

Tears glistened in the morning sunlight as they slid down Reeve's face. He didn't look at her. His solemn gaze was set on Mal.

Maeve's jaw relaxed, and she looked back down at Mal. "I want to honor him in his burial. Everyone will know what he did here today."

Reeve nodded once. "He is honored, whether we deem it or not. But yes, Maeve. Whatever you want, it is yours to have."

She looked back up at Reeve. His eyes were on her now.

"May I?" he asked so gently, so reverently, that more tears, impossibly more, spilled over her bottom lashes.

After a moment, she nodded, and Reeve crossed the rocky landing to them. He kneeled on the other side of Mal. He placed his hands across Mal's forehead and whispered Magic that Maeve couldn't recite, but, through their bond, she felt its holy intention all the same.

Reeve prayed over Mal, thanking him for his sacrifice. Thanking him for making Maeve strong enough to survive. Thanking him for Maxius, and vowing to never take his place, but to ensure Maxius knew a father's love.

"I'm so sorry, Maeve," he voiced at last.

Guilt slipped through her at the sincerity in his voice. His broad hand reached for her, tilting her chin up to his gaze. His touch was starkly warm, spiraling through her body and igniting her bones. Like she had forgotten his affection, his understanding, and his grace. She leaned towards him.

Their foreheads touched.

"Allow me to carry him," said Reeve.

Maeve relaxed her hold in silent answer, and Reeve's arms slipped around Mal's body, lifting him with careful ease.

The sculpture stood tall, towering over them. She'd erected it with her own Magic, ensuring every detail of Mal's face, his fingers, and his posture were perfect. Though the end of his rule as a monarch of the Dread Lands was fallen, Maeve would make sure his legacy remained pure. She'd ensure the history books wrote of his sacrifice, and the valiant way he paved their future with that sacrifice.

No one argued with his honorable burial, though she kept the ceremony small. Abraxas was at her side as Maxius laid hydrangeas across Mal's chest. It had been tempting to bury him near her father, on Earth, but she knew his place was in the Dread Lands, laid to rest in a monument that would live forever outside Castle Morana. A reminder to all that the era of peaceful Magic between all realms they entered was not gained or traded freely.

It was purchased with Mal's death.

Warm sunlight brushed her face, beaming down from the clear sky above where she reclined on the balcony, far from the Celestian Palace or Castle Morana, but nestled somewhere in between the two. An intimate home where Reeve's laughter could be heard anywhere in the house. Where Maxius was a step away.

She looked down at Spinel, who purred in approval, his black tail curled high as he jumped into her lap. Her fingers trailed across his fur as her eyes drifted to the open doors. Sheer curtains shifted in the warm breeze, revealing Reeve with Maxius on his hip. A shared smile on their lips.

"What once was cannot always be," she whispered to herself, "and what will be cannot always have been."

Her darkened veins, once black and racing with Magic, sat dormant. Their coloring faded to the memory of a scar. But sometimes, when Maxius' eyes landed on hers, or when she heard a certain melody, she felt a glimmer of Malachite Peur run through them.

Epilogue

Mal's Letter

Reeve,

I can admit that I hate you. I have felt disdain, disgust, and indifference for many whose paths have crossed my own. Never a loathing like this. Because I know that if you are reading this, it means I am gone.

And my Little Viper is yours.

I have known for a few years now that this conflict would likely end with my demise. I've known since the first time I watched another man press his lips to hers that I would die for her. I felt it take root deep in my core. It never withered. It only blossomed.

But the kiss Alphard Mavros placed on her lips in front of me was nothing compared to the silent and invisible, to a lesser Magical that is, way your Magic claimed hers the first night I met you. It was the Sacred Seventeen party. And at that time, getting through the evening without telling the Committee of the Sacred and the Orator I wish they'd all drop dead, seemed the greatest challenge of the evening.

Until you arrived.

You, and that Aterna Magic that oozes from you with perfect control, control I never mastered, sought her immediately. As if you knew exactly where she stood. Your Magic flared, reaching for hers at once. Like old friends. I watched, rather, I felt, as a part of her own Magic rose to meet you. She was completely unaware then that part of you was inside her, forged with her own power. I didn't quite understand it then, but as Maeve altered our own reality time and time again, I think I do now.

And that is why I hate you more than I could ever express.

I hate that I know you'll be good to her. I hate that you'll never hurt her. I hate that you made her smile when I couldn't. I hate that you protected her when I couldn't. That you were the one keeping my son alive. And not me. I hate that I know you'll raise him as your own. I hate that he'll love you. It's likely he already does.

I hate that she loves you.

But I love, I relish, knowing that her father blessed my union with her, and not yours. It may seem a low blow, but it's the last one I'll deliver to you. Because I'm certain that once you set this entry down, she'll be standing there. You'll get to hold her.

You won.

Neither of us could possibly deserve such a divine being. I've never seen anyone so beautiful. There was never another who saw the dark and deadly force coursing through me and stayed. There was never another whose mind was as sharp as hers, who bent Magic and reality to her will, even against my own desires and yours.

Make no mistake, Reeve, I do despise you and everything you ended up with that should have been mine. Despite that, I still ask, as someone who did not get the second chance you did, that you put Maeve and Maxius before yourself every slumbering and waking moment until the end of time. And during those years of life, know that such a thing is an honor.

If I have died for her, I urge you to live for her.

Malachite Peur

end of book three

The following is a teaser from
Dreadfully Yours, a Dread Series
collection of romance stories.

Vaukore, Maeve's second year

"What did I miss?" asked Abraxas, happily taking his seat in the oversized chair.

Maeve pressed the drink to her lips and downed it.

"Slow up, Maeve," whined Abraxas. "You didn't even 'cheers' me," he noted, raising his glass into the air between them with a pout.

Maeve didn't listen. She drank and drank until the glass was empty once more. With a small hiccup, she extended it to Abraxas, who hadn't even taken a single sip of his own drink.

"I'll cheers you this time," offered Maeve.

Mal and Abraxas watched her in silence.

"Well?" she huffed.

Abraxas took the glass from her, leaving his own behind, and hurried back to the bar.

Maeve's attention returned to Mal. He had, to his credit, taken Antony off her mind.

But it wasn't enough.

She reached for Abraxas' abandoned drink, her eyes growing heavy. She knew just looking at the dark amber liquid that it wasn't going to taste good, but couldn't find it in her to care. She tossed his drink back, grimacing as it burned across her chest. With a soft groan, she slammed the empty glass down, and her eyes snapped to Mal.

"Magic is merely the will of the mind. And if I deem it irrelevant, then it is."

Mal's brows raised. "That's quite arrogant. Magic may bend to our will, inherently ours, but it is a symbiotic and mutually beneficial relationship. What you are doing is unnatural in the order of Magic. And if you don't allow it to be what it is, it will control you in return."

"You have a lot of experience where that is concerned?" she asked lowly, in what was meant to be a blow.

Mal leaned farther over the table towards her that time. "Yes," he answered darkly. "I do."

Maeve was silent a moment, running over his words in her head.

"You have to face it," he said. "Or you risk falling out of balance within yourself."

"I don't want to face it," she admitted, ignoring the last part of his statement. "I want to run from it."

"And what are you using this vile liquid to run from tonight?" he asked, his voice low.

"Everything," she whispered and changed the subject. Her words came out soft and honest, thanks to her drunken state, before she could restrain them. "You're very handsome."

Mal accepted the compliment without complaint or argument, but his reply wasn't in keeping with her sentiment.

"I think you've had enough to drink, Sinclair," he said, his voice velvety smooth and without judgment.

Maeve shook her head, and the room twisted as she tried to find a steady breath to ground her.

"Yes," he said coolly.

"I don't want to stop," she slurred. "I want to forget the sight of my brother's mutilated and dead body."

Mal didn't flinch. He didn't recoil or react to her words. His eyes traced over her face, studying her expression.

"Again with the repressing of what's real," he said, and then his eyes were back on hers.

"Don't you ever want to live in a different reality?" Maeve said. "One you shaped and chose?"

"Such a thing isn't possible. And if it were, I would not choose it."

Maeve sighed, her body quickly growing heavy under the weight of alcohol. "I would."

A blur slid by her that she reckoned had to be Abraxas' returning. Mal's eyes never left hers, though he put distance between them once more, leaning back in his seat.

He really was beautiful. So dangerously dark.

He'd be a fine distraction, though she was certain he'd never entertain the idea.

At the thought, a spark of Magic kicked up under her chin and ran across her bottom lip. It was icy cool. Her eyes widened at the implication. The advance.

It was Mal's.

Her stomach flipped over. This time the butterflies *were* excitement.

Abraxas handed her yet another drink as he realized his drink now sat empty.

"Hey," he began in protest as Maeve's fingers moved towards the freshly filled glass.

They barely brushed the cold crystal before it vanished and appeared in Mal's hand.

"I said you were done. Abraxas can walk you to your dorm."

Abraxas' attention was suddenly on Maeve.

"No," said Maeve. "I'm having fun."

"The fun is over, Sinclair," said Mal as the Magic running along her jaw retreated, leaving her wanting. "You're practically incapacitated."

"I think I'd disagree," came a familiar voice. "The fun is only just beginning."

Alphard appeared behind her, one hand braced on the back of the couch and the other on her head. He yanked her neck backwards, bending over to slam a kiss on her lips. The sting of Dragon Whiskey burned from his mouth.

Roswyn, who entered with him, groaned and muttered, "I don't want to see that," as he plopped down in the chair Fawley had been in.

And Maeve didn't want him to. She didn't want any of them to see this. She felt too bare. Too vulnerable. She winced as Alphard's fingers dug deep into her hair, pulling her from her seat. She pulled away as his kiss became too much and his grip tightened.

Her intoxicated state slowed her down as she twisted in her seat, giving her back to Mal and the rest as she attempted to slip from Alphard's grip. But his brazen pursuit continued, and his hold on her only deepened.

The room tilted slightly, and she was pried from his lips and off the couch in one smooth motion. The arm encompassing her waist released her as her feet touched down, and she wobbled at once, weight shifting and stumbling into Abraxas, who caught her with ease.

"Shit, shit shit," he whispered as she slid into his grip.

Maeve groaned, feeling horribly nauseated at the sudden, unwelcome, movement. Despite the spinning room, she looked over her shoulder. Alphard hadn't moved. He stood facing Mal.

"Why—" she began softly, but Abraxas swiftly cut her off.

"Hush, cousin," he whispered. "It's about to get good."

Alphard laughed, a sharpness in his voice that sliced through his inebriation as he spoke to Mal. "What are you doing?"

The party quieted, and every eye, every drop of attention, moved to them and the scene unfolding between them.

"Stopping you," replied Mal smoothly.

"From kissing the girl who's kissed me back plenty?" Alphard laughed, both hands braced on the back of the couch.

"She was trying to pull away from you, Mavros," Mal countered calmly.

A smirk appeared on Alphard's face, but it was sinister. Twisted.

Angry.

"I don't appreciate the insinuation," said Alphard.

"I'm certain not."

Alphard's eyes moved to Maeve, still being supported by Abraxas.

"You've had too much as well," continued Mal, his eyes calmly locked on Alphard, drawing his attention back to him.

"Oh," said Alphard softly, a vicious and low laugh escaping him. "I get it."

Mal's head cocked to the side. The motion tightened Maeve's core, sending her Magic on high alert.

"What's that?" challenged Mal.

"You want her," said Alphard, his words slurring slightly.

As if he could feel the insult coming, Mal's Magic flared around him. It forced Maeve's breathing to halt completely.

Alphard's sinister smile faded. "Too bad, though. She wouldn't touch someone with your tainted blood."

The blow cracked across Alphard's face instantly, sending him sideways. Mal had barely moved his hand to deliver it.

"Stop," said Maeve, her voice too groggy and soft to be heard. Not that she was certain Mal would listen. Or Alphard, for that matter.

Roswyn settled deeper into his seat, silently watching, his face void of emotion.

Alphard straightened. He stood tall and pressed his hand against the red slice across his cheek.

Mal looked over to Abraxas. "Get her some water and walk her to her dorm." He turned back to Alphard, who rolled his shoulders. "Come on," said Mal. "Let's get it over with."

Continue reading this scene and others in Lauren Cate's novella *Dreadfully Yours*, a Dread Series collection of romance stories. Reeve may or may not say, "I've been so patient, kitten. I want a reward," in one scene.

Acknowledgement

To my Little Vipers,

I can't believe this is the end! I don't quite know how to express my love and gratitude for you all. You have changed my life with your love for these books. All my life, I have longed for the sense of belonging and community you bring. Each one of you is a part of that, and I don't think I've ever experienced anything quite so beautiful. You inspire me to write more, explore my creativity, and be myself in ways I've dreamed of for decades.

If you've followed me on socials (or read my first two dedications), you likely know I lost my mom just as I was entering adulthood at eighteen. She was a marvelous woman. She was everything warm and bubbly, magical and extraordinary.

Her greatest gift was love. She loved fully and without reserve. She loved every ballet student or theatre kid that crossed her path. She encouraged and uplifted those who couldn't do it themselves yet. It's been many years since her death, and I still have people tell me she changed their lives for good.

I will never feel that mother's love again, for it cannot be replaced. But you, and your love for my stories, come pretty damn close.

You have changed my life for good.

Lauren Cate

ABOUT THE AUTHOR

Hi! I'm Lauren Cate (yes I have a double first name, but the good news is if that blows your mind you can call me LC. All the cool kids do.)

I write fiction about the messed up and toxic love you should stay away from in real life (but he's fictional. . . so enjoy) and baddie women. Even if they are the villain. Still baddie.

I've been a performing artist my whole life until publishing. I have two cats and I am obsessed with cats.

You can follow my socials and my website for more information about me and my other works!

Thank you so much for reading! It means the world to me to have gotten Maeve's story into your hands.

XOXO
LC

TikTok @authorlaurencateleake
Instagram @laurencateleake
Facebook: Author Lauren Cate Leake

ALSO BY LAUREN CATE LEAKE

THE DREAD DESCENDANT SERIES
THE DREAD DESCENDANT
THE DREAD PRINCE
THE DREAD KING
DREADFULLY YOURS

MURDEROUS LOVE: AN ANTHOLOGY
FEATURING MARRY, KISS, KILL